CJ Carver is a half-English, half-Kiwi author living just outside Bath. CJ lived in Australia for ten years before taking up long-distance rallies, including London to Saigon, London to Cape Town and 14,000 miles on the Inca Trail. CJ's books have been published in the UK and the USA and have been translated into several languages. CJ's first novel, *Blood Junction*, won the CWA Debut Dagger Award and was voted as one of the best mystery books of the year by *Publisher's Weekly*.

www.cjcarver.com / @C_J_Carver

KNOW ME NOW

CJ CARVER

ZAFFRE

First published in Great Britain in 2018 by

ZAFFRE PUBLISHING
80–81 Wimpole St, London W1G 9RE
www.zaffrebooks.co.uk

A CIP catalogue record for this book is available from the British Library.

ISBN: 978–1–78576–031–0

also available as an ebook

1 3 5 7 9 10 8 6 4 2

Typeset by IDSUK (Data Connection) Ltd
Printed and bound by Clays Ltd, St Ives Plc

MIX
Paper from
responsible sources
FSC® C018072

Zaffre Publishing is an imprint of Bonnier Zaffre,
a Bonnier Publishing company
www.bonnierzaffre.co.uk
www.bonnierpublishing.co.uk

For my godchildren
Kate, Maddie and Monte, with love

CHAPTER ONE

Connor Baird couldn't believe it. He was lost.

Trying not to panic, he quickly dropped into the mist towards where he thought the main track into town should be. The rain increased. Torrential. And it wasn't mist, he realised. He was in cloud. Dodging a small rock fall, he tried to keep his sense of direction but it was almost impossible when all the rivers and mountainsides looked the same.

He pushed on.

As he rounded a corner, he expected to see the old shepherd's bothy dead ahead, which would show that he was barely a mile from Duncaid, but all he saw instead was a rock face.

He slid to a stop and at the same time, the cloud parted.

Below was a seemingly endless monochrome carpet of peat and waterlogged moorland. Nothing was familiar. He could have been on the other side of the Cairngorms for all he knew.

Shit, shit, *shit*.

Should he keep going, or retrace his tracks?

He dithered briefly before he decided to keep going downhill. How could he have been so stupid? Talk about teaching him a lesson: never storm off in a temper. He'd spent a great day at his grandpa's, but then his mother had ruined everything by asking him to babysit tonight. For the third time in a week! Hadn't she got the message yet? He was sick of the baby, the way everyone made stupid goo-goo noises at it, grinning like idiots. It was just a baby for Chrissakes, but when his little brother had taken his first steps last week you'd think he'd walked across the English Channel unassisted. And when little Dougie threw Connor's mobile phone on to the flagstone floor, smashing its screen into a thousand pieces, it wasn't the baby's fault. It was Connor's, for leaving the phone within the baby's reach. He was still without a phone a week later.

Connor wound down a snaking track, the tips of heather blurring into his peripheral vision. Why should his mum go out again and leave him alone with the baby? Why couldn't she get a proper babysitter? And what about his dad? Why couldn't he help out? Just because he'd had an affair shouldn't mean he could wriggle out of his parental responsibility. He was the sodding father after all.

Connor pedalled faster, squinting through the rain. He'd been out for hours now and he was hungry. He was fantasising about what he'd eat from the fridge when he got home, when a building loomed through the fog, its stone walls slick with rain. As he got closer his spirits lifted when he saw a long industrial-style building with a couple of cars parked outside. It looked like he'd come to the back of the Blackwater Industrial Estate. How on earth had that happened? He supposed it made a weird kind of sense he'd done a zigzag loop around the back of town but he wasn't sure how he'd done it, and if he was asked to do it again he wouldn't have a clue where to start.

Propping his bike against the wall, he went and knocked on the door. He wanted a hot drink, to dry off for a bit and maybe hitch a ride home. He knocked again, louder. Nothing. He waited a while, shifting from foot to foot. It may be September but it couldn't be called warm, not with the rain.

He tried the door, but it was locked.

Frustrated, he walked to the next building and had a look around. He glanced up at the security cameras. Was anyone watching him? He'd never seen anybody here. It was probably derelict inside and the cameras defunct.

When he saw one of the windows had a chink in its blind, right at the bottom, he bent to have a look. He saw a tiled floor and white-washed walls. The room seemed empty, except—

What the . . .?

He reared backwards, blinking rapidly. His brain seemed to have stalled. He stayed where he was for a moment. He was trembling, but whether it was with fear or from the cold, he didn't know.

He bent down to have another look. He needed to be sure. But he hadn't imagined anything.

At the far end of the room was a girl.

She was lying on a table.

She was naked.

She had short-cropped curly dark red hair and her skin held a weird green tinge and looked wet and waxy.

She had three soaring ravens tattooed on her wrist and although he was too far away to read the words beneath, he knew what they were.

Let it be.

She'd had more ravens tattooed on her back, spiralling out of a tree that covered the whole of her left shoulder blade and curled its delicate branches up her spine and along her neck. The accompanying text, in a dainty Brush script, read:

The worst thing is
holding on to someone
who doesn't want to be
held on to.

Connor's heart began pounding so hard he wondered how it didn't leap from his chest.

Nimue Acheson.

She'd been named after the 'Lady of the Lake', or at least that's what she'd said. Teachers thought she was fantastic: great grades, always neatly dressed, helpful and polite. But then she'd been dumped by her boyfriend, Rickie Finley, and things changed. She'd become depressed and struggled with school work. When she started talking about suicide, her family sent her to a shrink. But she still killed herself. Jumped to her death from Collynie Bridge and onto the rocks below.

Connor had been at her funeral two weeks ago along with the rest of the school. He'd seen her coffin, covered with pink and white hearts made out of miniature roses. He'd watched her being buried. Heard her dad saying he was going to get a beautiful headstone made out of marble for her and have a raven carved into its top. That he'd plant bluebells and snow-drops around her grave to welcome her each year into spring, her favourite time of year.

Connor moaned.

What was Nimue doing here?

Why wasn't she in her grave?

The moan began to rise into a shout of horror from the back of his throat.

At that moment he heard something behind him. He spun round and jumped in shock. The man was *so close!*

'I just . . . I mean . . .' Connor stammered. He held his hands high. 'I'm s-sorry . . .' He wanted to step back but couldn't. Not with his back thrust against the window.

The man moved so fast Connor didn't have time to react. One second he was standing there, both hands behind his back, the next he'd rammed something sharp into Connor's thigh.

'Hey!' Connor scrambled aside, yelping with pain.

The man watched him without expression.

Connor looked down to see a syringe hanging from his jeans. 'What the . . .' He pulled it free. Held it up. The hypodermic needle dripped blood. Then he took in the fact that the plunger had been pushed almost to the end of the barrel and that any liquid that had been inside was now inside *him.*

'Shit.' He looked at the man. 'What's in it? What the fuck . . .'

The man didn't move. Didn't blink.

A thought formed in Connor's head: *I have to get out of here.*

He started to move for his bike but he'd barely gone a few paces when his legs collapsed. He fell to the ground, gravel scraping his face.

No, no, no!

He tried to get up, but his limbs wouldn't move. He tried to shout but his mouth wouldn't work. Terror flooded him.

He was paralysed.

He heard the man's footsteps coming towards him. Connor desperately tried to open his mouth to scream as a dark wave enveloped him.

No breath.

No feeling.

No thought.

Nothing.

CHAPTER TWO

Grace Reavey was pulling wallpaper off the wall, great chunks of damp plaster coming with it, when her phone rang. Pushing her hair back with her wrist, she grabbed it off the windowsill.

It was still light, sunset another three hours away. One more hour of daylight than she was used to in England, which was great, but what about the winter months? She was already dreading the notoriously short and dark days, but she hadn't said anything to Ross. If she went stir crazy for sunshine, she'd get a sunlamp.

'Dr Reavey,' she answered her phone.

'Oh, Doctor,' a woman said. 'I'm so sorry . . .' She started to sob.

Grace made a murmuring, soothing noise, and waited.

'I don't know . . . I'm so sorry . . .' The woman was forcing her words out. 'I'm trying to see . . . but I don't know if he's dead or not. He's jumped, you see. Just like that girl . . .'

Alarm filled Grace.

'Dead?' she said.

'I don't know.' It was a wail. 'I don't know what to do!'

Grace gripped the receiver. 'Dial 999 immediately. But first, what's your name?'

'Mary Gibson.'

'Mary, can you tell me where you are?'

'I'm on the Collynie Bridge. I was walking Billy home, you see. Wanting to get back for our tea.'

'That's on the other side of Duncaid, am I right? On the road to Knockstanton?'

'Aye. That's the one.'

'I'm on my way.' She was already moving across the room as she spoke. 'But call 999 *now*, OK? They'll send an ambulance straightaway.'

'Aye, OK.'

After frantically scrubbing her hands clean, Grace pulled on a fleece, grabbed her doctor's bag and raced to her car. Flinging her bag on the passenger's seat she started her Golf in such a hurry she nearly stalled. *Steady*, she told herself. *You'll get there just as fast if you're not in a panic.*

Grace tore down the drive, stones spitting from her tyres. She couldn't see Ross. He was probably in one of the cottages, clearing it of debris. She rumbled over the cattle grid. Turned right on to the road to Duncaid. As she drove, she called the emergency services who confirmed they'd heard from Mary Gibson. They'd sent a blue light.

Although Collynie Bridge wasn't far from Duncaid, it always took longer than you expected because of the narrowness of the road and the countless hairpin bends. Luckily, she only met one tractor en-route, which she overtook easily, and made it to the other side of town in under twenty minutes and well before the ambulance, which had to come all the way from Elgin.

Grace parked her car on the narrow verge and jumped out. She could hear the roar of the water and smell the peaty spray from the river before she stepped on to the cast-iron bridge. Mary Gibson rushed to greet her, grey hair askew beneath her waterproof hood, expression distraught. A damp looking West Highland terrier tagged alongside. Billy, Grace assumed.

'I cannae get down there,' Mary gasped. 'I'm too bloody old.'

Grace looked past the floral tributes to Nimue Acheson, who'd jumped here just three weeks ago. A mountain bike was propped next to them. *Please God, let there not be an epidemic of copycat suicides.* Heart in her mouth, she peered into the ravine.

Straightaway she knew he was dead from the catastrophic angle between his head and neck, but she still had to check. She scrambled down the bank, grabbing handfuls of heather and grass to stop her falling. The bridge was single span, two car lengths at the most, but the drop had to be at least a hundred feet. A waterfall thundered past, dampening her face and hair. She passed the spot where Nimue's body had been found, marked by several strings of police tape strapped around some rocks. As the bank steepened, she braced herself, sliding her way down, and by the time she reached the bottom her hands and clothes were covered in mud.

Carefully, Grace crabbed her way over some boulders to the edge of the river and quickly washed her hands before squatting beside the body. He'd not only broken his neck, but both legs were also broken along with his right arm. Without any hope she tried his pulse. Pressed her fingers against his carotid artery. Zero. He'd died not long ago as the skin was still in early rigor mortis. Less than six hours, she guessed.

She gently pushed the hair back from his face.

Her heart clenched.

'Ah, no.'

CHAPTER THREE

It was Connor Baird. She'd met the boy a fortnight ago in her surgery when his mother, Sam, brought him in to treat a nasty gash after falling off his bike.

He was so *young*. His features were smooth and clear, surprised and uncomprehending, maybe even disbelieving, and she had to force down her emotions. She was a professional. She mustn't let sentiment get in the way.

She looked up at Mary Gibson and shook her head. The woman brought her hand to her mouth and turned away. Grace pulled out her phone to ring the ambulance, tell them there was no rush, but she had no signal. Great.

She wasn't a police officer or a forensic physician, but her training demanded that she discreetly inspect the body to ensure that there were no concealed findings which might be relevant to death. She could see a messy wound on the boy's right thigh that seemed at odds with his fall, but she decided not to move him to study it. She couldn't assume it was definitely a suicide, and whilst there was a possibility of death from unnatural causes the area was a potential crime scene.

She checked Connor over and frowned when she saw lividity on his upper right arm, an area of the boy's body that hadn't been in contact with the ground. Had the body been moved?

She was studying his hands – no defensive wounds that she could see – when someone shouted above the din of the waterfall.

'Hoy there!'

She looked up to see a burly man in a florescent jacket heading down the river bank.

'Hello,' she called.

Like her, he arrived at the bottom of the bank soaked and with mud up his trousers.

'Lachlan,' he told her cheerfully. 'Your local paramedic.'

'Grace Reavey.'

He came and squatted beside her. 'Ach,' he said, shaking his head. 'Two jumpers in less than a month. A crying shame.'

'I wouldn't be so sure he jumped.' She hated it when people made assumptions.

Lachlan gave her a sideways look. 'Why is that?'

'Well, there's this small patch of lividity . . .' She swallowed her words when Lachlan raised his head and yelled, 'Dave!' His voice boomed as clear and loud as a trombone. 'Get Murdoch on the phone, would ya? Tell him it's Connor Baird we've found.'

Dave's affirmative yell was faint against the constant beating sound of the waterfall. 'Aye, OK!'

'So,' said Lachlan. 'You've an opinion on Connor here. Are you from the polis?'

'No. I'm a doctor.'

He gave a low whistle, sinking back on his heels as he looked her up and down. 'I've heard about ye. Aye, that I have.'

Grace didn't know what to make of this, so she kept quiet.

'How are you finding us up here?' he asked, sounding genuinely curious.

'I'm finding you pretty good, thank you.'

He smiled a big broad smile that showed twin rows of large white teeth.

'That's all right then.' His cheerful expression remained. 'How're the renovations coming along?'

'Fine, thank you.'

Her tone must have given something away because he said, 'Not so keen on DIY yourself, then?'

'The house will be beautiful when it's finished.'

'Aye.' His gaze turned shrewd. 'But there's a long way to go yet. It's a bit of a wreck, that place.'

'We'll get there.'

'Aye,' he said again. This time he nodded. 'He's a strong worker, your man.'

She wasn't sure if this was a compliment to Ross or a rebuke to her. She hadn't admitted it to anyone but she loathed DIY, and the thought of spending every weekend of the foreseeable future scrubbing mucky old flagstone floors did nothing but make her feel monumentally depressed.

Luckily Lachlan changed the subject, asking where she'd trained, where her first placement had been, diverting her from Connor's cold body until Murdoch, a uniformed policeman, slithered down the bank to join them.

'Crying shame,' he echoed Lachlan. He had his hands on his hips and was shaking his head. 'Hate it when it's kids. They tend not to realise that when they jump it's forever.'

'Aye,' Lachlan agreed.

The policeman turned and looked at Grace. 'You don't have to stay,' he told her not unkindly. 'Lachlan and I can bring him up.'

Grace blinked. 'You're moving him?'

He frowned. 'Can't leave him here, can we?'

'But what about forensics?'

He sucked his teeth. 'You're the new doc, right?'

'Yup.'

'Well, not wanting to be rude or anything . . . I know you probably do things differently down south, but here we're a bit more practical, OK?'

'Practical,' she repeated. Her voice may have been even, but inside a coal of indignation began to burn.

'We dinnae have the resources.' His voice hardened. 'You'd better get used to it.'

She lifted her chin. 'I can't issue a death certificate.'

A look of disbelief crossed his face. 'You cannae confirm the cause of death?'

'No, I can't.' She repressed her natural urge to add 'sorry' because she didn't want to appear weak.

He flung up his hands. 'Jesus fucking Christ.'

'There's lividity on his arm that concerns me,' she pointed it out. 'It could well be that his body was moved after he died.'

'You're fucking kidding me.' Then his gaze turned sly. 'This isn't the first time, is it? That you've insisted on a post-mortem.'

'No,' she agreed.

'And how many of those were proven to have died in suspicious circumstances?'

None, she thought, but she refused to give in. She wasn't going to let him get away with it and bully her into submission. Connor deserved more than that.

'This isn't the same,' she told him.

They locked gazes.

She could feel Lachlan's tension, riveted by the confrontation, but she didn't look at him. She was concentrating on Murdoch.

Finally the policeman looked away. He rubbed his hands over his face, took a deep breath and blew it out again. 'OK, then. I'll ring my boss. He'll be thrilled to hear you'll be blowing his already-stretched budget to kingdom come for fucking nothing, but if you insist . . . He'll be the one who'll decide if it's a crime scene or not. Satisfied?'

'Thank you.' She smiled sweetly but dislike rose in his eyes. Ross had warned her about alienating people in such a small community, but what was she to do? Let every unexplained death go unexplored?

She'd attended a rash of sudden deaths recently. All of the victims had been in their early sixties and all had died from a range of afflictions from strokes to cancer and liver disease.

When she'd questioned the high mortality rate for such a relatively young group, the pathologist had said in a cheerful tone, 'We all die young up here.'

But not as young as Connor Baird.

CHAPTER FOUR

Dan Forrester was staring at a road sweeper outside his office window. Jenny had told him not to go to work but it wouldn't have done any good. He hadn't slept much last night and thought it a waste to lie there in the dark when he could be catching the early train to London. He had stacks of things to do, and he hadn't even started to get his head around arranging the repatriation of his father's body, let alone sending an email to all of his dad's friends and work colleagues to tell them he'd died. He'd do that when he got home tonight.

His father had died in the Golf-Klub Isterberg near Braunschweig in Germany. A massive heart attack. He'd just come off an eighteen-hole course where he'd been playing with his friend Arne and they were headed to the club house with Arne's wife, Anneke, to celebrate Arne's beating his handicap. A good day out for both of them until Bill had dropped dead, but as everyone said – including his German friends, who admittedly had been a bit shell-shocked at the time – it was a great way to go, dying with no warning and doing something you loved. No hanging about in hospital. No lingering in a hospice waiting for God.

Even Dan had to agree it was probably a good thing as his father would have hated any form of debilitation. Bill'd always enjoyed robust health and had been incredibly active through his seventies and into his eighties. That said, Dan could remember when his father had been forced to stop sailing three years ago. He'd become a real liability on the boat, and when Gordon, his yachting buddy since they were at university, broke the news he couldn't take Bill on board anymore, he hadn't spoken to Gordon for the rest of the year. And even then, when Bill eventually started speaking to Gordon again, it was only because Gordon had admitted he wasn't so steady on his pins either and had sold the boat.

Stubborn old goats, Dan thought, shaking his head and smiling ruefully.

The landline rang on his desk and he picked it up. 'Forrester,' he said.

'Dan, it's me. Christopher.'

Dan blinked. 'I was just thinking about Gordon.'

'Christ . . .' The man's voice broke. 'I'm sorry . . .'

Without realising, Dan got to his feet.

'What is it? What's wrong?'

'It's Connor. He . . . he's . . .'

Dan felt a cold wave wash over him. *Not Connor, please, not my godson.*

'T-they found him . . . at the b-bottom of a ravine. They say he j-jumped off Collynie Bridge.'

Dan sat down abruptly. He felt sick.

'They say it's suicide. That he *killed himself*. But it's not true. I know it's *not true*. But I don't know what to do. Dan, please. Tell me *what to do*.'

Dan's fingers were already at work on his computer keyboard. He glanced briefly at his wall clock. In its centre was a man in a suit with a bowler hat and briefcase. His legs were the minutes' and seconds' hands, making him look as though he was always running. 'Running home to us', Jenny had told him, smiling.

'What I want you to do,' Dan said, 'is meet me at Inverness Airport this afternoon. I'll text you my flight details.'

'But you can't,' Christopher protested. 'Bill just died. You can't come up here when—'

'Unless I say differently, I'll be on the eleven twenty-five flight, arriving at twelve forty-five.'

'Dan, seriously—'

'See you there.'

He hung up, knowing it was the only way to silence his friend. There was no way he could stay down here with Connor dead. Bill would have agreed. He could almost hear his dad's voice in his mind, a strong baritone, brooking no argument.

Of course, you must go. Not much you can do about me, is there? Send them my love.

Dan began moving around his office, grabbing the essentials. The scar on his stomach tightened at the activity, making him wince. He'd been lucky that the bullet had passed through the muscles and never entered the abdominal cavity, and even luckier that he'd healed so fast. Yet another scar to go with the rest. Another wound for Jenny to tenderly kiss.

Passport – he never went anywhere without it – his tablet and phone, the chargers, his wallet. Everything went into his grab bag, the contents of which he'd overhauled after he'd returned from his last assignment a fortnight ago. Underwear, clean shirt and socks, toothbrush and paste, electric shaver. And a tie, just in case.

He moved swiftly through reception. Their receptionist wasn't in yet. His boss was, though, and also Julia from the sound of the coffee machine whirring through her open door, but he didn't have time to explain. Outside he hailed a cab to take him to Paddington. He caught the Heathrow Express with three minutes to spare. Sitting in an aisle seat with his tablet on his lap, his grab bag between his feet, he rang Jenny.

'Hi, Daddy,' his daughter answered.

'Aimee?' he said, surprised. 'Aren't you meant to be at school?'

'We're late 'cause Poppy hid my shoe! Mummy's driving really fast . . .'

He heard Jenny say something, and Aimee giggled. 'She says she's not driving fast. She's driving effici . . . effi . . .'

'Efficiently.'

'Yes!' There was a short pause before she said 'Daddy?', drawing the word out to indicate she was posing a serious question. He could almost see the frown appearing on her face.

'Yes, sweetpea?'

'Who's going to babysit me when you and Mummy go away?'

She didn't have to add, 'now Granddad's dead.' because Dan knew that's what she meant.

'We won't be going away for ages,' he assured her. 'But if we do, Granny Becky and Grandpa Adam will look after you in Bath.'

Another short pause.

'OK.' Her voice suddenly brightened. 'Look, there's Tara! She's late too . . .'

It was one of those times he felt glad she was still young enough to be easily distracted. He heard a flurry of activity at the other end of the phone which he assumed meant they were pulling up outside the school gates and that Aimee was unbuckling her seatbelt – always too soon in his opinion – and grabbing her backpack.

'Aimee?' he called.

'We've got relationship education today!'

Aimee may have just turned seven but even so, Dan wasn't sure how to respond. 'Great,' he said.

'Byeeee!'

'Bye,' he responded but she'd already gone.

'Dan.' Jenny sounded cautious; he rarely called her from work and when he did it was usually to say he was running late. Hence the wall clock she'd given him.

'Jen, I'm sorry but something's come up. I'm on my way to Heathrow.'

She didn't say anything, just waited.

He leaned back and closed his eyes, belatedly realising he should have held off calling her until she was home. 'I don't know if this is the right time to tell you . . .'

'What is it?' her voice was alarmed.

'I don't want you driving—'

'Jesus, Dan. It's too late now. Just tell me, OK?'

'I'm really sorry . . .' He rubbed his forehead with the tips of his fingers. 'Christopher rang. He told me Connor died.'

'What?' She sounded blank.

He repeated what he'd said.

'Oh, no.' It was a whisper. 'How?'

'They say it's suicide.'

'Dear God. That's awful. I mean, really . . .' Her voice thickened into tears. 'Shit. He was such a great kid.'

'I know.' He rubbed his forehead. 'I can't believe it either. Christopher sounds a mess so I'm going to Scotland. Will you be OK? I can always go up tomorrow if you—'

'No, you must go.' Her tone started to firm. 'They need you far more than I do, Dan. I'll be fine.'

'If you're sure . . .'

'I'm sure. There's nothing to keep you down here, is there?'

'It was only stuff to do with repatriating Dad's body, which can probably wait.'

'Let me do that. What about the death certificate?'

'I need to get a provisional one, apparently.'

'I can do that too . . .'

Not for the first time he thanked his lucky stars for his wife. She was upset over Connor but she wasn't falling apart. She was supporting him the best way she could, by freeing him to go to Christopher. They'd been married fourteen years, and although they'd had their ups and downs – some resembling the cliffs of Everest in a snowstorm – he didn't think he'd ever loved her more than he did right at that moment.

'Concentrate on Sam and Christopher,' she told him. 'They really need their friends right now. And poor Gordon . . .'

Gordon and Bill had met at Magdalen College in Oxford. It was thanks to their friendship that their sons, Christopher and Dan, had also become friends. Since he was a toddler, Dan and his family had spent three weeks of every summer holiday at the Bairds' place, a Scottish estate with a loch and a boathouse, and red deer on the front lawn. For Dan, a London boy brought up with pavements beneath his feet and streetlights keeping the night at bay, those weeks in Scotland had been frightening and exciting in equal measure, and he'd been inordinately gratified to learn that when Christopher came and stayed with him in London he'd felt just as challenged. Not that either admitted it until they'd been down the pub one evening as adults. How they'd laughed at their childhood insecurities.

'Thank you,' he said.

'Just send them my love.'

'Look . . .' He took a breath. 'Will you be OK if I stay up there overnight?'

'I'm pregnant,' she told him with a sigh. 'Not disabled.'

He wasn't so sure about that since she couldn't sleep comfortably, couldn't eat without heartburn and her ankles were the size of watermelons, but he wasn't going to mention any of that to her.

A stab of grief that his father had died before his second grandson was born pierced him. Bill had already promised to teach him how to fish, like he'd taught his first grandson, Luke. Bill had adored Luke, and Luke had adored him back, riding around on Bill's back shouting 'Horsey!' Not that Dan could remember this. He'd lost great chunks of his memory from the shock of what everyone believed to be his 'breakdown' when he'd witnessed Luke's death, and it was only thanks to Jenny that he had any kind of mental map of what life had been like with his first son.

'Love you,' Jenny said, and he could almost see the softness in her eyes as she spoke.

'Love you too.'

After he'd hung up, he called his boss.

'Take the week off, Dan.' Philip was brisk. 'More, if you need it. Help your friend then get started on your father's affairs. What's outstanding here?'

'Most can wait,' Dan told him, 'except for Norse.'

Dan talked Philip through the case. DCA & Co specialised in political risk analysis, and this particular client of Dan's was looking at investing in a company in Brazil and needed impartial, professional advice on the potential risks and benefits, before he sank his considerable amount of money into it at the end of the week.

'I'll take Norse, then,' Philip told him. 'The rest will be covered by Julia. OK?'

'Great. Thanks.'

At Heathrow Dan bought a cappuccino and a panini which he devoured at the gate. He hadn't eaten much since his father had died, he realised. It was only now he'd been given a mission to help someone else that his appetite had kicked in. He licked his fingers, glad to be feeling a bit more normal until he remembered what he was doing here.

Connor Baird, thirteen years old, mountain biker and all-round pretty decent kid, was dead.

Had he really committed suicide? Dan pictured Connor's vivid expression, always curious, questioning everything. He'd thought him an intelligent, well-balanced boy, outgoing and active, and about as far from being suicidal as he could imagine, but what did he know? He hadn't seen the boy for two years and who knew what had gone on behind closed doors, behind the screen of his computer. Had he been bullied? Lost any friendships? Had his school let him down somehow? Had he been abused in some way? Dan supposed any one of those things could trigger suicide.

Connor had been so vital, so enthusiastic and *alive* when Dan had last seen him. Had he really changed that much?

He guessed he'd soon find out.

CHAPTER FIVE

When Dan disembarked he spotted Christopher straightaway. Tall, slim, with sandy hair and freckles, he usually wore an open expression that people warmed to immediately. Christopher made friends easily and, unlike Dan, would happily chat to strangers, finding them interesting and engaging, but today he wasn't chatting to anyone. He was standing on his own, his face grey and frightened, and the crowd stood apart as though they knew there was something wrong with him and didn't want to be contaminated.

'Christopher.' The men embraced. Dan could feel the tension vibrating in his friend's body like a high-voltage wire.

'Dan.' His voice shuddered. 'You didn't have to come. Bill only died –'

'Dad would have wanted me here.' Dan was firm.

'But you must have so much—'

'What are you driving?'

As Christopher said, 'Polo,' Dan put out his hand.

Christopher gave a twisted smile and delved in his jacket pocket to pull out a set of car keys which he handed over. Outside it felt unseasonably cold and, in the distance, heavy grey clouds had sunk low enough to obscure the mountain tops. Dan unlocked the car and climbed inside, repositioning the driver's seat, mirrors and steering wheel. Christopher didn't say a word because he knew that Dan's previous job had been as a high-performance instructor, training racing-car drivers along with high-pursuit police and ambulance drivers. Dan had once taken Christopher on a high-speed drive across country while at the same time giving him a running commentary, and from that day forward Christopher let Dan drive. *To save me the embarrassment of looking like an idiot*, he'd said.

Dan eased out of the car park, nipping in front of a Mercedes whose driver appeared to be more absorbed in inspecting her mascara in her rear-view mirror than the traffic.

'What happened to the Baby Rangie?' The last time Dan had seen Christopher, he'd been enamoured with his brand spanking new Range Rover Evoque.

'Sam's requisitioned it.'

Dan was startled but he didn't react. He let the silence hang.

'She kicked me out six weeks ago,' Christopher told him. 'She relegated me to the Polo. Said it was all I deserved.'

Dan opened and closed his mouth. He wanted to say, 'What's going on? You've just had a baby . . . you were both so happy when I last saw you . . .'

Christopher made a deep groaning sound. The sound of grief.

'I fucked up, Dan. Christ, I've fucked up.'

Dan flicked on the windscreen wipers. Rain was pushing in from the west and clouds were beginning to thicken. He automatically split his awareness between Christopher and his driving. The A96 was notoriously dangerous due to driver frustration. He kept his senses alert.

'But just because I fucked up, it doesn't mean Connor killed himself.' Christopher's voice strengthened. 'He's not like that. He's not that stupid. Yes, he was angry. He was furious with me and furious with his mum. He didn't want me to move out. He wanted Sam to forgive me, but she wanted to punish me first. Connor knew things weren't permanent. We *talked* about it. He was OK. He knew the score. *He was OK.*'

Dan flicked his gaze across. Christopher was trembling. His whole body in distress.

'I know he finds . . . *found* little Dougie a pain in the backside. Dougie's a baby. Connor's a thirteen-year-old boy. When Sam told him he'd be babysitting while she went out with the girls again for the third time in a week – what was she *thinking?* – he saw red. Stormed off apparently. A lot of it was because Sam refused to call me and have me babysit instead. Which I would have done like a shot. Anything to get back inside the house . . .'

Christopher put his head in his hands and started rocking back and forth. 'Why didn't she call me? Then Connor wouldn't have gone who knows where and ended up . . .'

Long silence.

Clumps of faded wildflowers flashed past. Wind farms, low rolling countryside, brown sweeps of recently harvested wheat. As they crossed the Findhorn, Dan automatically glanced at the water level.

A bit low, his father said in Dan's mind. *Could do with a spate to bring the salmon up.*

If they were fishing today, they'd probably use a bog-standard Ally Shrimp with a hot orange bucktail. Dan still found it strange how he couldn't remember Luke or anything about his old job at MI5 but he could tell you every detail of the fishing rod Christopher's father had let him use each summer. Some memories had been lost forever but he could recall the fly patterns – Hares Ear, Pheasant Tail, Prince Nymph – as if he was holding them in his hands.

He could also remember the look of horror on Christopher's face when he lost control of the Land Rover that day. They'd been twelve, and it had been Sophie – as usual – who'd goaded them into doing something they shouldn't. Sophie was a year younger than they were but she made up for that by being twice as audacious.

'Nobody's here!' Her face shone with excitement. 'Nobody'll know we've driven it!'

Their parents were all on the hill, shooting, and the one father who'd stayed behind because he didn't like guns – Rafe, Sophie's dad – had been called to the neighbouring estate to help with a fisher who'd broken his wrist. 'You be good,' he'd told them sternly. 'Or none of you will come up here again.' He towered over them, a powerful presence. He was a fell runner, super-fit, but he still smoked like a chimney. Whenever Dan smelled cigarette smoke he always thought of Rafe.

'But I will know.' Gustav snatched the car keys out of Sophie's hand. He was three years older than them at fifteen and invariably acted as a brake on their more adventurous exploits. At first Dan had thought Gustav stuffy, but soon came to realise it was simply that he came from Germany. He was OK though, and kept out of their way most of the time.

'Oh, come on, Gus,' she wheedled. 'Don't be a spoilsport. You can drive first if you like. I bet you're really good. Like a Grand Prix driver.'

Dan waited for Gustav to fold. He had a soft spot for Sophie and was rarely able to resist her entreaties.

'No. It is too dangerous.'

'It's only an old banger!' she exclaimed. 'It's not like it's a Ferrari or anything!'

Gustav scowled. Pocketing the keys, he marched outside.

Sophie raised two fingers at Christopher and Dan – *two minutes* – and pattered after Gustav. Secretly, Dan was relieved Gustav had taken charge. The thought of driving the car was exciting but also terrifying. The only time he'd held a moving car's steering wheel had been when he was a little boy, sitting on his father's lap. Looking at the Land Rover he doubted his legs would even reach the pedals.

Sophie reappeared. To his dismay, she was holding up the keys triumphantly.

'Gustav gave them to you?' Dan was astonished.

'No, silly. I grabbed the spare set from the kitchen.'

Christopher looked at Dan. Dan looked back. Dismay quickly turned to excitement.

'Me first,' Sophie announced. 'Dad's already shown me how.'

She had to sit right on the edge of the bench seat and stretch her lower body forwards to reach the pedals, and with a single choking roar the Land Rover erupted into life.

Beside Dan, Christopher gave a high-pitched giggle. Dan felt a sickening combination of fear and exhilaration as Sophie released the handbrake and the clutch at the same time.

The vehicle bounded forward at a terrifying rate, straight for Rafe's Vauxhall.

'STOP!' yelled Christopher as Dan braced himself against the dashboard shouting, 'BRAKE!'

Sophie nearly vanished from sight as she rammed both feet on the brake. The Land Rover bucked to an abrupt halt. Silence fell.

Sophie caught Dan's eyes and grinned.

'That was fun.'

'Fun,' he repeated. His voice came out as a croak.

'I want to go to Blackwater.'

The derelict farm buildings were situated along the Ben Kincaid track – they used to play there, but they had been out of bounds for the last two years because they were, apparently, dangerous.

Sophie leaned past Dan to look at Christopher. 'You're the tallest. You drive.'

CHAPTER SIX

Luckily Christopher had had some experience driving the Land Rover, albeit under the watchful eye of his father, Gordon, and they only did about five kangaroo hops before they rattled over the cattle grid and were away.

Sophie had slid back her window and was leaning outside looking behind at the lodge when she suddenly gave a shriek.

'Faster!' she shouted. 'Gustav's coming!'

Being in the middle Dan couldn't see what was happening. All he knew was that Christopher pushed his foot on the accelerator, making the engine howl, and they were bounding down the drive.

Sophie was whooping as she dropped back into her seat. 'He's still running. Do you think he'll run after us all the way?'

Before Dan could answer to say that Gustav didn't know where they were going so how could he? she reached into her back pocket and brought out a lighter and a packet of cigarettes. Benson & Hedges. Her father's cigarettes. 'Who wants one?'

She smiled and shook one out and Dan and Christopher were looking at her as she put a cigarette between her lips – even though Dan knew smoking could kill, she managed to make it look so *cool*. Sophie flicked the lighter at the same time the car gave a massive great BANG! and left the road.

They all screamed as the steering wheel whipped free of Christopher's grip and the Land Rover careened across the grass and straight for the river.

Dan tried to grab the steering wheel but it jerked away as the front wheels bit into an ant hill. The impact slewed the car sideways, slowed it down, but the river bank was still fast approaching. A steep, grassy drop that would plunge them beneath the surface of the water.

Dan was shouting as the Land Rover's bonnet dipped. Started its slide down the river bank.

A soft shudder ran through the framework as the vehicle collided with another ant hill and then it stopped abruptly, resting at a sickening angle, just yards from the river.

'I've got the brakes,' Christopher gasped. He was half in the foot well, legs stretched out. 'I've got both feet on the brakes . . .'

Sophie shouldered the door open, falling out of the Land Rover. She was shouting for them to follow her.

Dan scrambled across the bench seat and tumbled outside and into a heap on the grass. When Christopher didn't appear he raced back. 'You've got to come too.'

'I can't,' Christopher bleated. A look of despair crumpled his face. 'If I take my feet off the brakes it'll go into the river.'

Christopher, Dan remembered in horror, hadn't yet learned to swim.

Dan tried the handbrake but it was loose and didn't bite as it should. Even if Dan wanted to, it would be virtually impossible to swap positions without Christopher releasing the brakes.

'I'll run and get help.'

Dan had barely reached the road when Gustav arrived, red faced and panting. He seemed to understand the situation at a glance and ran past Dan to the Land Rover, straight to Christopher.

Dan saw him try the handbrake then he bent down and manoeuvred himself to push both hands on the brake. 'Go,' he told Christopher.

'But what about you?'

'GO!'

Christopher scrambled outside. He stood there looking shell-shocked.

Dan held his breath waiting for Gustav to take his hands off the brakes and jump out.

The Land Rover began to move and Dan saw Gustav frantically trying to push himself free but he wasn't fast enough and the next second the vehicle plunged into the river taking him with it.

All three of them raced to the edge of the water. The Land Rover bobbed its way down the river, doors open, sinking fast. Gustav was nowhere to be seen.

'Gus?' Sophie whispered.

'We've got to get help,' Dan said just as Gustav's head broke through the water. He was coughing, water and spittle flying from his mouth, but Dan had never seen anything that looked so good.

They helped Gustav onto the bank. He had scrapes on his hands and a bruise on his cheek. He was shivering like mad. 'If y-you *ever* do *anything* like this ag-gain, I will k-kill you.' He was looking at Sophie.

'Promise,' she whispered.

There had never been four more silent children on the walk back to the lodge. They were too stunned to cry or talk.

That evening, when Christopher's father discovered the Land Rover missing, Gustav put his head on one side, frowning. 'A man, he came to the door earlier.'

Gordon switched his gaze to pin Christopher with an eagle stare. 'What man?'

Christopher looked his father straight in the eye as he answered. 'He wanted work. I told him to come back tomorrow when you'd be here.'

'And where were you while I was tending to the fisherman next door?' This came from Rafe, who was gazing at his daughter. 'What were you up to?'

Sophie squirmed. 'Nothing.'

Rafe's eyes narrowed. 'Tell me,' he ground out.

'We . . .' Sophie hung her head.

Dan held his breath.

'We played in . . .' a furtive look at Gordon '. . . the workshop.'

The workshop was another place that was out of bounds because it was full of dangerous tools and sharp objects.

'I've told you before . . .' Rafe launched into a diatribe of rebuke but Dan wasn't listening. He was watching Sophie in sheer admiration for coming up with something so brilliant which not only sounded totally genuine but neatly deflected everyone away from the Land Rover.

'And you, Dan?'

The voice he'd been dreading.

He'd never lied to his father before. Heart beating faster, he met his father's eyes. Held them.

'We were in the workshop,' he said clearly then added in a mumble, 'sorry,' as he looked away.

Later Sophie disappeared and after a while Dan went to find her. She'd tucked herself in the corner of the boot room and was hugging one of the spaniels, crying silently, her nose and eyes red and swollen.

Dan sat with her, stroking the dog and murmuring that everything was OK, they were all safe and hadn't been found out. At least not yet anyway.

'You were amazing,' she eventually choked. 'I didn't know you could lie so well.'

'Nor did I.'

'And what about Gustav and Christopher?' She scrubbed her face of tears. 'They were amazing too. Dad really believes some pikey nicked the keys from the house and stole it.'

Dan wasn't so sure their parents had been fooled; in fact at the end of the summer his father said in a voice that sounded troubled and full of unease, 'I'm not sure I like it that you lot can dissemble quite so well.'

Dan had to look up the word *dissemble* and putting the meaning together with the way his father had said the word made him feel guilty and slightly sick.

*

Now Dan glanced across at his friend who was staring dead ahead through the windscreen. No lying today, no dissembling. He just wanted help finding answers as to why his son had died.

'Connor didn't commit suicide.' Christopher persisted.

Dan overtook a logging lorry laden with stacks of Scots pine.

'Can I ask one thing?'

'Of course. *Of course.*'

'What does the fiscal say?' It was the Procurator Fiscal's job to decide if a crime had been committed and if there was enough evidence to prosecute, or not as the case may be. The fiscal was a powerful figure in Scotland; their word was the law.

Christopher leaned his head back. 'Suicide.'

'Who attended the scene?'

'A GP and a police officer.'

Dan digested this.

'What else?'

'Nothing.' His voice was laced with despair. 'The police report states it was a suicide, that's all I know. A girl from his school jumped from the same bridge a few weeks ago and everyone assumes he's copied her. But why would he do that? She wasn't his girlfriend. She wasn't even in his *class.* Everyone keeps telling me it's normal to be in denial when someone you love has committed suicide, but *I just know he didn't kill himself.*'

Dan thought of Jenny and Aimee, his clients at DCA & Co, his father's repatriation and the funeral that needed arranging. Then Jenny's voice came into his mind. *Concentrate on Sam and Christopher. They really need their friends right now.*

Dan looked across at his childhood friend.

'You want me to try and find someone to help get some answers?'

At that, Christopher turned his head. Hope flared in his eyes. 'Yes, Dan. *Yes*, thank you!'

'Even though you might not like what you hear?'

Christopher bowed his head and clasped his hands together as though he was praying. 'I have to know what happened.' He raised his head and Dan could feel the intensity of his gaze practically burning his cheek. 'Who do you know?'

'A GP and a cop.'

CHAPTER SEVEN

Detective Constable Lucy Davies was interviewing a leggy brunette who was telling her how she'd crept through the kitchen window of her ex-husband's home and tried to seduce him.

'Why use the window?' Lucy asked. 'Why not knock on the front door?'

'I did, but he didn't answer.'

'He was inside?'

'He came to the door and looked through the peephole.'

'Since he didn't answer the door,' Lucy said evenly, 'didn't you think you might not be welcome?'

The woman gave Lucy a blank look. 'But the window was open.'

'It's not your house.'

The woman looked baffled.

'Look,' Lucy said patiently, 'if someone knocked on your door and you didn't answer, how would you feel if they climbed through your window and walked into your kitchen?'

'But it wasn't *my* house. It was *his*. And the window was open.'

She's not getting it, Lucy thought. She just doesn't see that she is totally one hundred per cent *nuts*. Lucy didn't dare look at the DS who was letting her lead the interview, in case it triggered a bout of hysterical laughter. *Honestly*, she thought, *the people I meet in my job.*

Lucy had started to explain to the woman that not every ex-husband wants to have his ex-wife break into his house and bare her breasts at him in his kitchen while his new wife is upstairs, when someone tapped on the door and opened it.

'Lucy.' It was Howard, her old partner. 'Call for you. It can't wait, sorry.'

She managed to supress the urge to do handsprings and shout, 'Yippee!' and simply leaned over, called out the time and switched off the tape. 'We'll resume in half an hour.'

Outside she looked at the DS and immediately wished she hadn't. He appeared to be holding his breath against the laughter threatening to erupt. His eyes were watering from the effort. 'Don't you dare,' she warned him. 'Or her brief will have your balls for breakfast.' But as she turned aside she couldn't stop the snigger at the back of her throat, and at that the DS gave a half-shout, half-laugh and bolted down the corridor, shoulders shaking.

Howard watched him go. 'What was that all about?'

'Don't ask.' She rolled her eyes.

'She looked all right to me.' Howard was referring to the brunette she'd been interviewing.

'She looks all right to anyone. Until you start talking to her.'

In the sector office, she picked up the phone. 'DC Davies,' she said.

'Lucy.'

One word and her nerves jumped to attention, quivering like a pack of hunting dogs being called to task.

'Dan?'

'Yes. What are you doing right now?'

'Interviewing a woman who's been accused of stalking her ex.'

'Sounds exciting.' His voice was dry.

'At least I'm not running around some junkyard with two Rottweilers about to tear me to shreds.'

'There is that,' he said agreeably. 'Look, something's come up. Any chance you can come to Duncaid, Scotland? If you left now, you'd get here around 8 p.m. and in time for a whisky and a home-cooked dinner.'

Her mind showered rainbows of yellow and lavender. Thanks to a neurological phenomenon, a type of synaesthesia, her mind lit up with colours when emotionally stimulated in some way, becoming particularly lively when her brain was trying to make disparate connections to do with an intricate police case. It was particularly useful in warning her that she might have missed something, rather like a flashing amber traffic light trying to get a driver's attention at a busy junction.

'Is this official?' she asked.

'Sorry.'

Not again! She put her hand on her forehead trying to think, but she couldn't get past the fact that each time she saw Dan she invariably ended up in trouble. Mind you, if it hadn't been for the case they'd originally been involved with, she would never have been fast-tracked to become a detective so it wasn't all bad. Besides, she was never bored when Dan was around. Terrified, yes. But the excitement more than made up for it.

'What's it about?'

'I'll tell you when you get here.'

Inside, she gave a groan. That was the trouble with dealing with an ex-spook. Not only was Dan laconic at the best of times, but he only gave out information when he absolutely had to and usually only at the last minute.

'How long do you need me for?' she asked.

'A few days. All expenses paid. The air's great too. It's like breathing champagne.'

For Lucy in her current mood – ebullient, filled with energy, her mind crackling – it was a no-brainer. She'd do anything not to have to go back into that airless interview room with that nutcase of a woman.

'I'll ask Mac, OK? I'll go and see him now and ring you back.'

'OK.'

They were about to hang up when she said, 'Hey, did you say Duncaid?'

'Yes. Why?'

'Did you know Grace moved up there with Ross? She's working out of the Duncaid Medical Centre.'

The silence told her she'd surprised him.

'Are you sure it's Duncaid?'

Quickly she checked her contacts list. 'Yup. The surgery's there but she doesn't live in town. Ross bought a ruined farm that he's doing up. Middle of nowhere apparently. Would you like her number?'

'Thanks.'

After they'd hung up Lucy jogged along the corridor, her thoughts whistling.

Dan's called me, he wants me for a mission and I'm important, vital, I can solve his case with one hand tied behind my back, and then there's Grace, my friend and confidante, who I haven't seen for ages, and now I get to see the farm and see Dan and help him . . .

Ten months ago, Grace, Dan and Lucy hadn't known one another, but the death of Grace's mother had set off a chain of catastrophic events that had brought them together. Unlike friendships made day-to-day through mutual friends or work, theirs had been forged in fear and desperation, bonding them together as tightly as soldiers who'd fought a war side by side. Lucy couldn't wait to see them.

When she arrived outside Mac's office, she stopped. *Hell,* she thought. *She couldn't go in there in her current mood, could she?* Grace had warned her against feeling over-confident when she was riding one of her highs, and to be more mindful at work to avoid making a disastrous mistake of some sort.

You're vulnerable at each end of the mood spectrum. When you're high you must be careful not to think you're invulnerable, and when you're low you have to make sure you eat well and keep up your fluids or you could feel so low you don't want to go to work.

She'd met DI Faris MacDonald two years ago on a team-building exercise in Wales. She could remember the first time she'd seen him, how her skin had tightened all over when she'd seen his hands – big and strong – yearning to feel them on her body, his lips on hers. She'd never felt such a powerful attraction before. And it appeared he hadn't either because he'd immediately invited her for a swim. Which turned into a five day long fantastic, mind-blowing affair; bunking off for a drink, a cliff top walk, a search to find a sheltered cove where they made love as though they were the last people on earth. It had been crazy, out of control, and she'd panicked. She'd been going out with someone then, and so had he. She'd ended up leaving the course early, blanking his calls. A year later he'd turned up in Stockton as her boss. She'd struggled to keep him at a distance, and now she reminded herself not to drop her guard.

Mac is your boss, she told herself. *Yes, you've had sex with him (spectacular) and you like him (a lot) but you can't risk a relationship with him. Not just because it will undermine you – everyone will think you slept with him to become a detective – but the second he gets to know you he'll write you off as a loony tune. He'll run a mile. Much better not to go there, so your heart can't be broken.*

She lifted her chin. *You just have to go in there, explain about Dan and ask Mac if he can spare you for a few days. Mac already knows Dan, and that he's a bit special, so he shouldn't have a problem letting you go. Besides, you're not in the thick of anything that can't be covered by the team. And then there's the little fact you're way overdue your holiday . . .*

She squared her shoulders. Rapped on the door.

'Come!'

She stepped inside to see Mac frowning at his computer screen. Curly brown hair, strong jawline, broad shoulders and hands that could be as gentle as velvet. As she looked at his hands her mind emptied of everything but the need to feel them on her skin. A rush of desire, a pure clean bolt of heat shot through every vein, every cell in her body.

Shit. She had to go. Get out of here before . . .

Mac looked up.

Mismatched grey eyes met hers.

The oxygen in the room suddenly emptied.

'Jesus Christ,' he said.

One second Mac was at his desk, the next he was across the room and standing in front of her. His eyes were locked on hers, the pupils so large they appeared almost black.

'Lucy.'

A mute pounding started in her skull. Sound faded. *Keep it together,* she told herself. *Keep it cool. You mustn't lose control. You can do this. You have to.*

'I came to ask for some time off.' Her tone was stiff. 'Not long. Just a few days. Dan Forrester called. He wants me in Scotland.'

At that, his eyes changed colour from hot black to steel-grey. He glanced aside. Stepped back and took a deep breath. Cleared his throat. Folded his arms.

'Why?'

'He couldn't say.'

Mac didn't comment, but she could almost hear the cogs whirring inside his head, his thoughts. *Couldn't? Or wouldn't?*

'He needs me up there by eight,' she added.

'What, tonight?'

'Yes.'

Silence.

'I'm happy to help him out in my own time. I'm owed lots of holiday.'

'What about your boyfriend?' he asked. His tone turned uncharacteristically snide. 'Or will Baker go too?'

She'd met Nicholas Baker, ex-special forces, on her last big case. Nick wasn't her boyfriend and was never likely to be, but she wasn't going to tell Mac that. She wanted to keep Nick as her first line of defence.

'None of your business,' she told him.

Mac exhaled sharply, running a hand over his head and making the curls dance. His hair was incredibly soft, she remembered, nothing like she'd imagined. She looked away before she could give in to the temptation to reach up and touch it.

'OK.' Mac cleared his throat. 'I'll speak to Dan. He's on the same number?'

'Yes.'

As Mac moved to his desk she turned to leave the room but he said, 'Wait. Let's do this now.'

She tried not to look at him as he dialled, fixing her gaze on a poster offering a £1,000 reward for information on a series of rapes in Middlesbrough.

'Dan Forrester? It's . . . yes, I'm fine thanks . . . yup . . .'

Long silence while Mac listened. She glanced across to see his expression was distant, unreadable.

Then he said, 'It's nothing that will cause her any conflict of interests?'

Which was Mac's way of enquiring whether Dan was going to ask Lucy to do anything that might risk her job, from planting bugs to breaking the speed limit, both of which she'd done on Dan's behalf earlier in the year.

Mac listened some more before saying, 'OK, I understand. She says she has holiday due. She'll let you know her ETA, OK? But before you go,' – his tone hardened – 'I want you to know that Lucy is an invaluable part of my team, and I want her back unscathed.'

Mac didn't say goodbye, simply hung up. His face was grim. 'I don't like it,' he told her. 'Whenever you and Dan Forrester get together you're like—'

'What did he tell you?' she interrupted him, not wanting a health and safety lecture.

He surveyed her for a moment. 'He needs a cop's eyes. He wants to brief you himself. He's going to ring you later ... it's a personal matter, but knowing you two, what appears to be a simple task will no doubt turn into some sort of nightmare.'

She decided not to say anything.

He sighed. Looked away. Did the hand over-the-head thing. Sighed again. 'OK. I need you to tell me what you have outstanding so I can get you covered.'

She tried not to grin. It would only annoy him and make him think she'd won. Which she had, she supposed. As she ran him through her cases, he made notes on his computer, telling her who he'd get to do what. He was sharply efficient, and not for the first time she thought what a good policeman he was. Intelligent, confident and trustworthy. Tenacious too. And a bit of a risk taker. Just look at the long leash he gave her. Her old boss at the Met had hated her and tried to rule her with an iron fist. He'd called her a liability. Temperamental. Irritable. Obsessive. Exhausting. All of which Mac had cheerfully said were positive characteristics for a detective, but then he hadn't seen how crazy she got sometimes, or witnessed her crash. Hopefully, if she kept him at arm's length, he'd never see the real her. It was the only way she could protect herself.

When they'd finished he looked up at her. 'Keep me informed. Every day, please.'

It was their usual deal. As long as he felt he was part of whatever was going on, he kept out of her hair.

'OK,' she agreed.

'Be careful, OK?'

'Of course,' she said brightly, spinning on her heel.

'I MEAN IT!' he yelled after her as she jogged down the corridor.

CHAPTER EIGHT

Mac fought to concentrate on the briefing he was giving. What to do about Lucy? What was she going to get up to in Scotland? He couldn't blame Dan Forrester for wanting her professional view on his godson's suicide. Where some people thought of Lucy as difficult, struggling to pigeonhole her into a box labelled 'POLICE', Mac saw her unorthodox behaviour as a gift. As did Dan Forrester. Both of them appreciated the fact that Lucy's logic didn't always run along tramlines and although her judgement could be seen to be off-the-wall, sometimes bizarre, a lot of the time it got results.

He kept seeing Lucy's face in his mind's eye, the way her lips had softened as she looked at him, her eyes darkening the same way they did just before he entered her.

Jesus Christ, how the hell were they going to keep working together? Was she as affected as he was? Maybe it was all in his imagination. What about Nicholas Baker, the pretty-boy ex-soldier that dressed like a surfer and thought he was God's gift? Was she still seeing him?

It was over six months ago when he saw them together and the memory still burned. He'd been racing to see her, desperate to make sure she was safe, hold her, throw himself at her feet, he hadn't been sure which, when he spotted them walking across the car park. They'd been sharing an umbrella, Lucy touching Baker's arm and looking up at him laughing. They seemed so at ease together, comfortable, *happy*, it just about killed him. He'd sneaked away before they spotted him. Headed straight home where he'd got absolutely, totally, gas-guzzlingly drunk.

Since then he'd managed to keep his equilibrium pretty much in place when she was around. He'd gone online and found himself a couple of dates. Went out with a woman from Leeds for a while, but although she was attractive and very nice in bed and out, she wasn't Lucy.

Nobody was Lucy.

CHAPTER NINE

Grace rang Dan as she walked to the butcher. No delis here, and thank heavens the butcher sold more than just raw meat or they'd be forced to shop in Elgin every other day. She really had to learn to cook. She really had to learn to do a lot of other stuff, including catch fish and ride a horse, but cooking was at the top of the list; they couldn't live on takeaways for the rest of their lives.

Dan answered on the second ring. 'Any luck?' he asked.

He wanted to know if she'd managed to set up a meeting with the Procurator Fiscal to arrange a post-mortem on Connor's body.

'I'm seeing him on Wednesday.'

'Great.'

'Look, Lucy's staying with us. Why don't you come around for dinner? We can chat then.'

'Can I bring Christopher? It would be good for him to talk to you. He's got lots of questions.'

'Of course.'

She could understand Connor's father wanting answers. Suicide was a particularly devastating way to lose a loved one, the shock of which could be as violent as a grenade exploding within a family. Survivors were invariably left profoundly distressed, struggling with a complicated grief process often made harder by not knowing why it had happened. She purposely didn't picture Connor, the way she'd found the boy's body battered and broken at the bottom of the ravine. Too depressing.

With two big home-made game pies and a variety of re-heatable vegetables in foil dishes, Grace drove home. As she turned the last corner approaching the farm, she felt the same sense of looming disbelief descend.

Lone Pine Farm in the Highlands of Scotland was a heavenly place to be on a fine summer day with the crest of Ben Kincaid rising dramatically over the farmhouse, red grouse cackling in the heather, the river Lomhar glittering beneath the ancient stone bridge. It made your spirits soar. But when the weather turned, sleet driving from a sky the colour of a tar pit, the wind cutting like knives from the frozen wastes of Greenland, it felt so remote and hostile she had trouble believing she was in the United Kingdom.

Rumbling across the cattle grid she looked at the dilapidated buildings that Ross was going to turn into holiday cottages, the low-slung farmhouse that he'd partially done up. *Home.* She still hadn't got used to it.

When she'd been embroiled in a crazy manhunt with Lucy last year, she'd realised how much she loved Ross and how terrified she was of losing him. She'd made herself a vow: that no matter where in the world he went, she'd go with him. But now that the reality was here, she was struggling. Not with Ross but with her environment. She was used to shops and cafés on her doorstep, restaurants, cinemas, late-night bars. If she wanted to socialise she just had to walk down the street to the pub on the corner. Here she had to drive for miles to do the same and there wasn't a decent place to eat for love nor money.

Pulling up outside the house she heard her own voice as she spoke to Lachlan the paramedic – *it will be beautiful when it's finished* – and had the realisation she was nothing but a soft southerner used to endless privilege and luxury, and abruptly felt a wave of self-loathing.

Just shut up, she told herself. *You have so much to be thankful for. How can you be so self-centred?*

As she switched off the ignition, Ross came across, boots muddy, his overalls covered in dust and dirt, and leaned in to kiss her. She forgot all about the mud, the mounds of building rubble, and kissed him back. For a moment her disquiet at where she was living vanished.

'God, woman,' he said. 'You're looking good today.'

She grinned. 'You are so busted.'

'What?'

'I think you were talking to this.' She patted the butcher's box beside her.

He gave her a sheepish look. 'Did you get pies?'

'I got pies,' she told him, but as his eyes lit up she added sternly, 'but don't forget you have to share.'

Dan was the first to arrive with Christopher, who moved as slowly and painfully as if he had a sword buried in his heart. Dan was taller than she remembered but the careful reserve in his body language and expression remained the same. She was surprised when he embraced her, kissing both her cheeks with warmth in his eyes, but then she remembered saving his life last year. An embrace was the least she supposed she deserved and she returned it with affection.

Since the sitting room was a mess, piled with mouldy wallpaper and rotten plaster, she took them through to the kitchen where Ross had lit a fire. The kitchen was enormous, bigger than the sitting room, with plenty of space for the two armchairs and sofa in front of the fire. Grace suspected that even when the sitting room was finished they'd spend most of their time in the kitchen because it was, quite simply, the nicest room in the house. She was pouring them all whisky when Lucy arrived in a flurry of dynamism that she quickly tempered when Dan introduced her to Christopher.

'Dan rang me earlier and told me about Connor.' Her narrow face pinched in sympathy. 'I'm so sorry.'

Christopher nodded. 'Thank you.'

Grace hugged Lucy tightly feeling her spirit lighten at the energy Lucy brought into the gloom of the farmhouse. Although she knew Lucy occasionally crashed, suffering black moods, she'd never seen her friend functioning at less than top speed.

While Ross prepared dinner, they got down to business. As Grace suspected, Dan wanted Lucy to undertake an unofficial investigation into Connor's death.

'I'd like you to act as a friend of the family. Not as a police officer.'

'Fine by me, because if the local boys and girls know I'm poking about they'll probably put me in a giant wicker man and set fire to it.'

Dan's eyes went to Grace. 'You were the first person called about Connor's death.' He glanced at Christopher. 'You're sure about this?'

'I want to know *everything*.' Christopher's voice was intense. 'Please, Dr Reavey—'

'Grace,' she told him.

'Grace,' he amended. 'Don't hold back or hide anything. It will kill me slower if you do.'

Grace nodded. She took a sip of whisky and told them, word-for-word, what had happened.

'I'm sorry,' she said to Christopher when she finished.

The man didn't move, didn't give any indication he'd heard her. His face was ashen and immobile.

'Drink this.' Dan handed Christopher his glass of whisky.

Obediently he drank. His hands were trembling, but when he spoke his voice was surprisingly strong. 'Go on.'

Dan raised his chin at Lucy. 'First thoughts?'

Lucy turned to Grace. She said, 'Was any effort made, in your opinion, to look for the presence of a weapon or other means of death other than suicide?'

Grace shook her head.

'Was the body searched for a suicide note?'

'Not while I was there.'

'What about the Coroner?'

'They're not Coroners here,' Grace explained. 'They're Procurator Fiscals. The fiscal for the District tells me he spoke with Murdoch's boss and is satisfied that death was suicide and that there are no elements of criminality or negligence. He's asked me to provide a death certificate.'

'Which,' Lucy clarified, 'means he's not asking for an autopsy.'

'Correct.'

Lucy leaned back, a corkscrew frown between her brows. 'Were any photographs taken?'

'I don't know,' Grace admitted.

'Did they bag the body *in situ*?'

Grace thought for a moment. 'I didn't see a body bag.'

'Which means it's probably well and truly contaminated.' Lucy exhaled. 'And they transported it in the ambulance? Not a Coroner's vehicle?'

'Ambulance,' Grace confirmed.

'What about his bicycle? Dan said it was found on the bridge?'

'It's been returned to his mother.'

'They certainly do things differently up here,' Lucy remarked. She looked over at Dan. 'When can I visit the scene?'

'Any time you like. It's not out of bounds.' At that moment Dan's phone rang. He checked the screen. 'Sorry,' he murmured. Rising to his feet he walked to the far end of the room and stood looking out of the window at the woodland. He spoke quietly.

Grace got to her feet and put another log on the fire sending a shower of sparks up the chimney. Ross topped up their drinks and together they laid the table.

When Dan re-joined them something had changed. There was a restlessness in him now, anxiety perhaps, it was hard to tell.

'I'm sorry,' he told them, 'but something else has come up. I'm going to catch the first flight out tomorrow.'

Something to do with his job, Grace guessed. Freelance spy or whatever he was now.

'You'll be OK to investigate together?' Dan looked between Grace and Lucy. 'Grace is to get a post-mortem done if she can. Both of you talk to the pathologist. Lucy is to talk to Sam, Connor's mum, and his school . . .' He raised his hands half-apologetically at Lucy. 'Sorry. You know what to do. I'll let you get on with it.'

Later, after they'd eaten, Grace pulled Dan aside. He'd been withdrawn since his phone call, barely speaking to his grief-shattered friend during dinner, and his eyes were shadowed with emotions she couldn't read.

'Are you OK?' she asked.

He looked at her steadily. He said, 'My father's left me a letter.' At her blank look, he added, 'He died last week.'

Before she could offer her condolences he said, 'The bearer of the letter is a friend of my father's.'

She could tell he wanted to say more but she also knew he hated giving anything away if he could avoid it.

'You don't have to tell me,' she said.

He looked into her eyes.

'Someone has to know. Someone I trust.'

'I won't tell anyone.'

'Except Lucy.'

'Except Lucy,' she echoed.

He took a breath, and she knew he was finding it difficult to speak, so she remained quite still, quite silent.

'Dad's friend, Olivia, says he may not have died of a heart attack after all. She says he may have been murdered.'

CHAPTER TEN

From Heathrow Dan took a bus to Reading Station and a train on to Bristol where he caught a taxi to Clifton. He spent the journey in a state of stunned incredulity, unable to comprehend what Olivia Laing had told him.

His dad, murdered?

If his father had been in a military theatre, on a war operation, Dan wouldn't have a problem with this, but he'd died in his friend's golf club. Doing something he loved.

When Dan wasn't staring blankly into space he was replaying the phone conversation he'd had with Olivia Laing and, when he could, he used his tablet to research everything about her. When he'd taken her call last night, her name rang a bell but that was all. Dan had never met this particular friend, and didn't know anything about her. He found this slightly disturbing although he couldn't pin down why. Was it because he thought he knew all his father's friends? He was familiar with Christopher's father, Gordon, along with their other university friends, Rafe and Arne. But he couldn't say the same for his father's work colleagues.

His father had been an officer in the Royal Marines. He was tough, fit and intelligent, and when he'd retired at fifty-five he'd founded Tor & Associates Ltd, a global security and risk management company that he'd eventually sold for a small fortune to three former Royal Marines who kept him on as a consultant. Dan couldn't remember meeting many of his father's colleagues and as his taxi turned into Victoria Square he realised he'd had no reason to.

Olivia Laing lived on the ground floor of Victoria Square West, a grand Georgian terrace of houses overlooking a broad stone pavement and leafy gardens. Having attended Bristol University, Dan was already familiar with the place and knew it was one of the oldest and most affluent areas of the city, filled with art galleries, restaurants, and boutique shops and bars. He'd always had a vague notion at the back of his mind that he and Jenny might move here in their dotage so they could shuffle along and have a good coffee with friends, also in their dotage, before reading the newspaper sitting by a window in the sunshine and then shuffling back home.

Was that what Professor Olivia Laing did? Her page on the University of Bristol website showed she had retired in 1996 having reached pensionable age, but it didn't seem like she did much shuffling. She'd just completed a book on constitutionalising the European Union after the Brexit vote and was co-authoring another, along with advising on a project funded by the Office of the Prime Minister. Her biography made her sound like an academic spinster, one of those elderly, dignified, frighteningly intellectual women living alone with a cat and sustained by little more than deep thought, so when she opened the door in a flurry of colour and jangling bracelets, Dan made a swift mental adjustment.

'Dearest Dan, I can't imagine how you must be feeling. I'm so sorry for ringing you like I did but I only returned from Brussels last night and when I heard about your father I knew I had to do something straightaway . . .'

She took his arm and led him inside, silk scarves trailing. She was small and delicately boned, with short-cropped jet-black hair threaded with silver. From her biography she had to be at least seventy-eight years old but she didn't look anywhere close, which Dan put down to her Asian genes.

'He told me if he died suddenly and without warning, to get in touch with you immediately. I know he died of a heart attack and that very many people die of heart attacks, but he also died suddenly and without warning . . .'

'Yes.'

'I'm so sorry.' An upsurge of sorrow washed across her face. 'Your father was a very good friend to me. I shall miss him very much.'

Dan touched her lightly on the shoulder and she looked up at him with a sad smile. 'He loved you, Dan. Dearly.'

'I quite liked him too,' he responded with ironic Britishness to cover his pain.

'Come and sit down. Let's have something to drink.'

He opted for a glass of mao-tai, a Chinese liquor and something his memory told him he'd had before but that he couldn't remember ever drinking.

'*Gambai!*' he said. Bottoms up. He didn't know where that came from either, but he'd learned not to get stressed over his ruined memory. One day he might discover he'd been to China, but in the meantime there was no point in getting frustrated over his inability to recall it. As he'd worked out with his psychiatrist, it was a waste of mental energy and merely made him angry if he dwelled on it for too long.

Olivia Liang smiled at the toast, and at that moment, he saw her age in a multitude of tiny wrinkles radiating from around her eyes. '*Gambai.*'

They drank in silence for a moment. Then Dan put down his glass and leaned forward. 'I need you to tell me everything my father said.'

Carefully she put down her glass. Her gaze went to the window, her expression withdrawing a little. 'It wasn't much, I'm afraid. He said he'd discovered something that might put him in danger. He stressed the word *might* several times. He honestly wasn't sure. He told me he'd read something in the newspaper that had scared the "living daylights" out of him. He was looking into it, in case it was true.'

Dan remained silent, not wanting to interrupt her reliving the memory.

'I asked him what he'd do if it was true. He said he'd take it to you.'

Dan wanted to ask whether his father had seen him as a son when he had said this, or as an ex-MI5 officer, or a political analyst, but he held his tongue. Bill would trust the son, and Dan guessed he'd also trust his son's professional experience in a global and political world.

'What else?' Dan pressed.

Olivia rose and fetched them another glass of mao-tai. She paused in front of a huge painting of red and orange swirls that was outrageously bright, almost gaudy, but which Dan found oddly restful.

'He didn't say much,' she told him, 'because I'm sure he didn't want to worry me. He was very light-hearted about it. He said he was probably being paranoid and that we'd have a laugh about it when it turned out to be nothing.'

'When did he see you?'

'Last Tuesday. In the evening. We had dinner at Fishers. He had a huge bowl of mussels followed by the most enormous piece of cod. And sticky toffee pudding. I could never work out where he put it all.'

His father had always eaten heartily, and it was only later in life he had begun to put on a bit of weight around his middle, which he battled against by keeping active.

'Which newspaper had he read?'

'He didn't say.'

'I don't suppose he mentioned what day he read it?'

Olivia shook her head. 'Sorry.'

Dan took a sip of his drink. He let his eyes rove over a variety of contemporary art, from a pair of bronze lobster claws to a vibrant neon chandelier hanging over the dining area.

'When he gave me your letter,' Olivia added, 'he said to keep it safe. *Very* safe. Shall I fetch it?'

'Please.'

The envelope was standard plain white, press seal, medium weight, sized to take an A4 sheet folded into three. There was no name on its front, nothing on the back. It wasn't sealed either. It looked like an unused envelope, aside from the fact there was a sheet of paper inside. It was the type of envelope Dan himself might have left with a trusted friend, something that a burglar wouldn't notice and that could easily be overlooked. He put it on his knee.

Olivia returned to her seat.

'Where did you keep it?' he asked, curious.

'In an envelope holder with the rest of the envelopes on my desk.'

Hiding in plain sight.

'Have you read it?'

'No.'

He believed her.

'Do you know what's in it?' he asked.

'No.'

'Dad didn't intimate what he might say?'

'No.'

He heard a car door slam outside, then an engine starting up. When the car had gone he picked up the envelope and opened the flap. Withdrew a single sheet of paper. Unfolded it. His father's bold, slanted writing scrawled across the page.

My dearest Dan,

If Olivia has given you this, then I am dead. I'm sorry to do this but I would like you to ask a pathologist to check my body for any signs of foul play. If you don't find any, then I died suddenly and without knowing anything about it, which has to be a good thing.

If, however, you are convinced otherwise, then I am mad as a cut snake and I want you to place an ad in The

Times *saying you love Elizabeth very much and how sad you are that she can't be with you on your anniversary but you will be sitting on your special bench on the day so she can picture you there.*

The bench, son, is the one facing the pharmacy on Chelsea Green. The day is the day after you place the advertisement, 10 a.m. sharp. Have the newspaper with you.

All my love,

Dad x

'Don't tell me,' Olivia said, raising both hands. 'He told me not to get involved and in all honesty, I'd rather not know.'

Normally Dan was pretty unreadable – which sometimes drove Jenny crazy – and he wondered what had shown on his face to alarm her. Disbelief? Astonishment? Or was it something more profound, like cold fury? He took a breath and gave a twisted smile. 'Don't worry, I won't be sharing it.'

'Will you be all right?' She looked at him anxiously. 'You look as though you could use another mao-tai.'

'I'll be fine.' He held up the envelope. 'Would you mind looking after this for a little longer?' He was thinking he might need it as evidence and couldn't think of a safer place to keep it.

'Of course not.'

They both rose. He handed her the envelope.

'Thank you,' he said.

She leaned up and kissed his cheek. 'If you ever need me or my help, you only have to ask.'

CHAPTER ELEVEN

Dan spoke to the funeral directors who were arranging the return of his father's body. They suggested he speak to the Staatsanwalkt, the Public Prosecutor of the area in which the death had occurred, and gave him a number to ring. After several attempts Dan finally got through to the right person who, luckily, spoke English.

'I am absolutely satisfied your father died from natural causes,' he was told firmly. 'The death certificate has been issued. I am very sorry for your loss but I see no reason to have a post-mortem.'

It transpired that in Germany, if the doctor attending the body was sure about the cause of death, they would simply issue the death certificate and arrange for the body to be taken by a mortician and prepared for a funeral.

When Dan started to ask how he could get a private autopsy done, the man said, 'You will be paying for this yourself?'

'Yes.'

After a long pause, the man cleared his throat. 'In that case I will review the situation but I am not guaranteeing anything, understand?'

'Thank you.'

Dan hung up. Thought for a while. Made several phone calls, after which he headed for his father's apartment located a block from the Bristol Channel in Weston-super-Mare. When he arrived a westerly wind was blowing hard and the tide was out, showing acres of dark sand, coloured brown-grey by river silt. Aside from a couple of dog walkers, the beach was empty.

His father had moved here when Dan's mother had died over a decade ago, and when Dan had asked why – they'd never holidayed in Weston-super-Mare or had any connection to the place that he knew – his father had said, 'I find it extremely cheerful'. He hadn't said any more and Dan hadn't pressed any further since his father had seemed so very content.

As he walked down his father's street, and without a conscious effort, he took in who was around. A young couple at a bus stop. A woman with a buggy. A family of four in the café opposite. Nothing out of the ordinary that he could see, but his senses were more alert than usual. Olivia's voice echoed in his mind. *He said he'd discovered something that might put him in danger.* Now his father was dead, Dan thought he had every right to be cautious.

He let himself into the apartment. He'd come here the day his father had died to check it was secure and that all the appliances were switched off, the heating set to sixteen degrees. The air felt bitterly cold, but it wasn't the temperature as much as the lack of life that made it feel so. A surge of sorrow rose within him when there was no welcoming holler, no shout of happy greeting.

Dan moved from room to room to find that everything was, as far as he could tell, exactly as he'd left it, from his father's spectacles by the phone and notepad on the hall table to the neat stack of books by his bedside. He paused to pick up a framed photograph of the Fearsome Four, as his dad used to call them, taken by the fishing hut at Glenallen. Gustav, the broadest and tallest, followed by Dan, then Christopher the beanpole and Sophie, looking at the camera through her eyelashes.

Out of nowhere he was ambushed by the vision of Sophie arriving at the lodge that year. She had missed a summer and it had been two years since the boys had seen her, and when she stepped out of the taxi all their jaws dropped. At fifteen years old she was no longer the tow-headed tomboy they remembered but an unbelievably sophisticated and striking-looking girl.

None of them had known how to act around her at first but the second the four of them were alone together she'd reached into her voluminous handbag (when had Sophie ever had a *handbag?!*) and brought out a bottle of vodka.

'Fancy a drink, boys?'

Not even Gustav demurred and they'd drunk straight from the bottle, exhilarated and euphoric at the summer stretching ahead before them.

Putting the picture down, Dan went to the sitting room to find a copy of the *Daily Telegraph* folded to the cryptic crossword. His father had filled in just over two thirds, and if he'd lived he would have finished the remainder when he'd returned from his golf trip.

Had someone really murdered his father? It seemed unlikely but with his father's words echoing in his mind, *check my body for any signs of foul play*, Dan quickly scoured the apartment for any newspaper clippings. There were none, so he collected the newspapers from his father's recycling bin and laid them on the kitchen table. He started with the Saturday *Telegraph* and moved to the *Sunday Times* but there were no clues. No scribbled notes, no marks, not a single indication that any article meant anything in particular. He moved to the colour supplements but had no more luck. Part of him wasn't surprised. His father wouldn't have wanted to leave any clue for an enemy. What had Olivia said? That Bill was looking into it, in case it was true.

Dan picked through the newspapers again, concentrating on things military along with the political commentary, but since there was nothing that raised the hairs on the back of his neck, he bagged the previous week's newspapers to take home. He'd have to work through them until something jumped out at him, but in the meantime there was more he could be doing. Like working through his father's emails and seeing where he'd been recently, who he'd been in contact with, who he'd visited. Fortunately, his father had shared his usernames and passwords with Dan – *no point in making things painfully difficult for you when I pop my clogs* – so he wasn't worried about accessing any of his father's devices. It was just the time it was going to take as he bet his father wouldn't have left any trace of what he was 'looking into' for anyone to find.

Dan propped his father's laptop and newspapers by the front door along with the leather pouffe his father had bought on a trip to Morocco years ago and that Aimee loved. Beautifully hand crafted and embroidered delicately with silver, it would last a lifetime and be something for her to remember her grandfather by.

Heading to fetch his car, he had barely taken three steps outside when a shifting, uncomfortable feeling brushed over him. Something was lurking at the corner of his vision, something that wasn't quite right.

He didn't slow down or change his pace in any way. He kept walking. But his senses switched to high alert.

He looked at the people along the street. A man at the bus stop, another in a car on his phone. Two women in the café opposite, chatting. He continued to scan. Everyone seemed to fit into the environment, but then he realised that the couple he'd seen earlier at the bus stop had split up and the woman was now behind him, ostensibly on the phone.

When Dan reached the end of the street, instead of turning left toward his car, he turned right heading for the Sovereign Shopping Centre.

The woman followed him.

He passed McDonald's on the left, began to cross the road for the High Street. The young woman remained behind him. He committed her face, her size and style of movement to memory in case she altered her appearance in any way in order to confuse him.

Shoulder-length brown hair. An ordinary face. Oval, slightly pallid. No noteworthy features. Nothing outstanding, everything muted, unexceptional. Small, wiry body. Her clothes were bland –jeans, plain white shirt under a wind breaker, a pair of black high-top sneakers – nothing to remember. Mouse Woman. She was the perfect surveillance tool. If it hadn't been for his father's letter the sixth sense of an ex-spy wouldn't have kicked in and he'd never have known she was there.

When he came to a Vodafone store, he ducked inside. Browsed for a while, had a chat with one of the sales staff. When he exited, he glanced about, seemingly for traffic, before he committed to cross the street. No young woman. Dan walked to Boots where he bought an energy drink. Still no young woman but his nerves tightened when, in a shop window opposite, he saw the man from the bus stop exit Poundland and fall into step behind him.

Dan continued his surveillance until he was certain there were just two of them. Tracking jobs were usually done in threes, minimum. Why just two? Whatever the reason, it made things easier for him. He didn't want them to know he'd spotted them, so he concentrated on disguising his evasive moves as ordinary behaviour, finally losing the man by ducking inside the shopping centre – a haven for counter surveillance operatives – but Mouse Woman was more persistent. She was good. She needed shaking fast before her partner could catch up.

He stopped suddenly and pulled out his phone as though he was answering a call. He spoke quickly, making his body language tense and angry, pretending he was having an argument. After he'd hung up, he broke into a fast walk. Annoyed, wanting to get somewhere in a hurry. He walked too fast for her to follow without breaking into a run. She wouldn't want that.

Dan headed back the way he'd come. He zipped past the shopping centre, past Poundland, past the Vodafone store. He outdistanced her quickly. He kept his eyes open for her partner but didn't see him.

As he passed McDonald's he increased his stride and at the same time saw her drop her pace a fraction. He felt a moment's satisfaction. She'd fallen for it. She thought he was returning to the apartment. At the next corner he turned right and then switched left, but when he reached Oxford Street, instead of walking down Union Street, he ducked right and right again into St James Street. From there he dry-cleaned assiduously as he worked his way back to his car ensuring there was nobody else on his tail. Another day he might ignore them. Let them watch, for who knew who was watching the watchers? But Dan knew the secret world and that they might already know who he was. They might know the make of his car, his number plate, and that he was married with one daughter, a son on the way. However, if they didn't know that, then he'd like to keep it that way.

He scrutinised his car for tracking devices and felt a wash of relief when he found nothing. He drove home carefully, checking behind and around him all the time. He only pulled into his driveway when he was a hundred per cent sure he was on his own.

The breeze was damp and scented with grass as he climbed out of the car. He could see Jenny in the sitting room, working. She was frowning, absorbed in whatever she was doing. He did a perimeter check of the property before heading inside.

'Hi, Pops.' He greeted the family dog, a Rottweiler he'd rescued last year. Stumpy tail wagging, she greeted him back. 'Heard you hid Aimee's shoe earlier. Hope you didn't chew it.'

Next he went to check in with his daughter, who was in her bedroom creating a 'museum'. When Aimee had started collecting various things – bird's feathers, shells, the odd animal bone from the moor – Dan had built a cabinet for her to store them, and now she was putting a broken blackbird egg alongside one of Jenny's earrings.

'Hi, Aimee.'

'Hi, Daddy.' She finished what she was doing and turned around, expression serious. 'Will Connor have a wake like Grandpa will?'

Aimee didn't remember Connor that clearly but she certainly knew who he was. Two deaths in the same month was quite a lot for her to be getting her head around but she seemed to be coping pretty well.

'I would think so,' Dan replied.

'Will I go?'

'It might be a nice thing to do, to say goodbye to him. We can also say hello to all the people who'll be there, and share their sorrow.'

She came over and put her arms around his waist. 'I miss granddad.'

Dan cleared his throat as he hugged her back. 'I do too.'

Finally, he headed downstairs where Jenny was propped on the sofa, calculator on one side, papers and pen on the other.

'Hi,' he said.

'Hey.' She made to rise.

'Don't get up.' He went over and gave her a kiss.

'Was it awful?' she asked.

'Yes.'

She touched his face, expression sad. 'I'm so sorry.'

He took her fingers and kissed them. 'You shouldn't be working,' he chided her gently.

'It distracts me.'

Jenny was an accountant, looking after the books and tax returns of local businesses, and as word had spread about her efficiency and speed in getting things done, her client list had grown. If she wasn't careful, he'd warned her, she'd be busier than she'd been when she'd worked in London.

She looked at the mess on the sofa and gave a sigh. 'I got so uncomfortable upstairs, I moved.'

He wasn't surprised. The baby was due any time now and even though she felt exhausted, she found it almost impossible to settle for any period of time. Her belly was too big, her breathing shallow. Her body ached and she felt permanently hot. 'I've had enough of being pregnant!' she kept telling Dan. 'I can't wait to have this baby!'

'Can I get you anything?' he asked.

'A cup of tea would be lovely.'

'I'll put the kettle on.'

He stood in the kitchen looking at the array of family photographs stuck on the fridge door along with several of Aimee's drawings. He was thinking about normality, where he came home every Friday and dropped his briefcase by the front door where it remained untouched until Monday morning. He was thinking about his wife, his baby boy and Aimee playing on a beach. He was thinking how the secret world refused to let him go, how its tentacles kept reaching out and enfolding him, drawing him back in.

Then Jenny walked into the kitchen and he took her in his arms. He held her and she kissed him and there were no words between them, just love. He wondered how to protect her while he finished what his father had started.

That question kept him awake for most of the night.

CHAPTER TWELVE

Lucy leaned over the strip of blue and white barrier tape strung sloppily on one side of the bridge. POLICE – DO NOT CROSS. More tape had been strung to prevent people from entering the ravine, but the bridge itself hadn't been shut, giving walkers and other traffic their usual access.

She hadn't been able to have a look yesterday thanks to Constable Murdoch's presence. He'd been nice enough when he'd told her she really shouldn't be rubber-necking and for a moment the urge to tell him she was a fellow police officer had almost overcome her, but she'd swallowed her ego and simpered at him, her eyes watering from the effort. God, she'd make a crap undercover officer.

No Murdoch today. Nobody, thanks to the weather.

It was chucking it down, sheets of rain, and even though she wore a pair of Grace's waterproof trousers and jacket, water still managed to work its way beneath her hood and trickle down her neck. Bunches of flowers were piled to one side, some for Nimue Acheson, some for Connor, and all had collapsed into a soggy mess. There was a sodden teddy bear with a tartan scarf and a waterlogged looking Eeyore lying on its side.

Lucy did her best to study and analyse the site, checking to see if any lichen had been disturbed, whether a vehicle had struck the bridge leaving behind any paint or paint chips, but found nothing. She made a note of where Nimue's body had been found in comparison to Connor's resting place. Lucy didn't go into the ravine. Anything that might have been useful would probably have been washed away.

Stripping off her waterproofs, she stuffed them in the back of the car and headed to Elgin. As she drove she listened to the news. Another terrorist attack, another lorry driven into pedestrians, killing six and injuring dozens more. This time in India. When was it going to stop?

When she arrived at the Crown Office she found Grace waiting just inside the door.

'Perfect,' Grace said smiling. Lucy's mind hummed a soft peach. Grace always had that effect on her; soothing and restful. After they'd checked in at reception they settled on a pair of plastic moulded chairs in a waiting area that seemed to be caught between two centuries. Blue commercial carpet tiles, maroon flocked wallpaper dotted with sepia hunting and sporting prints.

Lucy's phone rang. She looked at the display. 'Dan,' she told Grace as she answered it.

'You're OK to talk?' he asked.

'Yep.'

When he didn't say anything she realised he was waiting for her to fill in the gap. She really must sharpen up. Give him information faster. 'I'm with Grace. We're at the Crown Office in Elgin.'

'Was Connor suicidal?'

'I'm not a shrink,' she answered, 'but at first glance it doesn't look like it.'

'What does it look like?'

'I'm not sure yet,' she admitted. 'We're going to talk to the fiscal in a minute and see what he says.'

'OK. Anything else?'

'Well, I visited Connor's school. Spoke to the head teacher as well as two of his class teachers.'

'And?'

'They were all shocked. But not disbelieving. Suicide among kids is rising. They're under huge pressure these days, not just from parents and SATS, but keeping up with their peers. When you think ChildLine received over thirty-five thousand calls from under-eighteens who had suicidal thoughts last year . . .'

'That many?' He sounded dismayed.

'Sadly, yes.'

'OK. I'll let you crack on.'

'And you?' Lucy said hurriedly. 'How are you?'

'Bearing up.'

Small pause and then he said, 'Thanks,' and hung up.

'How is he?' Grace asked.

'Bearing up, apparently.'

Grace nodded, and at that moment a man appeared in the doorway. Tall, almost stately, with silver hair and a serious expression, he was wearing the sort of suit men would pay hundreds of pounds for.

'Dr Reavey?' he enquired.

'Yes.'

'If you would follow me.'

Grace and Lucy got to their feet, walked down a corridor where the man was striding ahead, his gait athletic. He paused at an open doorway waiting for them to go inside. He closed the door behind them.

'Please.' He gestured at the two chairs in front of his desk while he took the one behind. A steel office sign was propped in front of him as though to remind those facing him who he was.

Brice Kendrick. District Procurator Fiscal.

The fiscal steepled his fingers in front of his face. Nicely kept nails, Lucy noticed, possibly manicured. His eyes were pale grey, his gaze sharp.

'You say you would like an autopsy done on Connor Baird?' He spoke to Grace. Lucy was there under the guise of a 'family friend'. No chit-chat to put them at ease, no offer of tea. He was all business. His voice was firm, with a strong Scottish burr.

'Yes.'

'Tell me your reasons.'

'He had no history of feeling suicidal. He appeared to be a well-balanced boy, with loving parents—'

'Who had recently split up.' He picked up a piece of paper from his desk along with a pair of gold-rimmed reading glasses, and scanned it. 'The father had an affair with his laboratory assistant. His wife threw him out of the house.'

'The father,' Grace went on in the same even tone, 'Christopher, talked everything over with Connor. Nothing was hidden or brushed under the carpet. The boy had a very good understanding as to what was going on. He also had a very good relationship with his father. They both expected Christopher to move back into the family home any day and—'

'Not according to his wife.' He picked up another piece of paper, scanned that one too. 'According to the police report she was furious and "wasn't having him back any time soon". Also, she'd just had a baby. The boy wasn't just struggling with having competition in the house, he hated the whole thing. He complained about it all the time at school. He said he "hated" the baby and wished he'd never been born.'

'In that case, I would have expected him to have murdered his little brother rather than take his own life.' Grace's voice was carefully modulated, her demeanour respectful, but Lucy had learned to read her friend by now and she could almost hear the words 'you condescending prick' echoing in the office.

A flare of what might have been annoyance crossed his face but it was gone so fast Lucy wasn't sure if she'd imagined it.

'Look.' Grace leaned forward, hands on her knees. 'His grades in school were good. He was planning on going to the UCI Mountain Bike World Cup in Fort William next week. He had tickets. He'd also organised to go mountain biking with friends this coming weekend—'

'His mother wanted him to babysit on Sunday. He didn't want to. They had a row over this on the day he died.'

'But the biking event was the following weekend. He was looking *forward*. Suicides don't do that.'

The Procurator Fiscal just looked at Grace.

'He left a note,' he said.

It was the first Lucy had heard of it and she knew her gaze had intensified because he glanced at her for the first time.

'It was in his jeans pocket,' he added. 'It said "I'm sorry".'

'In his handwriting?' Lucy asked.

The fiscal didn't look at her this time. He ignored her.

'The police,' he continued, 'have interviewed relatives, school teachers and friends who have provided information about the circumstances of the death. I am confident Connor Baird committed suicide.'

This time Lucy leaned forward. 'Did anyone mention the positioning of Connor's body?'

Again, he didn't look at her. It was as though she hadn't spoken. 'I see no reason to have an autopsy,' he told Grace. His tone was final. He put his hands on his desk preparing to rise.

'What about the lividity I mentioned?' Grace asked. 'I saw some on Connor's upper right arm, an area of the boy's body that hadn't been in contact with the ground.'

He stared at Grace. 'Are you suggesting the body was moved?' He made it sound as though she'd suggested she might start levitating.

'I'm asking for another opinion.' Grace's tone was steady but Lucy could see the tension in her fingers which were twisted together, her knuckles showing white.

Lucy let the silence hang for a moment. Then she said, 'When suicides jump from a bridge, they don't actually *jump*. They don't fling or throw themselves, they step off the structure into the air. A suicide will usually be found near the top of any place where they have fallen. For example, Nimue Acheson's body was found near the top of the falls, which coincides with stepping into the void. Connor's body, however, was right at the bottom of the ravine. In order for him to be there he would have had to have flung himself off the bridge with force, which would be considered highly unusual.'

You could have heard a pin drop.

'Also,' Lucy went on, 'as Dr Reavey has said, Connor hadn't mentioned any suicidal thoughts to his family or friends. The police report states the word "suicide" was only found on his computer due to his talking to friends about Nimue Acheson's death. It also says he hadn't explored any suicide sites or shown any suicidal tendencies.'

'He also explored several sites to do with life after death and what happens when you die,' the fiscal told her.

This was news to Lucy but she didn't let it show. Even though she was hampered by not knowing when Connor had accessed these sites, she continued to defend her position. 'Wouldn't any kid be curious as to what happened to their classmate after they'd died?'

The fiscal still didn't look at Lucy. He said to Grace, 'You *will* provide a certificate as to the cause of death.'

Silence again.

Lucy's frustration began to rise. 'This case,' she said, concentrating on keeping her tone calm, 'started with a potential miscommunication. Which may have resulted in serious errors that are affecting the outcome. It is my belief that the police officer who responded to the call as well as the investigators have made a critical error in thinking. Psychologically everyone is assuming the death to be a suicide case, when in fact this is a basic death investigation, which could very well turn out to be a homicide—'

'From the way you're talking,' he remarked, 'I take it you're not just a family friend. What are you? A solicitor?' His voice carried a faint sneer even though he would have started out as a solicitor himself before climbing up the greasy pole in the Crown Court.

Lucy hadn't planned on blowing her cover, but he was being such a dick, such an *unprofessional* arse, trying to bully Grace into doing what he wanted, that she was about to grab her handbag and pull out her warrant card when Grace put a hand on her arm stopping her.

'Lucy is here as a concerned family friend.'

This time he looked directly at her. He took his time, taking in her jeans, her brown leather belt, her tatty sheepskin jacket. Her hair was tied back with a scrunchy as usual, but no matter how hard she scraped it back, wisps always kept escaping. No make-up and, except for her father's old watch, no jewellery.

'And as a concerned family friend,' Brice Kendrick said acidly, 'you expect me to arrange a post-mortem, at the public's expense, on your whim.'

With difficulty she hid her dislike behind a mask of neutrality. 'Considering the facts, yes.'

'Very well.'

She raised her eyebrows.

'I shall reconsider.'

You could have knocked her over with a feather. She'd honestly thought he'd dug himself in for the long haul, but here he was, saying he would think again. It was, she speculated, the best outcome they could have hoped for, and when they walked outside she and Grace high-fived one another like a couple of schoolkids.

CHAPTER THIRTEEN

Dan was searching through his father's old emails when his phone rang.

'Herr Forrester?'

'Speaking.'

'My name is Nicola Stangl.'

It transpired Nicola was the Staatsanwalkt Liaison Officer. She informed him that the post-mortem on his father was going ahead that morning and asked if he'd like some preliminary information about the examination. He was surprised things were moving so fast. He'd only rung the Staatsanwalkt yesterday – talk about German efficiency.

'Yes, please.'

'Will you perhaps be available if we make a video call later?' she asked. '2 p.m.?'

'Yes.'

Dan made some phone calls, filling in time to try and take his mind off his father's body lying on a slab and being examined by strangers. He talked to Julia in the office, who appeared to have everything under control in his absence. Although this was exactly what he wanted to hear, he still ended up prowling around the house unable to concentrate on anything in particular until his computer finally alerted him that Nicola Stangl was online. In her early forties, she had wiry brown hair and a brisk attitude. 'I'm sorry for your loss,' she told him.

'Thank you.'

'I gather you asked for the post-mortem?'

'Yes.'

'You suspected something about your father's death wasn't due to natural causes?' Her eyes were sharp.

'Yes.'

'Well.' She puffed out a breath. 'I'm sorry to tell you that you were right. The pathologist found he died from a poison – digitalis – that induced heart failure. An injection site was found on his thigh, along with traces of the poison in his blood and organs.'

Dan could practically feel the blood leaving his face.

'I'm sorry,' she added.

I am angry as a cut snake.

Nicola Stangl looked away, then back. 'I'm afraid I have to inform you that the post-mortem examination has prompted the Staatsanwalkt to instruct the police to investigate your father's death.'

'As a homicide.' His voice rasped.

'Correct. The Staatsanwalkt won't release your father's body just yet. We will let you know when this will happen, and then the repatriation can take place.'

A high-pitched hum started at the back of his head.

'Would you like me to put you in touch with bereavement services in your—'

'I would like a copy of the post-mortem.' Dan put his hands on his knees. He suddenly felt nauseous.

'There will be a fee.'

'I can pay now if you like.'

'Online will be fine. I will make sure the report is emailed to you promptly.'

'Thank you.' Dan reached forward and closed the application. He rose to his feet. His legs felt unsteady. *Dad's been murdered.* The words looped endlessly around his head. He wasn't immune to death. He'd held his dead son in his arms, or so he'd been told, and in his old job he would have seen people killed and may even have killed people himself. He knew he had a ruthless streak from what he'd done to a Russian spy earlier in the year. When Jenny had been kidnapped and spirited secretly to Russia, Dan had kidnapped an FSB officer in return and tortured him in order to find her.

Now Dan placed the advertisement as his father had instructed. He would go to the bench on Chelsea Green tomorrow and see what happened.

Who had killed his father? What was at stake to have caused his murder? Olivia Laing had said he'd read something in the newspaper that had scared the *living daylights* out of him. He'd been investigating whatever it was and someone hadn't liked it.

CHAPTER FOURTEEN

'It's m-my fault that Conner's d-d-dead.' Samantha Baird stammered.

They were in the kitchen with Sam's mother and a large marmalade cat that was napping on the windowsill. Little Dougie was upstairs asleep.

Sam was white-faced with glassy eyes that told Lucy she was on some kind of sedative. Normally she'd be a pretty woman with her auburn hair and creamy skin, but grief had taken hold of her and turned her grey, giving her grooves around her eyes and mouth and making her appear older than her years.

'I asked him to b-babysit while I went out with the girls. I should never have d-done it. He was so angry with me . . .' She buried her face in her hands. 'Oh, God.' She started to sob. 'I can't b-bear it.'

'I'm sorry,' Lucy murmured.

Sam's mother came over, putting her arms around her daughter and rocking her back and forth. Tears streaked her cheeks.

Past the cat, Lucy could see the rain had stopped and that the sun was flashing between fast-moving clouds, forming moving shadows on the cars parked in the driveway. 'I don't want to be a bother . . . but can I have a look at Connor's room? Dan asked if I could look at his computer too . . .'

At the mention of Dan's name, Sam raised her head, wiping her eyes, trying to regain control. 'Yes, Dan . . . he mentioned it. Upstairs. Second on the right.'

'Er . . . do I need a code to access his computer?'

Sam gave her eight numbers. 'It's his father's date of birth. So we can all access it.'

'What about his phone?'

'The police have it.'

Connor's room wasn't that messy but it wasn't neat either. Clothes and sneakers were dumped seemingly without thought along with an array of socks, empty packets of crisps and random bicycle parts. There was a half-burned candle on a table, along with a tube of acne cream and a handful of biking magazines.

Lucy quickly searched the room. After a while she stood back, hands on hips and frowning. Didn't every teenager have something to hide? She searched under the mattress, in his shoes and pockets, inside the speaker system, his computer case. She even checked his candle and books in case any had been hollowed out. No luck. Not even a teensy baggie of marijuana.

She moved to his computer. A screensaver with the word MUDE appeared. Beneath it, *I am not happy or sad, I am mude.* Really? Lucy clicked on to find downloaded movies, computer games galore, a lengthy shopping history, nothing alarming on his web browser history, but she wasn't an expert and Connor was no doubt well ahead of her. No porn that she could see, but with his parents able to access his computer he probably wouldn't—

'What the fuck are you doing?'

Lucy jumped and spun around to see a tall elderly man with a shock of white hair and a beaky nose. He held a cane and it wasn't to help steady himself. He was holding it as a weapon.

'Hi,' she said, 'I'm—'

'This is my grandson's room.' He didn't put the cane down. 'He's barely dead and you're—'

'Lucy Davies,' Lucy firmly overrode him. 'I'm a friend of Dan Forrester's. You must be Gordon. I'm so sorry for your loss. Truly, I am.'

The man blinked twice. He may be old but he held himself ramrod straight and his eyes were bright and alert. The cop in her immediately did a scan, taking in his expensive leather brogues and slender gold watch, so thin it had to have cost a fortune.

'What sort of friend?' His gaze wasn't unfriendly but it was definitely wary.

'We've worked together a few times,' she told him. 'Along with Dr Grace Reavey. Grace moved up here—'

'Yes, I know who Dr Reavey is.' The rheumy eyes narrowed.

Sensing a growing mistrust Lucy said, 'Christopher knows I'm here.' She didn't know whether to mention she was here as a policewoman or not and decided against it until she'd spoken with Dan.

'Does he indeed?' The rheumy eyes didn't change their guarded expression.

'I'm sorry for your loss,' she said again, unsure how to proceed.

This time he gave a nod. 'Sam didn't say you were here,' he told her, his severity relenting a little. Was this his way of apologising?

'Nor did Margaret,' he added. 'When I came in I heard someone up here and I . . . well. I wanted to scare you off.' His gaze went from her sturdy brown boots to the top of her head and down again, reminding her of the fiscal's careful appraisement earlier. 'Not that you look as though you'd be scared off. You look remarkably self-possessed.'

Before she could acknowledge him in any way, he went on, saying, 'Dan sent you, you say?'

'Yes.'

He held her gaze. 'His father just died. Did he tell you that?'

'Yes.'

'Good.' He was brisk. 'Now, tell me what you were doing in here.'

'I was trying to see if Connor was suicidal or not.'

'Are you a psychologist?'

'Dr Reavey wasn't convinced that he was suicidal,' she prevaricated.

'And what does Reavey say about Connor's death?' He accented Grace's name with a hint of gravity, which Lucy took to mean he might value her opinion.

Cautiously, Lucy said, 'She's concerned about some things.'

'Concerned how?'

When she didn't answer he said irritably, 'Come on, come on, woman. Getting information from you is like getting blood from a stone. You can't just say the doctor is *concerned* and not elucidate.'

OK, he asked for it. 'She wants an autopsy done.'

At that he stared. 'And how is she going to get that?'

'She went to see the District Procurator Fiscal this morning. I went with her.'

A long silence fell. He moved across the room, walking past her to take up position in his grandson's study area where he stood gazing outside. 'Christopher remains unconvinced that Connor killed himself, but I wasn't sure if it was because he didn't want to take the blame for fucking everything up.'

Lucy remained silent. She could hear traffic at the end of the drive, and then came the happy squeal of a baby, no doubt little Dougie waking up next door.

Eventually Gordon turned around to face her.

'The fiscal. What did you make of him?'

'I think he's got a difficult job.'

'That's not what I asked.' His gaze was steely.

'He has to make sure he has enough evidence before he can instigate an investigation.' Lucy remained firmly neutral. This was a small community and she didn't want to take sides. She could almost see the wicker man burning in the garden below.

'But he was reluctant.'

'He said he was going to reconsider.'

'Reconsider?' he repeated with a snort of derision. 'Ha!'

Still looking at her he pulled out a phone. Dialled. He listened a moment then said, 'Call me back. Immediately.'

There was an odd little pause. Then Lucy said, 'I was looking at Connor's computer. Checking his browser history.'

'Find anything?'

'Nothing obvious so far. No suicide sites, for example.'

He grunted. 'Keep on with it, then.'

Lucy turned back to work. She was looking at Connor's Facebook page, filled with photographs of teenagers drinking, laughing, biking, having fun, when Gordon's phone rang.

He looked at the display but when he answered he didn't greet the caller. Just jumped straight in.

'I hear you're *reconsidering* doing an autopsy.' His tone could have stripped paint.

Shit, she thought. He knew the fiscal.

'From now, you're not *reconsidering*, you're authorising it.'

Even from where she stood she could hear the tinny squawks of protest from the phone's speaker but Connor's grandfather didn't seem to be hearing them.

'If Dr Reavey's got her concerns then they need to be satisfied,' he snapped. 'I know she's English but that doesn't mean—'

She watched as he took a huge breath and said, *'Do not interrupt me again.'*

Silence.

Holy crap, thought Lucy. Who was this man that he could talk to the fiscal like this?

'As I was saying, you're already aware that the English autopsy anyone and everyone, no matter how they have died, but this does not mean that Dr Reavey is wanting it done for no reason. What justification did she give?'

He listened for a bit then said firmly, 'I want to do it.'

Shit, she thought a second time. He was a medical examiner of some sort.

'I know he's my fucking grandson.' Gordon Baird's voice hissed. 'But I'm the most fucking qualified person you know and I don't want to leave it to some wet-behind-the-ears incompetent imbecile who won't know their dactylography from their diploid.'

He listened for a few seconds. 'OK, OK.' He began nodding. 'I'll observe. But give me Elena. She's the only one who might do a half-decent job.'

Without another word, he hung up and turned to her.

'He doesn't like you. He called you interfering, obstructive and self-opinionated.'

'Ah,' she said brightly. 'Those old chestnuts.'

He came and stood in front of her. 'I don't know who you are, or why you're representing Dan, but there's something about you . . .'

'There's something about you too.' She was beginning to like the old bugger, as obstreperous as he was. 'But would you mind telling me who you are? I mean I know you're Connor's grandfather, but if you're asking to conduct an autopsy—'

'I'm a pathologist.'

Lucy blinked. 'I see.'

'And Brice Kendrick' – his eyes gleamed satisfactorily – 'well, he's my nephew.'

CHAPTER FIFTEEN

'I met your cousin,' Lucy told Christopher.

'Which one?'

'The Procurator Fiscal.'

They were sitting in his VW Polo at the end of his drive. He was staring longingly at the house. She'd spotted him as she'd walked onto the street, and when she'd gone to speak to him he had said defensively, 'I'm not stalking her, I promise. I just want to see her. See little Dougie.'

'Any idea why he didn't deign to tell me or Grace he was related to you when we saw him yesterday?'

Now Christopher turned to face Lucy. His eyes were rimmed red and bloodshot.

'No.'

'You didn't tell Dan either.'

'I didn't ... I mean, it honestly didn't cross my mind. Dan asked me what the fiscal said, so I told him.'

'Are you close, as cousins? You and Brice?'

'We're family,' he said simply. 'We used to play together as kids. Dan too when he was up here. But after uni we went our own ways. We only see each other at Christmas and the like.'

Like a lot of families, Lucy thought.

'Does Dan know Brice now?'

He blinked. 'I don't think so.'

Silence.

'Will she take me back do you think?' Desperation stood out in every feature. 'I don't love Jasmine. Not at all. It was a moment of madness. And it wasn't as if I enjoyed it either. The sex, I mean. I thought I would, I thought it would be exciting, wild, different, but it was . . . ordinary.'

Lucy kept quiet.

'I'm such a fool,' he added. 'Just because Sam and I had drifted . . . Hadn't made love in . . . a long time, I thought I deserved some attention, some affection. God, how insufferable, how *arrogant* of me.'

'How did it start?'

'We went for a drink. That's all. But then we went for another and another. We had dinner . . . She was so *interesting*. She had so much to say . . . and it was nice to talk about my work with someone who could see what I hoped to achieve. It was refreshing . . . incredibly stimulating, to be with someone who *understood me*, understood how my mind works, someone who listened. We laughed a lot too, about work things that . . .'

He looked ashamed for a moment and Lucy filled in the gap. *Work things that Sam would never understand.*

'She's nothing like Sam,' he admitted.

A classic tale of adultery. Like most men, Christopher thought he could get away with an affair – did all men think their wives were stupid? – but then Sam found out.

'How?' Lucy asked.

'A friend of hers saw me leaving Jasmine's flat one evening when I said I was working late in the lab. She told Sam . . . When I got home later . . . Oh, God it was awful.' He put a hand over his eyes. 'Sam was so hurt . . . I've never seen her cry like that. I tried to tell her it wasn't because I didn't love her anymore, that it was a work thing . . . A period of madness . . . But she wouldn't listen.'

'What about Jasmine?'

'What do you mean?'

'How did she react when your affair came out? Did she want you to move in with her?'

Christopher's face contracted in surprise. 'Good God, no. Jasmine made it quite clear she liked her independence. It was what attracted me in the first place. Her free spirit. No clinging, nothing ordinary or boring. No washing up or mowing the lawn . . .'

Lucy had heard it all before and tried not to yawn.

'I still love Sam.' Christopher's voice was fierce. 'I've never *stopped* loving her. Jasmine was . . . a diversion. A crazy mistake. But Sam doesn't see it like that.' He turned a desperate gaze on to Lucy. 'What am I supposed to do? I can't lose her. I *can't.*'

'Give her time.' It was an old adage but one that Lucy depended on regularly. Time sometimes gave people the emotional space they needed, especially after an acknowledged affair, but she wasn't sure time was going to help much considering their son had just died.

'The one thing I don't have,' he gritted, 'is fucking time.'

To her astonishment he leaped out of the car and began striding up the drive to his house, his shoulders set, his footsteps hard and angry. For a moment she was tempted to go after him, find out what had made him snap like that – *because he's just lost his son, you idiot* – but since she was eternally nosy and alone in his car, she quickly opened the glovebox, had a look. A baby's dummy, a pink mini umbrella and a coral lipstick told her this used to be his wife's car. Lucy continued her search, keeping an eye on the street in case Christopher returned. She'd just checked the car's rubbish compartment (two Crunchy wrappers, several tissues and a dried-out apple core) when she spotted a small, black plastic device tucked above the car bonnet release.

She hadn't honestly believed she would find something and for a moment she thought she was imagining things. Checking outside again – still no Christopher – she wriggled closer.

Well, bugger me, she thought.

It was a spy bug. She knew what they looked like thanks to Dan giving her two on a previous case. Switching her phone to silent – she didn't want to tip off the listener – she took several photographs of it. Sat back in her seat.

Was it a case of a jealous spouse keeping tabs on their partner? Or was it someone else?

CHAPTER SIXTEEN

Christopher's anger had evaporated by the time he reached his front door. It wasn't like him to snap and he hoped Lucy would forgive him. He liked the young police woman, her energy and enthusiasm. He liked Grace too, and he wondered what Dan's other friends were like. His father always said you could judge a man by his friends.

What would that say about him? His closest friend had to be Dan, who he'd known since he was a toddler. He was pretty close to Sophie too, having advised her on countless occasions over her chaotic love life – thank God she'd married Nick – but the last time he'd seen Gustav had been at Sophie's wedding ten years ago. He had other friends, of course, but when the estate had to be sold a lot of them vanished.

Fair-weather friends, his father told him. Friends who were only interested in the shooting and fishing parties, and not in them as people.

Not Sam, though. They'd been going out for a year when his father made the announcement: *Glenallen has to go*. Sam said it was a shame because she loved the place too, but life was about more than living in a big house with endless guests. He had to agree with her on that point. He'd loved his home deeply, being able to fish practically from his bedroom, to walk five minutes and hear nothing but grouse cackling in the heather, but the guests he could take or leave.

It was the quietness he missed the most. He worked best in that endless highland silence. He supposed he would have liked to have inherited Glenallen not just for the sports but because he felt free there. His mother had understood. When they didn't have guests, she'd fish every day, irrespective of the weather. She died just eight months after they moved into the little lodge at the end of the drive. *Of a broken heart*, they all thought, but nobody said so.

He flinched when the front door suddenly opened. He hadn't expected Sam to answer.

'Hi,' he said. He suddenly felt devastatingly, appallingly awkward.

'Hi.'

Her face was swollen from crying. Pain hovered like a miasma around her. She was trembling. He wanted nothing more than to take her in his arms but he didn't dare.

'What do you want?'

'To see if you're all right.' *Be normal*, he told himself. *Then all will be normal.*

'How can I be?'

He saw she'd put the lights on in the sitting room, which weakly illuminated the corridor behind her. Familiar objects, like the three-legged stand where they hung hats and coats, and the console table with the ceramic lamp they'd bought in

France. Just standing there on the outside, looking in, made his knees feel weak. How had it come to this? His purpose in life had always been to provide and support his family, love them and protect them as well as give the children the best chance in life.

Had he got lost in his work somewhere along the way? He'd set up the Environmental Research Centre specifically to help people less fortunate than himself. He wanted to prevent starvation caused by population growth and feed the next generation for free. He didn't know where it came from, his altruism, but talking to Jasmine – who had known real poverty in China – he wondered if it was because he'd come from such a privileged background and felt the need to redress some kind of balance. Whatever it was, it had driven him into another woman's arms and had cost him what he'd once thought unassailable: his family.

'You can't be OK,' he admitted. 'Any more than I can.'

She looked at the ground, twisting her hands together. When she spoke it was almost a whisper. 'Do you really think he did it because I asked him to babysit?'

'Of course not!' He was shocked.

'It's what everyone's saying . . .'

'He didn't commit suicide. And if he did, it wouldn't be over something like that. You know that, deep down. He was a *happy boy*. He was incredibly excited about going to the bike championships, remember? He was looking *forward*.'

Sam turned her head away. 'I don't know anything anymore.'

His heart felt as though it was clenched in a vice. He made to move towards her but she held up a hand.

'When you feel your world shatter, you instinctively reach for something solid to hold on to, and when it's no longer there you feel cut loose, desperately adrift . . .'

'I am your anchor,' he told her fiercely.

'What about that woman?'

He hadn't done anything about Jasmine but now it seemed ridiculously clear. 'I'll ask her to leave.'

For the first time Sam met his eyes. 'I thought she was invaluable to your project.'

'Not at the expense of my family.'

She knew he meant it and gave a nod. For the first time he felt some hope that they might make it through this mess, together and not apart.

When he heard footsteps behind him he turned to see Lucy approaching.

'I'm sorry to interrupt,' she said, 'but I just need to ask you a question. Would that be OK?'

'Of course,' he replied and at the same time as Sam nodded.

'It's a bit of an odd one, I'm afraid.' Lucy directed her attention to Sam, but Christopher could feel her attentiveness embrace him too.

'I know you had your difficulties before Connor died . . . but I was wondering if you were ever tempted to bug Christopher's car? I mean the Polo . . . to check up on him?'

'What?'

'I just wondered, that's all.'

'Well, no.' Sam looked bewildered. 'Why?'

Lucy looked at Christopher. He knew his expression was perfectly blank because he had no idea what this was all about.

Police statistics on spousal surveillance? The fallout from infidelity?

'Sorry to have bothered you.' Lucy looked between them, shifting from foot to foot. 'Look, I don't often get personal but of all the couples I've seen going through an appalling patch . . . well, you need each other now, and who else can support and understand what you're going through? I know I'm not an expert, but . . .' She suddenly looked embarrassed. 'I'll be off then.'

Christopher watched her walk down the path. He was thinking again what good friends Dan had when Sam touched his arm.

'She's right, you know. Do you want to come in?'

CHAPTER SEVENTEEN

Twenty-five past two in the afternoon and Grace was thanking God she hadn't had lunch. She wasn't great with autopsies. She wasn't bad enough that she threw up, but she wrestled with the process and always had.

She hadn't wanted to attend but Lucy had insisted. *I'd go if I could,* she'd told her. *But since I can't, we have to have one of the team there.* The team being her, Lucy and Dan.

Elena Crofton, the pathologist Gordon Baird had insisted upon, was inspecting a messy wound on Connor's thigh. She was concentrating, she told Grace, on finding any wounds or injuries that would not have been caused by a fall into a ravine. She'd already weighed and measured the body, and collected scrapings from beneath his fingernails. She'd taken swabs for possible DNA analysis, and saliva samples as well as residues of dried blood, which had all been stored for later analysis.

They both looked around when the door opened and closed. Gordon Baird.

'Elena,' he said.

'Sir,' she responded. Her posture had straightened as though she was a foot soldier in the presence of a superior officer.

He looked at Grace in sharp enquiry. 'What are you doing here?'

They'd met when she first started at Duncaid Surgery. He'd come in specially to meet her and he'd grilled her as relentlessly as any medical board about her qualifications and particular skills for the job. Not wanting to alienate a local – a *big man* at that – on her first day, she'd taken it on the chin but inside she'd been simmering at his intrusive, God-like attitude.

'I asked for the autopsy,' she replied evenly.

He didn't respond. Simply went to the body. Elena stepped back, her head bowed slightly, her body language deferent. He looked down at his grandson. His face lengthened and Grace felt herself soften at his obvious sorrow, but when he turned back his sadness had vanished beneath a professional cloak.

'What have you found?' he asked Elena briskly.

'I'm not sure about this wound.' She pointed at the bloody mess on the boy's right thigh. 'His jeans are ripped at the same point, but whether it was from the fall, I'm not sure.'

Gordon withdrew a pair of spectacles from his lab coat and put them on. Then he pulled on a pair of vinyl gloves. Studied the wound. 'His jeans?'

She brought over a clear plastic bag and pulled them out. He studied them at length frowning. 'I see what you mean. The tears aren't necessarily consistent with a fall upon the rocks. They could have been done with a knife.'

He returned to inspect Connor's right thigh. 'I want you to concentrate on this area. I think someone could have made this mess in order to cover something else up. What else?'

'There's lividity on his arm. I think he was moved after death.'

A tension came over him. 'Show me.'

Elena lifted Connor's arm to allow the old pathologist to have a look. He studied it a while. Then he straightened up. 'The lividity isn't what bothers me,' he added, his expression troubled. 'It's the wound on his thigh that does. You'll be taking samples of bodily fluids? Samples of the contents of the stomach and intestines? Oh, and remove the liver and weigh it, please.'

Elena blinked several times.

'Do you have a problem with that?' he snapped, cold and authoritative.

'No, sir.'

'For the record, of all the teenage boys I knew, my grandson was the least likely to kill himself. I want every test done. And I mean *every* test.'

'Of course.' Elena looked as though she might salute.

He left the mortuary room without looking at either of them.

CHAPTER EIGHTEEN

Dan studied the photographs Lucy had sent him of the listening device she'd found in Sam and Christopher's car. He didn't like it at all because it wasn't a cheap, plasticky appliance a suspicious spouse would buy off eBay; it was a top-of-the-range professional bug that was specifically designed to be hidden away behind the dashboard and hard-wired into the vehicle electrics for long term deployment.

The purpose of this particular device was to provide the ability to listen to what was happening inside the vehicle from anywhere in the world.

What was it doing in his friend's car? Was the target Christopher or Sam? Or was it both of them?

Although his mind churned with questions, anxiety pressing, something in his soul came alive at being back in London. The constant muted roar of traffic, the whine of jet engines above, a police siren, a shop shutter rattling, the smell of coffee overlaid with diesel. He felt a million miles from his home in Wales and although he liked the huge skies there and the sharp, clean air, he missed London with a ferocity he never shared with Jenny.

His phone rang as he turned to walk along Elystan Place towards Chelsea Green.

'Daniel Forrester?' a woman asked.

'Yes.'

'My name is Detective Superintendent Didrika Weber. I am investigating your father's death ...' There was a small pause then she added, 'please accept my condolences.'

'Thank you.'

Didrika Weber was from the State Crime Desk in Braunschweig and was heading the murder squad that had been set up comprising local detectives and specialists, in order to find his father's killer.

'I know it's a difficult time for you, Mr Forrester, but please may I ask you some questions?'

He found himself adopting her formal approach. 'Please, go ahead.'

'First, I'd like to know why your father came to Germany. What you know about his visit. Who he saw, where he went.'

Pausing outside a restaurant, he told her that his father had been visiting his friend Arne, and felt a surge of frustration that that was the extent of his knowledge.

'Brussels Airlines confirm that your father landed in Hanover at ten twenty-five in the morning on Thursday the thirtieth of August.'

She seemed to be waiting for some kind of response, so he said, 'If you say so.'

'He hired a car for the day. His mileage was 179 kilometres. He stayed with his friends, Arne and Anneke Kraus that night.'

'I see.'

He heard her sigh gust down the line. 'So you don't know who else your father might have visited? Where else he may have gone?'

'I'm afraid not.'

'Hmmm. Would you have any idea why he might visit Isterberg Cemetery?'

Dan straightened. 'He was seen there?'

'He visited a commemorative plaque.'

'A memorial? What to?'

'I'm not sure if it's relevant.'

'Please,' he said.

'It's dedicated to the victims of World War II. Babies who died in an orphanage. They were born to Polish workers who were taken from their mothers.'

Although he couldn't think what his father would be doing there he murmured, 'I'd be interested to see it.'

'Of course.' Her voice was dismissive. 'But you are in England.'

'Yes, I am.'

Something in his voice must have given away his frustration because she said, 'If you are maybe thinking of coming over here, please let me know. You could tell me about your father. I find if I know the victim better I have more of a chance in finding out what happened.'

After they'd hung up Dan didn't go straight to the bench his father had told him about. Instead he switched right to walk around the miniature green, passing a smart-looking deli with a queue of well-heeled clientele waiting for their cappuccinos, and when he reached the next junction he stopped, pretending to check his watch. A woman with a small white dog gave an irritated explosion of breath as she swerved past him, but he wasn't concerned about her. His attention was on another woman, who was buying what looked to be a lettuce from the open-fronted fish-cum-grocery on the north-east side of the green.

Shoulder-length brown hair. An ordinary face. Oval, slightly pallid. Nothing outstanding, everything muted, unexceptional. Small, wiry body. He felt a cold rush of tension in his stomach.

Mouse Woman.

Today she was wearing a black skirt and white shirt, a pair of low-heeled black shoes.

She'd followed him from his father's flat on Tuesday. Was she following him now? Or was she the person he was supposed to meet?

Not wanting to flush her out or get too close and unnerve her into doing something she hadn't planned – he was pretty sure she didn't know he'd pinged her the first-time round – he kept walking up Elystan Street, eyes clicking around the area, looking for the woman's partner, the man who'd tracked him in Weston-super-Mare, but although he couldn't see him he knew any of the suits in the area could be on point.

9.55 a.m.

Dan walked back to Chelsea Green. Nobody sat on the benches. His watcher appeared to have vanished, but he knew she'd be around, maybe lurking in the pharmacy or one of the real estate agencies.

At the precise moment he moved to stand next to one of the benches, yesterday's *The Times* in one hand, a woman moved into view from Jubilee Place. She was smiling, her face filled with warmth.

He felt his jaw soften in surprise.

The last time he'd seen her had been a decade ago, at her wedding. The old gang had all been there – Christopher, Gustav, Dan – and Sophie. They'd all drunk far too much and behaved like the kids they used to be, culminating in Christopher and Dan having a mock-fight some time after midnight and both of them ending up, black ties and all, in the swimming pool.

Back then she'd worn a shimmering medieval dress with layers of lace and embroidered with pearls. The gown had a deep open back, her smooth skin tantalisingly naked all the way to her sinuous waist, and Dan had had great fun watching not just Gustav but every male in the room trying not to salivate. He was as affected as the next man, he supposed, but he could never shake the picture of her as a little girl, grubby from playing in the orchard, knees always scraped, hair a tangled mess, clutching a worm, a bird's nest, something she'd found and wanted to show off.

'Sophie?' He couldn't help it. His voice showed his incredulity.

'Dan.' Amusement shone in her eyes.

He looked beyond her and around the green. Then back at her. 'What's going on?'

She came and stood next to him. She wore a navy-blue, tailored single breasted jacket above a simple A-line skirt. How she managed to exude sexuality wearing something so business-like was impressive.

'Are you alone?' she asked.

'Yes.' He wasn't going to mention Mouse Woman.

'How have you been?'

'Mixed blessings.'

'I heard Bill died.' Sophie touched his arm, as light as a moth. 'He was a great guy. I'm really sorry.'

'Who told you?'

A tiny frown marred her brow. 'Dad.' Her tone implied, *who else?*

Dan decided not to mention the fact that his father had been murdered. Not until he knew more about what was going on.

'And you?' he asked politely. 'How's Nick?'

'Perfect, thank you. He works from home, leaving me to roam the city streets as much as I like.'

Home, if Dan recalled correctly, was a pretty little cottage on the seafront in Bosham, near Chichester.

'You still sail?' he asked.

'Very much,' she replied. 'You?'

'Not really.' Jenny hated sailing – the wet, the spray, the cramped conditions. She much preferred a brisk country walk followed by a pub lunch somewhere warm and dry.

'Shame. I seem to remember you were rather good.'

'We do other things.'

She put her head on one side, encouraging him to explicate, but instead he said, 'So,' and raised the newspaper. He wasn't interested in small talk no matter how many childhood memories they shared.

She got the message.

'So,' she repeated. 'It actually shouldn't be me here. It should be Dad.'

'I see.'

'He's really ill, which is why he sent me. He couldn't come himself, much as he wanted to.'

He raised his eyebrows into a question she immediately understood.

'He's had me check *The Times* every day for that particular message. He used to do it himself until last weekend, but he's taken a turn for the worse. He can't do much of anything anymore.' Her face lengthened in sorrow.

'I'm sorry.'

She looked away. 'He makes a terrible patient as you can imagine.'

'My father would have been the same.'

Sophie leaned back a little. Rearranged her handbag on her shoulder. 'What are you doing for the rest of the day?'

'Seeing your father?' he suggested.

'Perfect.' She smiled. 'Shall we go?'

CHAPTER NINETEEN

Sophie drove fast and efficiently and, unusually for Dan, he sat back and relaxed because it was obvious she'd had some advance training. When he asked after her job, she gave a beautifully bland response that had his antenna quivering.

'Nothing terribly exciting, I'm afraid,' she told him. 'I'm a drone in the Home Office.'

The Sophie he knew as a kid would never settle for something mundane. She had a quick and enquiring mind, and an adventurous spirit, but it was more than that. She needed to be challenged and continually stimulated or she'd become irked and irritable.

'How come I don't believe you?' he said.

She sent him a quick look.

'An office drone?' He gave a snort. 'Seriously?'

'OK, OK.' She flung up a hand in mock-surrender. 'You got me. I'm part of a performance, analysis and research team for HMIC.'

Now, that was more like it. Her Majesty's Inspectorate of Constabulary. Not so dull after all, monitoring, inspecting and reporting on police forces in England and Wales, as well as other national law enforcement agencies. She expanded a little and he realised that her job, despite its dreary title, sounded like it suited her very well.

'I don't normally tell people,' she admitted, 'because they invariably get it wrong and think I'm a cop and when I try and correct them, they still don't get it and start to moan about their speeding ticket.'

Thanks to light traffic, it took them just over two hours to get to Salisbury. Sophie's father used to live in a handsome Victorian townhouse, within a stone's throw of the cathedral, but now he was in a hospice on the outskirts of the city. Climbing out of the car, Dan scanned the area for watchers but didn't see anyone to concern him. During the journey he'd dropped his visor and flicked the mirror cover aside to check the vehicles behind them, but even using the wing mirror on his side of the car it was difficult to check whether they were being followed or not. He had to assume they were, and his mind continued to gnaw on who it might be and who would have planted a listening device in Christopher's car.

Inside, they scribbled their names and arrival time in the reception book before walking past a little shop selling fresh flowers and cakes and down a broad corridor. Dan had never been in a hospice before and it was nothing like he had imagined. No doctors or nurses rushing around, no beeping machines or smells of disinfectant. There were squashy sofas and armchairs, tables with lamps and neat piles of magazines, views of gardens. It felt more like a hotel than a place where you came to die.

Sophie paused outside a half-open door. A rattling, wheezing sound reached them.

'Chronic obstructive pulmonary disease, COPD. You remember he smoked?'

Dan didn't think he'd ever seen Rafe without a cigarette.

'He was on forty a day, sometimes sixty. He stopped five years ago but it was too late. His lungs are a mess.'

Her face contracted and for a moment he saw she was battling to contain her emotion.

'I'm sorry,' he said gently.

Her smile wobbled. 'Thanks.'

She pushed open the door. Soft grey carpet, easy chairs, a TV on the wall and a vista of bird tables. The only concession to Rafe Kennedy's terminal illness was the electrical medical bed.

'Hi, Dad.' Sophie went and greeted her father. 'I brought Dan with me.'

A hacking cough erupted from the bed, wet with phlegm.

'Let's get you up,' she said. The coughing worsened and Dan stepped forward wanting to help, but Sophie motioned him away.

Using a handset, she adjusted the bed. Intellectually, Dan knew Rafe wouldn't be looking too good if he was so close to death, but emotionally it still came as a shock. Gone was the tall, strong and ebullient man who spoke four languages and was a well-known fell runner, and in his place was a scrawny creature with skin the colour and texture of dry cement. His eyes were clouded, rheumy, and his lips pale and dry.

'Rafe,' Dan said. He was glad his tone was even and didn't betray his dismay.

'Daniel.' The word came out on an exhale that preceded another bout of coughing.

Sophie walked to the window and opened it a little, scaring off a couple of sparrows that had been on a feeder.

'Thanks . . . for . . . coming,' Rafe managed.

'It's been a while.' Dan moved a high-backed armchair closer to the bed and sat on it leaning forward, his hands between his knees.

'Sophie's . . . wedding.'

'Best party I've ever been to.' Dan smiled. 'Shame you didn't have another daughter so I could have ruined another set of shoes.'

The skin around the old man's mouth stretched as he smiled, showing a set of strong ivory teeth. No dentures for Rafe. If he hadn't smoked, Dan guessed he would have been as fit as Gordon and Arne.

'One is quite . . . enough.' He swivelled his eyes to look at Sophie who rolled her own at him. 'Darling daughter. . . would you mind . . .'

'Leaving you two alone? Of course not. I'll wait outside.'

Dan looked at Rafe. 'I'm sorry,' he said.

'Bloody fags.'

'Yes.'

'Wish I'd died . . . years ago.' Anger poured from him. 'I'm wearing . . . a fucking . . . nappy. Can you . . . believe it?'

'I'm sorry,' Dan said again.

'Fucking ... old age. Demeaning. Humiliating. The nurses call me ... "lovey" and talk to me as though I'm ... two fucking ... years old.' His eyes suddenly focussed on Dan, turning razor sharp. 'Wouldn't you rather fucking ... drop dead like your father ... fit as a flea at, say, sixty, rather than ... suffer an interminable, undignified ... demise?'

Rafe fixed him with a glare. 'Well?' he demanded.

Before he spoke, Dan considered his father's letter, the precautions in contacting his old friend via an advertisement in *The Times*, and knew he had to be honest.

'Dad didn't drop dead as you think,' Dan said evenly. 'He was murdered.'

The rattling and wheezing stopped. Rafe's eyes widened and for a moment Dan thought the old man was having a heart attack. He sprang up but Rafe took a gasping breath.

'Who?' he croaked.

'I'm trying to find out.'

'Christ.'

Dan sank back into the chair. 'He left me a letter with instructions to place the advertisement. I had no idea it was to contact you.'

'That's the fucking ... point. No ... names.'

'Why?'

'Your father was worried ... that he might disturb a hornet's nest. He wanted to ... protect us both until he knew there was no danger. We set it up after he came to see me ... last week.'

'A friend of his told me he saw something in the newspaper that frightened him.'

Rafe continued to look at Dan but he didn't say anything. Finally, he took a slow breath.

'Did Bill ever . . . tell you where I worked?' he rasped.

'You all got a medical science degree. I know that much.' Dan frowned as he thought further. 'Dad was the only one who didn't use his.'

'Joined the fucking . . .' Rafe's words disintegrated into more coughs but he managed to eject, 'marines.'

A childhood memory inched into his mind, of Rafe giving Bill a hard time over wasting his degree and Bill's energetic response: *I'd rather hump a fifty-pound pack through a bog than spend my life locked up in a lab.* Rafe had told Dan he'd tried to get Bill to change his mind about joining up, saying he could have got his fix of the outdoors training and running fell races like he did, but Bill defended himself with a sly look in the eye, *We have the same employer, doesn't that count for anything?*

'I worked on . . .' Rafe made an effort to speak, eyes watering, chest heaving.

Dan waited.

'Pro—' Rafe shuddered as made a massive effort to get the rest of the word out '—ject.'

'Project,' Dan repeated.

Eyes streaming, bony fingers clawed on the sheets, Rafe fixed his gaze on Dan. Urgency and desperation twisted between them as Rafe struggled to inhale. Dan began to rise, to go and find a nurse, but Rafe shook his head violently. Skin springing with anxious sweat, Dan sank back. 'Are you sure?'

Rafe shook his head again. Ghastly sucking noises bubbled from his chest. He was fighting to speak and as Dan watched he found himself holding his breath in sympathy. He thought: *I'll give him another five seconds, and then I'm going to go and find a nurse, a doctor—*

'Snowbank.' The word came on an explosive outbreath triggering a massive coughing fit that shook the old man's frame like a tornado.

'Project Snowbank,' Dan repeated, leaping out of his chair and tearing for the door but Sophie had already flung it open and was calling for a nurse. Dan stood aside as the nurse affixed an oxygen mask over Rafe's face but it didn't seem to help much. He continued coughing, his eyes closed, tears coursing down his withered cheeks, and then he suddenly fell quiet and his body went limp.

Dan felt a moment's horror.

'It's OK,' Sophie quickly assured him. 'It's what happens when he talks too much.' She ushered Dan outside. 'He'll be out of it now for at least a couple of hours. I'm sorry.'

'It's OK.' He touched her shoulder.

'There's not much point staying.' She glanced up and down the corridor. 'I'll just say goodbye to the nurses. See you in reception.'

The receptionist was occupied on the phone, booking a taxi for someone, so under the pretext of signing himself out, Dan checked the previous week's visitors in the reception folder. His father's bold handwriting jumped out at him. He'd visited Rafe last Tuesday, twenty-eighth of August. The same day he'd seen Olivia. Three days before he died.

He looked up Project Snowbank on his phone to find nothing but pictures and YouTube videos of huge banks of snow in America. He put his phone away when Sophie appeared.

On the journey back she was distracted, unfocussed, her driving not as sharp, and he knew she was far more distressed by her father's illness than she let on. He didn't want to bother her but he didn't see he had a choice.

'Soph, can I ask . . . where did your father work?'

'Oh. TSJ. TarnStanleyJones. In their life science wing.'

Although he'd heard of them – they were in the top FTSE 100 – Dan looked them up on his phone. A science-led global healthcare company, their banner was that they were a company with a mission to help people to live better and enjoy an enriched quality of life as they aged. *Age well. Live well.*

Dan felt a wave of pity for Rafe, his strong body ravaged by age and disease.

Wish I'd died . . . years ago.

CHAPTER TWENTY

Lucy had just parked outside the Duncaid Environmental Research Centre when Mac called.

'Hi,' she answered brightly.

'I thought we had an agreement.'

'Ah.'

'Ah?' His voice rose. 'You've sent me three texts, Lucy. The last one was on Tuesday. It's now—'

'Thursday. Yes, I know. I'm sorry.' Inside, she kicked herself for being so slack. Mac would happily let her do her own thing but only if he believed he was in the loop.

'So,' he said. 'What gives?'

She filled him in as she watched the latest deluge through her windscreen. Being a Londoner, Lucy wasn't used to so much rainfall and couldn't think how people managed to keep their spirits up with this amount of grey. Grey skies, grey stone houses, grey rivers.

She finished by telling him that an autopsy on Connor had been done. They were waiting for the results.

'They suspect foul play?' He sounded incredulous. 'Why? He was a thirteen-year-old boy!'

'I know it sounds crazy, but . . .' She nibbled her lip as she considered whether to tell him about the listening device or not.

'But, what?'

She sighed. She couldn't withhold something so important.

'Come on, Lucy. Spill it.'

'I found a listening device in the Bairds' car,' she confessed. 'Dan's concerned it's professional.'

A silence ensued, during which she knew Mac would have a huge scowl on his face.

'You two . . .' His words were strangled.

'Three,' she corrected quickly. 'Don't forget Grace. She's working with us too.'

He muttered something she thought sounded like *God help me*, but then he said, 'What about the local police?'

'Everyone's pushing for suicide.'

'There might be a reason for that,' he remarked testily.

Lucy remained quiet.

'OK, OK,' he relented as though she'd been arguing for hours. 'Just keep your nose clean, OK? And when you're back, let's talk it through over a drink. Or is your boyfriend so possessive we have to do it in the office?'

Mac and alcohol? She didn't think so. Alcohol lowered her inhibitions and sure, it helped make her more relaxed but it also made her do some really stupid things. 'The office is my preferred option,' she told him.

'Oh, he's the jealous type, is he? I wouldn't have thought you'd take too lightly to having a controlling—'

'Ooooh, Mac,' she rode over him. 'My interviewee has just turned up, gotta go.'

She hung up. Stared some more at the rain-washed windscreen. She wasn't sure how long she could keep up the pretence that Nick Baker was her boyfriend. She hadn't actually *lied* outright to Mac, but it was as near as dammit. She realised they were both trying to keep things professional, at least she was, but Mac kept pushing that little bit more, winding her up about Nick, pushing for a drink . . . Why couldn't he find someone else? That would distract him nicely. She'd heard he'd been seeing someone a couple of months back – had they split up? If so, why?

Lucy spent the next few minutes trying to make a plan on how to deal with Mac, most of which involved her tearing his clothes off and making love with him on his desk, in her flat, in his house, on the moors, on the beach, and by the time she climbed out of the car she was almost cross-eyed with sexual tension. Maybe she should just give up and jump back into bed with him and see where the cards fell, but that little voice of self-preservation wouldn't let up.

If I let him get too close, he'll see who I really am and I can't let that happen.

She pushed open the door to the Duncaid Environmental Research Centre to be welcomed by the smell of freshly made toast. Lucy loved toast almost as much as she loved chips and could eat it any time of the day, preferably with lashings of butter. As she crossed the little reception area, empty aside from a modular reception desk and swivel chair, her mouth watered.

'Hello?' she called out.

She rang the chrome desk bell. 'Hello?'

Seconds later a woman of Chinese appearance, dressed in a white lab coat, appeared. She was licking her fingers. 'Sorry,' she said, looking abashed. 'You caught me—'

'Making toast,' Lucy said with a smile. 'Smells delicious.'

The woman brushed her hands together. 'How can I help you?'

'I'm Lucy Davies. I'm here because I'm a friend of Christopher's and—'

'You're looking into Connor's death.' The woman's eyes widened. 'Yes, he told me.' She held out a hand. 'I'm Jasmine. His lab assistant.'

Lucy did her best not to show any surprise. She'd expected Jasmine to be more glamorous, maybe even beautiful considering Christopher's affair with her, but she was plain-featured and surprisingly dumpy. Lucy tried not to flinch as they shook hands. The woman had the handshake of a sumo wrestler.

'It's been awful.' Jasmine pulled a face. 'Poor Christopher. Poor Connor. I can't believe he'd commit suicide.'

'Why do you say that?'

Jasmine repeated the litany Lucy had heard over the past few days; that he was a positive boy, popular with his friends, and that he had lots to look forward to.

'He wasn't too happy about little Dougie,' Lucy remarked. 'With a new baby in the house I've heard he wasn't getting the attention he was used to.'

Jasmine put her head on one side and studied Lucy. Her gaze was cool, assessing. She said, 'That didn't bother him. Not really. It was his father's affair with me that really did the damage.'

Inside, Lucy applauded Jasmine for being so honest. It would make her job a lot easier than if she had to drag a confession out of the woman.

'Come inside.' Jasmine was brisk. 'I'll make us tea.'

The smell of toast increased as they stepped into a corridor with a long window that overlooked a laboratory where three people were working. Long benches were covered in glass beakers, flasks and test tubes and stands.

'We've got several PhD researchers here,' Jasmine told her. 'As well as a Research Fellow.'

'What is it that you do exactly?'

'Crop science. Agri-technology. Finding crops resistant to pests, that are more efficient, grow faster and give a higher yield. Christopher's done some incredible work here.' Her eyes brightened. 'Has he told you about his *Mĭ quiáng*? Strong rice?'

Lucy shook her head.

'Oh.' Jasmine pulled a face. 'I can understand it, I suppose with everything that's going on . . . but the thing is, he's been researching C3 and C4 plants, developing a strain of rice that isn't just incredibly resilient but grows faster and has higher energy too. So you can eat say one bowl of rice where you used to eat two and actually get more energy and nutrients than before.'

'You're talking GM?' Lucy asked. 'Genetically modified rice?'

Something in the woman tightened slightly. 'You have a problem with GM?'

'I don't know enough about it,' Lucy responded neutrally.

'Most people don't realise they're eating GM foods every day,' Jasmine sighed. 'The supermarkets are full of it. Apples bred to the right shape, root ginger without the knobbles, tomatoes with less pips. It's all about getting the most out of your harvest, whatever it may be. And that's what *Mǐ quiáng* is all about. That's why I'm here. I want to help Christopher bring his strong rice to the world.'

'Wow,' said Lucy, impressed, but inside her mind was buzzing. The subject of GM was highly contentious, inciting powerful emotions and arguments both for and against. She'd once arrested five people at a GM talk in London where a scientist had lost his rag against a 'bunch of pig-ignorant, lefty do-gooders that needed a map to find their own arses.' Insults were returned, hotly followed by some scuffling, a couple of punches thrown, nothing serious, but the hatred that had flared between the two sides was as dark and violent as any religious disagreement.

'Was Connor for or against GM?' asked Lucy.

Jasmine looked surprised. 'I have no idea. I'd rather assume he'd be pro, with the work his father does.'

Lucy knew that may not necessarily be the case – not every kid followed their parents' beliefs – but she didn't comment. Instead she said, 'How many of you work here in total?'

'Seven including Christopher and me. Part of our research is funded by the EU. Who knows what's going to happen with Brexit. We might have to shut down.' She looked depressed.

Lucy followed her into a tea room just around the corner. A couple of chairs, a table with stacks of scientific magazines mingled with dirty cups and plates covered in crumbs.

'Sorry.' Jasmine scooped up the dirty dishes and stacked them in the dishwasher set to one side. Next to the kettle sat a plate with a slice of half-eaten toast. Jasmine flipped it into the bin.

'Sorry to interrupt your toast,' Lucy told her.

'No matter.' Jasmine put the kettle on and brewed tea in a delicate pot the colour of cornflowers. Matching cups.

'They're beautiful,' Lucy remarked.

'My auntie sent them from Fouzhou.' She pronounced it *Foochow*. 'My childhood town.' She'd come to the UK when she was twenty to attend university and over the next ten years had only been back for the odd holiday. 'I like it here,' she admitted. 'Less poverty, more freedom.'

Lucy turned the subject back to Connor.

'He came and saw me,' Jasmine said. 'He wanted to know if his father and I were going to get married. Live together. I told him absolutely not.' She lifted her chin and levelled a steady brown gaze at Lucy. 'I don't want to live with anyone, let alone get married. I like my independence too much.'

Just as Christopher had said.

'How do you and Christopher get along now?'

Jasmine's expression turned distant. 'We rub along. We're not the friends we used to be but we're OK. I like the work here. I'm good at it, and Christopher appreciates that.'

Pretty much everything tallied with what Christopher had told Lucy, except for one thing. 'When did Connor come and see you?'

'Last Saturday.'

The day before he'd died.

'Where?'

'Here. Everyone knows I work Saturdays. It's quiet and I can get on, undisturbed.'

They both turned when a Chinese man stuck his head around the door. Swarthy, blocky body, fleshy lips. He took one look at Lucy and barked something in Chinese – Mandarin? Cantonese? – at Jasmine who snapped something back in the same language. The man flushed.

'Sorry,' he said. His English was heavily accented. It came out as *Sow-ee*.

'This is Bao Zhi,' Jasmine introduced them. 'He's from the Kou Shaiming Company in Beijing. Bao Zhi is helping test Christopher's strong rice with a view to possibly taking it to China.'

'It's that far advanced?' Lucy asked.

'Oh, yes.' Bao Zhi nodded, his face suddenly alight with enthusiasm. 'It is looking very good. It will help many people.'

With a strangely formal little bow, he left the room closing the door behind him with exaggerated care.

'Do you want to see Christopher before you go?' Jasmine asked as she walked Lucy outside.

'He's here?' For some reason Lucy was surprised. She hadn't seen his car outside. Nor had she thought him capable of functioning in the lab.

'He finds work helps.' Jasmine's hands lifted then fell in a helpless gesture.

After they'd said goodbye Lucy climbed into her car and checked her phone to see she had two missed calls. One from Grace and one from Dan.

Since Dan had called just two minutes ago, she rang him first.

'Lucy,' he said. Something was wrong with his voice. It sounded strangled, as though he was having trouble speaking.

'What is it?'

'Grace just rang me with Connor's autopsy results.'

Bloody hell, she thought, *that was quick*. Elena Crofton must have worked through the night, which wasn't surprising considering she had Gordon Baird breathing fire down her neck.

He cleared his throat. Lucy saw Bao Zhi watching her through the window of the research centre. She gave him a little wave which he returned tentatively before ducking back out of sight.

'They found phenol in his system.'

Lucy's mind fired a single crimson rocket along her synapses.

'It's what the Nazis used to execute individuals and small groups of people in World War II.'

Jesus Christ, she thought.

'Approximately one gram is sufficient to cause death. The toxic effect of phenol causes sudden collapse and loss of consciousness. It's pretty immediate, I'm told.'

She fixed her gaze on the granite-grey wall ahead of her.

'He was injected in his thigh. Someone tried to mess up the injection site but the pathologist said her findings were conclusive.'

'He was murdered,' said Lucy. Her voice was faint.

'Yes.'

'Why?'

'I don't know. But I want you to find out, Lucy. Fast.'

CHAPTER TWENTY-ONE

With Aimee at school, and wanting to give Jenny a bit of space, Dan went to Chepstow for a lunch of fish and chips and half a pint of bitter. While he ate he opened his father's laptop and had a look. He purposely didn't think about his murdered godson. He'd delegated the hunt for Connor's killer to Lucy not just because he knew she'd do an exemplary job but because he trusted her one hundred per cent. Dan didn't trust people lightly but knowing Lucy was on the case released him to concentrate on finding his father's killer. Once that was done he'd turn his attention back to Connor.

Carefully, Dan checked his father's email and Internet browser history to see he'd been in regular touch with Gordon, Rafe and Arne, but that was nothing new. Their subjects ranged from electro-magnetic weapons, whether they were morally acceptable or not, to the pros and cons of euthanasia, which had turned fairly heated recently, particularly between his father and Rafe. Rafe was violently in favour of assisted suicide, his father against.

There was a long history of emails between his father and Olivia, and smatterings of chats between more friends. Nothing to do with newspaper articles or anything that Dan could think might scare his father so badly. He turned to check his father's Internet browser and the bookmarks he'd made, occasionally lifting his gaze, and it was only because of sheer luck that he saw her.

He felt a bite of alarm.

She was stepping out of the pub door. If he hadn't looked in that direction at that precise moment he'd never have spotted her. Today she wore a blonde wig and a big blue baggy sweater over faded jeans. She looked much younger, almost in her teens, which he guessed was the idea. He recognised her by the curve of her face, the lightness of her step. He was glad he'd memorised her so well all those days ago.

Mouse Woman.

He stared at the space she'd vacated. She had to have followed him here from his house.

She *knew* where he lived.

Pushing his food aside, Dan sprang to his feet, grabbed his father's laptop and shoved it inside his satchel. Slinging the satchel across his chest he ran for the door and yanked it open.

An icy wind snatched at his hair as he walked quickly through the car park, glancing around, trying not to look as though he was searching for her. If he lost her he didn't want her to know she'd been pinged.

There!

He spotted her blonde wig moving between a panel van and a Mazda MX-5. He broke into a low run, the scar across his stomach a taut line of pain as he tried to keep a short profile. He used parked cars as cover but to his dismay, as he ran past the back of a blue sedan, she turned her head and looked right at him. He didn't slow down. He accelerated hard and fast straight for her. Her expression turned to fright. She spun round and at the same time he heard two beeps and saw the MX-5's hazard warning lights flash as the driver's door opened.

He got to the car just as she slammed the door and snapped the locks in place.

'Open up,' he told her.

She shook her head.

'I'll ask one more time . . .'

The second he saw her hand go to start the engine he leaned over and punched the side of his fist into her side window. A crack appeared.

Her face went white.

As he drew back his fist again, the engine started with a roar. A crunch of gears as she rammed it into reverse.

Dan turned and sprinted for his BMW. Not far, maybe thirty yards, but it could be far enough to give her a disproportionate advantage. He reached it in a clatter of gravel, skidding to the driver's door. Hauled it open and dived inside. Turned on the engine. He saw the MX-5 turn left out of the car park. He tore after her, engine roaring. The seatbelt ring tone came on but he ignored it. He couldn't waste a second buckling up. He had to get behind her before she could vanish.

The street was active with shoppers and delivery vehicles, kids, pushchairs. When he saw Mouse Woman was boxed in between a Waitrose van and a VW Polo he hung back a little, not wanting to push her into doing something stupid on such a busy road, like overtake blindly and hit a pedestrian. He followed her at a sedate pace, buckling up at last, his heart hammering, adrenaline pumping.

Gradually the centre of town fell away and Dan pushed closer. She accelerated, and then suddenly dived right down the next street. Was she using a satnav or acting on instinct? No matter. He knew the area well, better than she did probably, so he had the advantage. Soon they were out of town and as he swept round the next bend he saw she was flat out on a long, smooth straight. He floored the accelerator, topping eighty miles per hour, the wheels bouncing and thudding as they leapt over potholes. Then came a sharp right-hand bend and he waited until the last second before he stamped on the brakes, dropping into third gear and powering round the curve roaring to the next straight.

She took the next right, then left after a farmhouse, her little MX-5 fast and nippy, but the BMW was more powerful and Dan the more experienced driver, which he could tell after watching her driving through town: her observation and hazard management were almost non-existent.

Dan closed in.

At the next corner Dan rode tight behind her through the bend, then on the next straight he brought his car right up to her bumper and gave it a tap. The MX-5 wavered briefly. He tapped again. He was hoping she'd pull over, but no. She was still going flat out.

They came to a steeply cambered road. As Dan popped out of the bend, he was inches from the MX-5's bumper. No traffic was coming the other way. He floored the accelerator and before she could block him, he was level with the MX-5.

Keeping pace with her he gestured at her to pull over.

Her face was pale and resolutely faced forward.

He sounded his horn. Gestured again.

Ahead, on his side of the road, a tractor suddenly appeared.

Dan kept level with her. Kept gesturing. Kept sounding the horn.

The tractor switched on its headlights. It was getting closer and closer at a terrifyingly fast rate.

Dan held his nerve.

He heard the tractor's horn. He was still racing toward it but he wasn't going to brake. Not until the last—

The MX-5 suddenly vanished.

She'd braked to let him in.

Just as he'd planned.

Dan yanked the steering wheel over. As the tractor's snout flashed past his window, inches away, its horn shrieking at him, he swerved further across the road, right in front of the MX-5, and slammed on the brakes.

The BMW had one of the best braking systems in the world. Even when applying the full force of braking power the vehicle remained under his complete control.

The MX-5 on the other hand had good brakes but not exceptional ones. In his rear-vision mirror he saw the little car trying to skid to a halt and he suddenly pulled out, allowing her to almost come level, and then he rammed her straight into the ditch.

As her car came to rest, Dan pulled over and reversed back. Ignoring the pain across his stomach he bolted outside, not stopping to switch off the engine.

The Mazda was tilted to one side, the driver's front wheel in the air, spinning lazily. Muddy water had sprayed over the bonnet and windscreen.

He raced over.

Mouse Woman was struggling with her seatbelt but otherwise looked OK. She was the colour of curdled milk and even from where he stood he could see she was shaking badly.

'Open up,' he said, rapping on her window.

In response, she leaned away from him, snapped open her glovebox, and when she turned back, she was holding a pistol. Which she aimed straight at him.

CHAPTER TWENTY-TWO

With its grey stone foundations and grey rendering around stained PVC windows, Duncaid's Police Station wasn't a building to lift the spirits. Grace had passed it plenty of times on her way to work, but had never had cause to step inside. Until today, when Murdoch had insisted upon her 'dropping by'. He had made it clear that he expected her to come to him, and not him to her.

Grace waited for him in reception, her eyes taking in the posters on the wall. END WILDLIFE CRIME. STOP POACHING. Another showed an eagle in full flight. OPERATION APRIL, EAGLE WATCH. There were the usual posters on drugs and alcohol but it certainly made a difference having dramatic pictures of wildlife on the walls.

A door banged behind her. 'Dr Reavey.'

She turned to see Constable Murdoch. His face was stony. 'Follow me, if you would.'

He led the way into an interview room. Small, blue, no windows. A two-way mirror was set in the wall over a bolted-down table and two chairs. It was where the police interviewed suspects and Grace had no doubt Murdoch had brought her in here to unsettle her. *Don't give him anything. Pretend this is completely normal. Smile.*

Murdoch closed the door firmly. Although he didn't lock it, it felt as though he had. It was like being in a cell. With as much aplomb as she could muster, Grace took a seat. Folded her hands on her lap. Murdoch sat opposite.

'Well,' he said.

Grace waited.

'It appears Connor Baird was murdered.'

He glowered at her. She thought of saying, *apparently so*, but there seemed little point since he'd now raised a forefinger and was stabbing it at her.

'This does *not* mean you can demand a fucking autopsy at the drop of a hat in the future. This does *not* mean you can tell us, the polis, how to do our jobs and it does *not* mean you're fucking God around here.'

His face had turned puce, the veins on his nose standing out. She hoped he wasn't going to have a heart attack. Her de-fib was in the car and since the tiny car park at the back of the police station had been full, she'd been forced to park down the street and it would take her at least two minutes to fetch it.

'Do you *hear me*?' he added furiously.

'I hear you,' she said mildly. She decided not to tell him she'd just requested another autopsy, this one on a sixty-six-year-old woman out of Bridgeorth who'd died the day before yesterday. Two weeks ago Iona Ainsley had come to her with an infected finger. Grace had put her on antibiotics and things had seemed to improve but then, to Grace's horror, the infection suddenly deepened and Iona's health dropped into a severe decline. Despite having been blue-lighted to hospital, Iona had died that afternoon.

'Right.' He nodded several times. 'OK then.' He brought out his pocketbook and a pen. 'I need to ask you some questions now.'

'OK.'

More nodding. 'OK,' he echoed on an exhale. To her relief, his colour began to subside. No de-fib required, thank God.

He opened his pocketbook and clicked the nib of his pen. 'Tell me what you saw when you first arrived at the crime scene.'

She talked him through her first impressions, which led to more questions. His writing was surprisingly small and angular, which suited his tense and irascible attitude. After a while he moved on to how she knew Connor as a patient, his parents, her thoughts on them as a family.

He said, 'You know Samantha's husband Christopher was having an affair before Connor died?'

'Yes.'

'Jasmine Zhang doesn't have an alibi for the day Connor was killed.'

Grace stared at him.

'She says,' he went on, 'that she was at work. In the lab. But nobody can corroborate her statement.'

Grace said, 'Surely you can't mean—'

'No alibi,' he said carefully, as if he was stating something obvious to a three-year old.

'You can't seriously think Jasmine murdered Connor?' Her voice was high in disbelief. 'For God's sake, *why*?'

'By setting it up as suicide she made sure Christopher and Sam would never get back together.' He held her gaze, absolutely firm, absolutely resolute. 'She had access to countless drugs in the lab. She'd seen Connor on his own before. No reason why he wouldn't go and see her again. She had the means, motive and opportunity.'

'The lab researches crops, rice. GM plants. You really think they'd have something like phenol there?'

'We'll soon find out.' He sat back, folding his arms and looking smug.

'And you think I waste public resources.' She couldn't help it; her tone was scathing. Sending a forensic team to scour the lab would cost a fortune.

The skin around his mouth tightened. 'At least I have good reason. A *real* purpose behind my request.'

'You think I ask for autopsies for *fun*?' Grace's blood pressure began to escalate. 'When someone dies and it's not obvious why—'

'Iona died of an infection.'

'Oh.' She was taken aback. 'You know about that.'

'Too fucking right I know,' he snapped. 'She died of natural causes and you throwing money away isn't going to change that.'

'But she *shouldn't* have. That's the point! According to her medical notes she'd never shown a vulnerability to infections before, and I want answers so if someone else suffers from the same problem, I know *what to do*.' Her voice had risen and she fought to temper it. 'Look, if you cut yourself tomorrow and you got a similar infection, wouldn't you want to know I was giving you the right treatment? I might learn something vital from Iona's autopsy that might just save your life.'

He drew his lips back in a sneer. 'As if.'

She could have been talking to a stubborn, obstructive teenager and it was at that point Grace realised she could say the moon orbited the Earth once every lunar month and he'd still disagree.

'If that's all,' she said coldly, 'I'll take my leave.'

She got to her feet. She didn't move to the door but made him open it for her. A trivial bit of point scoring but it helped make her feel better. God, she couldn't believe his attitude. Her bad mood was still with her when she walked into the surgery. Two early-bird patients glanced up as she passed, murmuring greetings.

'All right?' Susan McCreedy, the surgery's practice manager, looked at her askance when she checked in at the nurse's station.

Grace made an effort to relax her shoulders, which had bunched up around her ears. 'I was just at the police station, discussing Connor's case.'

'Ach. It's a terrible thing.' A flamboyant redhead with freckles scattered across her nose and cheeks, Susan was usually robust and cheerful but now her expression sobered into one of dismay. 'Who'd want to kill a child like that? Terrible, just terrible.'

'Terrible,' Grace echoed. 'Any messages for me?'

'Nae. But Mr Baird is wanting to see you.'

Grace raised her eyebrows in a question: *Which Mr Baird?*

'That'll be Professor Gordon Baird. He's waiting for you in your office.'

'What?' For a second, she thought she'd misheard.

'What?' Susan looked baffled.

'Gordon Baird is in my *consulting room?*'

'Well, yes.' Susan was still perplexed.

Grace stepped close to the woman. She said, 'My consulting room is private for very good reason. I have confidential files in there along with sensitive medical equipment. The only people who are allowed inside when I am absent are the cleaners and anyone working in this surgery. Nobody else.'

'But it's Gordon—'

'I said *nobody* else.' Jaw clenched, she held the woman's gaze. 'And that includes the Archbishop of Canterbury and Brad Pitt. Obviously if the Queen wanted a look I might make an exception but since that's highly unlikely I think we'll stick to *nobody*. Understand?'

'If you say so,' Susan said, obviously reluctant and sulky. Grace could practically hear her chanting, *oooh, la-di-da* but she wasn't going to back down. Even if it made her unpopular, she was determined to maintain standards and avoid any Tom, Dick or Harry wandering in and potentially stealing drugs, or accessing her computer. She didn't want to make an exception for even one person. Christ, this never would have happened in Ellisfield, her last surgery, where doctor's offices were pretty much sacrosanct.

'Thank you.' Grace swept out of reception and along the corridor to her room where she found Gordon Baird standing with his hands behind his back, studying her wall shelves and the folders, medical journals and books stored there.

'Murdoch kept you for longer than I thought he would,' he said without turning around. 'I'd hoped to have more than a few minutes with you but you have a surgery at four, don't you?'

Inside she raised her eyes to the ceiling. Was nothing secret in this town? Then she took in his bowed shoulders and felt something inside her relent. She'd been about to order him out but she couldn't. He had probably just learnt that his grandson had been murdered. However, it was still no excuse to muscle into her personal rooms. Was it a territorial gesture? Or was it because he was deeply upset and wanting privacy? Or was it more self-regarding? Because he didn't want to be seen waiting like a member of the general public in reception?

'Yes,' she said instead. 'Surgery's in five minutes.' She put her handbag on the chair behind her desk. 'I'm so sorry about Connor.'

At last he turned. His skin had turned a sickly colour and his eyes looked rheumy. For the first time he looked his age. 'What does Murdoch think about it?' he asked.

She wasn't going to tell him the policeman thought Jasmine Zhang was in the frame. Instead she said, 'I think you should ask him yourself.'

'Aye. I will do that.'

He came and sat in the seat beside her desk. 'I like this,' he told her. 'That you're not behind the desk and the patient in front like at a job interview. I expect your patients feel as though they're on the same level as you. More equal.'

'That's the impression I like to give.' She looked at him straight. 'How can I help you?'

'It's more how I can help *you*.'

She frowned. 'What do you mean?'

'It's a funny old thing. I was talking to a colleague of mine yesterday. John Buchanan. He's got a practice in Edinburgh. The Queensferry Medical Practice. He's looking for a top GP to join him. Not just anyone. Someone at the top of their game. He's recruiting from London but I told him to wait a moment because I thought I knew of the perfect person for him.'

Grace stared.

'You're wasted here,' he told her. 'Don't tell me you don't know it.'

She opened and closed her mouth. 'I like it here.'

'Liking is all very well, but you're hardly challenged, are you?' He gave a long sigh. 'Look, John's got a two-bedroom garden flat that he'll let to whoever gets the job. You can walk to work. It's in the city centre. You could stay there Monday to Friday and come to the farm at weekends. It's only a three-hour drive away.'

'I like it here,' she repeated. She couldn't think of anything else to say against the surge of traitorous hope that leaped in her breast.

He put a card on her desk. 'Call John. Talk it over. You've got nothing to lose. That said, I have to tell you that you'd be missed here as you're bloody good, a breath of fresh air compared to most of the junk doctors we get, but in all honesty you're under-achieving in this practice and you could do so much better, be so much happier . . .'

It was like an electric shock beneath her breastbone. What the hell did *he* know about her happiness? She pushed her chair back. 'You'd better go, surgery has started.'

'Of course.' He rose. He looked at her carefully. 'I've offended you. I'm sorry. I didn't mean to. I just hate it when I see talent squandered.'

CHAPTER TWENTY-THREE

The instant Dan saw the gun levelled at him he backed off, hands raised, but Mouse Woman didn't lower it. Kept it trained on him.

She was holding a Glock 17 that would fire a bullet straight through the driver's window without losing much accuracy. She was still shaking but not as much. The gun had given her confidence.

'OK,' he called. 'I just want to talk. OK?'

She shook her head.

Still holding her weapon she brought out a mobile phone. Flicking her gaze between Dan and the phone she made a call. He couldn't hear what she said, but whoever she'd rung was obviously coming to her rescue because when she hung up the colour in her face began to return.

Dan walked back to his car. Switched off the ignition and pocketed the key. Then he brought out his phone. Dialled.

'It's me,' he said. 'I need a number plate run. Fast as you can.'

When he finished the call he pushed his phone into his back pocket. Walked to a tree that stood between his car and Mouse Woman. Propped a shoulder against the bark. Crossed his arms. Settled to wait.

When a car approached, Mouse Woman pushed the gun out of sight. Dan waved the car past and the instant it had gone she brought her weapon up again. Unerringly trained it back on Dan.

Over the next hour he waved a variety of lorries and cars past. Only two people stopped to lower their windows, good Samaritans making sure they couldn't help. Dan assured them the tow truck was on its way and that his girlfriend, Charlotte, was fine, thank you. As soon as he said the word *Charlotte*, they nodded, feeling safe in the belief he was telling the truth and that everything was in hand.

Eventually, an Isuzu truck – no decals, plain blue – arrived. Right behind it was a black Ford transit van. Tinted windows. A crumpled off-side wing where it could have rammed or been rammed by another vehicle. The side door opened and three men climbed out. Jeans and sweatshirts, boots. Hard faces. Dan didn't move. Just stood against the tree and watched.

One man moved to stand between Dan and the MX-5. Dan shifted his position, uncrossing his arms and standing squarely on the balls of his feet. An alert posture that suggested he was ready for anything. As he moved, the man's hand went to the small of his back to check his weapon. Dan raised his hands to show he wasn't a threat. The man nodded. Let his hands dangle at his sides.

Another man went to the MX-5 and opened the driver's door. Helped Mouse Woman out. She was clutching a handbag, big enough to carry her handgun. The third man stood by the van, gesturing traffic past, keeping an eye on Dan. All three men wore earpieces.

Dan's phone rang as Mouse Woman clambered inside the van.

'Yes?' he answered.

'The car belongs to Joanna Loxton, Holland Road, Kensal Rise.'

'Can you run another two plates for me?' He rattled off the truck's and the Ford transit's number. He didn't wait for confirmation and hung up.

The car was loaded on to the back of the Isuzu. The men stood around, half-watching the process, half-watching Dan. When Dan pushed himself forward, away from the tree, one of the men stepped forward putting a hand up in a STOP gesture. Dan began to walk across. The man put both hands up. Dan stopped where he could be heard.

'Who are you?' he asked.

The man's mouth pinched as he shook his head.

'Who do you work for?'

Again he shook his head.

Dan took another step towards them but this time the man's hand went to the small of his back.

'What? You're going to shoot me?' Dan looked pointedly at a car driving past.

There was a clank and a rattle of chains as the MX-5 was made safe on the back of the tow truck. The truck driver and his buddy gave the men the thumbs-up and climbed into their cab.

'Come on,' Dan spread his hands. 'Your colleague was following me. Why? What are you after?'

Two of the men turned and clambered into their black van. The last man said, 'Throw me your car keys.'

'No.'

This time he showed his weapon. A Glock 17. Same as Mouse Woman's.

'You want me to put a bullet in your tyre?'

'Not particularly.'

'Then throw me your car keys.'

'No.'

Dan folded his arms.

'For Chrissakes . . .' a Scottish brogue erupted. One of the men inside the van leaped outside, pulled out his gun and aimed it at Dan's right knee. 'Just fucking hand them over. And don't think I won't shoot you because I fucking will, OK? I don't care who sees, either.'

From the way the man's dark eyes burned into his, Dan knew he meant business. He brought out his key and threw it to the other man.

The Scot turned and climbed into the van. The other man brought back his arm and threw Dan's car key through the air, into the vegetation on the other side of the ditch. As best as he could, Dan marked the spot between a weary ragwort and a beech sapling.

The man joined his pals inside the van. Dan didn't bother watching them go. He was already leaping across the ditch, looking for his key.

CHAPTER TWENTY-FOUR

'Hi, it's me again,' said Lucy brightly down the phone.

'Don't tell me,' said Mac, sounding weary. 'You want another favour.'

'How did you guess?' She didn't pause but ploughed straight ahead. Momentum was the key. 'Another number plate. Two actually. One apparently belongs to a black Ford transit van, the other, a tow truck.'

'He's broken down?'

Mac was being droll, but before he could ask what Dan was up to, Lucy said, 'No, he's on a mission.' She didn't know any such thing but thought it prudent to give Mac something. Now she thought about it, if she hadn't known Dan as well as she did, she would have thought him exceptionally rude. No words of acknowledgement on the phone, no salutation. Just: 'I need a number plate run'. Luckily Mac hadn't quibbled the first time round, but now? How long could she push her boss's goodwill?

'I am not Dan Forrester's personal link to the DVLA,' Mac grumbled.

'It's really important,' she wheedled. 'Pretty please? I'd do it myself but obviously I can't as I'm on holiday.' Which wasn't strictly true as she had a contact she could use, someone she'd carefully cultivated when she'd been at the Met, but she didn't want to blot her copybook if it came out she'd used him for personal reasons. She'd only been a detective for seven months.

'You'll owe me a drink,' he told her.

'Ohhhkay.' She was hesitant.

'At the Swithenbank.'

'You mean the one on the moors?' She was slightly taken aback he'd choose one well out of town and on the edge of the North York Moors National Park.

'That's right,' he agreed. 'I like it there.'

'But isn't it more of a restaurant?'

'It's still a pub.'

She rubbed her forehead. It was a bit like doing a deal with the devil. The bad news was that it was a charmingly romantic stone pub with blazing fires and candles on the tables, but the good news was that she'd have to drive there so she couldn't have more than one drink and would remain stone-cold sober. 'OK then,' she relented. 'I'll buy you a drink at the Swithenbank.'

'And I'll call you back with the info,' he said, suddenly sounding cheerful.

Before she headed back to Lone Pine Farm, Lucy rang Grace.

'Yes.' Grace sounded tired.

'Where are you?'

'Surgery. But I'm going home now.'

'Can I pick something up for supper?' Lucy offered. 'I make a mean chicken curry if you fancy it.'

'That would be fantastic. Would you mind?'

'Of course not.'

Lucy picked up the ingredients on the high street, enjoying the fact she could park outside each shop if she wanted and that there were virtually no queues. It would have been the most restful grocery shop she'd ever experienced if it hadn't been for the panic over Connor's murder. Everyone had a view. There were open outpourings of fear and grief, and demands for the authorities – the police in particular – to do something. The newspapers were filled with photographs of Connor and his family, and on the radio journalists speculated endlessly.

'I bet Nimue Acheson was murdered as well,' said one woman. She rolled her r's so the word *murdered* was drawn out and rumbling.

'Ach, I dinnae believe that. She was proper unhappy, that lassie. She was on anti-depressants according to Susan in the surgery.'

'And that makes it gospel? If little Nimue wasn't murdered, then I bet it was an accident. Kids stealing drugs from all them labs and shooting up.'

'All the labs?' Lucy remarked. 'Why, are there many around here?'

'Well, there's Christopher Baird's environmental lab, and several others too on the other side of town, like the Green Test Lab. What do they do, Liz? Something about contaminated land and water—'

'They also do things for Christopher sometimes. To do with the environment. Or is that Biofoods? I can never remember.'

'And there's the veterinary laboratory.' She pronounced it *vetin-ry labortry*. 'And the Turfgrass place. They test turf and—'

'Soil,' Liz supplied firmly. 'Sand and rootzone for golf courses and the like. I know, because Carol's boyfriend works there.'

Carrier bags banging against her thighs, Lucy headed to the car. Once inside she looked up Biofoods and Green Test Lab to see both were located on the edge of a mini-industrial estate at the base of the moors. She checked her watch. It was 4 p.m. Not the best of timing it being a Friday afternoon and she crossed her fingers that not everyone had decided to bugger off early for the weekend.

CHAPTER TWENTY-FIVE

By the time Dan found his car key, his shoes and trousers were soaked and he had stinging nettle blisters on his hands and wrists. Even though he knew it was futile, he ran for his car, started it up and hared in the direction the truck and transit van had gone. Despite driving as fast as he dared to on a public road, he didn't see either vehicle again. He'd have to wait for Lucy to supply the information he needed. In the meantime he had an address for Mouse Woman's MX-5 in Kensal Rise, London, which he punched into his satnav.

He rang Jenny as he drove but she didn't pick up. He leaned his head against the headrest, letting his hands rest lightly on the steering wheel as he wondered whether to leave a message or not. On balance, he thought he probably should in case something came up that prevented him from making another call, like those men reappearing and separating him not just from his car but from his phone too.

'Hi, love.' He spoke to her messaging service. 'I'm on my way to London to see someone. Something came up when I was in Chepstow, a lead into . . .' He stopped as with a little shock he remembered that Mouse Woman knew where he lived. Where Jenny and Aimee lived.

'Actually, I'm not going to London at all. I've changed my mind. I'm coming home.' He took a breath. 'Things are . . . well, potentially, er . . .' He didn't want to use the word dangerous, so settled for saying, 'unsettling.'

He suddenly wanted to get home *now*. He wanted to make sure Jenny and Aimee were safe. He pressed the accelerator until he was inches from the rear bumper of the car in front. Riding tightly through the bend he popped out at the exit in the perfect position to overtake. He zoomed past.

'I love you, OK? Love you very much. See you in twenty minutes.'

He was haring over the Severn Bridge when Lucy rang him. She said, 'The information you wanted.'

'Yes.'

'Both vehicles are registered to Top Car Leasing in London. When I rang them – with my DC hat on, of course – they told me their biggest client was the Home Office and that both vehicles were currently in the hands of Home Office employees.'

He'd already guessed that was the case, but that didn't stop the sensation of what felt like a large tarantula creeping down his spine.

'Buddies of yours?' she asked, openly curious.

'Not today, they're not.'

'Oh.'

'What news?' he asked.

She filled him in on where she'd been and who she'd spoken to. She'd visited a small industrial estate on the west side of town but apparently nobody was there. She sounded frustrated. 'They've all left for the weekend.'

'You think one of them might be involved in Connor's murder?'

He flicked his indicator on before he overtook a lorry hauling a container.

'I won't know until I start ferreting about.' She sighed. 'I'll give it a try tomorrow but if nobody's around I might go home for the rest of the weekend. Come back Monday.'

'It sounds like rather a long shot. Are you sure it's a worthwhile lead?'

'Not particularly. It was the phenol that got me going. Where would the killer get it from? It's *horribly* toxic. They have to work in some sort of lab, surely?'

'I would have thought so but I'm no expert.'

'Nor am I. God, Dan. I can't stop thinking about poor Connor.'

'Yes.'

'I wonder what he did. If he stepped out of line, was in the wrong place at the wrong time. If he saw something. Witnessed something ... I know he was your godson, but was he into drugs? He could have been buying them from one of the labs, supplying the kids at school, or being a gofer of some sort ...'

'I'd like to say no, but I guess anything's possible.' Dan moved to the inside lane as he approached the Severn Bridge.

'I'll let you know how I get on,' she told him.

'Thanks, Lucy.'

Jenny was propped on her bed with her tablet on her belly but when she saw him she pushed it aside and started to clamber clumsily upright.

'Hey, don't get up . . .'

She suddenly started to cry. He swept her in his arms. 'My love, what is it?'

'It's m-me. I'm sorry.' She sobbed against his chest. 'It was you saying you were going to London and even though you changed your mind and said you were coming here I thought *what if he's in danger* and I remembered how much I love you and realised what a crap wife I've been . . .'

He couldn't help it, he chuckled.

'You're not allowed to laugh!' She leaned back, wiping her eyes. 'You're meant to tell me I'm a brilliant wife and that even though I'm a whale and hideously ugly and behaving like some kind of insane madwoman, I'm still beautiful and look as young as I was when you first saw me fourteen years ago.'

'You are definitely more beautiful than you were then.'

'Liar.' She swiped at his arm but she was smiling.

He pulled her into his arms again. Rested his chin on top of her head and rocked her gently. Breathed in her scent of wild bluebells and mimosa.

'How's the baby?' he asked.

'Much calmer than I am. I can't wait to pop.'

He led her back to the bed. He sat and cradled her in his arms as he told her about the recent events, about Mouse Woman. She didn't look at him as he spoke, just listened.

When he finished, she twisted around, looked him in the eyes. Her gaze intensified and when she spoke, her voice was calm and firm. 'You must go to London,' she told him, 'and talk to this Joanna Loxton. Find out what's going on.'

CHAPTER TWENTY-SIX

As he trickled through the streets of London, Dan stopped to buy a big, expensive bunch of flowers. He then invested in a baseball cap and a cheap wind-breaker. A pair of thick-rimmed glasses followed. When he checked himself in a shop window, he figured his appearance was altered enough to satisfy a cursory inspection.

Makeshift disguise in place, Dan drove to Holland Road to find that Joanna Loxton, aka Mouse Woman, lived in a neat Victorian terrace with white-painted bow windows and a deep red front door. No MX-5, which he guessed was in a garage somewhere, being fixed. From the quantity of bins in the front garden, he guessed the house had been converted into flats. His guess was confirmed when he checked the doorbell. Two flats. Joanna Loxton and Mark Roll lived on the ground floor.

Dan pressed the bell.

'Who is it?' A woman's voice.

'Delivery for Loxton.'

'I'm not expecting anything . . .' Her voice was wary.

'Flowers,' he added. 'From the Fresh Flower Company. I can leave them on the doorstep if you like.'

'That would be great. Thank you.'

Dan put the flowers down. Then he walked out of the garden, turned left, pausing behind a huge hedge in next door's garden. He counted to ten then strode up the neighbour's path and stood waiting in their garden, next to the low wall that separated the two houses.

The instant he heard Loxton's latch click he hurdled the wall and launched himself at her front door.

Mouse Woman didn't stand a chance against 190 kilos of moving muscle. His shoulder crashed the door open and at the same time he grabbed her and spun her inside her hallway. She started screaming but stopped when he wrapped an arm around her waist and clapped a hand over her mouth.

'Quiet,' he told her.

She fell perfectly still.

He took in the door on the left, which stood ajar. He could hear music coming from inside. Jazz of some sort.

'Who else is there?'

She shook her head.

He waited.

'Sweetheart?' A man's voice came trailing out, along with the smell of frying onions.

'You are going to tell him I'm a friend,' Dan told her. 'We are going to walk inside and you are going to introduce me as Barrie from work, and we are going to have a civilised chat because I have a gun and I do not want to use it. Clear?'

She nodded.

He eased his hand from her mouth. She turned to look at him. 'Barrie?' she said, wiping her lips with the back of her wrist.

'Whatever.'

'Sweetheart, is everything OK?' the man called out.

'It's just a friend from work,' she called back. 'Baz, sorry Barrie Dix. He's come for a chat and a glass of wine. He's HR's Ops Manager in our Kensington branch.'

'Nice embellishment,' Dan muttered. He nudged her forward.

The flat was open plan, with the kitchen at one end and living space the other. A long kitchen bench created a dividing line between the two.

'Sit,' he told her, gesturing at the sofa.

She sat. Folded her hands in her lap. She looked far more in control than he liked and put it down to her being on her own turf.

'Sorry, sorry . . .' A man arrived, looking harried, anxious. To Dan's surprise he didn't introduce himself but went straight into the kitchen area and opened a cupboard, brought out a wine glass. 'Red, Baz?' he asked. 'Or white?'

'Red, please.'

'You, darling?'

'Vodka, please.'

'Give me a moment.' The man vanished.

'Joanna Loxton.'

'Dan Forrester.' She tried to hold his gaze but her eyes slid away. Not so confident after all.

'Why were you following me?'

'I was asked to.'

'By whom?'

'A friend.'

'Like a friend with the firm?'

She considered his question. 'Yes.'

'Why?'

'I wasn't told.'

'What was your brief?' Dan asked her.

'To tell them where you went, who you saw.'

'Why?'

'I wasn't told that either.'

'Who's the friend?'

She shook her head.

Dan held her eyes. *'Who's the friend?'*

'Sorry.' Her voice was surprisingly firm against the fear in her eyes.

She glanced past him as her companion returned. He came into the living area and put Dan's glass on the coffee table. 'I'll join you in a minute,' he said.

'You really want to piss me off?' Dan whispered, looking pointedly at her companion walking back outside. 'I could break his arm before you made it halfway across the room.'

'Don't.' Her face pinched.

'Then tell me what I need to know.'

She chewed her lower lip.

'You used your own car to follow me,' he stated. 'But called in the firm when you needed it. Does this mean you're following me in your own time?'

From the flash of anxiety that crossed her face he took the answer to be *yes*.

'You're off the books.' He clicked his tongue and wagged a finger at her. 'I wonder what your boss will say when they find out.'

She closed her eyes briefly, as though she was saying a prayer.

'I need a name, Joanna. Give me a name and I'll go. Leave you alone. But until you do, I am going to stay here and—'

The doorbell shrilled.

Joanna jumped. Turned her head to the bow window but the curtain was drawn.

'Who are you expecting?' Dan wanted to know.

'Nobody,' she said, but her face turned hopeful.

The doorbell shrilled again, long and loud, setting Dan's teeth on edge. When Joanna's companion didn't turn up to answer it, he pulled Joanna to her feet. Marched her over to the window. Had a look.

A man in his fifties, dressed in a double-breasted camel coat with a fedora and a pair of leather gloves, stood on Joanna's doorstep. As Dan stared, unable to believe his eyes, the man turned his head and looked straight at him. He raised a hand and made a beckoning motion with his finger.

Dan dropped the curtain. Spun to face Joanna.

'What the hell is Sirius Thiele doing here?'

'Who?' She sounded genuinely puzzled.

He pulled back the curtain, pointed at Sirius. 'Him.'

Sirius raised his hat to Joanna.

'Oh, God.' The colour drained from her face.

'You know him,' Dan stated.

'Well, yes . . . He's, er . . .'

'A cleaner.'

She gulped.

'Who is wanted for multiple murders,' Dan added.

'I didn't realise it would be him who came . . .' She was still staring at Sirius. 'I mean, we have a panic alarm but I expected a couple of colleagues . . .'

He could have kicked himself. Of course she'd have a panic alarm, and no doubt her boyfriend had activated it when she'd given him a prearranged code earlier, probably the name *Baz* or *vodka*, even the mention of an *HR Operations Manager* could have been a tip-off. No wonder the man hadn't introduced himself. He'd known Dan was a threat.

'How come he got here so soon?' Dan asked.

She swallowed audibly. 'We thought you might come here. He must have been on standby somewhere near.'

Whoever was pulling Joanna Loxton's strings were one step ahead. He didn't like it.

'Let him in,' Dan told her.

When she hesitated, he snapped, 'You invited him.'

She went to the intercom. Buzzed the door. Nothing happened.

'Mr Thiele?' she said. 'Could you come in?'

'No,' Sirius said, and even though his voice was small and tinny through the speaker, Dan still felt a chill brush over him. 'If you could send Dan Forrester outside, I would be grateful.'

Joanna looked at Dan.

'Don't make me do something you will regret,' Sirius added.

Joanna threw a look at Dan. *Please?*

Dan shook his head.

'Please tell Dan Forrester that I'm not here to harm him. I just have a message to deliver.'

Dan stepped to the intercom. 'Really?' His voice was disbelieving.

'You have my word.'

Dan closed his eyes for a moment, recalling the events of last year. Sirius was probably one of the most frightening men he knew, and one of the most dangerous. He wasn't just a cleaner but an assassin – one of the best and most ruthless in the business. That said, Sirius was renowned for having his own peculiar code. He was also known for never having knowingly broken his word. If he said he was going to strangle someone to death, he did it. If he said he was going to save a drowning kitten, he did it. Dan didn't want to trust Sirius but he needed information from him.

He fixed Joanna Loxton with a hard look. 'We haven't finished, OK?' Then he stepped into the hallway. He heard Joanna Loxton close and lock the door behind him. As he opened the front door, the chill running through him turned to fire. Although he looked relaxed, his shoulders dropped, arms loose, his hands open, every muscle in his body was ready to fight.

'Hello, Dan.'

Sirius moved back a few paces, giving him plenty of room. His gloved hands were open wide and spread at his sides, showing he wasn't holding a weapon.

Dan moved on to the path, his steps steady and careful, braced for Sirius's slightest move.

'Sirius,' he said.

'My message is simple and perfectly clear,' the man said. He spoke calmly and with absolute clarity. 'You are to stop investigating your father's death. You are to let the police do their jobs and not interfere. You are to go home to your wife and daughter and return to work as normal.'

'My father was murdered.'

Sirius tilted his head fractionally. 'My condolences.'

'If your father was murdered, wouldn't you want to know why?'

'My father died before I was born.'

Both men stood in silence as a car drove past. Only when it had gone, did Dan speak. 'Sirius, who sent you here?'

A little moue touched the man's mouth. 'You know I can't divulge such information.'

'Have you heard of Project Snowbank?'

There was no change in his expression, no indication Sirius had even heard Dan speak. He just looked at him, face perfectly blank.

'What can you give me?' Dan said.

Sirius thought for a moment. Then said, 'Do you know why I didn't come through the back door as requested?' The man's shiny black eyes held his, as emotionless and cold as pebbles. 'Why I didn't disable you and threaten you with death to convince you to leave your father's case alone?'

Dan opened and closed his mouth but couldn't think of a word to say.

'I chose to be civilised about this because you are a friend of Grace Reavey's. I thought you deserved more respect than what was asked of me.'

'Grace?' Dan's voice was incredulous.

'She's a very brave woman.'

'Well, yes. But—'

'Now I have warned you, I shall go. Please send my best to Grace.'

Dan wanted to race after Sirius, grab his arm and demand more information, but there was no point, not unless he wanted a full-on street fight. He watched Sirius walk down the street, his gait jaunty, as though he was out to meet a friend for a drink. Dan didn't move until he was completely out of sight.

CHAPTER TWENTY-SEVEN

Grace wouldn't normally conduct a home visit on a Friday evening unless it was urgent, but she felt the need to get away, to try and settle her thoughts before the weekend. So she'd offered to go and see Alistair Tavey, who was, according to his wife, suffering from a particularly nasty bout of flu.

Grace wasn't entirely convinced about making a house call for someone too stubborn to come to the surgery, but when she remembered her chat with Dr John Buchanan in Edinburgh earlier (what was she going to say to Ross? Dare she say anything to Ross?) she knew she needed some time out before she headed home to Lone Pine Farm.

The Taveys lived in a bothy on the other side of Ben Kincaid at the end of a long, rutted track. Even at low speed, her Golf bounced and juddered, making her flinch at each *thump* into another trench. If she stayed up here she really ought to invest in a 4x4 of some sort, a sturdy Land Rover that would take this sort of punishment in its stride. But she didn't *want* a 4x4. She loved her Golf. She could feel herself becoming petulant and told herself to *grow up, dammit*, but her mind couldn't drop the vision of John Buchanan's smart modern surgery on the website – she bet his practice manager wouldn't allow anyone into the doctor's rooms without permission – or the photographs he'd sent of the flat he'd let to her if she took the job. The master bedroom was huge, the kitchen sleek and modern, the bathroom to die for. No mould or damp patches. No rotten floorboards. No building site.

Plus, the flat was around the corner from a street lined with restaurants. Italian, French, Moroccan, Mediterranean. She wouldn't have to learn to cook if she lived there during the week. She wouldn't have to catch her own fish and gut it. Boil haggis and burst it, or whatever you did with it.

And what about John Buchanan? They'd Skyped for forty minutes, an informal interview, and his energy and enthusiasm for proper consulting were infectious. She'd hung up bubbling with excitement, which quickly turned to dismay when she pictured herself returning to the flat alone without Ross. She couldn't live apart from him. It was ridiculous, what was she thinking?

Confused, muddled and getting more distressed by the minute, Grace wished her mother was still alive so she could talk things over with her. She hadn't asked her often for advice but when she had, her mother had always listened carefully and objectively and the ensuing discussion invariably helped Grace see things more clearly.

Talk to Ross. Her mother's voice echoed in her mind.

But he'll go berserk. Won't he?

Grace was so absorbed in rehearsing what she might say to Ross, *I just happened to be offered a spectacular job in a spectacular practice, and I'll be home every weekend* – that she almost ran over the Labrador that suddenly appeared in front of the car.

Grace rammed on the brakes, forcing the Golf to slide sideways and it was only thanks to the fact she'd been driving so slowly that she narrowly missed being plunged into the ditch. Sweating, heart pounding, she inched forward, trying to ignore the dog trotting alongside. She groaned when she saw her way ahead was barred by a rickety five-bar gate.

When she'd started her journey the evening had been beautiful, the hills drenched in sunshine, but as soon as she turned off the main road the clouds had rolled in and it was now pelting rain.

Idiot, she thought. *You left your waterproof in the boot.* She opened the door and scrambled out into the wind. Head ducked, cursing, she popped the boot and hauled out her waterproof, pulled it on. The dog pottered around her, tail wagging.

By the time she'd driven the car through the gate and closed it behind her, she was pretty much soaked.

Bloody weather, she thought. *Bloody everything.*

As she made to open her car door, she heard a whistle. She couldn't see anyone at first, but then she spotted a figure standing to one side. Barbour, wellies, tweed cap. He was whistling for his dog, which was ignoring him.

'Go on,' she told it. 'Go back to your owner.'

The dog looked up at her, tongue lolling.

Grace decided to let the two get on with it and hopped inside her car, out of the rain. She watched the man, obviously reluctant, walk over. Put the dog on a lead.

When she saw who it was, she buzzed down her window.

'Christopher? Whatever are you doing all the way out here?'

'Don't tell anyone, will you?' His face was anxious.

'Why ever not?'

'I'm trespassing.'

'A fine day to be doing it.' Her voice was dry.

'It's the only time I can.' His mouth twisted. 'When I know everyone's indoors.'

'Like who?' She was curious.

'The new owner. A horrible Russian oligarch.'

When she frowned, not understanding, he added, 'We used to own this estate. Dad had to sell up fifteen years ago.' He looked into the distance, expression haunted. 'Glenallen was in the family for three generations. I miss it. And with Connor . . . gone, I find it's the only place where I can find any kind of solace.'

He was so obviously troubled, in such pain, her heart went out to him. 'I won't tell anyone.'

'Thank you.' He wiped his face of rain. 'I expect you're visiting Alistair.'

'Yes.'

'He's worked on this estate since he was sixteen.'

She wasn't sure what to say to that, so she put the car into gear. He gave her a nod and turned away. Grace left Christopher walking up a long knoll, his dog loping alongside.

CHAPTER TWENTY-EIGHT

Dan awoke after too little sleep, his mind unable to stop replaying every minute of yesterday's events, and he felt tired.

Could he risk ignoring Sirius's threats? What if the German police didn't find his dad's killer? What if he got no answers? What had his father stumbled upon? It was serious enough to involve some pretty heavy types, and he didn't like the fact that Joanna Loxton had been working off the books. If whatever had scared his father was true, what should he do about it? He was itching to get back into the fray, and despite Sirius's warning, he knew he couldn't turn his back on what had happened to his father, let alone allow whoever had killed him get away with it.

Sirius threatening him hadn't warned him off. It had, in fact, had the opposite effect.

'Hi, love.' Jenny wandered into the kitchen. 'Couldn't sleep?'

'No.'

She came and kissed him. 'Me neither.'

'I'm sorry.'

'It's not your fault someone murdered your poor dad.'

'I know. But even so . . .'

He'd got home after midnight. He hadn't meant to wake her, intending to sleep in the spare bedroom, but Jenny was a light sleeper and the moment he'd stepped into the hallway Poppy had given a soft *woof* awakening Jenny. She'd pottered downstairs in her dressing gown and poured him a brandy, made a mug of hot chocolate for herself.

They'd talked well into the small hours. He hated doing it – he wanted to protect her, not send her into paroxysms of worry – but he'd laid everything out for her. How things were far more complex and dangerous than he could have imagined. His father dead, an old friend of his using codes to meet. Project Snowbank, and now a team backing up the woman who'd been following him. And then there was the DSI in charge of the case, who'd told him about his father's visit to the Isterberg Cemetery.

Jenny looked at him, an expression of resignation on her face. 'You want to go to Germany.'

'I can't see how else I can find out what's going on. It wouldn't take long. Two days, three max. I want to meet the detective in charge of the case as well as visit Arne.' He looked at her straight. 'But I want to be with you too.'

She returned his gaze steadily. Then she sighed.

'I have to be honest, Dan. I don't like it, but I think you should go. Otherwise it will drive you crazy. Plus, if I stopped you going, it could come between us. You might blame me . . .'

'I'd never do that,' he protested.

Her mouth twisted. 'I'd rather not risk it.'

While she went back to sleep, he crept around the house, picking up an overnight bag and some spare clothes, a razor, his passport. He also unlocked the gun cabinet and withdrew a passport in the name of Michael Wilson. Although he'd used it in January and it didn't expire for another six years he couldn't be sure it still worked. He should have handed it in to the security services but since they hadn't asked for it, he hadn't surrendered it. He'd also kept the wallet litter; a credit card, a couple of membership cards and receipts in Wilson's name. He took the lot.

Finally, he packed some photographs of his father, including one taken at Christmas. He'd come and stayed for three nights, making himself useful not just by helping fix a broken gutter, but taking Aimee out for lunch and giving Dan and Jenny some luxury time to themselves on Christmas Eve. Jenny had taken the photo in an unguarded moment as Bill was telling Aimee a story. His face was in repose, relaxed and content, but it also held a sense of concentration too. It was his dad to a T.

Now Jenny was looking at his carry-on bag, which was on the kitchen floor, all packed. Her expression was guarded.

'Are you still OK with my going?'

'I know you must go, because if you don't . . .' She bit her lip. 'What I hate is that you'll be overseas . . .'

He should never have contemplated it. She was almost due to give birth. How could he think of leaving her? He lifted the bag on to a kitchen chair and started to unpack.

'What are you doing?' she asked.

'It was wrong of me to even think it. I won't go.'

'What? And have you pacing around the house like a caged tiger? Please, Dan, go because if you don't you'll only drive me and Aimee nuts. And as you said, you'll only be gone a couple of days.'

'Are you sure?'

'As long as you promise you'll be with me when I have this baby.' It was both a challenge and a plea.

'I will be there,' he promised.

CHAPTER TWENTY-NINE

Lucy splashed her way around the Green Test Lab, trying to peer inside, but all the blinds were drawn. Her jacket pattered with raindrops and she was glad she was wearing her waterproof boots otherwise the leather would be soaked through by now.

Around the back were four industrial-sized waste bins chained together and locked to a steel bar. Two had double lids and were plastered with yellow hazard notices. Her eyes went to the security cameras secured on each corner of the building, then to the double lock doors and windows: *what are they trying to hide?*

Using her phone, she went to the Companies House website to see that Green Test Lab, a private limited company, had been dissolved on the thirteenth of July the previous year. Its last annual return had been made up to the twentieth of February the year before that. Nature of business: soil research. She made a note of the registered office address, in London N14. Was it still in use?

She walked around the rest of the trading estate, deathly quiet on a sopping wet Saturday except for an auto-electrical workshop.

'Sorry,' the electrician told her. 'I don't think I've seen anyone I could recognise as working at Green Test Lab. That goes for half the places here, really. Unlike some trading estates, we don't have a snack van, which makes it harder to get to know one another.'

'How about Biofoods?'

'Oh, you mean Christopher? Sure, we know him. Awful what happened to his kid.' He shook his head. 'Nice lad, that. Damn shame.'

'When did you last see Connor?'

Luckily the electrician didn't seem to find her question odd and said, 'Not in ages.' He glanced to the sky as he thought. 'Probably in town last month sometime. On his bike. Went everywhere on that thing.'

'Did you ever see him here?'

He shook his head. 'Not exactly the place for kids, is it?' he said, looking pointedly around at the rows of industrial-style buildings and aluminium roller doors.

'Some kids might like the fact it's quiet.'

He pulled a face. 'You mean drinking and taking drugs? Never seen that around here. They tend to go to the other side of the park, under the bridge by the river. It's out of sight and if it's raining they get a bit of shelter.'

He was opening his mouth again and the expression on his face told her he was about to ask *why all the questions?* so she said goodbye cheerily and walked away.

After skirting a handful more business units, which included a clock repairer and a funeral director's – THE ULTIMATE

FUNERAL PROFESSIONALS – she came to a stand-alone build-ing. Biofoods. Here all the blinds were wide open. Talk about a contrast to Green Test Lab. Even though she'd already peeked through the windows yesterday, she had another look. A cou-ple of offices, both utilitarian. A storage area, half-filled with large white plastic sacks with VERM MEDIUM stamped on their sides.

As she moved to the other side of the building, she saw a battered old Renault arrive. A young guy in his early twen-ties hopped out, gave her a wave. Gangly, brown hair tied back in a ponytail, jeans and hoody, which he pulled over his head in an attempt to keep the rain off. He was jingling keys as he approached, his face open and friendly.

'Hi,' he greeted her.

'Hi.'

'Can I help you?'

'You work here?'

'Yep. I'm on watering duty. My official title is "laboratory assistant" but rather than give me anything interesting to do, I'm charged with making everyone tea, running errands and water-ing a shed-load of plants.' There was no resentment in his tone and his manner was jovial.

'I'm Lucy.' She stuck out her hand. He gave it a shake.

'Tim.'

'I'm a friend of Christopher Baird's,' she told him. 'I'm help-ing him to try and find out what happened to his son, Connor.'

At that, Tim's face sobered. 'Awful. I never met Connor – I come from Elgin – but what a shock.'

'Would you mind if I asked you some questions? Maybe out of this weather?' She glanced ruefully up to the sky. The rain was now falling heavily and her jeans were getting wet.

'Sure.'

She followed him to the lab door. Watched him unlock it and step inside to the sound of a beeping security system. He flicked back his hoody and punched in a number, 5793, and she said, 'You really should hide the code from someone standing right behind you.'

'Oh, sorry.'

'And now, you really should change the code so I can't come back later and steal all your drugs.'

'We don't keep drugs here.' He seemed indifferent.

'Even so' – the police officer in her wouldn't let it go – 'you wouldn't want an anti-GM mob coming in here and trashing the lab would you?'

The dismay on his face was all she needed.

'Change it,' she told him.

'Yes, yes,' he agreed hastily. 'I'll get Jasmine to do it when she gets in. I'd do it but I don't know how.'

The mat was sticky underfoot and as she glanced down he said, 'It's to pick up any seeds when we leave.'

They were in a small lobby lined with pictures of people wearing conical straw hats, knee-deep in vivid green rice paddies. On the back of the door was a life-sized poster of a cute looking baby being fed from an overflowing bowl of rice.

Lucy pointed at the poster. 'Jasmine told me about Christopher's strong rice.'

A flash of excitement crossed his face. 'You want a look at the chamber?'

She had no idea what he was referring to but she said, 'I'd love to.'

She followed him down a corridor to a door in which was placed a small window. As she peered inside, her eyes widened. She'd never seen anything like it. Endless rows of perfectly spaced grasses. Some were short and vivid green, others tall and wispy, the colour of straw. There were chunky grasses, stubby grasses, elegant fronds and broad leaf blades. As she marvelled, she realised a lot of them had seeds. Some were tiny, almost microscopic, but others were thick and oval, and belatedly she realised she was looking at rice. Lots and lots of different varieties of rice.

'It's incredible,' she said.

'Incredible all right, it's like walking into a tropical rainforest.'

Everything was labelled. Every pot had a number, along with each bench. There were arrows as well as more numbers marked on the heavy plastic surrounding each container.

'How long have you worked here?'

'I've only been here for the summer,' he told her. 'It's just a holiday job. I go back to uni next week. Jasmine wants me to stay on but I can't. It was Jasmine who told me about Connor. Jesus.' He sucked his teeth. 'I can't believe he was murdered.'

'Jasmine said she works here most Saturdays. Is she due here today?'

'Yeah.' He looked at his watch. 'Any time now. She says she likes a bit of a lie-in in the morning, but she works late sometimes. She says it's nice and quiet without anyone else clattering around.'

'Do you know the Green Test Lab?'

'Who?'

'They're the next building next door.'

'Sorry.'

'They've got some quite serious security.'

'They'll have stuff worth stealing, then.'

'Like what?'

He gave a shrug and when she realised he assumed she knew what he meant, she said, 'Seriously, give me an example. I'm really interested.'

'Oh.' His expression cleared. 'Well, at the lab I worked in last year, we caught a meth head trying to steal an ammonia tank. Umm . . .' He thought further. 'We used to lock up the disposable syringes because the janitors were notorious for nicking them. Jesus, can you imagine shooting up with an 18G needle?' He gave a theatrical shudder. 'I also knew someone who lifted a ton of stuff from his grad school lab to manufacture meth in his basement. He had an entire lab's worth of Roundbottoms and Erlenmeyers, some brand new bottles of solvent and even a vacuum pump.'

'What if a thief wasn't interested in making meth? What else might someone want to steal?'

'Well, hexanes make great fuel. Vermiculite's pretty useful . . .'

He paused when Lucy held up a hand. 'Sorry, neither name means anything to me.'

'OK. Hexanes are significant constituents of petrol. Vermiculite's used as a moisture-retentive medium for growing plants. We have loads of it here.'

'What about phenol?'

He blinked. 'You mean benzene?'

'Is it the same thing?'

'Phenol's also known as carbolic acid, if that helps.'

Not much, she thought.

'Would any laboratory have phenol around?' she asked. He obviously didn't know that Connor had been killed with a dose of phenol.

'I can't say,' he told her. 'But any tame chemist can make phenol. It's easy.'

CHAPTER THIRTY

Dan drove down the M4 filled with energy, his fingertips tingling. Jenny was right. He would have gone crazy if he'd been forced to stay at home, infuriated at not being part of the investigation and, potentially, not finding any answers.

Germany was an hour ahead of the UK, making it 10 a.m. He called DSI Didrika Weber.

'I'm flying over today. Can we meet, perhaps tomorrow?' Then he remembered it was the weekend and hastily added, 'It's Sunday, will that matter?'

'Not at all. You will be staying in Isterberg?'

'Yes.'

'Perfect.' She sounded pleased. 'I shall collect you from your hotel. Please text me the details in due course.'

He'd planned on booking his hotel as well as an open return flight to Hanover under his own name – keeping Michael Wilson's passport as an emergency backup – but when he realised he had a watcher on him, he decided to use Michael Wilson's passport instead of his own. Whoever was behind the watchers were obviously part of the security services. If they'd been agitated enough to use Sirius to warn him off, then his guess would be that they'd have his passport flagged at all ports.

Whether they knew about Michael Wilson's passport was a different matter, but he was hoping they didn't and by the time someone noticed he'd used it, he'd be back home. On balance, he thought using Wilson's passport was worth the risk but more importantly, if he got away with it, nobody would know he'd been overseas. And with Sirius around, that had to be a good thing.

Now all he had to do was to get to Heathrow without being seen.

Earlier, he'd rung his boss, Philip Denton, to ask for his help. In case his phone was tapped, he'd taken the precaution of using the public phone box in the village. He kept waiting for it to be taken out of service, but it was still operating, albeit for credit cards only, and was a godsend today.

'I won't ask why,' said Philip when Dan made his request, 'but you will tell me when I next see you.'

'Yes.'

'I will leave the key in the usual place.'

'I'll owe you.'

'Oh you will, Dan.' Philip's voice sounded pleased. 'And don't worry, I won't forget.'

As far as Dan could tell, when he arrived in Mayfair he had one watcher following him – the man who'd crewed with Joanna Loxton to follow him in Weston-super-Mare – but when he left Mayfair, however, Dan was in Philip's Jaguar having lost that watcher. He had to cross his fingers the simple car swap had done the trick.

Dan queued at the airline desk, trying not to imagine what would happen if Michael Wilson's passport was flagged up on the system. Even though he'd booked his flight late, he knew the API – Advance Passenger Information – would have been cross-checked on a database, and if the airline agent saw an alert against Wilson's passport, they'd signal the authorities.

He pictured Aimee as he last saw her, building a blanket fort in the sitting room. Jenny had looked slightly weary at having the sitting room requisitioned, along with clothes pegs and sheets, but you couldn't fault the idea as Aimee was one hundred per cent occupied stocking her new home with a sleeping bag, torch, apple juice and crisps.

'When's the housewarming?' he'd asked.

'Now.'

She'd created a front entrance using a cardboard box as a tunnel, but it was too small for Dan and he'd lain flat on the floor with just his head inside instead, which had made them both laugh.

'Sir?'

Dan heard the airline agent's voice and roused himself in a nicely relaxed fashion, handing over his passport, saying, ''afternoon.'

The agent gave a nod. He opened Wilson's passport at the page with Dan's photograph and slotted it into a scanner, withdrew it. Was it his imagination or had a tension fallen over the man? He watched as he tapped on a keyboard out of sight. He didn't return Dan's passport.

Dan waited.

At the next desk, a passenger who had arrived at the same time as Dan was waved towards the departure gate.

Dan kept his breathing level but he could feel his skin starting to warm.

'Business or pleasure, sir?' the agent asked.

'Pleasure. I'm visiting an old friend.'

More taps on the keyboard.

Next to him, Dan watched another passenger being processed.

'Is something wrong?' Dan asked.

'Sorry, sir. My system's slow, that's all.'

He didn't believe him. Something was up. There was nothing he could do, however, except wait and try and think calm thoughts and not picture himself being thrown into a tiny windowless room for hours before being interrogated by an officer with hunched shoulders and bags under his eyes from a decade of shift work.

Dan had already visualised three scenarios on how to deal with being arrested when, to his surprise, the agent returned his passport. 'Apologies for the delay, sir.'

'No problem.'

Dan didn't realise how tense he'd become until he was sitting on the plane. He wasn't shaking but he was jumpy, his nerves feeling as though they were on the outside of his skin.

Was he under surveillance?

Dan spent the flight reviewing everything he knew, which wasn't much. All that was certain was that someone in the establishment didn't want him digging into his father's death. Why? Was it something to do with Project Snowbank? He still hadn't found any mention of it anywhere and knew he'd have to speak to Rafe again. And what about Connor? Why in the world would someone want to murder a thirteen-year-old boy? He'd spoken to Lucy earlier and neither of them had managed to come to any conclusions. The tracking device in Christopher's car continued to worry them both, but as Lucy had said, there was no point in calling her off until the job was finished. She was nothing if not determined.

'I'll owe you,' he'd told her, repeating the same words he'd spoken to Philip earlier.

'Yup,' she agreed. 'When I find myself banged up in some Turkish jail I'll call you directly, don't worry.'

To his relief, the immigration officer at Hanover gave his passport a cursory glance, waving him through without fuss. Dan zipped through arrivals to find Arne waiting. Dan's heart hollowed. When he'd last seen his dad's old friend, his skin may have been speckled with age but his eyes had been bright behind his spectacles and gleaming with intelligence. Now he'd shrunk, his wrinkles deepened into canyons of grief. The light had gone out of his eyes. For the first time, he looked every one of his eighty years.

'It is good to see you again,' Arne told him. 'But I am so sorry it is in such circumstances.'

Dan embraced him. For all the solidity of Arne's frame, Dan couldn't shake the feeling the old man felt fragile.

'Who would do such a thing?' Arne raised rheumy eyes to his. 'What do you know, Dan? What tipped you off to make you ask for a post-mortem? Did Bill tell you something?'

Dan warred against revealing his father's letter. Even to friends, he hated giving away information. 'He mentioned something,' he admitted. 'But it wasn't anything concrete. Just that he was concerned for his safety.'

'I see,' Arne said. 'Let us go to the car. We can talk on the way.'

Arne's car was a Mercedes S-Class Saloon, top of the range and with a price tag to match. It felt effortlessly fast and smooth once on the road, but Dan couldn't say the same for Arne's driving, which was overly fast and erratic.

'Are you sure you won't stay with us? Anneke would really like it.'

'I'd love to,' Dan lied. 'But I have other business in Isterberg.' Until he knew what was going on, he didn't want to involve his father's friends and had booked himself into a hotel in the centre of town.

'You'll come now for some refreshment? Afterwards, I can drive you to your hotel.'

'That would be nice. Thank you.'

They made it to Isterberg in just over half an hour. Dan peered through the windscreen to see a picture-postcard pretty old town with ancient timber-frame houses leaning over cobbled streets. He immediately thought of the fairy tale *Hänsel and Gretel.*

'It is beautiful, yes?' Arne asked, swinging down a street empty of pedestrians.

'Jenny would like it,' Dan replied.

'She and Aimee should come and visit. We could take you walking in the Harz Mountains. Now, they are *really* beautiful.'

He eventually pulled up outside the last house on the road out of town and overlooking a small river. At first glance Arne's house looked like any other fifteenth-century building except, Arne told him, its timber frames were false and every brick brand new.

In the distance were some other dwellings. Dan stared. He couldn't think of a starker contrast to Isterberg's historic charm. Instead of ancient, warm coloured houses, stood blocks of stained concrete. An old fortress, Dan guessed. A watchtower loomed between the two settlements; a sharp reminder that Germany used to be divided.

'A lot of people wanted to destroy it,' Arne told him when he saw Dan gazing at the fortifications. 'But Anneke and I campaigned to keep it. It is where we used to live, you see. It is now a museum. I think it is a good thing, not to forget.'

Intrigued, Dan turned to look at Arne.

'I have my parents to thank for living here,' Arne confessed. 'When they were awoken by the East German army, instead of letting themselves be herded into trucks and taken away from their home – never to see it again – they escaped over here. They had to start again, but their life was much easier than if they'd stayed in the East.'

Arne glanced at the watchtower, then at his handsome house. 'Everyone knows our story. The hardship we suffered and how we survived. How we made our way in the West – became successful. Someone even wrote a book about my family.' He looked proud.

Inside the house, Anneke greeted Dan warmly. Tall and slim, she was like a willow beside Arne, who resembled a stunted oak. Her skin was lined with wrinkles, her hair faded blonde, but she had the same fire in her eyes as Arne used to have, the same gleam his father had had, he realised, and probably the same lust for life. No wonder they'd all been such good friends.

'I can't believe what has happened. Bill, murdered?! It is unbelievable. He was such a dear friend. Please, come inside. Make yourself comfortable.'

While Anneke went to make tea, Dan took one of the large squashy armchairs. Arne took the other.

'Would you mind,' Dan asked him, 'telling me everything? I'd like to know how Dad . . . spent his last few days.'

Arne leaned forward, pudgy age-spotted hands between his knees. 'I understand. The police wanted to know the same thing. I told them everything that happened, that he arrived on Thursday, the thirtieth of August. His flight got in at ten thirty in the evening. Hanover is only half an hour from here so I went to collect him . . .'

Dan tried not to react. *10.30 p.m.?* DSI Weber had told him that his father had landed at ten twenty-five in the morning. Not at night.

'Anneke was already asleep when we got home so we didn't stay up. Friday morning, we played eighteen holes. We were both very pleased we were doing so well considering our venerable old age and then . . .' Arne spread his hands, shaking his head.

Dan didn't share the fact that the police had said that the day he arrived his father had hired a car and driven 179 kilometres before meeting his friends. Trying to hide his disquiet, he ran his eyes over a display of framed photographs hanging on the wall. Arne playing golf, shooting pheasant, roe deer, holding a massive salmon with three other fishermen crowded around. They were all grinning. It was the same photograph his father, Rafe and Gordon had in their own homes.

'Is that . . .?' Dan pointed it out.

Arne looked over at the photograph. 'Forty-two pounds. Biggest fish caught on the Glenallen Estate. It took thirty minutes to land.' He sighed. 'We had a big party. But it wasn't for the fish.'

Dan knew the story. How Arne had visited from Germany one spring and Gordon had arranged for the four old university friends to meet at his lodge in Scotland where they'd all got wildly drunk and behaved pretty appallingly, if the stories were to be believed.

'Gordon rang me about Connor.' Arne raised a trembling hand to cover his eyes briefly. 'Christopher must be devastated.'

'He is.'

'Gustav rang him to say how sorry we all are,' Anneke remarked as she arrived with tea.

'That was kind. Did Dad see Gustav when he was here?'

'No, not that we . . . know of.' As Anneke faltered something flashed between her and Arne. Dan thought it was dismay, but it was gone before he could analyse it.

'I'd like to see him.'

'He's at the Klinic. I know he'd like to see you too. Arne can drive you there, if you like.'

'I don't want to be a bother.'

'It's no trouble,' Arne said. 'I have work to do there.'

As Dan raised his eyebrows, Anneke smiled. 'Arne never retired. Too much to do. Too active.'

'What about you?' Dan asked, curious. He couldn't imagine Anneke sitting around the house waiting for her husband to come home.

'I work part-time in the mayor's office. Sometimes I go to the Klinic to help out. You know I used to be a nurse?'

'No,' Dan admitted.

'It was the best job I ever had.' Her voice was wistful. 'I still enjoy going to the Klinic. It makes me feel young.'

After they'd finished tea, Arne rose. 'Is there anywhere else you would like to visit while you're here?'

'Yes. I want to visit the Isterberg Cemetery . . .'

He was unprepared for their response. Arne flinched. Anneke's face tightened.

'Why?'

'There's a commemorative plaque I'd like to see.'

Arne turned his head to look at his wife. His face had turned cold and smooth, like marble. 'Yes, we know it.'

Anneke fixed Dan with an icy stare. 'Here, we're not afraid to look at our past.'

Dan wasn't sure if it was a challenge or a statement and didn't respond. He experienced the strange and disturbing sensation of the family member who has made an embarrassing gaffe but nobody would tell him why.

CHAPTER THIRTY-ONE

The Klinic was a fifteen-minute drive from the old town and housed in the west wing of the university hospital. Arne dropped Dan at the main door.

'Reception will let Gustav know you're here.'

'Thanks.'

Ultra-modern, the Klinic had a bright and airy atrium. Oil paintings lined the wall behind the reception desk. In the centre stood a portrait of Arne looking proud, very patrician. Beneath it was a large bronze plaque with an inscription. Since there was a queue, Dan looked it up on Google translate.

GERMAN MEDICAL ASSOCIATION FOUNDATION OF EXCELLENCE IN MEDICINE AWARDS: COMMITMENT TO SERVICE, COMMUNITY INVOLVEMENT, ALTRUISM, INSPIRATION, LEADERSHIP AND DEDI-CATION TO PATIENT CARE.

Impressive.

When he asked to see Gustav, he was directed to a waiting area set to the west of the atrium. A man sat to one side, reading a car magazine. A woman was opposite, talking with a girl that Dan took to be her daughter. He was immediately reminded of Aimee. She had the same vivid expression and looked about the same age, maybe a little older. He offered her a small smile. She held his eyes but didn't smile back.

Dan turned his attention to the photographs on the walls. Views of mountains and forests, aerial photographs of tree-fringed lakes and people mountain biking, kayaking and picnicking.

'*Es ist schön, nicht wahr?*' The woman smiled at him.

'I'm sorry,' Dan said, 'but I—'

'You're English?'

'Yes.'

'I just said "it's beautiful, isn't it?"'

He looked back at the photograph of the kayakers. 'Yes.' Then he looked pointedly outside. 'But I'm not so sure about the weather.'

'But if you're kayaking,' the girl piped up, 'you'd get wet anyway.'

Her English, although heavily accented, was excellent.

'Good point,' he agreed. 'You have a kayak?'

'No, I used to borrow George's.'

'Is he your friend?'

'He used to be,' she said shyly. 'But he died.'

Dan blinked.

'Shush, Christa,' her mother told her. 'He doesn't have to know that.'

'He asked me.' Christa's voice was plaintive.

The mother sent her daughter a warning look.

'I'm sorry,' Dan said to Christa. He couldn't imagine how hard losing a friend at that age had to be.

'He had a heart attack,' she told him. 'When his mother went to wake him up for school he was—'

'Christa, I've told you before—'

'Why can't I tell anyone?' Christa said, twisting aside. 'What's the big secret?'

'There's no secret!' Her mother looked at Dan apologetically as if to say, *kids, you know what they're like.*

'He had a heart rhythm disorder,' Christa told Dan. 'But Alice died of cancer.'

'Christa, *sei sill*,' her mother snapped, gripping her arm and giving it a shake but the girl wasn't going to stop. She was staring straight at Dan, her whole stance determined.

'Our town is cursed. That's why George and Alice died.'

Her mother responded as though she'd been slapped. *'Wie kannst due es wagen?!'* How dare you?!

She sprang to her feet and grabbed the girl.

'Ow, Mama!' Christa protested but her mother didn't seem to hear. She'd flushed bright red as she marched Christa across the atrium, a stream of angry German spilling from her lips.

Dan looked at the man with the car magazine who shrugged his shoulders. 'Kids,' he said. He looked unperturbed, unlike Dan who'd found the whole scene alarmingly disturbing. Poor Christa, with two friends dead and a mother who refused to let her talk about it.

Footsteps approached. It was Gustav. He wore a white medical coat with two pens in his top pocket. A pair of reading glasses dangled from a cord around his neck.

'Herr Taube.' Gustav acknowledged the man with the car magazine before coming to Dan and shaking his hand. 'My sincere condolences.'

'Thank you.'

Being the eldest when they were kids meant Gustav always played the parental role. When they first met, Dan had been ten, Gustav thirteen, and the age difference had meant they'd had little in common until Gustav had seen Dan struggling to fly his kite one day. It was darting violently, and not wanting to look stupid Dan had tried to pretend everything was OK but Gustav simply came over and without saying anything showed him the bridle intersection was too low. They'd flown the kite together for the rest of the day and he remembered racing into the lodge over-excited and eager to show off his new kite-flying skills. *Gustav showed me how to re-rig my kite and now I can do stalls and spins!*

Dan surveyed Gustav, remembering how he and Christopher used to mercilessly wind Gustav up – usually over Gustav's crush on Sophie – and then laugh as hysterically as only teenage boys can when Gustav rose to the bait flushing beetroot to his hair roots.

Despite the reason why he was there, Dan felt a certain satisfaction that his childhood memories appeared intact. Although his intellect told him that the only memories damaged were the ones of his old job at MI5, he could never be a hundred per cent sure of that, and now he stood quietly enjoying the memory of Gustav's puppy dog's eyes following Sophie's lithe form everywhere.

'I'm sorry I don't have time for you today.' He touched Dan's arm in a gesture of what Dan thought was conciliation. 'I know it's a weekend but I have many patients to see and tomorrow is also busy. Perhaps one evening next week?'

'Perhaps. I just wanted to ask if you saw Dad when he was here?'

Gustav shook his head. 'No, he only saw my parents.'

'Apparently he visited the Isterberg Cemetery.'

Gustav blinked. 'Why?'

'I don't know.'

There was a tiny electronic buzz and Gustav flinched and looked at his watch. 'I'm sorry, but I must go.' He didn't give any explanation. He turned on his heel and left the room.

As Dan walked out to the street, he saw the girl Christa. She was standing forlornly beneath an awning outside a grocery store, watching him go.

CHAPTER THIRTY-TWO

Christopher had been hoping to catch Jasmine at the lab, her usual haunt at the weekend, and he wasn't sure whether he was relieved or annoyed she wasn't there. He was dreading telling her she had to go. How would she react? With her latest icy-cold demeanour, or a hot-headed slap? He'd fired people before, but this was going to be different. Frighteningly different.

Would Bao Zhi stay? He knew the man was instrumental in conducting the assessments required for the Kou Shaiming Company, but as he thought about both of them leaving he suddenly felt a surge of emotion that was almost akin to joy.

It would be so good to have his lab back.

As he locked his car, he heard footsteps and turned to see Lucy walking towards him.

'Hi,' she said.

'Hello.' He walked to meet her.

'Tim's just shown me the chamber, I hope you don't mind. All those plants! It's amazing.'

He made a noncommittal gesture.

'You must be really proud,' she went on. 'I mean, creating something that will potentially feed the world. That's one hell of a thing.'

He looked away. Pride wasn't on his list of emotions right now.

'I'm sorry.' She touched his arm gently. 'I know you're going through hell . . .'

Tears sprang to his eyes at the kindness of her gesture. 'Thank you. And thanks for saying what you did outside the house. Sam and I, well . . . we talked. For a long time. I'm moving back in. For a trial period, but I stayed last night.'

Sam had cooked spaghetti and he'd sat at the table with his mother-in-law and little Dougie kicking in his carry cot. Later, after Sam's mother had gone to bed, Sam had asked him to stay the night. They hadn't made love. They didn't even kiss. In bed, they lay facing each other for a moment and then he raised his arm, inviting her into his embrace. They fell asleep entwined, his arm wrapped around her shoulders, her leg between his, her head on his chest.

When he awoke, it was dawn and he needed the loo, but he didn't move. He lay there breathing in Sam's scent, enjoying the weight of her in his arms. He owed Lucy more than he could express.

'That's good to hear.' Lucy nodded, cleared her throat. 'Has anyone talked to you about how Connor died?'

'No.' He frowned. 'Why? What do you know?'

'I'll let your father tell you if that's OK. He was at the post-mortem on Connor.'

'I'll ring him in a moment.'

She glanced over her shoulder at the lab then back. 'Did you know Dan's gone to Germany?'

Christopher blinked. 'No.'

'He's visiting friends, who I believe you know. Arne and Anneke, and their son, Gustav. When did you last see them yourself?'

'At a wedding, over a decade ago.'

'That would be Sophie Kennedy's wedding, who married Nick Matthews?'

'That's right.'

'When did you last see Sophie?'

'Gosh . . .' He had to think. 'Six months ago? I was in London on business. We had lunch.'

The way she was looking at him had his nerves jangling.

'Why do you ask?'

'Both Dan's father and Connor died the same week.'

He stared at her in astonishment. 'You can't think they're connected?'

'Put it this way.' Her eyes hardened. 'In my job, we don't believe in coincidences.'

CHAPTER THIRTY-THREE

Dan was ensconced comfortably in his hotel in Isterberg by
6 p.m. His room overlooked a picturesque cobblestoned square.
Lots of cafés and restaurants, a tourist office. Nobody was
watching him that he could see.

He had a simple dinner, no alcohol. He wanted a clear head.
In his room, he spoke to Jenny and Aimee. Then he trawled his
father's photographs, and his father's emails again. This time,
however, he carefully read each one for signs of covert messages.
There were a handful that might fit the bill, including one from
someone going by the name of Firecat.

Firecat had apparently watched a film Bill had recommended
on Monday the twenty-seventh of August. *It wasn't the best
movie I've seen but it was powerful enough with an unknown
party threatening the protagonist not to continue their investigation. It was seriously frightening and seriously scared me. It would
take a lot of money to persuade anyone to stand up against such
forces, but then again, everyone has their price.*

He dropped Firecat an email explaining his father had died
and that he'd like to talk. He didn't say that Bill had been murdered. Then he went to bed. He was surprised he slept so well

and woke early, feeling refreshed. He texted DSI Didrika Weber and by the time he'd showered and had a breakfast of cold meats and cheeses, she had texted back asking him to meet her outside his hotel.

An ancient VW Beetle, tea green with what looked like its original wheels, idled on the kerb. Dan's eyes passed over it for the smart Audi pulling up next to him but then he turned back to the Beetle when a woman climbed outside. Tall, black hair scraped back hard into a ponytail, she was built like a shot-putter, all thick limbs and bulky muscles. She held her chin high with her shoulders back, obviously not self-conscious about her massive breasts, which stuck out before her like a pair of missiles.

She strode over, offering her hand. 'DSI Didrika Weber.' Her shake was as strong as he'd expected.

'Dan Forrester.'

'Let's go.'

He climbed into the Beetle and buckled up. 'This is your car?'

'Yes. My father worked for VW in Wolfsburg, and his father before him. This was my grandfather's car. He gave it to me.'

'It's beautiful,' he said, admiring the worn – obviously original – leather and carefully touched up paintwork.

'Thank you.'

The car started with a roar, rumbling over the cobblestones and making a heavy clanging sound.

'Sorry,' said DSI Weber. 'I think it's the shock mounts.'

Dan listened a bit more. 'It could be more simple, like a loose strut gland nut,' he offered.

He felt her gaze appraising him.

'My mother had a Beetle,' he told her. 'Years ago.'

She gave a nod as she turned out of the square.

'How's the investigation going?' No point in beating about the bush.

'It is difficult,' she said slowly. 'Trying to re-trace where your father went, who he saw – apart from visiting his friend Arne Kraus, of course.'

'Did you tell Arne that my father arrived on Thursday morning?' Dan asked.

'Yes.'

'What did Arne say to that?'

'He was puzzled.'

Dan's disquiet deepened. If Arne had known his father had arrived earlier, why hadn't he mentioned anything to Dan yesterday?

As they drove out of the old town, the streets widened and the buildings became more modern, with double glazing and off-street parking. Low hills rose to the south.

She said, 'Could you please tell me everything you know about why your father came here to Germany.'

He talked while she drove. She was a good driver, brisk but careful, indicating at the right moment and keeping a defensive position through the town. Dan told her about the friendship forged between four university students in the 1950s, and how their children had holidayed together each summer. After she'd asked some questions, he asked one of his own.

'How did you discover my father visited this memorial?'

'The hire car company remembers him asking how to find Isterberg Cemetery. I showed a photograph of your father around. The cemetery caretaker remembered him.'

In another five minutes they were there. DSI Weber parked to the side of the cemetery gates. 'Mr Forrester—'

'Please, call me Dan.'

'In that case, I am Didrika.'

He gave a nod.

'Dan. May I ask what you do professionally?'

'I work for a company that specialises in political risk analysis. I advise companies whether it's wise to invest in a particular country or not.'

'How do you do your analysis?'

'We have experts around the world that give us information on the markets in which they operate.'

'Experts.' She put her head on one side, studying him. 'Have you always done this?'

'Before that I was a high-performance driving instructor.'

She held his eyes. 'And before that?'

'This and that.' He put his hand on the door handle.

'Not a policeman? Or something like it?'

He gave her a wry smile. 'Whatever makes you say that?'

'There is more to you than meets the eye, I think.'

Short pause.

'The memorial?' he prompted.

She led him to a large, black stone obelisk set to one side in a square of fiercely mown lawn.

'What does it say?' he asked.

'Here in 1944 . . .' She was slightly hesitant as she translated. 'Are buried two hundred and forty-three babies. They were . . . born to Polish slave labourers and forced from their mothers to die in an orphanage in Isterberg. Their sufferings are part of the history of twentieth century Europe.'

Dan felt a sadness creep over him.

'It was a terrible time,' she said, her face sorrowful.

They stood in silence, gazing at the black stone.

'Can I meet the caretaker?' he asked.

'Of course.'

CHAPTER THIRTY-FOUR

Together Dan and Didrika Weber walked to the cemetery gates. Lines of headstones in the shape of stone crosses stretched between neat rows of trees. The DSI led the way past two magnificent tombs and an area filled with perfectly aligned, small bronze crosses pattée. Tucked behind a stand of beech trees stood a neat wooden shed. Its door was open and Dan could see a ride-on mower and a variety of strimmers inside. Didrika rapped on the doorframe.

'Herr Keller?'

A man in overalls appeared almost immediately. He had soulful eyes and sported the largest moustache Dan had ever seen. One gnarled hand held a pair of pliers, the other a piece of wire, both of which he quickly placed on a bench to one side. 'Detective Superintendent Weber.' He looked at Dan with faint curiosity.

'Herr Keller, this is Herr Forrester. The son of the man who was murdered.'

'My condolences,' the man murmured.

A buzz came from Didrika's jacket. She quickly brought out her phone, glanced at the display and, murmuring an apology, moved aside.

Dan turned back to Herr Keller. 'DSI Weber tells me my father came here last Thursday morning.'

'Yes.' Keller nodded. 'He wanted to know where the most recent cemetery plots could be found. I showed him.'

'Would you mind showing me?'

In answer, Keller grabbed a ratty old fleece from a hook inside the shed and stepped outside. With Dan at his side he headed back past the crosses pattée and tombs, walking to the northern end of the cemetery.

'Was anyone with him?' Dan asked.

Keller shook his head.

'Did you see his car?'

Another shake.

Keller stopped in a grassy area and made a wide gesture that included maybe twenty pale grey, new looking gravestones. 'Here. This is what he wanted.'

Dan looked at the nearest gravestone dedicated to Jacob and Louisa Meyer, who'd both died just a few years ago, within a year of each other.

He said, 'What was his mood like? Was he in a hurry maybe? Did he seem upset in any way?'

'I think maybe . . .' Keller glanced over his shoulder at Didrika, who was still on the phone. 'The detective superintendent didn't ask this.'

'Please.' Dan held the man's eyes. 'Tell me.'

Keller shuffled his feet. Looked around. Dan waited.

'I think maybe he was a little bit angry,' Keller finally said.

Instead of simply saying, *why?* Dan said, 'What did he do to make you think that?' He hoped it would make Keller think more deeply about his father's behaviour, and he seemed to have got it right because the caretaker smoothed his moustache several times before answering.

'He did not look at me after he saw this.' Again, he made a gesture to encompass the new gravestones. 'Before, we had a nice talk. After . . .' He shrugged his shoulders. 'He left without speaking to me.'

Dan began to move around the memorials. 'Which one in particular do you think made him angry?'

'I am not certain, but I think maybe . . .' He pointed out a pink granite monument with the sculpture of a white rose carved across its shoulders.

Dan stood before it. 'What does it say?'

'It is for a girl called Alice Lange. She was nine years old.'

Immediately he thought of Christa, the girl he'd seen at the Isterberg Klinic. Was this the same Alice she'd known, who'd died of cancer?'

'Did you know her?' Dan asked.

Keller shook his head saying, 'Her father comes and visits every Sunday.' He walked to the next gravestone. 'This is for a boy called George Müller. He was at the same school as Alice.'

'Which school?'

'Grundschule Isterberg.'

George Müller, Dan saw, died four months ago, just seven years old. A shiver took hold of him. Could it be the same boy who used to loan Christa his kayak?

Dan walked the area, checking the names on each headstone, but no other name was familiar.

'Apologies for the interruption.' Didrika Weber appeared and looked between the two men. 'Anything new?'

Dan returned to the pink granite headstone. 'Herr Keller believes this headstone made my father angry.'

The detective brought out her phone and took a photograph of it. '*Gut.* Anything else?'

Keller shook his head. Dan walked around the area again, taking several photographs before shaking Keller's hand, thanking him. Once again Keller offered his condolences. All three of them walked to the cemetery gates. Didrika gave Keller a wave as they drove away.

It was purely out of habit that Dan pulled the sun visor down and checked to see who was driving behind them. While Didrika asked him more questions, Dan continued to keep half an eye on the traffic following. He wasn't expecting to see anyone or anything to alarm him. Not Mouse Woman now she'd been pinged, or her companion who'd lost Dan once before. But after they'd been driving for twenty minutes, Dan's concentration intensified.

The same Mercedes had been following them since they'd left the cemetery – a silver three-door Coupé – and it was still with them when Didrika dropped Dan back at his hotel. Dan checked on it last thing that night to see it was still there. Tucked in the furthest recesses of the cobbled square, the streetlights made its low shape gleam.

CHAPTER THIRTY-FIVE

'Are you all right?' Ross looked at her closely. 'You've been twitchy all morning.'

'I'm just worried about a patient, that's all.'

Liar, Grace told herself. *You want to broach the subject of this fabulous new job but daren't. You're not just a liar, you're a coward too.*

They were in the kitchen having a lazy Sunday morning; Ross on his tablet reading the news, Grace flicking through a copy of *Good Housekeeping* trying to picture what the house was going to look like in three months' time. Lucy had gone home for the weekend and wouldn't be back until Monday.

Grace turned the page of her magazine.

'I'll have to get some tartan decorations,' she announced.

'What?' Ross looked startled.

'Christmas.'

'Dear God, is it that time already?' He looked faintly horrified.

She waved the magazine at him. 'The countdown to Christmas starts here!' she quoted. 'Do you think we should order a turkey?' She glanced sideways at the Aga. 'Will it fit in that? How many potatoes should I do? Parsnips? Carrots? Does everyone like bread sauce, or—'

'Gracie.'

He stopped her mid-flow, voice firm. 'I am not going to discuss Christmas until the clocks go back.'

'Oh.'

'That's on the thirtieth of October at 2 a.m.,' he added.

'Ah.'

'I don't want you panicking, OK?'

'I won't panic,' she lied. His family were coming to stay; his parents, his brother and sister-in-law and their two-year-old along with their dog.

'And because I know you will, there's something I have to tell you.'

Apprehension rose. 'What?'

'I, well . . . I . . .' He looked sheepish.

'*What?*' Please God he hadn't invited another branch of the family or his younger sister, who was going out with a drummer from a rock band and had four unruly kids under the age of ten. Thanks to Ross, the rock drummer had proudly shown her his tattoos the last time they'd visited, in the mistaken belief she had one too.

'It's not a tattoo, it's a birthmark,' she had told him, sending Ross a filthy look for winding the guy up. She'd pulled her hair back so the drummer could see the dark red stain on her neck just behind her ear.

'Wow, cool,' he breathed. 'It looks just like a poisoned ivy tattoo.'

From then on the drummer had insisted on calling her Ivy, which was confusing for everyone but which Grace simply found weird.

'So,' said Grace with a sigh. 'Who else is coming for Christmas?'

'Nobody.' Ross looked bemused. 'It's just that I, well . . . I've started a cookery course. We're learning how to cook Christmas lunch next week. Gravy, plum pudding and all.'

She was so stunned she just stared at him. 'I was going to do one.'

'I know. But you're so busy with work . . . and me? Well, I'm just a self-employed labourer and can take time out when I want.' He glanced pointedly at the rain lashing the windows. 'Especially when it's like this.'

'But I really wanted—'

'You can still do one,' he said hastily. 'But I thought it might take the pressure off you. Besides, I think I might actually enjoy it. I've always wanted to learn how to make custard from scratch.'

She rolled her eyes. 'To go with your spotted dick, I suppose. Your most favourite pudding in the whole wide world.'

'Correct.' He then gave a filthy chuckle and started to reach for her. 'I don't suppose you'd like to take a look at a real live specimen with perfect propor—'

A loud ringtone sounded making them both jump.

'Jesus,' said Grace. 'Couldn't you have your mobile turned up any louder?'

'I can't hear it when I'm working, sorry.' He snatched it up. 'Hello? Oh yes, Graeme.' He covered the receiver briefly to look at Grace, saying, 'the damp-proof guy.'

Oh, joy, she thought, her mind drifting to picture the immaculate, luxurious flat in Edinburgh. *Traitor,* she told herself. He's doing a cookery course for you. How can you throw it back in his face? *Because I'm lost up here. I don't fit in.* Hating herself and the way her thoughts kept returning to the Queensferry Medical Practice, she walked into the hall and picked up her doctor's bag. Ducked back to the kitchen and raised it up to Ross.

Although he frowned, he gave a nod along with a thumbs-up. 'Yes, we'll have to tank the cottage and DPC the main house . . .'

Grace left him still talking condensation and basement waterproofing and climbed into her car. She didn't drive far. Just down the road to a lay-by that overlooked an old stone bridge. She lowered her windows, listening to the distant baa-ing of sheep, the rush of water churning past, the cackle of a nearby grouse lurking in the heather. She sat there for a while, but no matter how she looked at it, she couldn't make up her mind what to do.

'I didn't realise you had a patient to see,' Ross remarked on her return.

She looked into his eyes. His expression was concerned. He was concerned for *her.*

'I didn't. Not really.'

He widened his eyes a fraction.

'I needed some space to think.'

'I see.' His tone was cautious.

She sank into the chair next to him. Her heart was bumping as she realised she hadn't given him any warning about her feelings or her anxieties regarding living on the farm. She'd never even confessed her disquiet about moving to Scotland. She'd just plunged right in, in the belief that love would conquer all.

'You know I love you,' she began.

He closed the lid of his tablet. Folded his hands on his lap. 'Yeees . . .' He drew the word out warily.

'But I've been . . .' She took a breath. 'Struggling.'

Ross remained perfectly still. 'Go on.'

'With this . . .' As she waved a hand around she saw how much work he'd done, not just in the kitchen, but in the yard, the outbuildings. He'd worked incredibly hard, much harder than she had, how could she detonate the bomb of her misery at his feet? She suddenly felt appallingly selfish. She knew it had been Ross's dream to move up here but she'd joined him voluntarily, one hundred per cent on board with his plans. Now he was watching her carefully and she felt a rush of love so strong her throat constricted. Oh, God, she couldn't risk losing him. She loved him *so much*. Tears rose. She tried to swallow them down but they kept coming.

'Gracie,' Ross said. His tone was gentle. 'You know I want to leap up and hug you, but first I have to know what you're struggling with.'

'I've been offered a job.' It came out in an explosion of breath.

The sound of the rain against the window panes was suddenly incredibly loud.

Ross cleared his throat. 'I didn't know you were looking.'

'I wasn't.'

'But you're tempted.'

She bit the inside of her lip. She didn't dare to speak. She felt duplicitous and faithless and wished she'd kept her mouth shut.

'I see.'

Something cool crept into his eyes. She'd never seen it before. Her mouth turned as dry as dust.

'Where?'

'Edinburgh.'

The coolness washed away, replaced by a frown. 'But that's in Scotland.'

'Well, yes.'

The frown deepened. 'Not England.'

'God, no!' She leaned forward, wiping tears from her eyes. 'There's a flat too. I mean, it's not free, but it's discounted to whoever takes the job. It's just around the corner from the surgery. The idea was that I could spend weekdays there and come home for weekends.'

'Whose idea?'

She licked her lips. 'Gordon Baird's.'

The coolness returned. She ploughed on.

'The practice belongs to a colleague of his, John Buchanan. John was looking for someone and Gordon thought of me . . .' She trailed off. The muscles in Ross's jaw had bunched like rocks.

'Gordon Baird suggested we live apart?'

'No!' she protested. 'It wasn't like that!'

He looked at her for what felt a long time. The tension in his jaw remained.

'You're that unhappy here?'

'I'm not unhappy *unhappy*.' Grace fought to find the right words. 'I know how lucky I am . . . you and me . . . you're the love of my life . . . It's just that it's so different. I'm not used to . . .' *Living in a mess of a building site. Working with people who don't seem to like me.*

Ross looked at her for another few seconds. Then he rose, pushing his chair back on the flagstones.

'I'm going out.'

Although he didn't storm out of the house, didn't slam any doors or cupboards, it still felt as though he had.

CHAPTER THIRTY-SIX

First thing the next morning, Dan checked on the Mercedes to see it had moved and was now tucked behind a blue van on the other side of the square. He wasn't entirely sure what to do about it, whether to let it follow him or not. More importantly, should he tell DSI Didrika Weber? She would be able to find out to whom it belonged in a nanosecond.

Didrika was apparently in meetings for most of the day but said she'd pick him up from his hotel late afternoon, which suited Dan fine. He was perfectly happy to have the time to conduct his own investigation. After calling Jenny and Aimee, he checked his emails to see that Firecat had responded.

Sorry to hear of your father's death. My sincere condolences. If you're around, why don't we meet up? We can drink some Highland single malt scotch whisky – 17 years old, double cask, first fill sherry and bourbon cask, of course.

Dan stared. Firecat knew his father's favourite tipple. And not just any tipple either, because you could only buy that particular whisky directly from the distillery. He'd bought Bill a bottle when they'd undertaken the Aberlour Distillery tour years ago. Unbeknownst to his father, he'd gone back and bought another bottle, which he then later presented to him as a Christmas gift. Whisky didn't *age* in a bottle, simply became a little more intense as a small amount of liquid evaporated, and his father still had half a litre or so sitting in his drinks cupboard waiting for a special occasion. *Like when my grandson is born*, his father had told him cheerfully.

Dan shot off a reply to Firecat, asking where and when they could meet. Having no idea where Firecat might reside, he suggested Thursday, which meant he could be pretty much anywhere that day, as long as it wasn't Australia or New Zealand.

As he stepped out of the hotel, he was surprised to see the Mercedes had gone. Had it been replaced by another watcher? He looked around but couldn't see anything to concern him, but that didn't mean nobody was there. Were they connected to Mouse Woman? he wondered. Or was this another team of some sort? What on earth had his dad gotten involved in? Out of nowhere, he felt a surge of grief so strong his throat closed up.

He would miss his father, miss their talks. Their occasional disputes and differences of opinion. But above all he'd miss his father's laugh, because when his dad laughed it was always genuine and whoever heard it couldn't help looking around, their faces already alight and wanting to know what was so funny.

With the photographs of his father to hand, Dan walked across the square to a café. He ordered the house special, which his dad would have loved: slices of local cheese, dried ham, hard boiled eggs and two warm rolls and butter. He showed the pictures to the waitress but she shook her head.

'Maybe one of the others might be able to help?' he suggested.

Her gaze flickered between the gingham aproned staff and the kitchen hatch. 'For sure.' She took the photograph. 'It's not so busy now.'

'Thank you. Could you also ask them if they knew Alice Lange or George Müller? They were children at the Grundschule Isterberg.'

She came back as he was finishing his coffee. 'Sorry,' she said. She handed back his photos. 'No one has heard of the children either.'

Dan continued his trawl of shops and cafés but with no luck. The morning slipped away. Breakfast menus turned to lunch. Without holding out much hope, he entered a rustic looking restaurant that his father would have liked, which boasted the best Jägerschnitzel as well as having its own micro-brewery. Waiting staff flickered around the restaurant like busy fireflies, taking orders, bringing back trays of beer, sausages and bratwurst.

To his astonishment the first waitress he spoke to took one look at the photo of his father and said, 'Oh, yes. He was here all right.' Her tone was aggrieved.

'He did something wrong?'

She rolled her eyes to the ceiling. 'We had to throw them out. They were fighting.'

'They?' he repeated. 'When was this?'

She looked again at the photograph, frowning. Then her hand went to her mouth. Her eyes rounded. 'He was murdered. I saw it in the papers.'

It was obviously the first time she'd put the man she'd seen having an argument in her restaurant together with the man who'd been killed on the golf course.

'That's right.'

She stared at Dan, her mouth agape.

'It's OK,' he tried to assure her. 'He's my father. I'd like to know what they were fighting about.'

She returned her gaze to the photograph. Rubbed her forehead.

'Can you describe who he was with?'

She glanced behind her, then at her watch. 'Give me ten minutes. I'm due a break then.'

'That's fine.'

He watched her sturdy form wind its way with practised ease through the crowded room. His dad had been thrown out of a café for fighting? He didn't think he'd ever seen his father lose his temper; his marine training had taught him to keep tight control of his emotions. Had the other person attacked him in some way? Forced him to defend himself?

Dan settled at the brauhaus bar, opting to order a fresh orange juice. He sipped it while he checked his phone. Another email from Firecat.

The Fiddichside Inn, Craigellachie, 6 p.m. Tomorrow night.

A tight frisson of shock ran through him.

Craigellachie? He knew the village. He'd even fished there years ago, his dad teaching him how to handle the fifteen-foot salmon rod. He fought to get his mind around it.

When he looked up the Fiddichside Inn he saw it was just outside the village, on the road to Keith. White walls, red trim, it looked homely and traditional. Apparently Firecat couldn't make it past Tuesday as he was going overseas.

Dan decided he'd fly back to the UK tomorrow. The cost of his air travel at the moment was depleting the family travel fund more than usual, but he didn't see he had a choice. From Firecat's caution, he was pretty certain he had some important information about his father and the sooner he got it, the better.

He emailed Firecat, confirming their meeting.

The reply was immediate.

You'll bring the money?

Dan had no idea what money was being referred to but emailed back:

Of course.

He re-read Firecat's previous email.

It would take a lot of money to persuade anyone to stand up against such forces, but then again, everyone has their price.

He guessed his father was paying for information. A whistleblower maybe? Dan wondered if his father and Firecat had met and if it had been in Scotland. If so, his dad hadn't mentioned it, which was unusual. When he was up there he'd always stay with Gordon – and Aileen until she'd died fourteen years ago – and he'd tell Dan all their family news.

He had heard nothing new from Lucy after her report on Green Test Lab, which hadn't come to much. Even though it had high security, nobody seemed to work there. Perhaps it had been abandoned for some reason? He wondered how the police were getting on, and thought it was maybe time to let Lucy reveal she was also police. That should stir things up. He'd see her tomorrow. Talk it through.

'Hi.'

He looked up to see the waitress wriggling onto the stool next to him, hastily removing her apron with one hand while she dragged her fingers through her hair with the other. The brauhaus had quietened a little, taking a breath before the next rush, he guessed. She asked the barman for a jug of water and poured herself a glass. 'I've only got ten minutes, sorry.'

He checked her name tag. 'Viveka,' he said, 'you say you threw them out?'

'Yes. They were yelling at each other. Everyone stopped to watch.'

'What were they arguing about?'

Viveka pulled a face as she tried to remember. 'Your father . . . he was very angry. He kept shouting "how dare you!" and . . . well, he swore a lot.' She looked slightly uncomfortable.

'Who was he arguing with?'

'A woman.'

Dan blinked. For some reason, he hadn't expected that.

'She was giving as good as she got. She yelled . . .'

When she hesitated, he said, 'Please, tell me exactly what he said. It's important.'

'She shouted, "you fucking bastard" several times. Then she slapped him.'

'Describe her.'

'Elegant,' Viveka told him. 'Same age, perhaps. Late sixties. Tall. Slim. She would have been beautiful when she was younger.'

Dan felt his stomach swoop. Was she talking about Anneke? Hurriedly he brought out his phone. Scrolled through his father's photographs that he'd downloaded yesterday. Opened the 'people' album and scanned until he found a recent close-up portrait of Anneke. It was dated June last year. 'Is this the woman?'

Viveka had a good look.

'Yes, that's her.'

'What else can you remember?'

'He called her a selfish, self-centred bitch, which was when she hit him. That was when we asked them to leave. She left first. He paid the bill.'

CHAPTER THIRTY-SEVEN

Dan couldn't put the picture of Anneke yelling abuse at his father together with the calm and controlled woman who now sat opposite him.

When he'd asked Viveka if it was OK for him to use a table for a while, she'd moved him to one in the centre of the brauhaus. From there, he'd called Anneke at her house. He didn't beat around the bush. He said, 'I gather you had a row with my father last Thursday.'

There was a silence then she said, 'Arne doesn't know.'

'I'd like you to come to the Brauhaus Isterberg.'

'All right.'

Now he was aware of everything around him, the tide of conversation from other diners, the smell of frying potatoes, the waiting staff watching them out of the corners of their eyes. Anneke had asked for a glass of Reisling, which had come with a tense smile from Viveka. Dan stuck to water.

'What did you fight about?' he asked, getting straight to the point.

She raised a hand and pushed back a strand of silver-blonde hair. Held his eyes as she spoke. 'Rafe.' Her voice was husky and she cleared her throat. 'We fought over Rafe.'

'Rafe?' he repeated. 'Why?'

She picked up her glass of Reisling and took a sip. 'Rafe wanted your father to kill him.'

Dan exhaled, leaning back in his chair as he recalled the vigorous discussions his father and Rafe had had over the subject of euthanasia.

'Except Bill wouldn't.' Anneke's mouth tightened. 'He didn't believe in it. I told him he was a selfish bastard.'

'What about Arne?'

'Rafe didn't ask Arne to help,' she said sharply. 'He asked your father.'

Long silence.

Dan took a sip of water. Anneke took another sip of her wine.

'Does Arne know Rafe asked Dad to do this?'

She looked away, her expression turning distant. 'I'm not sure.'

Dan considered Anneke

'Did you have an affair with my father?'

Her gaze flew to him, shocked. 'Absolutely not. I've never been unfaithful to Arne.'

At that moment Viveka came over with two menus, which she put on the table. Neither Dan or Anneke touched them.

'As far as Bill is concerned,' Anneke went on, 'well ... he wouldn't countenance such a thing, let alone with me, the wife of his close friend. He was an honourable man. You know this. Besides, he was still in love with your mother.'

Dan's mother had died eleven years ago. Had his father ever had another relationship? He'd never met any girlfriend of his and he suddenly felt sad, hoping his father hadn't been lonely.

'How did you find out about Rafe's request?'

'Rafe emailed me. He knew Bill was coming to visit. He thought I might be able to persuade him.'

Dan thought of the wasted figure that was Rafe, coughing his guts up, hating the indignity of his care. *Wish I'd died years ago.*

'Are you sure that's all you argued about?' Dan pressed. 'Rafe's euthanasia?'

She lifted her hands. It was a weary gesture. 'Isn't that enough?'

As he recalled the passion in Rafe's and his father's emails, he thought Anneke was probably right. Rafe had applauded Martin Amis and his call for euthanasia 'booths' on street corners where the elderly could 'terminate their lives with a "martini and a medal"'. Bill had protested against the thought of a giant super-loo where you put a pound in a slot and got a lethal drink in return. *It's too open to abuse*, he'd said. Dan could remember the email quite clearly. *Families getting rid of their doddery old parents early because they can't be bothered to care for them and want their money.*

Dan's breathing tightened as grief nudged him, reminding him his father's life had been snatched from him.

'Do you happen to know Alice Lange or George Müller? Dad went to see their memorials.'

She raised her eyebrows, considering Dan intently. 'I've never heard of them.'

'What about Project Snowbank?'

A tiny frown appeared. 'Project?'

'Snowbank.'

'It means nothing to me. What is it?'

She finished her glass of wine and raised a hand to indicate to a passing waiter that she wanted another.

Dan didn't answer her question. Instead he said, 'What about Firecat?'

'I don't understand.' The frown remained. 'Firecat? What does it mean?'

There was a pause, then Dan said quietly, 'Who do you think murdered my father?'

Her eyes widened. 'You think I know?'

'Do you?'

A flash of horror mingled with dismay crossed her face. 'Of course not! You can't believe I do, surely?'

'I don't know what to believe.' His tone hardened.

'Oh, dearest Dan.' Her face fell. For a moment she looked as though she wanted to reach across and take his hand, but thought better of it. 'I can't think what you must be going through. Please, ask me more questions. As many as you like, no matter how ridiculous or personal. Maybe I can remember something that might help you or prompt you on another avenue of questions. How is the police investigation going?'

He'd just started to speak when Viveka came over and said, 'Your guests are here. Shall I find you a bigger table?'

Surprised, Dan looked past Viveka to see Gustav, who was standing just inside the door with his arm around the waist of his companion. As Dan watched, the woman leaned up and kissed him fully on the mouth. They were lovers, no doubt about it.

He felt the shock of it against his breastbone.

Sophie?

Sophie and Gustav?

'What the—'

'I got Gustav's secretary to persuade them to lunch here,' Anneke said carelessly. 'Arne's coming too. I thought it would be fun for all of us to have lunch together.'

Dan stared at her. 'Do Gustav and Sophie know I'm here?'

'No.' A sly look crossed her face. 'I thought it would be a surprise.'

It was more than that, he realised. Anneke wasn't just exposing Gustav and Sophie's affair to him but ensuring a limit on the amount of time Dan had with her alone.

'What are you trying to hide?'

Anneke blinked. 'Nothing, Dan. Honestly. I thought you'd enjoy seeing your old friends.'

Like hell, he thought grimly. She'd engineered the whole situation to her own agenda. He rose from his chair, his eyes on Gustav and Sophie. They hadn't seen him. He walked over.

'Gustav,' he said. 'Sophie.'

He'd been prepared for the shock on Gustav's face but not Sophie's. She was normally so imperturbable, so cool, but the second her eyes met his, she blanched.

'Anneke's getting us a table,' Dan said. 'Apparently, Arne's coming, so we can have a bit of a party.'

Sophie's gaze snapped to Anneke, who was standing by a new table – one laid for five – smiling. Her posture was relaxed and friendly, but there was something in the way she looked at Sophie that made Dan cringe. She would hate it, he thought, that her only son wasn't just unmarried, no kids, but that he was involved with a married woman.

Gustav's mouth was opening and closing. No sound came out.

'Let's join Anneke,' Dan said briskly, stepping back and indicating Gustav and Sophie forward.

'Do we have to?' Sophie hissed and Dan pushed her forward saying, 'Yes, we do.' He wanted to see how things played out. It may have nothing to do with his father's murder but he was curious just the same.

'No,' said Sophie, and she could have been a little girl again for all the anger and petulance in her voice.

'Yes,' said Dan, and he held her upper arm like he used to all those years ago to prevent her bolting from the room.

'You shit.'

'Yes,' he agreed, but he was grinning.

'You haven't bloody changed, have you?'

'Nor have you. As stroppy as ever.'

'OK, OK. You can drop the strong-arm bit. I'm going over.' She slapped his hand away.

'Make sure you eat all your main course,' he told her, 'or you won't be allowed pudding.'

She smacked his arm. He saw the colour had returned to her face. A smile began to appear. 'You're a pig.'

'You're a sow.'

Childish insults from way back.

When they headed for their table, Viveka looked at Dan with raised eyebrows. He raised his eyebrows back at her along with a tiny gesture of his hands saying, *I have no idea what's going on.* She smiled and gave him a wink. He winked back.

As Anneke ordered a bottle of Riesling for the women and beer for the men, Dan leaned over to Sophie. 'Gustav?' he questioned in a low voice.

'Yes, Gustav,' she whispered.

'How long?'

She gave a casual shrug but despite their earlier sparring he could tell she was deeply rattled by the way she pleated her napkin, her fingers restless.

'Long enough,' she replied.

'Six months, isn't it?' Anneke said with a pretence of lightness.

'Mama.' Gustav still hadn't sat down. 'I don't think—'

'Sit, sit. We all want to hear about your love affair with the delectable Sophie.' She seemed amused, but Dan caught the animosity seething beneath.

'There's nothing to tell,' Gustav said. He still didn't sit down. 'I'm going to leave now and Sophie is coming with me.' He held out a hand.

For a moment, nobody moved.

Then Sophie got to her feet and put her hand in his. She looked at Dan. 'Call me.'

When they had left, Anneke rose. 'Thank you for the wine.'

'Wait. I thought Arne was—'

'I think we're done here, don't you?' she said archly.

At the door, he gave Viveka enough money to cover the bill along with a generous tip.

'Friend of yours?' she asked him.

'To be honest,' he answered, 'I have no idea.'

CHAPTER THIRTY-EIGHT

Grace had spent the morning trying to work her way through some paperwork but she found it almost impossible to concentrate. She kept replaying last night's scene with Ross.

He'd come home early evening and to her dismay he was still cool. He stood in the doorway of the kitchen, arms folded.

She wanted to ask him where he'd been but didn't dare. She wrung her hands together. Inside, she was trembling.

'How long have you been so unhappy?' he asked.

'It's not—'

'Grace, please don't bullshit me.'

'But I feel so pathetic.' She spread her hands. 'People up here are so *tough*. They never complain. I feel such an outsider . . . I can't plaster a wall or fly fish, let alone chop wood or make a clootie dumpling.'

A whisper of what might have been a smile made her spirits lift.

'Nor can a lot of people up here.'

A pane of glass rattled in the wind. Neither of them gave it any heed.

'Would you like to return to England?'

She hadn't expected him to be so blunt.

'No.'

'Why not?'

'Because you're here.'

'But if I'm making you unhappy—'

'It's not *you!*' she cried. 'It's the mess! I just want to walk through the rooms of our house without collecting an inch of dust! I want a hot bath without having to bang the bloody boiler first! I want the central heating to work ... Carpets would be nice too, and I know they're coming and that I'm being horrible and demanding but it's just taking so long ...'

She drew a breath and at the same time a gust of wind threw what sounded like a bucket of water against the windows. She looked around to see water dribbling through a crack in one of the panes and puddling on the windowsill.

'I'm afraid I can't do anything about the weather.' His voice was dry as he unfolded his arms and stepped into the kitchen.

'I know.' She put her head in her hands. 'I'm sorry. I sound like such a selfish, self-centred bitch.'

'Hey.'

Grace felt the warmth of his hands on hers as he pulled them gently down. He looked at her. 'What else?'

'What do you mean?'

'If we're airing things, then we have to be totally honest here, OK?'

She nodded, anxiety rising as she wondered where this was leading.

'Personally,' he told her, 'I've been missing home-cooked meals in the evenings—'

'Oh, God, Ross—'

'Which is why I'm doing a cookery course.' He held her eyes. 'Your turn.'

She squirmed.

'Come on, Gracie . . .'

It was the fact he'd used his nickname for her that gave her the strength to continue.

'Well, um . . . I'm not sure if I'm . . . well, very keen on doing DIY.'

She could see the surprise in his eyes.

'I thought you were OK with it.'

'I thought I was too. But it's kind of . . . getting me down a bit.'

'OK, so we'll find someone else to do it.'

'Really?' Her eyes widened.

He dropped his hands from hers. 'Jesus, Grace. Don't you get it? I'll do anything to make you happy! I'd do all the DIY myself but if you want the house perfect by the end of next week, it's not going to happen!'

Silence.

'Can we afford it?' Her voice was small.

'Yes, we can afford it.'

He put his arm out and she stepped into his embrace.

'I'll do anything for you Grace Reavey. Don't you know that by now?'

She raised her face and kissed him. Relief flooded every cell, every vein. She closed her eyes for a moment. 'I don't deserve you.'

'I'm not sure about that,' he said, but he smiled. 'What about this job? Do you really want to take it?'

She studied his face, the slightly crooked nose, the laughter lines around his eyes.

'I'm not sure.'

'Perhaps you just need a holiday. With knee-deep carpets and a boiler that works . . .'

'And no damp in the bedroom.'

'And a three course—'

'Home cooked meal—'

'With spotted dick for pudding . . .'

A wicked gleam came into his eye. 'I seem to recall I had something else in mind when that particular pudding was mentioned earlier but we were rudely interrupted—'

'By the damp-proof guy,' Grace finished just as his mouth swooped on hers.

CHAPTER THIRTY-NINE

On the street Dan dialled Sophie's number. When she answered, he said, 'Gustav? Are you kidding me?'

'Where are you staying?' Her voice was brusque.

'The Hotel Isterberg.'

'Give me thirty minutes, OK?' she said. 'I'll see you there.'

Killing time, Dan began tracking down shops that sold children's clothes, asking the assistants if they'd heard of Alice Lange or George Müller. Lots of shaking heads. Everyone knew of the school, though, the Grundschule Isterberg.

He returned to his hotel to find Sophie at the bar with a large glass of something rust-coloured poured over ice.

'Punt e Mes,' she told him. 'Italian vermouth.' She pushed the glass over. 'Try some.'

He took a sip. Bittersweet, it had a syrupy edge overlaid with astringent herbs. Sweet and sour, he thought, not unlike Sophie.

'Interesting.'

'What would you like?' She gestured at the barman who was looking at him enquiringly.

'Beer,' he said to the barman. 'Something local. Not too strong.'

Sophie propped her foot on the bronze foot rail, sipping her drink while looking at him from beneath her eyelashes. 'So, you caught us out.'

'Yes.'

'What are you going to do about it?'

'Sophie, it's really none of my business.'

She grinned. 'I hoped you'd say that.'

'I thought you were happy with Nick.'

'I am!' she protested. 'I love him to bits, you know that! And I have no intention of leaving him or anything. He's a great guy. It's just that . . . well, being married can get a bit dull.'

'You're having an affair with Gustav because you're *bored*?' He couldn't help the incredulity in his tone.

'Don't get all prissy on me, Dan. You weren't exactly snow white, remember?'

It was like a punch to his midriff. Nobody outside the firm knew about his affair. *Nobody.*

'What are you talking about?' he said. His voice was perfectly puzzled but inside his nerves were fizzing.

'Oh, shit.' She put a hand over her eyes. 'Fuck, fuck, fuck. I can't believe I said that . . . Shit, Dan. I'm sorry.' She lowered her hand. Her mouth was twisted. 'You don't remember, do you? It was before Luke died. You came to me for advice. It was tearing you up.'

'I don't remember having an affair,' he agreed. But he knew he'd had one because of the evidence presented to him last year. He thought back to when he and Jenny had visited their son Luke's grave on his birthday, the second of December. Jenny had thought Dan was in love with one of his colleague's wives, which was why she'd lied to him about his past. She hadn't wanted him remembering his old lover. She'd done just about everything to stop him uncovering the truth and her lies had nearly broken them apart. It was only when he discovered that he'd engineered the affair in order to uncover a mole in MI5 that they'd managed to save their marriage.

'Fuck it,' she said. 'I'm really, *really* sorry, OK?' She looked mortified.

'What was her name, do you know?'

'How do you know it was a woman?' Her gaze turned sly.

'For God's sakes—'

'Sorry, sorry!' She held up her hands. 'I couldn't resist it, sorry! You're right, it was a woman, but you never mentioned her name.'

At that his nerves untangled their tension and his shoulders loosened. 'OK,' he breathed out.

'OK,' she echoed. 'Sorry.'

'It's OK.'

He took a long pull of his beer. She drained her Punt e Mes and ordered another. They sat in silence for a while.

Dan couldn't help it. He arranged his expression into one of total disbelief and as he looked her in the eye he said again, 'Gustav?'

Her eyes creased at the corners and he felt a bubble of humour rising. Suddenly, they both burst out laughing. They laughed so hard tears came to their eyes, Sophie clutching his arm as she creased up. Dan couldn't remember when he'd last laughed so much, and when they finally stopped, wiping their eyes, the scar across his stomach was aching. It felt good to laugh, especially with an old friend.

'You used to look at him with such contempt,' Dan told her.

'That was years ago. We were just kids.'

'And now?'

'He's fun. He adores me. He buys me gifts.' She turned her wrist to show him her watch.

He raised his eyebrows. 'Are those diamonds?'

She pulled back her hair to expose a pair of elegant long-drop earrings that dazzled and glittered when she moved her head.

'They're a girl's best friend,' she purred. 'I love being spoilt.'

'Doesn't Nick do that?'

'Well, yes . . .' For the first time, she looked uncomfortable. 'But graphic designers don't earn much. I love Nick, but I want so much *more*.' Her expression suddenly turned impassioned. 'I want to sail around the world. I want to moor my yacht in the Caribbean and drink cocktails as the sun goes down.' Her eyes gleamed. 'And since I can't do that, Gustav keeps me entertained. He's *different*.'

Was she really so easily bored? he wondered. He felt a stab of pity for Gustav as he recalled his puppy-dog eyes following her everywhere. 'I think he's been in love with you since he first saw you.'

'I wouldn't know about that.' Sophie gave a careless shrug. 'We're just having a bit of fun. That's all.'

Dan decided to let it drop. As he'd said, it wasn't his business, but even so, he didn't fancy being around when Sophie dumped Gustav.

'How's Christopher bearing up?' she asked, changing the subject.

'As expected.'

'Poor guy.' She shook her head slowly, staring into her drink. 'I can't imagine what it must be like, losing a child.'

'It's one of the worst things that can happen.' His tone turned tight.

'Fuck!' She screwed up her face. 'I can't believe it. I'm a walking diplomatic disaster today, aren't I? It's not that I forgot Luke, it's just me and my big mouth, speaking without thinking first.'

'Hey.' He touched her arm. 'I know you didn't mean any harm.'

'OK.' She exhaled noisily. Took a gulp of her drink. 'Can I ask . . .' She thought for a moment. 'How is the investigation going? God, I still can't get over what happened to your dad. He was such a terrific bloke. What an awful way to go. What was he involved with, do you think? Was it to do with his consultancy work?'

Dan hadn't found anything suspicious in his father's affairs but he still hedged. 'Maybe. I'm not a hundred per cent sure.'

She looked amused. 'You're as reticent as ever. Do you think we'll ever change? As people, I mean?'

'I don't think so.'

'I hope not.' Her expression turned wistful. 'It's nice knowing we're the same underneath as we were all those years ago.'

Dan took another pull of the beer called, apparently, Golden Barbarossa. The colour was surprisingly dark and although it was full of flavour, it wasn't too strong. His father had always liked German beer and now he could see why.

'I hate to ask,' Dan said, 'but how's Rafe?' He decided not to tell her what Anneke had said. That Sophie's father had asked Bill to help him with his assisted suicide.

She pulled a face. 'Pretty awful, to be honest. I find myself wishing he'd just die. Does that make me a terrible person?'

He shook his head. 'I think it's entirely natural.'

Sophie rattled the ice cubes in her glass, expression sad.

'Sophie, can I ask ... Did Rafe ever mention a Project Snowbank?'

Her brow furrowed. 'I don't think so. Why?'

'I think it might be to do with Dad's death. But I can't find out anything about it.'

Sophie mused for a while before shaking her head. 'He's worked on loads of projects over the years, but Snowbank? It doesn't mean anything to me.'

'I thought I'd go and ask his old work colleagues at TSJ. Would that be OK?'

Although she said it should be fine, she gave him an odd look that made Dan feel as though he'd stepped over some invisible line, but what it was, he had no idea.

CHAPTER FORTY

Grace looked through a handful of discharge summaries, her body flushing at the memory of last night's love-making. She couldn't stop replaying it. Ross had been exceptionally attentive, and she had been too. It had been powerful as hell, and later, wrapped in thick dressing gowns and slipper socks, curled up in front of the wood burning stove with glasses of red wine, they'd talked everything through.

'Are you sure they're that unfriendly?' Ross asked her. He was talking about the surgery staff as well as Constable Murdoch.

'No. They just look at me differently.'

'I think they just want you to prove yourself.'

'I order too many autopsies,' she admitted to Ross. 'Except I don't, not really, because I'm actually very concerned at the high death rate.'

'What's worrying you in particular?'

'It's just that I've lost four people to cancer recently . . . All of them had retired of late and should have been enjoying their new lives.'

'Four?' He looked shocked.

'There are more, but every time I bring the subject up at the surgery, everyone just says *We all die young up here.*'

'That's awful.'

'I know.'

'What do you reckon is going on?'

'I think it's linked to their diets,' she sighed. 'Most people up here have porridge for breakfast, meat-filled sandwiches for lunch and more meat for dinner with the odd pea thrown in on Sundays. But bad diet or not, I can't keep demanding autopsies or I'll get run out of town.'

'If you're that concerned, you've got to keep at it, love. You're damn good at your job, and if you're worried you must get to the bottom of it.'

It was all very well for him to say, but she didn't want to make herself any more unpopular than she already was. Could she do a little digging around the edges, without letting anyone know?

Before she could lose her nerve, she picked up the phone and rang an old uni friend who had a PhD in pharmacology and was now heading the research department in one of the most famous teaching hospitals in the world: St Bartholomew's, otherwise known simply as Barts.

'Grace Reavey?' Ben sounded disbelieving. 'Isn't that the gorgeous doctor who moved to the Outer Hebrides?'

'The Highlands, you twit,' she told him fondly. 'It's not *that* far away.'

'Far enough that we don't meet up anymore,' he grumbled.

'You're welcome to come and stay anytime.'

'What? Me, actually breathe some fresh air for a change? It might kill me.' He chuckled. 'Now, what can I do for you? I'm guessing you're at work so I take it it's not a social call.'

'Correct. Look, I was wondering what you knew about red blood cells mutating due to a bad diet. I've had seven patients die recently, all in their sixties. Four of cancer, one of heart disease, one of an infection, and one of liver disease. They were all massive meat eaters and if they saw a green vegetable it was probably once a year at Christmas. What's really weird is that none of them showed any symptoms until they were really close to death.'

'How close?'

'Days, weeks.'

'Hmmm. There is some work being done in this area. Our cells are constantly exposed to reactive molecules that can cause DNA damage, so they need anti-oxidants to mop them up – which as you know, fresh foods supply. If red blood cells mutate, they can be easily spotted if you're looking for them.' His voice suddenly brightened. 'You want to send me their blood samples? I could have a look for you?'

'Too late.'

'Nothing post-mortem?' He sounded surprised.

'Ben, when someone dies up here, they're buried faster than I can say the word pathologist. No frills.'

'Jesus.' He cleared his throat. 'Look, you could well be right, and if you have another patient go the same way, grab a blood sample and send it down. It wouldn't harm to have a look.'

'Thanks, Ben.'

'I love looking at weird stuff.'

After writing a couple of referrals and processing a dozen clinic letters, she turned to the surgery's patient records to have another dig around. Interestingly, the people who'd died in their sixties had all been locals, born and brought up here. The Polish and other European immigrants seemed unaffected by the early-death rate, but that could be due to the fact many of them hadn't reached their fifties yet.

She'd just returned to her admin when her phone rang.

'Dr Reavey,' she answered.

'It's Disa Tavey,' said Sara the receptionist. 'Alistair's just taken a turn for the worst but he refuses to go to hospital. He says if he's going to die, he wants to die at home.'

Grace was already up and reaching for her doctor's bag.

'Tell her I'm on my way.'

CHAPTER FORTY-ONE

The Grundschule Isterberg was on the edge of a forested valley. Unprepossessing, built out of concrete and dark brown aluminium cladding, it looked tired and dated. Basketball hoops graced the front drive along with some benches and great clumps of hostas. Dan couldn't see any children but he could hear their chattering through an open window.

Didrika had collected him from his hotel at 3 p.m. Today she drove what he took to be a pool car, a bog-standard Ford Mondeo. Her cheeks were pink, her hair freshly washed, and the energy in her stride as she walked to meet him reminded him of Jenny before she was pregnant.

'*Guten Tag*,' she greeted him.

'How has your day been?'

'Busy. Yours?'

He told her about Anneke and Bill's row in the brauhaus. She gave it serious consideration before she spoke.

'How well do you know Mrs Kraus?'

'I don't really,' Dan admitted. 'I only knew her when I was a child, when we used to go to Scotland on holiday together.'

'Did she know the children whose memorials your father visited?'

'I don't think so.' A hint of reservation laced his voice and when she sent him an enquiring look he added, 'I don't know her well enough to know when she's lying.'

'I see. And her husband?'

'The same.'

Now the *Direktor*, the headmaster of the school, came to greet them. A short, slim-built man of around forty, with large brown eyes magnified behind his wire-rimmed glasses. The silky brown-grey hair combed over his pate and the neatly clipped beard gave him an academic air.

'*Detecktiv*,' he said, shaking her hand. He looked at Dan expectantly.

'This is Dan Forrester, from England,' Didrika said. She didn't say anything more.

Dan didn't either. He was pretty sure she wouldn't normally have the relative of a murdered victim accompany her like this, let alone interview the headmaster, and he put it down to the fact she thought he used to be a policeman or something like it.

'I shall speak English then,' the *Direktor* said genially.

After shaking Dan's hand, the head ushered them inside the building. Although it appeared spotlessly clean, it was slowly disintegrating into shabbiness. Steel bookcases were stained with rust and the linoleum floor worn in the centre. The head's office wasn't much better with a threadbare green carpet and condensation trickling down the windows.

'So,' he said, taking his seat behind the desk and offering them the two chairs opposite. 'How can I help you?

Didrika brought out a notebook and pen. Crossed her legs.

'We would like to talk about Alice Lange and George Müller,' stated the detective.

'Poor children.' The headmaster's face grew pinched. 'Alice had cancer. Very unusual in one so young. The first we knew about it was when she didn't feel like playing basketball. She said she was tired and that her bones ached.' He turned his head to gaze at the wall where a picture of the school hung. 'She died four weeks later.'

Cancer, Dan already knew, accelerated much faster in a young body than an old one, but even so this seemed unnaturally fast.

'George Müller had a heart rhythm disorder. Nobody knew he had it until his mother went to wake him one morning and found he'd died in the night.'

Just as Christa had told him at the Isterberg Klinic.

Dan waited while the detective asked a variety of questions before asking one of his own. 'Do you have a girl called Christa here?'

The head looked surprised. 'Why yes. Christa Braun. Do you know her?'

'I met her briefly. She said the town was cursed. What is your view, considering the children's deaths?'

Dan's voice had been utterly without inflection but the man still flinched. He looked at the detective. *'Müssen wir dort wirklich hineingehen?'* Do we really have to go into this?

'*Ich fürchte ja.*' Didrika's voice was hard. '*Dies ist eine Mordermittlung. Bitte beantworten Sie die Frage.*' I'm afraid we do. This is a murder investigation. Please answer the question.

From the way the headmaster's nostrils flared, Dan took it he wasn't happy. He looked at Didrika but her gaze was fixed on the headmaster.

She said without looking at Dan, 'The *direktor* is reluctant to go into this. I have told him to answer your question.'

Dan watched the man with interest.

'Isterberg has a dark history,' the head said quietly. 'During WWII, several state institutions were located here, including a Hitler Youth Academy for Leadership.' He swallowed, gazing at his desk. 'Isterberg also had a *Ausländerkind-Pflegestätte*, a foreign child-care facility. Unintended pregnancies were common among Polish and Soviet female forced labourers . . .'

Didrika spoke up, her voice still hard. 'This was due to rampant sexual abuse at the hands of their supervisors.'

'Correct.' Again, the head swallowed. 'When a slave worker fell pregnant, if the probable father wasn't a German or otherwise Germanic in origin, they were either forced to abort the baby or their child was sent to an *Ausländerkind-Pflegestätte*, where they were, ah . . .'

'Exterminated,' Didrika supplied stonily. 'Over ten thousand infants were purposely left to die in what were called the baby-huts. They were checked off as stillborn. Isterberg had the largest facility in the country.'

Although Dan knew his expression wouldn't show it, inside he felt a wave of horror.

There was a long silence.

The head finally cleared his throat and looked at Dan. 'The children at the school know the town's history. It doesn't surprise me that Christa says the town is cursed. George Müller was a good friend of hers, and she's probably looking for something or someone to blame.'

Although what the head said made sense, Dan still didn't get it. Why would his father visit Alice and George's memorials? Maybe he'd known the children? Anneke said she hadn't known them, but since he wasn't sure he trusted her anymore, he'd take that with a pinch of salt. But what about the children's parents?

Didrika brought out a photograph of his father and pushed it across to the head. 'Did this man come to the school?'

The head picked up the photograph. He stared for a moment then looked between them, saying 'This is the Englander who was murdered last week?'

'Yes.'

Alarm filled his face. 'What has this to do with the school?'

'Please, answer the question.' Didrika was steely.

'No,' he said. 'I've never seen him before. I mean, just in the newspapers . . .'

Dan leaned forward. 'Do you know Anneke or Arne Kraus?'

'Everyone knows them.' The head frowned as he put down the photograph. 'They're our local celebrities.'

Dan raised his eyebrows. 'In what way?'

'Their story about escaping to the West just before the fence went up resonates with a lot of people. The fact they made such a success of their lives starting from nothing . . .' He shook his head admiringly. 'They showed us what could be done.'

'Would they have known Alice or George?'

The head looked blank. 'I have no idea.'

'Maybe their parents?'

The head's shoulders raised, then fell. 'I wouldn't know.'

Despite Dan and Didrika asking more questions, they didn't learn anything to further the investigation. They were walking outside, dodging a troupe of shrieking children who were on a break, when his phone rang.

'Dan.'

Just the one word from Jenny, but from the half-gasp in her voice, he knew what was happening.

'I'm on my way.'

CHAPTER FORTY-TWO

Didrika insisted on driving him to the airport after he'd checked out of his hotel.

'You don't have to,' he told her. 'I can easily get a taxi.'

'No way!' she protested. 'I want to be part of your journey to your baby! Besides, we can talk on the way. I have had some thoughts, OK?'

'OK.'

'Will we make it in time?' said Dan, checking his watch. He'd already managed to change his flight – at an exorbitant price – to the 19:25 departure, and if he missed it he'd have to take another flight with a different carrier which would stop over in France, taking two and a half hours longer. He'd used the credit card in Michael Wilson's name and God alone knew what was going to happen when the bill hit MI5's accounts department, but he couldn't think about that now. He had to get to Jenny.

'No problem. Unless God has other plans, of course.'

He had to pray God was on his side. If he wasn't there for the birth, he couldn't even start to imagine what sort of trouble he'd be in.

Promise you'll be with me when I have this baby.

If everything went smoothly he could be at Bath's Royal United Hospital in just over four hours. Too long!

He could picture Jenny's face as she held their son in her arms for the first time and he wasn't there. Happy on the one hand, devastated on the other. *What decent father misses his son's birth?* He shouldn't have come to Germany. He should have been there, grabbing her hospital bag, taking it to the car, driving her to the maternity unit, dropping Aimee at a neighbour – an arrangement organised months ago – on the way.

She'll never forgive me if I'm not there.

'So, what are your thoughts?' Didrika prompted him into a conversation about where the investigation might go now, but he was tense and distracted, finding it hard to concentrate.

She'll never talk to me again.

Didrika slowed at the traffic queue warning ahead. The speed limit on the highway had been reduced to sixty kilometres per hour.

'It will still be quicker on the highway,' she assured him.

He checked his watch again. Tried to concentrate on what she was saying about euthanasia and the intensity of emotions it created.

'I wonder if your father's friend, Rafe – *Scheisse!*'

They'd rounded the bend to find the traffic at a standstill. In the distance, he could see blue flashing lights.

'An accident,' stated Dan. His tone was calm but his blood pressure began to rise.

'I will take another route.' She glanced across at him. 'I'm sorry I can't use my blue light. It's against the law.'

'I wouldn't want you to,' he lied.

It seemed to take an age to crawl to the next exit, and as soon as they were clear, she put her foot down, barrelling along a minor road. Her hands were relaxed on the wheel but her expression was intense. She'd stopped talking and was concentrating on the road.

'We'll make it,' she told him.

'OK.'

The road was narrow, winding cross country. Lots of twists and turns.

Just get me there, please God.

He kept quiet but his thoughts were leaping ahead. The next flight via France wouldn't get him into the UK until past midnight, and thence to the hospital around three in the morning, by which time Jenny would have already had the baby. If it was Jenny's first birth, things might be different, but apparently second and third babies could come really fast. He'd read stories of third and fourth babies shooting out like rockets in an hour. He tried to cling onto the fact that nothing was set in stone, and that they knew of one mother who'd said her third child took seven hours.

He saw Didrika risk a glance at her watch. 'We still have time,' she said determinedly.

Dan was doing the calculations. Thirty seconds to run to the check-in desk, a minute to check in, ten minutes to clear passport control, ten for baggage, five to run like hell for the gate . . .

He knew he was totally at fault. Although Jenny had told him to go to Germany, he'd taken her tolerance for the situation too far.

Why hadn't he been able to resist coming here? What was it with him? He hadn't needed to go. It hadn't been life-threatening.

Please God, just get me to the hospital on time and I'll never let her down again.

For five more minutes they bounded along the minor road and then they were at a junction and back on the highway, the traffic light, travelling smoothly, but he couldn't relax. They still had to get around Hanover. Finally, they came to a junction with the highway from Braunschweig and Didrika indicated right, pulling off to do a clockwise loop to head north-west to the airport.

'I'll drop you outside departures,' she told him. 'The British Airways check-in is to the left.'

He already knew this but didn't say so. He said, 'Thanks.'

As a precaution, he called for late-passenger instructions. He was told they couldn't help, sorry, and that the plane wouldn't wait for him. They only did that for passengers with a connecting flight at the other end. When he said he was trying to get to England for the birth of his son, the man on the phone said, 'Oh well, in that case we'll do everything we can.' He told Dan to go to the usual check-in desk where he'd be met by a member of staff who would accompany him through the queues to the aircraft. 'Good luck,' he added.

Didrika pushed on, the car bombing along in the outside lane. Half a mile or so ahead, he saw a passenger plane, wheels down, preparing to land.

They were nearly there.

Dan made sure his passport was easily reached, his ticket ready to be viewed on his phone.

'Scheisse!' Didrika cursed again.

Dan looked up to see overhead gantry's flashing white in warning.

'Another accident!' she exclaimed. 'I don't believe it!'

'No!'

He prayed it had already been cleared away. That the emergency services had already cleared it away and that the traffic would keep moving.

The traffic began slowing down. Eighty kilometres per hour. Sixty. Forty.

Please, don't stop.

As they cruised around a long corner the car ahead jammed on its brakes. Twenty kilometres per hour.

Please.

They came to the end of the bend and his heart plummeted. Ahead was a river of red tail lights, stationary traffic all the way to the horizon. Slowly, Didrika came to a halt. The next exit, for the airport, was another two miles.

In the distance, Dan heard a siren. He flipped down his sun visor to see blue flashing lights approaching.

'We're so *close*,' said Didrika. Frustration laced her tone.

But we may as well be a hundred miles away, thought Dan. If the emergency services were only just getting to the accident, they could be here for hours.

His stomach sank. He felt as though he'd swallowed a stone.

'We're not going to make it.'

CHAPTER FORTY-THREE

An ambulance raced past on the hard shoulder, hotly followed by two motorway patrol cars.

'Not going to make it?!' Didrika exclaimed. 'Yes, we fucking are!'

She leaned across and snapped open the glovebox. She pulled out a blue light. Set it flashing. Wound down her window and slapped it on the car roof. Began to inch her way into the left lane which was solid with traffic.

'You'll be disciplined,' Dan told her, but he didn't tell her to stop.

She didn't reply. She started pushing the snout of the Mondeo between an oil tanker and a VW sedan, blue light strobing. 'Come on,' she muttered, 'let me in, you bastards.'

The tanker crept forward a couple of yards but there still wasn't enough room.

Dan wound down his window and gestured at the driver of the VW sedan to go back.

The man put his car in reverse. The car behind sounded its horn – space was tight – but the VW had managed to create a narrow space for them to drive through. As soon as she'd straightened the wheels on the hard shoulder, Didrika accelerated after the ambulance.

18:55.

It didn't take long to get to the crash site. Maybe three minutes. A Citroën lay upside down across the hard shoulder and slow lane. A second car was crushed against the central reservation, the third behind it had a crumpled bonnet. Glass and bits of metal lay everywhere. The ambulance service team was already at work.

As soon as they appeared, an officer strode across. Didrika leaped outside. Started talking fast.

The cop gestured angrily behind us, obviously telling her to sod off and get back in the queue, but she persisted.

It didn't work. Things began to get heated.

Dan heard the traffic cop snarl something sarcastic, and just as he was wondering if he should get out and fall to his knees and start begging, his phone rang.

'Dan,' asked Jenny. 'Where are you?'

'You won't believe it, but I'm a hair's breadth from the airport and stuck in a traffic accident.'

'You're joking.'

'I wish I was.'

'We're on our way to the hospital.'

'I'll see you there,' he told her. 'As soon as I can, I promise.'

'OK.'

'I love you,' he said.

'Love you too.'

He twisted in his seat to see Didrika was on the phone, talking urgently. Then she passed her phone to the officer who spoke for a while, looking between Didrika and Dan. Then he handed Didrika's phone back. Things happened quickly after that.

Walking ahead, the traffic cop guided them between the wreckages and around the worst of the broken glass. As soon as they were clear, Didrika floored it. By the time she eased off, the needle rested on 185 kilometres per hour.

Gradually, traffic began to appear. Her blue light continued to strobe. She didn't take her foot off the accelerator until the traffic began to thicken, cars and lorries parting like shoals of fish to let them through.

It was 19:13 when the airport appeared.

Twelve minutes to go.

'Just jump out,' Didrika told him. 'Don't worry about shutting the door or anything. Run like hell.'

'One thing before I go,' he said. 'A favour.'

'Now you ask me?!' Her tone was disbelieving.

'A Mercedes has been following me.' He recited the number plate. 'Could you find out who it belongs to?'

'You . . .' She didn't finish her sentence. She was concentrating on accelerating for the terminal.

Dan kept his hand on the door handle as she slewed the car to the inside lane, heading for the terminal's automatic doors, slipping around a taxi and darting in front of a Mercedes. Dan began to open his door.

Didrika slid to an abrupt halt and he bolted outside.

'Good luck!' she yelled.

With his satchel slung across his chest, Dan sprinted into the terminal. Tore for the check-in desk. His flight was still lit up on the flight information board. *Final call.*

As he ran, heads turned to watch him go.

The check-in desk was twenty yards away when a man called, 'Mr Wilson!'

Dan swivelled round to see a man in Lufthansa uniform striding towards him, hand outstretched. Dan showed him his passport and ticket and the man said briskly, 'Follow me.'

As they strode out, he added, 'My name is Viktor. We have five minutes before the gate closes. We will make it in time, don't worry. They know you're coming.'

'Thank you,' Dan gasped.

'It is your first child?'

'Third.'

'Still,' Viktor smiled. 'It's an important event.'

'Very,' Dan agreed.

They bypassed the queue to immigration. Viktor passed Dan's passport to the officer, speaking rapidly, obviously filling him in. The immigration officer took Dan's passport. Slid it out of sight. The man's head was bowed as he tapped on a keyboard Dan could hear but not see.

The seconds ticked past.

'Gibt es eien problem?' Viktor asked.

'Gib mir nur eine minute,' the officer replied.

'He'll just be a minute,' Viktor said to Dan, but Dan didn't like the sudden anxiety that rose in Viktor's eyes.

Even though he kept his breathing level, he could feel the sweat beginning to form at the base of his spine. He had to hope there was none on his forehead.

He looked at his watch then at Viktor, but Viktor had moved away a little and was looking anxiously ahead, then back, as though he could will the officer to return Dan's passport.

Footsteps sounded behind them but before he could turn his head to see who approached, the immigration officer finally lifted his eyes. They were stone cold and devoid of emotion.

'I'm sorry,' he said, 'but there is a problem with your passport.'

Two Bundespolizei stepped into view and took up position on either side of Dan. He had no choice but to go with them.

CHAPTER FORTY-FOUR

Dan spent the night in a cell, in the detention centre. His shoes and his belt had been taken from him, and he'd been given a rough blanket to sleep beneath along with a hard, square pillow. They'd taken his satchel and phone from him straightaway while he was still at the immigration desk. Viktor had looked appalled as Dan was carted off by the two guards, but he hadn't intervened.

The interviews had been relentless. Same questions, over and over again. How long had he been planning his trip? How much money did he have for his trip? Whose idea was the trip? First time abroad? How much did he earn? Dan didn't want to give MI5 away since they'd provided him with the passport earlier in the year, so he didn't say much. He knew all the interview techniques and watched them being trotted out with vague interest. He wondered how long they'd keep him for. The German Immigration authority was the Bundespolizei, uniformed Police with the same ranks as the State Police Agencies.

Due to his refusal to cooperate, he'd eventually met the top dog, a small man with unnervingly wet and bulging eyes. Chief Inspector Richter. Dan said everything would be explained if he could be allowed one phone call, which was repeatedly refused.

He'd been in his cell all morning, listening to doors slamming, bolts clanking shut. Women and men sobbed and shouted. They couldn't keep him here another night, surely? Jenny would be going insane with worry. She'd probably think he was dead. Killed in a traffic accident. He couldn't think how she'd forgive him for missing his son's birth. He just hoped that everything had gone all right, that the boy and Jenny were doing OK and that there hadn't been any complications.

He did a set of press-ups before he returned to pacing his six-by-eight cell. He thought over everything he'd experienced since he'd learned that his father had been murdered. That someone in the security services was watching him, off the grid. That they had access to one of the most frightening people he knew: Sirius Thiele. That his father had visited a cemetery in Isterberg. That he'd rowed with Anneke. That his close friend, Rafe, had asked him to help him die.

Since they'd also taken his watch, he only had a rough idea what time it was and guessed it had to be mid-afternoon or so. He tried not to be angry with himself for being so impetuous, so *stupid* as to use a false passport – it was a waste of mental energy, he was where he was – but it was almost impossible. He shouldn't have been tempted. He should have left the damned thing at home and stayed with Jenny. Should, should, *should*. When would he learn?

He paused his pacing when the bolt outside drew back with a resounding clang.

'Come.'

Dan followed the guard to a large, rectangular room. There was a glass panel in one of the walls. Another interview room. He sat on one of the chairs and waited. Soon an immigration officer arrived, a file in one hand, Dan's passport – or rather Michael Wilson's – in the other.

More questions. Who was he really? Why had he used a false passport? What was his intention? What sort of criminal was he? People smuggler? Drug trafficker? Was he a terrorist? Was he even English?

Dan simply repeated his mantra. 'Everything will become clear when you let me make one phone call.'

'Who is that to?'

'My lawyer,' Dan lied. He had no intention of calling for legal representation, but since he knew his best chance of being allowed a phone call was by doing so, he stuck with it.

'Not your wife or your employer? What is it you do, could you remind me?'

'One phone call,' Dan repeated.

The officer halted the interview for a few seconds to review his notes. He looked up when the door opened. Chief Inspector Richter stepped inside and gave a nod to the interviewer. The interviewer stood up and Richter said to Dan, 'Come with me.'

He led the way to a small room which held nothing but an old-fashioned phone affixed to the wall.

'One phone call.'

Dan picked up the receiver and dialled. He knew he had to keep it short in case the phone was snatched from him. *Prioritise.*

When she answered, he said, 'Listen. Don't talk. I need you to do three things for me. First, ring Jenny at the Bath RUH and tell her I'm OK but detained. Second, call Philip at DCA & Co and tell him German Immigration have me in custody at Hanover Airport. Third, go and meet someone called Firecat at the Fiddichside Inn at six tonight. All are extremely—'

He ducked his head aside as Richter came close, reaching to cut off the conversation.

'Urgent!' he finished at the same time as the German slammed his fingers on the hook.

CHAPTER FORTY-FIVE

Lucy stood on top of Iron Ridge, gazing down at the Duncaid road snaking its way along the valley bottom as she replayed what Dan had said.

Sweet Jesus, he'd been lucky to get through. She hadn't had a signal all morning and it was only when she came into sight of Duncaid that she got connected again. She was walking the route Connor had supposedly taken the day he'd died, between Gordon's lodge and his house in the centre of Duncaid. Seven miles of heathland and rocks. The police had already walked it looking for clues, any signs of a scuffle, and apparently found nothing, but Lucy wanted to do it too. She was glad she'd borrowed Grace's sturdy walking boots along with her best, most expensive 3-in-1 waterproof jacket. She needed all the protective clothing she could get out here.

Quickly she googled the number for the RUH and dialled before the signal vanished. Her mind was spinning. What was going on that Dan was being held by German Immigration? Who was Firecat and where the hell was the Fiddichside Inn?

'Royal United Hospital,' a woman's bright voice answered her call.

'My name's Detective Constable Lucy Davies,' she said. 'I urgently need to speak to Jenny Forrester. She's either having or has had a baby.'

'Hold a moment . . . Ah, here she is. Post-natal Ward. Putting you through.'

Lucy spoke to two nurses before she finally got hold of Jenny. She started to shiver. She'd been baking hot climbing the ridge but now that she'd stopped her sweat was cooling and the wind cut against her face and wrists like cold knives, but she didn't dare to move. She didn't want to risk losing the signal.

'Lucy?'

Dan's wife sounded cautious.

'Dan asked me to ring you,' Lucy ploughed on. 'He's fine, OK? He's just been, er . . . detained.'

'Detained?' The woman's voice was faint.

'Yes.' She would have loved to have given Jenny more information but didn't dare without Dan's approval.

'He rang me yesterday,' Jenny told her. 'Not long after I called him to say I was on my way to hospital. He said he was caught up in a traffic accident—'

'No accident,' Lucy said firmly. 'He's fine.'

Another pause.

'Why doesn't he ring me himself?' Jenny asked. Her tone began to sharpen.

'He didn't say. I'm sorry.' Lucy found herself cringing. She'd kill Dan for this, she really would. *He* should be having this conversation with his wife, not someone standing on top of a bloody mountain in a freezing cold wind.

'Where is he?'

She took a breath and said, 'Sorry.' a second time.

'Where are you?'

'Actually, I'm on top of a mountain in Scotland. Investigating Connor's death.'

To try and prevent Jenny asking more questions, she said, 'How are you?'

Another short pause.

'I had to have a caesarean so I'll be here for another couple of days.'

'Oh, Jenny.' Lucy's concern was genuine. 'I am sorry.'

'But Mischa's doing fine.' The woman's voice lifted. 'He is seriously adorable but then I would say that, wouldn't I, being his mother and all.'

'I can't wait to meet him,' Lucy lied. She'd never been great with babies and always struggled to find something nice to say about them. She was never sure if that made her anti-motherhood or if she'd had the baby gene removed from her DNA. Her mum said she had been the same – she'd never liked other people's babies – but when Lucy came along she'd fallen in love straightaway.

'Give him a kiss from me,' Lucy added. 'And tell him I'll see him soon.'

'Thanks, Lucy.' Jenny's voice turned warm. 'Look, I know it's not easy being a go-between for Dan and me but I appreciate your call. Truly.'

Despite Jenny's words Lucy hung up still cringing, wishing Dan could do his own dirty work. She couldn't imagine how

Jenny was going to receive him when he eventually turned up. Personally, she'd throttle him, which she guessed Jenny would no doubt do.

She checked her signal to see it had gone from 4G to 3G. Flipping through her contacts she exhaled in relief when she saw she had Dan's business number, but when she rang Philip Denton it was to find he was out.

'Please get him to call me urgently,' Lucy told someone called Julia. 'Tell him it's to do with Dan Forrester.'

'Can I help? I'm looking after Dan's desk while he's away.'

'Sorry. I'll wait for Philip Denton to call me.'

'I'll make sure he gets the message.' Julia was brisk. 'In fact, I'll text him right now.'

Lucy googled the Fiddichside Inn but just as a picture of a low white building with a red trim appeared, the signal vanished and the page froze. She moved around the ridge top, holding her mobile high and low, but with no success. She looked at her watch. It was 3 p.m. No time to waste. She started walking fast, down the hill to Duncaid and hopefully to a signal as well as her car.

CHAPTER FORTY-SIX

Jenny Forrester walked back from the loo feeling tired and sore. She was finding it hard to rest on the busy post-natal ward, noisy with other babies and mothers. She'd pulled the curtains closed around her bed to try and get some privacy, but the noise continued non-stop. She couldn't wait to get home, get some proper sleep and start recovering properly.

She wasn't sure how she felt about Lucy ringing with a message from Dan. Part of her was relieved to know he was, apparently, OK, but the other part was upset, so goddamn *angry* she felt as though her blood pressure would burst. She'd thought he'd changed. She really had. But no, he was the same old Dan beneath it all. Give him a mission, a venture, any escapade, and he was off quicker than you could say 'Booking.com'.

Yes, he'd been in Germany. Yes, she'd agreed to the trip. Yes, he'd responded immediately when she'd called him, saying *I'm on my way*, but he hadn't got to her and she still had no idea where he was, Germany or the UK.

She loved Dan, but right now she didn't like him one bit. Another woman might be tempted to give him his marching orders but she could no more do that than cut out her own heart. She had to think positively, but how? She felt poleaxed by being abandoned to have Mischa on her own. Her mother had been with her but she hadn't wanted her mum, she'd wanted her husband.

Worry gnawed at her, making her restless and irritable. She wished he was here to see his son. She wanted him to hold Mischa, watch his expression as he gazed at his little boy. She suddenly felt like weeping. *Oh, Dan*, she thought. *How could you do this to me? To us?*

She pulled back the curtain, her gaze going automatically to the cot next to her bed where Mischa lay sleeping.

Her heart leaped to her throat.

The cot was empty.

She dived to the cot and flung the blankets back. No Mischa.

Her gaze flew around the curtained area. Nothing. No baby.

Pulse pounding, she yanked back the curtains. A nurse must have taken Mischa for some tests. Blood tests, hearing and heart screenings all needed to be done. Why hadn't they told her? Where was he?

She began to move along the ward, her head switching from side to side, searching for Mischa, a maternity support worker, a midwife, anybody who might know where her baby was. She felt a scream bubbling in her throat, a primal scream of fear and panic, but she quelled it, telling herself not to be so stupid, that her baby was fine and he'd be back any second.

At the other end of the ward she saw a man walking towards her with a baby in his arms. Despite the central heating belting out through the ward, he wore a double-breasted camel coat and leather gloves. Clean shaven, his shoes highly polished, he looked like a city businessman. He was looking right at her.

She stared. She didn't dare move. Was he holding Mischa?

As though he'd heard her thoughts, he nodded.

Her mouth turned as dry as sand.

She began to walk towards him. Her brain seemed to have frozen. She didn't recognise the man. Who was he? What was he doing with her son?

As she approached the man dropped his arms to show Mischa, wide awake and gazing at her with his huge blue eyes. She gave a little whimper. She held out her arms to take him but the man moved aside, saying, 'A little privacy, I think.'

He walked to her bed and, holding Mischa against his chest with one hand, he pulled the curtains around them with the other.

'Give him to me,' she demanded.

'No.'

She opened her mouth to scream for help but in one swift movement he brought Mischa high into the air, holding him upside down by his ankles. The baby blanket drifted to the floor.

'Don't, or I will drop him.'

Mischa gurgled, began to make a choking sound.

'No, please don't . . .'

'Listen to me,' he said. He didn't relax his grip on Mischa, whose face started to turn a dark pink.

'Please, the blood's going to his . . .'

'Listen.'

He may as well have slapped her. Her whole body flinched at his voice, laden with menace.

'Or this little boy will find himself with a crushed skull.'

A wave of cold nausea crashed over her. This couldn't be happening. Who was this man? What did he want?

'OK, OK.' She put her hands up. She was trembling violently. 'I'll listen.'

The man immediately brought Mischa upright to hold him against his chest, but his eyes never left Jenny's: twin shiny, glassy black marbles.

'I want you to tell your husband my name. Sirius. Then tell him to stop what he's doing in Germany.' His voice was quiet but even through the sound of crying babies and women's chatter she could hear every word. 'I want you to tell him to come home and stay at home, or one day he won't have a baby boy to come home to.'

'Whatever Dan's doing, it's nothing to do with me,' she said desperately. *'Nothing!'* The word came out on a half-sob.

'I wouldn't be here if he'd heeded my first warning.'

'P-please,' she begged. 'Give me my baby back.'

'He is to stop what he's doing. Do you understand?'

A whistling started in her ears. This was Dan's fault. Dan had brought this man to her and her baby. He'd put them in danger. She suddenly felt a wave of heat roar through her, the hot dry wind of sheer rage, and with no plan, acting on nothing but fear and anger she launched herself at the man.

She didn't think she saw him move. One second she was flying towards him, fingers hooked and reaching for his ghastly dead eyes, the next she was rammed against the wall with both arms twisted behind her and held high between her shoulder blades, so high she thought they might dislocate.

She was gasping, choking against the pain.

'I understand you're frightened,' he whispered into her ear. 'But I promise I won't hurt you or your baby if your husband does as I say.'

Her cheek was pressed into plasterboard and she rolled her eyes to see Mischa on the bed, fists and feet kicking. He started to cry.

'Do you understand?'

She nodded.

'Say it.'

'I understand,' she gasped.

'Good.'

He dropped her hands and as she began to turn around, he said, 'Don't.'

Jenny paused, her eyes fixed on Mischa, his sounds of distress, but her senses were also on the man and the second he vanished through the curtain she leaped for her son, pulled him against her breast. She was crying, sobbing with relief as she wrenched back the curtain.

The man was already at the end of the ward, moving swiftly. He'd be out of sight any second. Jenny took a huge breath and holding Mischa in one arm she pointed with the other, yelling, 'That man in the coat! The fawn coat! He just tried to steal my baby!'

CHAPTER FORTY-SEVEN

Lucy was halfway down the hillside when to her relief the signal kicked in again and the details of the Fiddichside Inn reappeared. No website, just a couple of photos and a dozen reviews. Thank God it was in the next village, Craigellachie, and not on the other side of the Cairngorms. She didn't want to let Dan down.

Firecat. It sounded like a code name. Would she be meeting a spook? An informant? A friend or a foe? Maybe they were a covert environmentalist, a greenie. When she'd gone back to Duncaid School she'd asked whether the kids supported any kind of environmentalism and met with Connor's art and design teacher, Lucas Finch. Dark hair, slightly tousled, topped a narrow intelligent face.

'I took Connor to a protest rally, if that helps,' he told her. 'Climbing the Scott Monument in Edinburgh.'

Lucy blinked. 'Is that legal?'

'No.' He grinned, unabashed. She'd bet he wouldn't look quite so smug if he knew he was talking to a police officer.

'I think I caught something about it on the radio,' she responded, carefully neutral. 'Wasn't it something to do with saving the Arctic?'

'Yes.'

'You were there as a protester?' Lucy was doing her best not to let her disapproval show, but it leaked through. She'd been policing a protest rally against fracking in North Yorkshire last November and had a can of soup thrown at her. She'd ended up in hospital with a cracked skull.

'Yes.' His amusement seemed to grow but she refused to let it bug her.

'Was Connor protesting too?'

'No.' Finch shook his head. 'His father's into GM and since he's a loyal kid . . .' He shrugged.

'Why did you take him with you?'

'I was introducing him to the power of the media. He was doing a project on advertising and I wanted to show him how a big event like that grabs headlines.'

When Lucy checked Lucas Finch out it was to find he'd been arrested several times for a variety of protest stunts, but although she couldn't think how he might be involved in Connor's murder she didn't want to drop the greenie or GM angle just yet.

It was only after she bypassed a small rock fall that she realised Duncaid's clock tower was over her right shoulder. She hoped the path would double back soon, or she'd end up on the wrong side of town. Wasn't she supposed to have come across a bothy of some sort? As she rounded a corner she was met with a rock face. She was definitely not on the right path.

She pulled out her map, had a look. Studied Duncaid. It was only walking the trails that she'd come to realise how easy it was to get lost, and she was thankful the weather was clear or she could well be in trouble. Was that what had happened to Connor? The weather had been appalling when he'd done the same journey, rain and fog, virtually no visibility. Plus, he was angry and probably hadn't been concentrating on where he was going.

Lucy tried to imagine what Connor would have done if he'd come to the same point as her.

Head downhill. Find a stream and follow it to some kind of habitation. Which would, she realised, bring him to the east side of town and near the Blackwater Industrial Estate. Or had he cycled down the hill and into town as normal? However, nobody had seen him. Had he been snatched off the hill? If so, why? Every instinct told her he'd been murdered near a lab of some sort where any tame chemist could make phenol. *It's easy.*

He'd witnessed something, she was sure of it. She just had to find out what.

The path steepened, forcing her to edge sideways, and when her phone rang she hurriedly wedged a boot against a flat-topped rock to stabilise herself and whipped it out of her jacket, hoping it was Philip Denton, but instead the screen told her CALLER UNKNOWN.

'Hello?' she answered.

'Lucy?'

Just one word filled with panic and tears. All the hairs on Lucy's body rose. She'd heard that tone often enough in her job to recognise something was very wrong.

'What is it?'

'A man j-just' – Jenny's voice quavered – 'threatened my baby. He told me to tell D-Dan to stop what he's doing in Germany or ... or he'd ...' She desperately tried to contain her tears. 'H-hurt Mischa. C-can you get hold of him? He's not answering his phone. I've left several messages ...'

'I'll certainly try. Can you tell me exactly what happened?'

When Jenny described the man – camel coat, long pale face, dark eyes – Lucy felt a wave of horror drench her.

'I screamed for help, b-but he vanished. The police came but h-haven't been able to do anything. They w-want to talk to Dan but in the m-meantime, they've moved me to a private room and p-put an officer outside.'

'Did the man give a name?'

'Sirius. No surname.'

Lucy knew her blood pressure was in freefall and she hurriedly sat on the rock and bent over, her head between her knees. Sirius. The man who Lucy had tried to arrest and who had tasered her before handcuffing her and Grace to a radiator pipe last year. A professional assassin, he was well known throughout the security services and was wanted for murder in several countries. Lucy hadn't heard anything of him since that incident.

'The p-police know him,' Jenny added. 'He's wanted for GBH, kidnapping, k-killing ... you name it ...'

Lucy raised her head. Took several gulps of fresh air to try and steady herself. What the hell had Dan got them into? Even though Jenny said she had a cop with her, was that enough to protect her from Sirius?

She said, 'You need to go somewhere safe, where this man can't find you.'

There was a small pause.

When Jenny spoke, her voice was quite calm. 'No,' she said. 'I won't go into hiding again. If Sirius comes to me a second time and harms me and Mischa, then on Dan's head be it.'

Without another word, she hung up.

Fuck, fuck, *fuck*. Lucy was sweating but she felt cold.

Sirius fucking Thiele was back in their lives.

FUCK.

She squeezed her eyes hard together before opening them again and fixing her gaze on a spray of autumn-brown heather by her boot. What to do now? Her mind careened along various avenues at dizzying speed, tongues of green and yellow flickering as it picked up thoughts, discarded them and picked them up once more.

She decided she would meet Firecat and then she'd head south and, whether Jenny liked it or not, she'd stay with her and try to protect her until Dan returned.

But first, she had to warn Grace.

CHAPTER FORTY-EIGHT

Grace had tried to persuade Alistair Tavey to go to hospital, but he wouldn't have it.

He'd rolled his head to look at the sweeping moorland outside his bedroom window and said, 'I'm staying here.'

He'd died eighteen hours later.

Now Grace was driving along the rutted track to the Taveys, and when her phone rang she lifted it off the passenger seat and answered it. No police out here to bust her.

'Pull over,' Lucy told her. 'Handbrake on.'

'I'm fine. I'm on a private road. There's no traffic for miles. Just the odd rabbit or two.'

'I want you to pull over.'

Lucy's voice was tense. Grace felt the first inkling of something wrong. 'What is it?'

'Is your handbrake on yet?'

'OK, OK,' Grace grumbled and shoved her foot on the brake, flipped her gear stick into neutral and pulled on the handbrake. 'Do you want me to turn the engine off too?'

'No. That's OK.'

She heard Lucy take a deep breath.

'Jesus, Lucy, what is it?'

'I'm not sure how to tell you this . . .'

Alarm speared her. 'It's not Ross, is it?'

'No, not Ross. Sorry. It's just that Dan's wife Jenny has just been threatened. And the man who threatened her told her his name was Sirius.'

Grace felt the world tilt on its axis.

Her gaze was fixed on a grassy tussock but she wasn't seeing it. She was seeing Sirius Thiele's face last year, as he held her wrist in his hands, threatening to snap it in two. The man who had no hesitation in abducting, torturing and killing people. It didn't matter if they were women or children. She remembered him turning up after her mother's funeral saying he was a debt collector and demanding money her mother supposedly owed his client. She had no idea what he'd been talking about but it hadn't mattered. He'd threatened her until she was forced to do as he asked and after she'd found the money he'd thanked her as politely as any guest at a tea party.

'Hello?' Lucy's voice squawked. 'Grace, are you still there?'

'Yes.' Her voice was hoarse.

'I'm sorry, but I thought you had to know.'

'Yes.'

Grace listened as Lucy told her what had happened to Jenny and her newborn baby. Her mouth tasted bitter. She'd hoped she'd never hear that name again and now here he was, back in their lives.

'Where are you?' asked Grace.

'Still on the hillside.'

When Lucy said she was going to stay with Jenny after meeting a contact of Dan's, Grace swallowed her instinctive protests. She wanted Lucy with her, not heading off down south. She hung up feeling vulnerable and scared until she remembered that Ross had some guns. A rifle, a couple of shotguns. Would they be enough against someone like Sirius Thiele? Probably not, but they might give them a fighting chance.

Hands trembling, Grace put the car back into gear and stalled. *Do not let the memory of that man get to you*, she told herself. *Don't let him win.*

When she reached the bothy, it was to see the ambulance had already arrived. Grace let herself inside to find Alistair's twenty-year-old daughter sitting on the stairs. 'I'm so sorry, Sorcha.'

The young woman's expression was blank. 'Who are you?'

'Dr Reavey. I saw your dad yesterday.'

'Dad?' She frowned, obviously puzzled.

Grace put her confusion down to shock and made her way up the stairs. After commiserating with Disa, she checked Alistair's body. Despite being a tough, fit man of sixty-one, he'd died of pneumonia. A death by natural causes. But she still took two blood samples.

As she went back down the stairs, Sorcha looked up at her. 'Who are you? What are you doing here?'

Deeply disquieted, Grace decided she couldn't let it go. She took a blood sample from Sorcha as well. Back at the surgery, Grace carefully wrapped the test tubes in bubble wrap and sealed them in a Ziploc bag. By the time she'd called Ben at Barts and addressed the box, the FedEx courier was on the doorstep, hand outstretched.

CHAPTER FORTY-NINE

Lucy washed her boots clean in the shallows of the river Lomhar before heading through the Blackwater Industrial Estate and the main road that would take her into the centre of Duncaid and to her car, which Ross had kindly driven to Grace's surgery earlier.

As she clambered up the bank, she took in the van parked outside the Green Test Lab. Black, no decals, double rear doors. It looked like a mortuary van – she'd seen enough in her job – but if she remembered correctly, the funeral directors were on the other side of the auto-electrical workshop. What was it doing here?

She went and had a quick look but couldn't see inside thanks to the tinted windows. Since the van was the only sign of human interaction with the Green Test Lab that she'd witnessed, she texted Mac the number plate asking who owned it. If it belonged to the funeral directors, she'd nip around later and have a chat.

Checking her watch, she saw she had just enough time to duck back to Lone Pine Farm to change and collect her things before meeting Firecat. Afterwards, she'd drive to Jenny. She didn't mind a night drive when the motorways were quiet. And maybe when Dan was back, she might zip down the M4 to London and see her mum.

Inside her car, she had just buckled her seat belt when her phone rang.

'Hello?'

'It's Philip Denton.'

His voice was clipped and brisk. Lucy tempered her tone to match his.

'Dan Forrester called me at twelve twenty-five,' she told him. 'He asked me to tell you that German Immigration has him in custody at Hanover Airport.'

'What else?'

She told him she'd called Jenny to tell her Dan was OK. She didn't know whether to mention Sirius or not, let alone that she was meeting someone called Firecat. Dan was obsessively secretive and from her dealings with him he usually had good reason so she held her tongue. Jenny was under police protection after all, and Dan could fill Philip Denton in when he spoke to him.

'That's it?'

'Yes,' she lied.

'Thank you,' Denton said.

After picking up her stuff and changing out of her walking gear, she drove to Craigellachie. She used google maps to help direct her, her mind spinning cartwheels of colour as it tried to assimilate everything that was going on. Dan investigating his father's murder, now in custody in Germany. Sirius threatening Jenny and her baby. Connor's death . . .

She was so absorbed in her thoughts she didn't realise the vehicle ahead of the car in front of her had stopped to turn right and she had to slam on her brakes. The lorry behind her sounded its horn at her sudden stop and she hurriedly wound down her window and waved an apology.

Jesus, she had to stop reflecting on things when she was driving. Trouble was, she'd found it was one of the best places to think. No more, she must concentrate when she was behind the wheel.

The road wound around the bottom of the village, the majestic river Spey on the left, pretty stone cottages rising up the hill on the right. As she came around another corner, she saw the inn on the other side of a narrow bridge. *Cute*, she thought, taking in the whitewashed walls and dorma windows perched like eyebrows in the slate roof. Really cute.

The car park at the rear of the building was empty, so she parked at the far end, nose in to the grassy bank, leaving lots of space for other customers. She zipped up her fleece as she walked round to the front door. The temperature was dropping fast; it would be cold tonight.

She pushed open the door into the smallest bar she'd ever seen. Six people and the place would be full. As it was, there were two customers warming themselves by the open fire. Both of them looked at her curiously, as though she'd just stumbled into their living room.

'Evening,' she said.

Both men nodded and raised their glasses. 'Hello, there.'

Lucy looked at the handwritten list of drinks and their prices on the wall, the photographs of huge salmon caught in times past, and even though she was on edge, waiting for a sign that one of these two men could be Firecat, she felt the history seep from the walls and relaxed slightly.

A man with a mane of white hair appeared behind the bar. 'What can I get you?' he asked, at least that's what she thought he said but his accent was so strong she wouldn't have bet on it.

'Half a pint of McEwan's, please.' With the dozens of Scotch and beer bottles on display, she didn't think he'd take too kindly if she asked for water.

'You a walker?' he asked. 'We get a lot of walkers here, doing the Spey Way.'

'Sort of,' she responded. 'I walked from Glenallen Lodge to Duncaid today. I drove the rest.'

'You know the Bairds?'

'Yes.'

'Nice lodge they've got,' one of the men said behind her opening up the conversation and, realising it was one of those pubs where you went to socialise, she moved over to talk to them.

Plum on six o'clock the door banged and another customer hoved into view. Broken veins splayed over a pasty face. Fleshy lips, thinning hair. He wore fawn trousers and a checked country-style shirt beneath a windbreaker jacket.

'Jo,' he said.

'Murray. Usual?'

'Ta.'

Lucy watched Murray's eyes flick over the two men and her, then to the door and back to Jo, who dispensed a dram of Macallan and pushed the glass over. She felt Murray's eyes studying her as she sipped her beer. Although she appeared absorbed in what the men by the fire were saying, she was intent on Murray.

'Anyone else been in tonight?' Murray asked Jo.

'Just Dougie.'

'But he disnae drink.'

Jo shrugged and at the same moment she took in the sign behind the bar. *Service may vary according to my mood and your attitude.*

She began to like Jo.

'Nobody else?' Murray insisted.

Jo gave him a steady look that said, *I've already answered you once*, and Murray muttered, 'sorry,' but he kept glancing at the door as though expecting someone to walk inside.

Eventually, Murray tipped the remainder of his drink down his throat. 'Another, please, Jo.'

Lucy sipped her beer slowly. Continued to talk to the two men. Watched Murray as he ordered and drank two more whiskies. Finally, he said, 'Bugger it. They're not fucking turning up.' And left.

Making her apologies, Lucy put her glass on the table and hurried after him. She caught him up just as he beeped open his car, a tatty old Rover, and he turned, surprised.

'Firecat,' she said.

He stared at her. 'What?'

'You're Firecat.'

'What the fuck is this?'

'You're supposed to be meeting someone else but they can't make it. I'm here in their stead.'

He took a step back. 'Why can't he make it?'

'He didn't say. But he told me that meeting you was incredibly important, that he didn't want to miss it, and that I had to be here instead.'

'Fucksake.' He ran a hand over his face. 'I've got a fucking story to tell that's worth a fortune and he sends me a pint-sized fucking emissary instead.'

'What story?'

His eyes turned cunning. 'Give me the fifty grand and I'll tell you.'

'I don't know anything about fifty grand,' she said carefully.

'Why am I not surprised?' He flung up his hands. 'What a waste of a fucking journey.'

'Hey,' she said, putting out a hand. 'Wait a moment—'

He slapped her hand away. 'Fuck off. Get the big man to meet me himself next time, OK?'

The temptation to whip out her warrant card and scare the crap out of him for drink driving nearly crippled her. She forced herself to take several deep breaths to steady herself as she watched him climb into his shitty heap of a car. He gave her the finger as he left. Unbelievable. *What a misogynistic shitbag.*

The second he was out of view, she pelted for her Corsa, wishing she'd parked closer, wanting to follow him, but as she tore around the rear of her car a dark shape suddenly reared up out of the dark and wrapped its arms around her. A man. He wore gloves and a balaclava.

She opened her mouth to shout, scream for help, but there was no time.

The man slammed his forehead straight into her face.

She felt her nose break as the world exploded into white light. Her limbs went numb. Warm liquid poured down her face and chin. Choking she tried to call out but he leaned forward and punched her hard in the stomach. All the air rushed out of her lungs.

Disabled, gasping for breath, she was helpless when he grabbed her hands and yanked them behind her back. She tried to fight but she had no breath and her efforts were pitiful against his brute strength. He dragged her to a car. When she saw its boot was open panic flooded her, giving her a surge of strength. She gave a violent buck and felt his grip slip but then something slammed into the side of her head. This time there was no white light. Just black.

CHAPTER FIFTY

A junior Bundespolizei officer showed Dan into Chief Inspector Richter's office where Philip Denton was handing Richter some paperwork. Philip was almost obsequious in his apologies. Although the German was polite, Dan could tell the man was furious by the pinched skin around his eyes and mouth.

'*Sie haben nichts getan, aber unsere Zeit vershwendet.*' You've done nothing but waste our time.

Philip responded calmly. 'If I can help you or your team with anything in the future, please call me directly.' He handed Richter one of the cards that Dan knew Philip used only rarely and which held two mobile numbers.

'Thank you.' The German must have realised the importance of what he held because he looked surprised, and pleased.

'Quid pro quo.'

'Thank you,' Richter said again, nodding. He didn't delay releasing Dan any further. That was how Philip's world worked. Someone did you a favour and you reciprocated even if it took years. Personal obligations were worth more than gold in his business.

As they walked outside, Philip said, 'I thought you should know that after lending you my car, I went and visited little Joanna Loxton to see what was going on. I arrived at her flat at eleven on Sunday morning, but instead of a cosy, domestic scene I was faced with a cold and empty flat.'

'They've moved out?'

'On Saturday, a neighbour told me. Lock, stock, and barrel.'

'Where to?'

'No idea. They didn't leave a forwarding address either.'

Joanna Loxton was running scared and Dan wasn't surprised with a hired assassin like Sirius Thiele being on the scene.

At the airport, when their flight was called, Dan looked at his boss. 'Thanks.'

Philip stood and looked him in the eye. 'You owe me, Dan.'

'I know.'

'Remember this when I call upon you.'

'I will.'

CHAPTER FIFTY-ONE

Lucy came to in the back of the car. The blood from her nose was running down the back of her throat. It felt like she was drowning. Shuffling on to her side, she coughed trying to clear her airways. Her sinuses were scorching with pain. She couldn't breathe through her nose at all.

The car was lurching from side to side. They were on a rough track of some sort. Not a road.

How long had she been unconscious for?

She lay there gasping, trying not to let her panic balloon out of control.

Your phone. Find your phone.

She searched her pockets but it had been taken, along with her car keys and handbag. She had nothing on her. Not even a tissue.

OK, she thought. *You've got to escape. You're in a car boot. There's a latch that'll pop it open. You just have to find it.*

In the pitch dark she started groping her fingers along the boot lid for the release cable. The car gave a couple of bounces and she groaned as her elbow and knee smacked into metal.

To her dismay the car started to slow.

Not yet, she begged. *I need more time.*

The car stopped. The engine was switched off.

She heard the driver's door open and as the sound of footsteps approached the rear of the car, she frantically wriggled around so her boots would be the first thing he saw.

Clunk.

Fresh, cold air poured over her. For a second it felt blissful against the red-hot fire burning inside her sinuses.

It was still light but barely. She guessed the sun had just set or thereabouts.

As the man bent down she lashed out with her boots. She connected with his hands and wrists but he appeared impervious. She was shouting, her voice broken and filled with blood, fighting with every muscle, but he was much stronger than she was.

'I'm a police officer,' she gasped. 'DC Lucy Davies. When I don't show up tonight, every police officer in Scotland will be looking for me. Let me go.'

It was as though she hadn't spoken.

He hauled her outside, plucking her clear of the boot as though she was nothing but a pillow.

Snapshot glimpses. Moorland all around. A handful of rotting farm buildings with weeds growing out of the windows.

The man started carting her across the dilapidated farmyard. She bucked and twisted violently, her chest pounding, nose agonising now, specks dancing in her eyes. She turned her head, trying to bite him, force him to drop her, but he simply raised a fist and clouted her behind the ear.

Pain detonated like a bomb through her head and sinuses. She heard herself emit a scream, and then her head was lolling, her mouth spilling saliva and blood.

She was only half aware he was lugging her away from the farmyard, his gait lurching across grass and clumps of heather.

She wanted to speak. She wanted to tell him that if he let her go she'd protect him from the police, but all that came out was a deep groan of pain.

And then he stopped. Rotated and looked down.

Eyes streaming, her breath clogged and panicky, Lucy looked too.

Edged with heather was a black hole about the width of a washing machine. She couldn't see the bottom. It was too dark.

Fuck, no.

And then the man was shoving her downwards, obviously intending to push her inside the hole.

'NO!' she screamed.

She struggled, fought with all her might against his bulk of solid muscle, but she was too small and already enfeebled by pain. She tried to go for his eyes but he threw her downwards, forcing her into the hole.

She was screaming and gasping as she clutched at the heather, desperately thrashing at the empty air above the hole, and then he brought back his boot and before she could duck, belted her on the forehead.

A flash of white light exploded behind her eyes and she plummeted downwards.

She landed ankle first – she felt it give, then a sharp stab of pain – and folded to the ground onto her knees and elbows, dizzy, blinded.

Her vision turned cloudy. She must have passed out for a second or two.

She was conscious of a bulging pain in her skull and she couldn't help it, she retched. She heard herself moaning. She wanted nothing more than to curl up and lose consciousness, make it all go away, but she forced herself upright. Looked up to see the fading sky. Nothing else.

'Wait!' she shouted. Her voice was congested but her words were clear enough. 'Please! Just tell the police where I am! I won't tell anyone about you, I promise!'

Her words were swallowed by damp walls and moss, barely lifting above the heather-rimmed hole.

'Please!' she yelled.

She heard an engine start up in the distance.

This can't be happening. Please God make him come back, please.

Blood in her mouth, weak with terror, Lucy stood and listened to the engine disappearing until it had gone altogether.

CHAPTER FIFTY-TWO

By the time Dan got to the hospital it was past visiting time but that didn't deter him. He strode through reception and along a corridor looking straight ahead and as though he knew where he was going. When he came to a ward he ducked back out of sight, waiting until the nurse behind her desk moved away, at which point he stepped forward. Scanned the desk. Picked up a pen and clipboard, removed the papers from the clipboard and left them behind.

Nobody looked at him twice as he sped through the hospital. Finally, he was in the post-natal ward. Rooms with between four and six beds were on either side of the corridor. Fortunately, the occupants of each room were listed on a tab outside by the door.

Women talked quietly, and he could hear a baby mewling, the sound of a TV, but otherwise it was peaceful.

He strode on but didn't see Jenny's name. Anxiety building, he rounded the corner. When he saw a uniformed police officer sitting outside what he took to be a private room, he paused. The constable rose swiftly to his feet, stance wary.

'I'm looking for Jenny Forrester,' Dan said.

'Sorry, mate. Can't help you.'

The cop tried to look insouciant but his eyes were sharp and were scanning Dan. Was he checking for weapons?

Dan was about to move off to find a nurse to help him when the door behind the cop opened.

'Dan,' Jenny said. 'I thought I heard your voice.' She looked at the police officer. 'It's OK. He's my husband.'

The cop still insisted on seeing Dan's ID, and only after calling in his visit to Control allowed them to head inside the room.

'What's happened?' Dan put down the clipboard.

She looked at him as though considering how to respond.

'Jenny . . .' he warned her.

'Don't you want to see your son?' She tilted her head at the cot beside the bed.

'Not until you tell me why there's a policeman outside your door.'

She continued to look at him.

'Please,' he added.

Still she looked at him. He wasn't sure what to do, so he moved to the cot and looked down. He blinked then looked at Jenny. 'Gosh, he's a good size.'

'Tell me about it.' Her voice was dry.

'Are you all right?'

'Caesarean. Mischa was bottom-down.'

'Mischa?' He'd thought they'd decided on the name Michael for their boy.

Her chin rose. 'It's a diminutive of Michael.'

'I like it.'

As he moved towards her, wanting to touch her, hold her, love her, she added in the same quiet voice, 'Oh, and someone called Sirius came and visited.'

It was as though he'd been tasered. His body went rigid from head to toe. Every cell was electrified.

'Sirius?' His voice was hoarse.

'Yes.'

'Where's Aimee?'

'With Mum and Dad.'

'What did he want?'

'He told me to tell you to stop what you were doing in Germany.' Her gaze was glued to her fingers.

'And?'

'Or you wouldn't have a son to come home to.'

It was as though an ice pick had buried itself in his stomach. He knew what Sirius was capable of. In certain circles he was known for being the least discriminating person anyone knew because if he wanted to kill or torture someone, it didn't matter if they were black or white or brown, male or female, a child, a baby or a grandparent. It made no difference. It was a job, and he did it.

'He means it, Dan.'

Her voice was calm but then he saw the tears filling her eyes. The fear on her face. He went to her and held her close. Rocked her gently. Let her weep against his chest.

His mind churned. How did Sirius Thiele know he'd gone to Germany? Had it been Michael Wilson's passport that had alerted someone somewhere? Or was it someone closer to home? After all, several people knew he'd visited Isterberg, including Anneke, Detective Superintendent Didrika Weber, the headmaster of Grundschule Isterberg and Viveka, the brauhaus waitress.

Who had told Sirius?

Gustav or Arne? Anneke or Sophie? The caretaker of the Isterberg Cemetery?

'We'll have to find you somewhere safe to stay,' he said, 'until this is over.'

At that, she jerked out of his embrace. Her eyes were blazing. 'Don't you dare.'

'How else are we going to keep you safe?' He was baffled.

'You stop doing,' she hissed, 'what you are fucking doing!'

'But I want to find who killed Dad.'

'Then find another way because I am *not* going to another bloody safe house *ever* again.' Her voice began to rise. 'I am going *home* with my *son* where I will remain safe and sound because YOU WILL FUCKING STOP WHAT YOU WERE DOING IN GERMANY.'

Silence.

'I mean it, Dan.' Her expression was fierce.

'OK.' He held up both hands in surrender but her face was still flushed, her fists clenched.

'Ma'am.' A man's voice broke between them. Dan looked around to see the policeman had stepped inside the room. 'Is everything all right?'

'I'm just leaving,' Dan told him. He looked at his wife. 'I'd kiss you,' he told her, 'but I don't think now is the right time.'

'Correct,' she snapped.

'He's beautiful. I adore him. I adore you.'

She glared at him.

'I will stop what I am doing,' he told her. 'I have stopped, OK?'

Her look of doubt was the biggest rebuke she could have given him.

'I promise,' he added and made a cross over his heart.

CHAPTER FIFTY-THREE

Mac had tried Lucy's phone several times that evening without success. He'd got her text earlier requesting a number plate check on what transpired to be a funeral director's van, and he was using that as an excuse to ring her when in reality he just wanted to hear her voice.

She hadn't called in very often, but then she never did unless he nagged and he hated nagging. It made him feel small and mean, and when she looked at him with those deep brown eyes of hers he invariably ended up going on the defensive, which then made him look like a bully. God, could he ever win?

He made himself some spag bol. It wasn't bad but it would probably taste better if he hadn't been eating alone. *Oh, get a grip*, he told himself. Or go online and find another girlfriend but for Christ's sake stop being so fucking miserable. He washed up the dishes and then on impulse rang Ross and Grace's landline.

'Hi, Mac.' Grace sounded surprised and he couldn't blame her. Why would Lucy's boss be ringing her at nine-thirty in the evening? He wished he'd met Grace, then he might have felt more comfortable talking to her. Knowing Grace was one of

Lucy's best friends didn't help. It simply made him feel ridiculously shy and tongue-tied.

'Hi, is Lucy there?'

'No, sorry. She's gone south. To Bath. She collected her things earlier.'

'Bath?' he repeated but inside he was shouting *What the fuck?!*

'I'll get her to ring you, shall I?'

'That would be great. I've left a message on her mobile but haven't heard back yet.'

'No problem. 'Bye.'

He hung up. *Bath?* What the hell was in Bath? Roman ruins, he knew, but not much more. *Come on, Lucy*, he thought. *Ring me. Fill me in, would you?*

He switched on the TV and turned the volume down low while he did some paperwork. When the BBC *Ten O'Clock News* came on he settled on the sofa to watch it, but his mind wouldn't settle and he knew it wouldn't until Lucy had called in. He checked his phone's volume was on max. No missed call, no text. He turned back to the TV, started to watch *Newsnight*.

Mac fell asleep half an hour later with his phone on his chest.

CHAPTER FIFTY-FOUR

Lucy was in darkness. She couldn't even see her hand in front of her face. All she could hear was her own wet breathing. Her broken nose was throbbing and sending pulses of pain through the centre of her head and behind her eyes. Breathing was agony. Everything was agony.

She'd already checked the well out. At least that's what she guessed it was. An old well, partially filled in, but not enough that she could climb out. She'd already tried, several times, but the walls were slippery and sheer with no foot or hand holds, and she simply slid back to the bottom at each attempt.

It had to be at least fifteen feet deep and she'd been lucky the bottom was covered in vegetation, clumps of broken heather and moss, or she'd have done more damage when she'd been pushed. As it was she'd just twisted her ankle. It was sore, hot to the touch and already swollen, but it was nothing compared to her face. She didn't think she'd ever been in such pain before, not even when that greenie had thrown the soup can at her.

She began to shiver in earnest. Jeans were rubbish at keeping you warm and she wished she'd never got changed. She would have killed for Grace's winter walking trousers and snug 3-in-1 fleecy jacket. At least she *was* shivering, because that was a response to preserve heat. The time to start worrying was when you stopped. She wasn't sure of the best way to stay warm, whether to keep hopping across the well on her good foot or huddle in the corner with her arms wrapped around herself. She ended up doing a mixture of both. She couldn't sleep. She couldn't stop wondering when anyone would realise she'd disappeared. Had they found her car outside the inn yet? Or had her kidnapper hidden it?

She hadn't seen anything about the man that might help identify him in future. Dark eyes glittering behind a black balaclava wasn't much to go on, nor was the man's strength and obvious experience in handling a struggling victim.

She looked up at her patch of sky to see a handful of stars. It would be a clear, cold night. How cold would it get in the well? It was sheltered from any wind, but she wasn't sure about surviving for long here. She was all too aware of the rule of threes.

Three minutes without air.

Three days without water.

Three weeks without food.

It was the water that worried her. She was already thirsty and wished she'd had water instead of beer earlier. Beer was dehydrating.

Was anyone looking for her yet? And what about Mac? She hadn't rung him in ages. He would have called her by now and when she didn't ring him back she was fairly sure he'd try to find out where she was. His interminable nagging about keeping in touch, *to keep you safe* was how he put it, was a good thing, she finally realised.

She tried not to let fear get the upper hand. She tried to keep the ropes of self-pity from strangling her. Stop the words *you are going to die here* from forming in her mind, or she'd collapse into a gibbering heap.

So she concentrated on Mac.

Pictured him when she'd last seen him in his office, frowning at his computer screen, expression intent.

Come on, Mac. I haven't rung you in ages. You know something's up. Come and find me, goddammit.

CHAPTER FIFTY-FIVE

Dan tried Lucy's phone again. Nothing. He didn't leave another message. He'd left two already. He wanted to know how her meeting with Firecat had gone but he'd have to wait. She'd call him back when she could.

After seeing Jenny, he'd called Philip Denton and told him about Sirius. 'He threatened my family. I want him called off. How can I do that?'

'You can't. Once he's undertaken a job he sees it through until the end. It would be my suggestion that you do as he tells you.'

'Does Bernard know how to get in touch with him?' If the Director General of MI5 couldn't track Sirius down, then the world may as well go to pot.

'He wouldn't go near Sirius with a barge-pole. And I wouldn't ask him, Dan. I don't think he'd be particularly impressed.'

Dan rubbed his forehead. 'He may not be particularly impressed that he's got a dirty pair of fingers in the firm's pie that's using Sirius.'

'You find who it is,' Philip said smoothly, 'or find a direct trail, then I'll contact Bernard and we'll do something about it.'

Dan hung up. He had to admit he hadn't expected anything more but he hadn't been able to resist trying. If Sirius couldn't be turned or stopped, then Dan had to drop his investigation into his father's murder to protect Jenny and the baby. Who was paying Sirius? He guessed it was the same person who'd got Joanna Loxton to follow him. Loxton was scared of him, Dan knew, but whoever had pulled her strings was scared too. Scared he might lean on Joanna Loxton and get her to confess who was behind all this.

Once home, he showered and went to bed. He lay in the dark, mulling over his trip to Germany. His father's visit to Isterberg Cemetery. The Mercedes following him and Didrika. Anneke's fight in the brauhaus with his father. He wanted to visit Rafe's old workplace in the morning, TSJ, and see if they knew anything about Project Snowbank, but he knew he shouldn't. With Jenny refusing to hide with the children until this was over, he really ought to go to work and come home at the end of each day.

Sirius was a critical problem. Until he was neutralised, his hands were tied. But even with Sirius out of the picture, wouldn't someone else replace him?

He slept fitfully without Jenny at his side. He missed her steady breathing, her scent, the way she always ended up on his side of the bed, arm over his waist, knees in the back of his, her head against his shoulder blades.

He was awake before dawn, trying to make a plan. He'd visit Rafe, he decided. Surely Sirius wouldn't see his visiting an old family friend on his deathbed like a threat?

After he'd finished his first cup of coffee he texted Jenny, told her he'd be there at eleven, when visiting hours started. She responded with three large emojis. One was of a baby, one a smiley face, the last a single red rose.

Relief flooded him. Thank God for that. He'd thought she might not speak to him for days, but it seemed she'd forgiven him. A bunch of muscles in his neck and shoulders that he hadn't realised were tense eased downwards.

Dan was on his second cup of coffee when Didrika Weber rang.

'I can't be long.' Her words came fast. 'I'm using a phone box. I shouldn't be talking to you.'

He didn't waste time asking questions, simply said, 'OK.'

'The Mercedes that you say has been following you . . .'

'Yes?'

'It belongs to Gustav Kraus.'

Gustav? It wasn't often he felt flummoxed but this was one of those times.

'Why shouldn't you be talking to me?'

'I've been warned off the case.'

His stomach turned over. 'Me too,' he said.

Silence while they considered things.

'Who?' he asked her.

'An officer from the Bundesnachrichtendienst.'

His stomach flipped again, a lurch of cold fright.

The BND for short, Germany's top-secret spy service, the Federal Intelligence Agency. Was it the BND who'd picked up the fact he was using Michael Wilson's passport? Or had they simply been tipped off by whoever was pulling the strings inside Britain's security services?

'Be careful,' Dan told her.

'I hate it.' Her voice was angry.

'I do too.'

Another pause.

'You know Gustav Kraus from your childhood,' Didrika said.

'Yes.'

'When I asked him why he was following you, he denied it.'

'Could someone have borrowed his car?' Dan suggested.

'He says not.'

Sophie could have driven it, Dan supposed, along with Anneke or Arne.

'I think Gustav lied to me,' she said. 'But, of course, I can't be sure. I'm sorry I have nothing more.'

'Thanks for letting me know.'

Unsettled, anxious, Dan called Rafe's hospice, asking if it was OK to visit him later in the day.

'I'll just check,' said the receptionist. 'I'm sorry to say he's been particularly poorly lately . . .'

Dan thought of Sophie's sorrow at her father's interminable death. *I find myself wishing he'd just die. Does that make me a terrible person?*

A nurse called John Adams came on the phone. 'I'm so sorry,' he said. 'You just missed him.'

For a moment, Dan wondered what he was talking about – had Rafe gone somewhere? – but then he realised the nurse meant he'd missed him because he'd died.

'When?' Dan asked, more for something to say than wanting to actually know the time of his death.

'Quarter past seven this morning. His daughter was with him. She flew in last night.'

'I'll call her in a moment.'

'My condolences.'

He rang Sophie but wasn't surprised when she didn't answer. He left a message saying how sorry he was and that he'd call her later, and please could she let him know when and where the funeral was to be because he'd like to be there.

He was itching to go to TarnStanleyJones, where Rafe used to work in their life science wing. He wanted to know what Project Snowbank was. He wanted to know what Firecat had had to say. He tried Lucy again. Left another message.

Dan spent the rest of the morning trying not to tear his hair out in frustration.

CHAPTER FIFTY-SIX

Lucy had managed to doze in fits and starts during the night and by the time she saw the light breaking across her little patch of sky, she felt physically and emotionally exhausted. She'd been in danger before, terrified for her life, but not at the same time as being damp, cold, and in pain.

She knew she had to keep her spirits up, but all she had to do was look at where she was for her mind to drift. She'd been unable to stop herself from screaming occasionally. Panic taking over and releasing itself the only way it knew how. She'd done a lot of thinking too. Who was the man who'd snatched her? He hadn't said a word. He'd waited for her in the car park. He'd let Murray go, but not her. Why?

She looked up at the sky belching with slate-coloured clouds. Would it rain later? Her mouth was horribly dry. She could kill for a glass, a litre, two litres of water. Somehow, she had to get out of here. Mentally, she squared her shoulders and gave herself a pep talk even though part of her felt it was hopeless. She spent the morning desperately trying to climb out. Every movement she made sent jagged flashes of pain through her head but she didn't stop.

She attempted to build a ramp with the debris at the bottom of the well, but it was soft and only raised her up a couple of feet. Her fingernails became scratched and torn from scrabbling at the stone walls.

She wondered if she'd been reported missing yet. She imagined Mac putting out an appeal for witnesses. *Has anyone seen the owner of this Corsa, a woman in her mid-twenties, last seen . . .*

The fear in her heart and lungs chilled to ice at her next thought. Who knew she was going to the Fiddichside Inn last night?

Dan, that was all. She'd never mentioned it to Grace, or to Jenny. And where was Dan? When they'd spoken he'd been in sodding custody in Germany.

She wasn't one to cry but right then she couldn't help it. She bawled like a panic-stricken baby abandoned by its parents. She knew that she'd been left to die here. That if and when her bones were eventually found, people would say she'd stumbled into the well by accident and that it should have been blocked off. The floor was littered with bones. Thankfully even she could see they were remains of animals. How long would it take her to die? If they did an autopsy on her, she wondered what they'd make of her broken nose.

After a while her sobs lessened. She leaned against the wall, breathing noisily through her mouth. Her face felt swollen to twice its normal size and her nose felt as though someone had poured acid into her sinuses.

Fuck it, she suddenly thought. She would *not die here*. She refused to give the bastard who put her here the satisfaction.

She double-checked the floor in case she could dig her way out. Solid rock. Every inch.

She studied the hole for what felt like the thousandth time, trying to work out how to get up there. Impossible.

'FUCK!' she screamed. Her hands were clenched by her sides. Tears streamed down her face. 'I DON'T WANT TO DIE!'

CHAPTER FIFTY-SEVEN

After he'd seen Jenny and Mischa, Dan tried Lucy for the umpteenth time. Still nothing, so he called Grace.

'Where's Lucy?' he asked. 'She's not answering her phone.'

'She's not with Jenny?'

'What?' He was startled. 'Why should she be with Jenny?'

'She said she was driving down last night . . . Oh God, Dan, please don't tell me she's not there?'

'No.'

'Oh God, oh God, no, no no . . .' Her tone dissolved into panic.

'Hey, Grace, take a deep breath.'

He heard her gulp loudly. 'Sorry. It's been awful . . . Lucy told me Sirius visited your wife . . . and now you're telling me Lucy's not in Bath?'

'Not that I know.'

'Oh, God. Where is she? She's not here . . . do you think she's been in an accident? Sirius hasn't got anything to do with it, has he?'

Making sure he spoke calmly against the nervous pinching in his belly, he said, 'Start from the beginning, OK?'

In fact, Grace started from the wrong end of things, which was when she last spoke to Lucy, and it took a good five minutes of him asking questions to iron out the whole story.

'So the last time you spoke to her she was still "on the hill" yesterday.'

'That's right.'

'Around three o'clock.'

'Yes.'

'And she said she was going to see a "contact" of mine before she headed down south to Jenny to protect her from Sirius.'

'Correct.'

Dan stared at a battered sedan exiting the hospital car park.

'Something's happened to her, hasn't it?' Grace's voice was scared.

'Let me call DI MacDonald,' he told her. 'See what's going on.'

'He rang last night. He hadn't heard from her either.'

His nerves were now shrieking in alarm.

'In that case,' he said, 'I suggest you call the police up there and report Lucy missing. Right away.' He looked at his watch. 'The first thing they'll do is check the hospital and road accident records. I have something to do this afternoon then I'll fly up. I'll text you when I've landed.'

'I can't believe he's back.' Her voice trembled.

'You may find this odd,' Dan said, 'but Sirius told me he'd treated me more kindly than usual because I was a friend of yours. He, well . . . he sent his best wishes to you.'

'Jesus Christ.' She sounded shell-shocked. 'He nearly broke my wrist and now he's sending me his best wishes? Fucking hell. That is more than odd, it's seriously messed up.'

He'd never heard Grace swear before and fell quiet for a moment. 'I'd better call Lucy's DI,' he eventually said.

'Yes, yes.' She was distracted, unfocussed. 'Keep in touch, Dan, OK?'

He hung up and dialled Mac. He didn't always get on with policemen – some could be thuggish and closed-minded – but Faris MacDonald was sharper than most and had a direct, professional attitude that Dan appreciated. He also gave Lucy more slack than most DI's would, which showed he was confident in his own abilities and trusted others to do their jobs, both characteristics which Dan respected.

'Dan Forrester,' DI MacDonald greeted him. His tone was frosty.

'I'm trying to reach Lucy,' Dan said without preamble. 'Have you heard from her today?'

'No, why?'

Dan filled him in as best he could. 'She was supposed to meet a contact of mine last night, at the Fiddichside Inn at eighteen hundred hours. I don't know if she made it or not.'

As Dan considered Firecat, he wondered if his father's and Connor's deaths were connected in some bizarre way. The one thing they had in common was that they'd both died within two days of each other. Could they be linked?

'I have something to do first,' Dan said, 'and then I'll head straight to Duncaid.'

'I'll see you there.'

Dan was about to hang up when DI MacDonald said, 'Wait. There's something I want to say.' The police officer's voice was as hard and formal as if he was cautioning Dan.

'Whatever happens, if a single hair on my DC's head is harmed I will hold you personally responsible.'

CHAPTER FIFTY-EIGHT

Lucy had given up trying to fight her way out of the well and was huddled on one side, arms around her knees, trying to take her mind off the pain of her broken nose and swollen ankle by dreaming of Mac and when they'd first made love, on a beach with the sun blazing down.

She'd been going out with Nate back then, and although she thought she was pretty moral (very moral, almost obsessively moral actually), she hadn't been able to resist Mac. They'd been introduced in a car park – not the most romantic of places – but the surroundings had faded into nothing against her crazy desire to feel his mouth on hers, his hands on her bare skin.

Before she'd met Mac she'd always snorted when couples spoke about being struck by a *coup de foudre* – a bolt of lightning, love at first sight – and even now she found it hard to believe she'd experienced the same thing. He'd been seeing Chloe back then, which had made them both unfaithful, but she supposed the fact none of them had been married helped, but not much. She'd felt awful about it, and when she'd got home and Nate had wanted to make love, she'd locked herself in the loo and cried because she didn't want Nate. She wanted Mac. She still did.

Suddenly she saw how stubborn she'd been. How spineless. If she got out of here, she'd go to him, take his hand and lead him to her bed. And she wouldn't let him get out of it until she'd explained why she'd put him off for so long.

Because I'm a coward. I'm scared if you see the real me, you won't like me anymore. And you're now my boss.

If it didn't work out, then she'd have a broken heart. She wouldn't die from it. Or would she? She'd read an article about broken heart syndrome, where people suffered heart attacks due to the emotional stress caused by a loved one leaving or dying. But she'd rather die of a broken heart than sit in this fucking hole.

She shuffled across the well's floor, trying to avoid the area she'd been forced to use as a loo. She shuffled back. Her hands were tucked beneath her armpits but they were like ice bricks.

She tried to concentrate her mind on Connor's investigation. She made a mental list of who she'd spoken to, from Lucas Finch, Connor's art and design teacher, to Jasmine and Tim, Christopher Baird's lab researchers, and the staff at Duncaid School. Then she switched to think about Dan's father's murder, because it was the shit-head whisky-glugging misogynist called Murray who'd triggered her kidnap, she was certain.

I've got a fucking story to tell that's worth a fortune, he'd said.

Was he a whistle-blower of some sort, or simply an opportunist? Fifty grand would get the grubbiest criminals to crawl out from under their rocks. Murray was the answer. All she had to do was get out of this sodding hole and shake him until he told her everything.

CHAPTER FIFTY-NINE

Dan supposed he could have telephoned TarnStanleyJones, but he always found it more useful to actually visit a place. You could glean a lot in even the shortest visit to an organisation, from the way the receptionist greeted you to how helpful they were. In his experience, whatever was at the top filtered down. If you had a rude, unpleasant receptionist, you'd invariably find their ultimate employer pretty unpleasant as well.

He hadn't dared tell Jenny where he was going but with Lucy missing he couldn't sit still. He had to be doing something.

As he approached Salisbury, two buildings dominated the skyline. One was the elegant Salisbury Cathedral with Britain's tallest spire. The other was TSJ's office and research block. Parking in the visitor's car park, Dan looked at the gleaming glass and steel building which held the TSJ logo at the top, where everyone could see it.

AGE WELL. LIVE WELL.

Had Rafe lived well? he wondered. All he knew was that the man had been terribly angry at having to endure the ignominy of illness and old age. Rafe's gasping words came to Dan as he walked through the automatic doors and into a modern, smart reception area.

I'm wearing a fucking nappy. Can you believe it?

Dan wondered how Sophie was bearing up. He'd send her a text later. See if he could do anything for her.

'Can I help you?' A keen looking young man behind the acres of reception desk greeted him. His name badge read ADISA AKIWUMI.

'It's about Rafe Kennedy.'

'Mr Kennedy?' Adisa blinked. 'He doesn't work here anymore, I'm sorry.'

'When did he leave?' Dan was curious.

'He came in on a consultancy basis until he fell ill. He hasn't been here for . . .' Adisa's face bunched a little as he thought. 'Two years at least.'

'I'd like to speak with someone he worked with, please.'

'What's it about?'

Dan held the young man's eyes. 'I'd just like to speak with them. It won't take long.'

Adisa swallowed. 'Yes, sir. I'll see what I can do. Can I have your name?'

Innate caution made him lie. 'Dr David Harrow.'

'If you wouldn't mind taking a seat . . .'

Dan wandered around the airy room. It reminded him of the reception area at the Isterberg Klinic where Arne and Gustav worked. Why had Gustav followed him? And what about Didrika Weber getting warned off by the BND? Something big was at stake, and no matter how much Jenny pleaded, threatened or begged, he was finding it impossible to turn his back on it.

He just hoped Lucy was OK. She really was one hell of a friend. Extraordinarily brave too. Not just for planning to drive nine or ten hours to be with his wife, but to stand beside Jenny against one of the most frightening men in the business while he was banged up in Germany.

Dan looked around when he heard heels clacking across the floor. A tall, rather attractive woman with thinning grey hair was approaching him.

'Dr Harrow?' she said. Her hand was already outstretched.

He shook.

'I'm Claire Hill. I used to work with Rafe.' Her gaze was clear and candid. 'I wondered if you knew . . .' She paused delicately, watching his expression.

'Yes, I heard he died this morning.'

She visibly relaxed at the realisation she wouldn't be breaking the bad news to him. 'We're really sorry. He was such a part of our team for so long . . . His daughter rang us. She wanted us to know from her rather than read it in some obituary or other.'

'That was kind of Sophie. How is she bearing up? She loved her father very much.'

He saw her relax further when he spoke of Sophie, putting him into the friends' category rather than unknown.

'She's finding it tough.'

'Poor Soph, I'll ring her later.'

Formalities over, Claire Hill looked at him, waiting.

'I was a close friend of Rafe's,' Dan told her, 'and I'd like to talk about Project Snowbank. He told me about it last week and I'd like to know more about it.'

Her expression turned puzzled. It seemed quite genuine. 'I've never heard of a project with that name. Are you sure?'

'Yes.'

Still puzzled, she said, 'Would you mind waiting a minute while I make a call?'

'Not at all.'

She moved to the reception desk where she picked up the phone and spoke. Five minutes passed, then ten. She was still on the phone when a white-haired man in a lab coat appeared. He looked at Claire Hill who glanced at Dan and nodded. The lab coat came to Dan.

He said, 'You wanted to know about Project Snowbank?'

'Yes.'

'There's never been any project here called by that name. Perhaps it was something Rafe worked on before he came to us.'

'Where did he work before?'

'Er . . .' The man looked away then back. 'If you don't already know, then I'm not sure if I can divulge that information.'

It was the man's discomfort that kicked Dan's childhood memory into action. Of course. His father, Arne, Gordon and Rafe had all gone to uni together to study science. After they'd graduated, Arne had gone to Germany to set up his Klinic, Gordon had taken up pathology, Dan's father had gone into the marines, but Rafe had remained in the research field. A light bulb blinked on inside Dan's head. *Dad and Rafe had had the same employer.*

The government.

'Ah,' Dan said. 'I remember now. He used to work up the road, didn't he?'

The man's expression cleared. 'Yes.'

Suddenly, everything started to make sense.

'He used to work at Porton Down.'

CHAPTER SIXTY

Mac paced the car park of the Fiddichside Inn, on his phone. It was drizzling, freezing cold, but he didn't notice. He was concentrating on finding the next lead to Lucy. He'd already heard from the truck driver who'd had to stamp on his brakes behind her car on the A95 yesterday evening, and now he was after a man called Murray, no surname, who'd left the Fiddichside pretty much at the same time as she had. Murray could be the last person who'd seen her. He had to find him.

Constable Murdoch sat in his patrol car. He was also on the phone. Murdoch had been furious to discover that Lucy Davies was actually a Detective Constable who had been secretly investigating Connor Baird's murder. Cops rarely liked cops from other districts on their turf, and Murdoch had been no exception. Although on the surface he appeared helpful, Mac could sense the resentment simmering beneath.

Mac had arrived in Duncaid at six in the morning having driven like a maniac through the night, no doubt collecting a handful of speeding tickets along the way – losing his license was nothing compared to losing Lucy.

He'd already interviewed the owner of the black van Lucy had texted him about. Peter Kendrick, funeral director, seemed as baffled as Mac at her interest in his vehicle.

'It's a mortuary van,' he told Mac. 'I can't think why she'd have any concern over it.'

'Where was it around five o'clock yesterday?'

'Outside the office. Where it's been all day and all night.'

Mac thought for a bit. 'You share the same surname as Brice Kendrick, the Procurator Fiscal. Are you related?'

'Well, yes.' The man blinked. 'He's my brother.'

With no other connection to help him further in finding Lucy, Mac had prowled the area, unable to work out Lucy's thinking, monumentally frustrated that he didn't have more to go on. In future, he would *make* her report to him daily to prevent anything like this happening again. And if she didn't change her behaviour, well, he'd pull the plug on her autonomy and chain her to a bloody desk.

'Any ideas where I might go next?' Mac was talking to the editor of the *Northern Scot*. Jo, the owner of the Fiddichside Inn, had told him that he'd seen Murray a couple of times but didn't think he was local. Maybe from Aberdeen way. It wasn't much to go on until Jo said that Murray used to be a journalist.

'That's what he said, anyway,' Jo had added. 'He's a bit washed up now. Never got the big story, apparently.'

Since then, Mac and PC Murdoch had been on their phones, ringing around newspapers and journals, trying to track the man down.

'I'd try *Herald Scotland*.' The woman rattled off a phone number. Mac hung up and redialled, went through the same spiel he'd recited half a dozen times until he got through to the editor.

'Murray?' The man sounded startled. 'You mean Murray Peterson?'

Every cell in Mac's body came alert, quivering.

'Tell me about him,' Mac said. 'When you last heard from him?'

As the man spoke, Mac brought out his iPad and rested it atop the bonnet of his car. He googled the name Murray Peterson, to see he was a freelance journalist 'known for his contributions to national newspapers, popular UK magazines.'

'We haven't taken anything of Murray's in ages. I thought he'd dropped out completely until he called a couple of weeks ago. He said he had a story for us and when we said we weren't interested he got . . . well, quite aggressive. He told me to eff off, and that he was going to go to the *Mail on Sunday* and that I'd regret it.'

'Did he have any luck?'

'I have no idea. I certainly didn't look out for it if that's what you mean.'

'What was the story?'

'Er . . . If I remember correctly, it was something to do with the longevity of residents in one Scottish town compared to the shorter lives of residents in another, also in Scotland. He was investigating diets and lifestyle, whether if we all turned vegetarian we could all live to a hundred. We've done things on this before and in all honesty, it didn't sound as though he'd come up with anything different.'

'Do you have his contact details?'

'Shall I email them over?'

'Thanks.'

They came through almost immediately. Mac went to Murdoch's car, knocked on the window. The policeman glanced up, obviously irritated at the interruption. Mac gestured for him to wind down his window.

'What?' said Murdoch.

'I've found the journo. Aberdeen. I want you to find out if he's at home and if so, get a car sent there to make sure he doesn't go anywhere.'

Mac ignored the way Murdoch pushed out his lower lip, and walked away to make another call. This one to the *Mail on Sunday*.

'Sure, we took a piece from Murray,' the editor told Mac. 'It wasn't that great to be honest, but he had some fantastic photographs to go with his piece. That's what really made it.'

When the link came through, Mac could see what the editor had meant. The pictures were of farmers and fishermen, chefs and factory workers. They were poignant and haunting, even more so when you saw how young the residents of the second town were, and they'd all died in the town of Duncaid.

His gaze jammed on the word *Duncaid*.

He stalked over to Murdoch.

God alone knew what his expression was but Murdoch wound his window down double-quick saying, 'He's in. The Aberdeen lot are sending a car there now.'

'Tell them I'll meet them there.'

CHAPTER SIXTY-ONE

Stomach churning with anxiety, Grace had spent the morning with Ross, driving the roads around Duncaid looking for Lucy and her car to no avail. They'd rung everyone they could think of to check that Lucy wasn't with them, and then called the police again to double check she hadn't turned up in a hospital somewhere. Zero results.

Finally, Ross suggested she return to the surgery.

'I'll keep looking, OK?' he told her. 'You've got patients to look after. If I can think of anything you can do to help, I'll ring.'

Reluctant but unable to think what else she could do, she'd gone to work. Checking her emails, she saw she had one from her old friend and pharmacologist, Ben Sharman. She was surprised to hear from him so soon. She opened his email. He'd written two words.

Ring me.

She picked up the phone and dialled. 'Ben?'

'Grace. Thanks for calling me so quickly. I really wanted to talk you through what we found.'

'We?'

'Paul and I. I hope you don't mind, but I started work as soon as I got your samples. They came in at nine last night and I was so bored . . .'

'You were still at the lab at nine?'

'I'm *always* at the lab at nine.' He yawned. 'I'm an owl. Do my best work with the vampires.'

'You worked on them last night?'

'Yup. You know me, I love the fun stuff. I hope you don't mind but when I saw your notes and that we had a "father and daughter" sample, I dropped all thoughts of red blood cells mutating due to a bad diet.'

'Oh.'

'I thought something far more exciting was going on, so I did a genetic screen of the two samples—'

'Doesn't that take an age?'

'If you go through the normal channels, yes. Look, Grace, this is just between you and me at the moment, OK? I'm simply giving you a broad-brush stroke of my initial thoughts from a very hasty first look. We'll need days and weeks to nail things down and test properly but I thought you'd like to know the direction we're headed.'

'Yes, of course,' she said hastily. 'Sorry.'

'No problem.' He gave another yawn. 'So long as you understand where I'm coming from.'

'I do,' she assured him. 'Go on.'

'Right. So, I did a genetic screen but neither sample had a genetic link to any recognised inherited form of diseases.

I didn't like the fact your girl, Sorcha, had Alzheimer's so aggressively or so early, so I looked at her RNA – the messenger that carries instructions from the DNA for controlling the synthesis of proteins. Existing databases can now tell us the synthesis of *which* protein is associated with Alzheimer's, you see. And it's my belief that her telomeres are, for some reason, shortening faster than usual, which is why she's got Alzheimer's today and not when she's in her seventies or eighties.'

Grace put her head in her hand as she concentrated on what he was saying. A telomere sat at the end of each chromosome, which protected it from deterioration or from fusing with neighbouring chromosomes. The length of a telomere declined from when you were born until the day you died.

'There's a healthy ageing signature that's common to all our tissues, and then there's Alistair and Sorcha's signature.'

'Which is?'

'I'm not sure. All I can say is there's something really weird going on. Paul agrees. We'll keep testing until we find out what the score is. And if anyone else walks into your surgery and you think they might be at risk, grab a blood sample and send it down, would you?'

'Sure.'

'Right,' he said cheerfully. 'I'd better be getting on with some more research that'll put me on the front cover of *Genetica* and get me life membership in the Royal Society.'

She was glad Ben was finding it all so exciting, but then he hadn't watched Iona Ainsley's husband howling with grief when his wife died so young of an infection, or witnessed Sorcha's heartbreaking inability to recognise someone she'd only seen five minutes before.

CHAPTER SIXTY-TWO

'His name is Professor Sun Chia-Jen,' Philip Denton told Dan. 'He used to work with Rafe Kennedy before Rafe got lured away by the big bucks of big business. They were good friends apparently. Sun Chia-Jen saw Rafe at the hospice three weeks ago.'

Dan was still outside the TSJ building, tapping his fingers on the steering wheel.

'Amazingly,' Philip went on, 'he's prepared to meet you.'

'Where?'

'Even more amazingly, at the bear's den itself.'

Dan was so surprised he fell silent. Porton Down was involved in national security at the highest level, with much of its work classified, and few people were allowed past its hallowed fences of electrified razor wire.

'He says he knew your father.'

Dan had never heard of Sun Chia-Jen but then he hadn't known his Dad's Bristol-based friend Olivia Liang either.

'When?'

'Any time this afternoon.'

Porton Down was just twenty minutes away. He checked his watch. 'I'll be there at three o'clock.'

'I'll let him know.'

Small pause.

'You do realise—'

'I owe you.' Dan was curt.

Before he headed off he quickly checked his phone for messages. Saw there was some breaking news. Another terrorist attack. A suicide bomber had driven a van packed with explosives into a police station in Belgium, killing two people. India, China, Sweden and England, vehicles were now the weapon of choice for lone wolf attacks. He didn't envy the authorities, trying to foil the impossible.

He put his phone aside. Climbed out of the car into a stiff, cold breeze. As he bent double, the scar across his stomach protested but he kept moving around his vehicle, looking for tracking devices. Most trackers were linked to GPS satellites, so wouldn't function deep under the car where metal blocked the connection, so he focussed on the perimeter of the underside, looking for suspicious boxes, taped-on objects, and antennas.

At first glance there seemed to be nothing.

He checked the petrol tank, an easy place to stick a magnetic device. Nothing.

As he searched, he thought again of the listening device Lucy had found in Christopher's VW Polo. Why Christopher? Was it something to do with his research? He checked under the plastic guards of each wheel well. Nothing.

Finally, he looked inside the bumpers and bingo. A tiny device had been slipped under the front bumper. He left it there.

Dan drove away from TSJ to a public car park in town. He parked at the far end, between a transit van and a Range Rover. Fairly certain he was out of sight, he removed the tracker and affixed it to the Range Rover's petrol tank.

Tracker free, he worked his way out of the city, passing Old Sarum's iron age hill fort, then Old Sarum Airfield. His was the only car as he approached the government military science park, fields on either side.

Porton Down had been formed to combat the threat of chemical weapons in WWI. It used to be called The War Department Experimental Ground and had a long history layered with myths and misconceptions. Known for using British military personnel in human experimental research into chemical and biological warfare agents, it was one of the leading weapons laboratories in the world. It focussed on all modern weaponry, from advanced ballistics and protection for armoured vehicles to researching nerve agents, plague and anthrax. It also had an active research programme on Ebola.

All this was to protect the United Kingdom and its military from threat. Today it was as open as it could be without giving vital research away, but its past was murky and dotted with tragedy. Like the death of Leading Aircraftsman Maddison, who died after being involved in a trial for the nerve agent sarin.

Dan drove to the front gate where he was checked and processed before being given an ID badge with his photograph printed on it. A soldier accompanied him in the passenger seat of his car, directing him to a whitewashed building with a grey slate roof that was, he was told, just over a hundred years old.

Dan parked and followed the soldier inside the building and through an echoing hall with a wooden staircase and wood panelled walls. It would have been a handsome space except for the linoleum flooring, which hinted at slashed budgets and giving the public 'value for money'.

The soldier showed him to a room that reminded Dan of an old, rather tatty army mess. More wood panelled walls, lots of green carpet, a variety of faux leather armchairs. The view was of a fiercely mown lawn with a couple of trees and behind a neatly trimmed hedge stood a row of green aluminium sheds.

'Please, wait here.'

Dan didn't have to wait long. Barely five minutes passed before a man said, 'Dan.' His voice was filled with warmth.

They shook hands. Although the man was diminutive, barely five four and tiny-boned, his grip was strong.

'Professor.'

'Call me Charlie, please.'

'Charlie. Thank you for seeing me, especially ...' Dan gestured at his surroundings. 'I hadn't expected –'

'It's the least I could do, to show you where your father used to work.'

Dan could feel the shock on his face.

'Ah, so he never told you.'

'But he joined the marines.' Dan's tone was strangled.

'Yes, but not before he'd been here for a year or so. Come, let us sit.' He led the way to two armchairs. Dan sank into his, feeling oddly weakened. His father had worked at Porton Down?

'It wasn't for him though,' Charlie went on. 'Working in a laboratory full time. Bill was too active. Too bullish. When he joined the marines he became a great ally to Rafe and the team by reporting from the ground, giving them an honest assessment of what the armed forces really needed in order to protect it.'

'Why didn't he tell me?'

Charlie put his head on one side like a bird. 'Back in the day nobody advertised the fact they worked here. Not many people would admit to experimenting on animals, let alone humans. And don't forget the work was extremely controversial as well as top secret.'

He pointed at an old tin sign that hung above the door.

IF YOU WOULDN'T TELL STALIN, DON'T TELL ANYONE.

Dan stared at the sign, still reeling from the fact his father had hidden a chunk of his life from him.

'So, Dad worked here.' He cleared his throat. 'Did he work on this Project Snowbank?'

'Yes. We were all involved.'

CHAPTER SIXTY-THREE

Murray Peterson lived in a three-storey featureless block of flats that blended into the granite surroundings perfectly. Grey pavement, grey road, grey breeze blocks, grey roofs, grey sky. There was one tree at the end of the street and that looked grey as well. The only bit of colour came from the bright blue P on the resident permit holders sign.

Mac nodded at the cops in the patrol car keeping watch outside and went to buzz the intercom system. Before he reached the front door, however, it was already opening and a man was stepping outside. Thread veins showed he either drank a lot, or smoked, or had rosacea, but whatever the cause, it had the unfortunate effect of making him look rough and seedy.

'Can I help you?' the man asked.

'I'm looking for Murray Peterson, the journalist.'

Although he'd seen the man's picture online and was ninety-nine per cent sure he was looking at Peterson, Mac still wanted the man's ID confirmed.

'Well, well.' A broad grin spread across Peterson's face. 'The big man's come himself, has he?'

Mac hadn't a clue what Peterson meant, but didn't say anything.

'How the hell did you find me?' The man glanced at the patrol car on the street. 'Ah. Your father said you were something in the security business. Are you a cop?'

'Yes.'

The man looked at Mac's hands, then behind him. 'You brought the money?'

'Remind me, exactly what will I get for it?'

'The story.'

'"The Secret to a Long Life"?' He'd read the article Murray had written for the *Mail on Sunday*, published just over two weeks ago, and couldn't see anything out of the ordinary. He had to have seen dozens of features like it over the past few years.

'Yes, yes. That's what you wanted, wasn't it? What your father wanted?'

With no idea what the man was going on about but not wanting to stop what might turn out to be a lead he wouldn't otherwise get, Mac made a non-committal gesture.

Murray peered at him, the first inkling that something wasn't right finally permeating his brain.

'You are Dan Forrester, aren't you?'

Mac reached into his pocket and withdrew his warrant card. 'Sorry,' he said. 'No.'

For a moment, Murray looked as though he might weep. 'Fuck it,' he said. 'What are you doing here then? You're a long fucking way from Stockton-on-Tees, aren't you?'

'I want to know what's happened to a colleague of mine who went missing last night. You were probably the last person to see her. Outside the Fiddichside Inn. Around seven o'clock.'

At that the man's eyes widened. 'You're kidding me. That wee lassie was a cop?'

'DC Davies. Yes.'

'Fuck.' His eyes widened further.

'We want to know where she is.'

'Jesus Christ.' He rubbed his forehead. 'I wish I could help you but I can't. Sorry. Last I saw of her she was walking to her car in the car park.'

A gust of wind brought a flurry of leaves inside the hallway.

'Look,' said Mac. 'Can we talk inside?' He glanced at the patrol car to make his point that if Murray was difficult, he might be looking at having the same chat at the police station.

'I guess so.' The man looked defeated.

Murray's flat was surprisingly neat if bland. The only items of interest were the framed newspaper and magazine articles on the walls. STUDENT, 21, DEMANDS LIFETIME SUPPLY OF BREAD BECAUSE SHE HAD NO MAYONNAISE IN HER SANDWICH.

'Got good money for that one,' Murray said.

Although he was itching to ask about Dan Forrester – he was going to punch that man squarely in the face for endangering Lucy – he kept his cool. Lucy was his priority.

'You last saw DC Davies . . .' he prompted.

Murray told him about the meeting set up between him and Dan, and how Lucy had been sent to the Fiddichside instead.

'I didn't realise she was one of your lot. Sorry.'

Once Mac had ascertained Murray didn't know anything that might help him find Lucy, he asked about Dan and the money. He could tell Murray was reluctant to talk by the way he hedged and coughed, and finally said, 'Look, I don't have time to beat around the bush. You were the last person to see DC Davies, and I can pull you in to the station for more questioning or you can tell me what happened between you and Dan Forrester. And his father,' he added.

'Ah, hell.' Murray went and stood by the window looking out at another grey vista. He heaved a sigh. 'I always keep an eye on the obits, you see. That's what got me started. I just wanted to know why this town on a Hebridean island had such incredibly long-lived inhabitants compared to those in Duncaid. Whether it was the water or the whisky that kept the islanders so fit and well into old age. That kind of thing.

'So I wrote the article, "The Secret to a Long Life". I'd ended it saying we should do some genetic testing on the two places to see if there are scientific answers. People wrote in about it, offering to be the *Mail*'s guinea pigs. I could see this story expanding into a serial and the *Mail* began to show real interest . . . And then I had a visit.'

Mac waited.

'From a businessman.' Murray sighed. 'He wanted me to stop any potential serial. He was adamant he didn't want any mention of genetic testing in Scotland ever again. He offered me . . . quite a large sum to put the story to bed.'

'How much?'

'Put it this way, it was substantially more than I used to earn in a year when I was at the top of my game.'

Since Mac had no idea how much that might be, he said, 'And that would be?'

'Fifty grand,' Murray sighed.

'Did he give a name?'

'No.' Murray interlaced his fingers and squeezed them together, cracking his knuckles. 'He transferred the money straightaway. He'd brought a computer with him, and did it with me in the room. So I knew he was serious.'

Mac studied the subtle way the man's body language had changed. He said, 'He frightened you.'

Murray swallowed. 'Yes.'

'Describe him.'

Mac brought out his notebook and made notes. Long face. Dark eyes. Polite. Well dressed. Thinning dark hair. Fifties.

'And so you kept quiet,' Mac eventually prompted.

'Yes. When Bill Forrester contacted me I tried to fob him off, but he was persistent. Then he offered to recompense me for my time. He said he'd be generous ... We were all set to meet when he got back from some trip to Europe, but he never turned up. Then on Saturday his son emails me and says he wants to talk.'

'You were hoping he'd pay you for your time as well.'

Murray hung his head a little. 'A writer doesn't earn much, not considering his long working hours.'

He could have been a criminal, unable to resist earning easy money, except he hadn't done anything illegal that Mac could see. Morally, accepting the payoff stank, but he hadn't broken any laws.

'Weren't you worried that your mystery man might get wind of the fact you hadn't in fact put this story to bed?'

'Yes. Which is why I used a code name. Firecat. I also went to meet Dan Forrester well out of Aberdeen.'

'Except you met my colleague, DC Davies, instead.'

'Not really.' Murray bit his lip.

'You wanted to meet "the big man himself",' Mac guessed, 'and brushed her off.'

The journalist stared outside. 'Sorry,' he said again.

'Do you think this mystery man may have done her harm?' Mac's tone was tense. 'Would you think him capable?'

'Oh, yes.' Murray's expression turned grim. 'He had a killer's eyes, that one.'

CHAPTER SIXTY-FOUR

'Can you tell me about Project Snowbank?'

Charlie mused for a moment. 'It's not public knowledge, but it's not top secret either. It's something that was quietly dropped in the 1960s when there was a change of government.'

'What was it?'

'You have to understand where the United Kingdom was after the war. The country was broke. Food rations didn't end until 1954. Life was still a real struggle but the baby boom had just started.'

Charlie looked outside as a pair of rooks hopped across the lawn, looking for grubs.

'Project Snowbank was started between the War Office and the Ministry of Health. Their concern was a burgeoning elderly population that would prove impossible to care for in the next century. Euthanasia wasn't being discussed back then, and the idea was to give the British people another option from a potentially endless, demeaning old age.

'What if you could have a sudden, painless death instead? A death that came without warning some time after you turned sixty? There would be no long-term dementia to suffer, no shameful body degradation and no pressure on family members to look after you. You could also plan your finances to a perfect T if you wanted.'

All the hairs on Dan's arms stood bolt upright. *Rafe*, he thought. *I wish I'd died years ago.*

'The incentive?' Charlie looked straight at Dan. 'The State would guarantee to pay you a monthly stipend. You wouldn't get rich on it, but you'd never go hungry either. And you'd have to commit when you turned eighteen.'

Dan guessed that in those days when you were eighteen, sixty would have seemed ancient, but today it was shockingly young.

'For those opting out of Snowbank,' Charlie continued, 'you might live a healthy, lively life until a hundred, or you might spend the last thirty years of your life miserably incapacitated in some kind of hospital institution. And you'd have no monthly stipend to see you through any rough times during your working life.'

Dan watched the rooks fly away.

'Snowbank expected people with inherited diseases, from Parkinson's to multiple sclerosis, to sign up, but also those frightened of Alzheimer's and those who didn't want to become a burden on their families. Snowbank called upon pharmaceutical companies and religious groups, and at one point it was a relatively well-known project.'

'The pensions and insurance industries wouldn't necessarily have been best pleased,' Dan remarked.

'Quite so.'

'And the project was dropped due to a change of government?'

'Correct.'

'Whose idea was Snowbank?' asked Dan. 'Who dreamed it up?'

'It wasn't your father, if that's what you think. He wasn't a great fan of Snowbank, to be honest. He thought it smacked of a totalitarian regime lording it over a dystopian society.'

'Was it Rafe?'

'No.' Charlie shook his head. 'It was formed well before your father and Rafe came here. That said, Rafe would have loved to have been Snowbank's creator. He championed it well into the 1960s. He was furious when it was abandoned, which is one of the reasons why he left. He hoped to start up something similar in the private sector, but it never happened. He left all his research papers with his colleague, Arne Kraus.'

Dan's heart began to pound.

'Arne?' he repeated.

'Yes. Arne left maybe a year after Rafe. Like Rafe, he treasured Snowbank and was bitterly disappointed at its failure.' Charlie glanced outside, thoughtfully. 'He's doing rather well, I'm told, with his Klinic in Isterberg.'

CHAPTER SIXTY-FIVE

It was late afternoon and Lucy hauled herself up off the ground and began hobbling to keep her circulation moving, but her limbs had stiffened and gone numb. The pain from her face came in waves.

She looked at her patch of sky to see that the light was beginning to fade. Soon it would be completely dark. The thought of spending another night in this hole made her want to cry again, but she'd told herself not to cry anymore, she was stronger than that. So she made another list of things to do when she got out of here.

First, make love to Mac.

Second, see her mum.

No, let's amend that.

First, have a long hot shower. Then make love to Mac.

After seeing her mum, she'd try and find her dad. She wasn't sure why she'd been thinking of him – probably because she was looking at dying pretty soon – but she wanted to know why he'd left her. Left her mum to bring her up on her own. He was living in Australia now, but whether he was still in love with the Aussie yoga teacher he'd run off with, God alone knew. Her memories of him were vague and distant, not unpleasant, except for the ones where he'd lied.

Her dad was a champion liar. He'd lie about where he'd been, what he'd been up to, he'd lie until you didn't know what was truth and what was fiction.

She wondered if he'd changed. What he was up to now.

If she got out of here, maybe she'd find out.

Meantime she had to survive a second night out here. She'd made a burrow with the debris on the floor and when the time came, would heap it over and around her to keep warm. It was only twelve hours until morning. Help would come then. Mac would be searching for her.

Her mind kept chewing over conversations, questions she'd asked about Connor's death, until suddenly she'd see Mac's face, the way his brows drew together when he was puzzled and trying to work something out, or when he was angry, *furious* with her for something she'd done, like not telling him about her meeting with Firecat.

She could see him smiling at the breakfast table, could almost feel the warmth of his hand as he reached over and tucked a stray lock of hair behind her ear. The warmth of his kiss. The tenderness in his eyes.

'God,' she said out loud 'if you get me out of here, I'll tell him I love him. I swear it on my life.'

CHAPTER SIXTY-SIX

Dan spent two hours making sure nobody was following him. Only then did he slip to Dungeness. The man he'd arranged to meet had big shoulders. His hair was blondish, cropped close, and his handshake was hard.

'Julia's told me about you,' he said. 'That you know Philip Denton as well as boats, and that you pay well.'

Dan scrutinised him narrowly. He had intelligent green eyes and a way about him that told Dan he did more than take tourists out fishing for halibut. Little wonder he knew Julia and Philip.

'Very well,' Dan replied.

They haggled briefly before settling on what appeared to be a mutually agreeable price. Within the hour Dan was aboard a fishing boat and cruising across the English Channel.

In Calais, he picked up a hire car and headed east. He'd bought a pay-as-you-go phone earlier, specifically to thwart any eavesdroppers, and now he rang Jenny.

'Hi,' he said. 'How are you? How's Mischa?'

There was a long silence. Inside he cringed.

'Jen'?'

'Oh, just great, thanks. Staying with yet another stranger in a strange house while my husband swans off to do whatever he's doing.'

'Look, I couldn't think how else to keep you all safe except—'

'I know, I know.'

She was furious with him, but when he'd insisted he was going to Germany because he thought he knew who had killed his father, she'd finally relented. Even she had enough sense not to expose herself to another visit from Sirius.

'I have to do this. Please, understand.'

When Jenny didn't say anything further, he filled in the silence saying, 'Julia will look after you guys.'

Julia from the office was ex-CIA and highly trained, but the most important thing was that nobody knew that Jenny, the baby and Aimee were staying with her. Not even Philip Denton or Jenny's parents.

Still Jenny didn't say anything.

'Love to you. Love to Mischa and Aimee.'

He hung up fast, his palms sweating. Would she divorce him? He supposed he deserved it if she did, but he didn't know what else to do. He could no more stay at home twiddling his thumbs than deliberately crash his car. How could he not confront Arne? Discover what had happened between him and his father?

He was passing Dunkirk thirty minutes later, when he called Aimee.

'Hi, sweetheart.'

'Daddy!'

'What's Julia's place like?'

'She's got a cat! It's a tabby and it's so sweeeeet! Have you seen Mischa? Isn't he cute?'

'I saw your little brother yesterday, and yes, he's cute. How are you?'

'Julia's going to take me to the zoo tomorrow, I can't wait!'

Yet another person he owed big time.

Eventually they hung up. Family done, Dan turned back to business and rang Mac.

'Any luck on Lucy?' he asked.

Silence.

'I'm sorry.' If anything happened to Lucy, he would blame himself. And so would Mac. And Grace. And the rest of the world. Lucy had done him a favour by investigating his godson's death, and now she was missing. All thanks to him.

'You . . .' said Mac. He was so angry he was obviously having trouble speaking, Dan realised. He couldn't blame him.

'I think I may have found my father's murderer,' Dan told him. Of all the distracting statements he could offer the DI that was one of the best.

After a pause Mac said carefully, 'Lucy mentioned something about that.'

'I think it's connected to Connor's murder.'

'How so?'

Dan wanted to share his new-found knowledge with the detective, but not yet. He said, 'Who was the last person to see Lucy?'

'The man you told her to meet.'

'Firecat.'

'Aka journalist, Murray Peterson . . .'

As Mac filled him in, Dan began to put the picture together. This whole thing had started when his father had seen Murray's article in the *Mail on Sunday*.

Olivia Liang's voice rang though his mind: *He told me he'd read something in the newspaper that had scared the 'living daylights' out of him. He was looking into it in case it was true.*

His father had suspected that Project Snowbank was in play. He'd wanted to see Murray, but when Murray put him off he'd gone to see Rafe. His suspicions had probably deepened because before he flew out to Germany, he'd lodged his letter with Olivia.

If Olivia has given you this, then I am dead . . .

When DI MacDonald described the man who'd paid Murray not to serialise his story, adamant he didn't want any mention of genetic testing in Scotland ever again, Dan's soul shivered.

Sirius Thiele.

His mind fought with his next idea.

What if the government was still involved in Project Snowbank? What if Isterberg and Duncaid were its testing grounds?

CHAPTER SIXTY-SEVEN

It was 1.30 a.m. when he arrived in Isterberg. The ancient cobbled streets were shiny and lit with a soft yellow light from traditional iron lamps. It looked as pretty as before, but as he recalled his last car journey with Arne, he also remembered thinking about the gruesome fairy tale *Hänsel and Gretel*. This in turn made him think of little Christa, who was missing her dead friends.

He pulled up outside Arne's house. All the windows were dark, except for one upstairs that Dan guessed was a night light of some sort. Pulling out his mobile, he rang Didrika Weber.

'*Ja,*' she said, sounding sleepy. 'Weber *hier*.'

Dan told her where he was, but not why.

'*Scheisse*,' she cursed. 'What's going on?'

'I just want you to know where I am.'

'No! I will not be your alibi or whatever it is you want from me.'

Dan took a breath. 'His name is Mischa.'

Small pause.

'Your son?'

'Yes.'

'Congratulations.' Her voice softened a fraction.

'Thank you.'

Dan hung up. Climbed out of his car and walked to the front door. He pressed the doorbell hard. He could hear it ringing inside. A light went on upstairs, then another. He pressed the doorbell again.

A curtain was drawn back briefly, then dropped.

All was quiet. Seconds later, lights snapped on downstairs. Finally, the porch light was lit and the front door flung open.

'Dan! What the hell's going on?'

Arne stood there in blue pyjamas and a silk dressing gown belted around his waist. Leather slippers on his feet. He was blinking behind his spectacles, obviously trying to clear his head.

'I need to talk to you.'

'Of course.' Arne stepped back. 'Come in, come in. You woke Anneke too. She'll be down in a minute.'

'It's you I want to talk to.'

Arne started to walk for the sitting room but Dan stayed where he was, in the hall.

'I want to talk about Project Snowbank.'

Arne went quite still. He turned to face Dan. 'What about it?'

'You're using Isterberg as a testing ground for Snowbank.'

At that, the strength seemed to leave Arne's body. He stumbled but Dan didn't go to help him. He watched dispassionately as Arne fumbled for the chair next to the radiator and sank on to it.

'Who told you?'

'Come on, Arne. You think I couldn't work it out for myself?'

'Who else knows?'

'Did you kill Dad?' Dan stalked over and looked down at his father's old friend. 'Because he found out what you were doing?'

Arne stared at the floor. His shoulders were slumped, defeated.

'Who's bank rolling it? Is it your government? Or is it private?'

Arne didn't speak, didn't move.

'Arne!' Dan snapped.

'Private,' he whispered.

That one word triggered Dan's memory of the Isterberg Cemetery. The rows of new memorials. Dan's mind switched to Christa. *Our village is cursed. That's why George and Alice died.*

'You're killing *children*?' Dan hissed.

At that Arne looked up, shocked.

'No! That was never the intention, I swear! We figured the genetics of progeria and modified them – that was the basis of our work. What we couldn't imagine was that methylation would occur in the next generation . . . We had no idea that the children of our test base would start dying even younger . . . but this means we're even closer to finding the perfect solution.' His face became animated.

'Dan, even your father could see the project was a massive success! People dying naturally without suffering for years from some ghastly disease. Rafe was so pleased with what we'd done, I can't tell you.'

'Are you insane?' Dan said. His mind was reeling from the man's ego. 'You're not God. People aren't lab rats. I know Porton Down use volunteers to experiment upon but it's with their *permission*. You're not at Porton Down any longer and these are real people with real lives, real problems, real children, and you've taken all their choices about their lives away!'

In the sudden silence, Dan became aware of a clock ticking.

'How did you modify these people's genes?' Dan asked.

Arne shakily rose to his feet. 'An injection. It was 1958, don't forget, and things were—'

'You were at Porton Down?' Dan was shocked.

Arne looked away.

'Jesus Christ. Did anyone there know what you were doing? What you *did*?'

'No.' It was a whisper. 'I knew the . . . nurse at the hospital. We'd gone to school together. She told the young mothers their babies needed a baby booster for their health.'

'How many?'

Arne kept silent.

It wasn't often Dan raised his voice, but when he did, it roared. 'HOW MANY?'

Arne shrank back. 'A hundred and five.'

'And you killed my father to stop this from becoming public knowledge.'

'No!' Arne looked at him, appalled. 'I loved your father. I would never harm him. When he came over, he didn't say anything. It was only later—'

Dan moved towards him, angry that Arne was lying, wanting to grab him, shake him into telling the truth, and at that moment the roar of a shotgun blasted between them.

BOOM!

Dan heard the pellets hit something metallic next to him and he shoved Arne away, diving for the floor, rolling for cover, scrambling on his knees and elbows down the corridor.

Arne was shouting something, he couldn't discern what. His heart was pumping, his legs driving him into the kitchen. Pushed on by fear and adrenalin he leaped up and grabbed a knife from a block on a worktop. Raced into the room next door. A utility room. A door led to the back garden. Still holding the knife, he shouldered the door open and slipped outside. He'd barely gone four paces when there was an infinitesimal movement of air behind him but before he could move, he felt the barrel of a gun pressed in the crease between his neck and his skull.

'Don't move.' The words were English, cut glass. 'Raise your hands.'

'Sophie?' he said disbelievingly.

'Fuck.' The gun dropped from his neck. 'Dan?'

He spun round.

'What the hell?' Her face was ghostly white in the shadows.

'I've just been shot at,' he hissed.

'Jesus. I heard a shotgun go off but—'

'What the hell are you doing here?'

'Anneke pressed the panic alarm. It goes straight to Gustav's phone, as well as the police. I came along for the ride.'

He grabbed her wrist and pulled her along with him but stopped when a figure appeared around the corner, just two yards away. Dan's eyes went to the shotgun aimed straight at his chest. His head went light. If it fired, he would die from the blast. There would be no second chance.

'You think you're so high and mighty,' said the shooter. 'You can't see the future. You can't see the great work that's been done.'

Slowly, Dan put up his hands. He dropped the knife with a clatter on the paving stones, wanting the shooter to see he wasn't a threat.

'The work is incredible,' he said. 'I'm not arguing with that.'

'You're a destroyer.'

'No.'

'You and your father. You are so liberal, so self-*righteous*. You don't understand anything.'

With his fingertips, Dan wiggled at Sophie to move away. She stepped slowly and carefully to the side. She still held her gun but it was out of sight, behind her back.

'You administered the injection,' Dan said. 'You were the nurse who told the mothers their babies needed a booster.'

'And none of those babies grew to suffer the endless debilitation of old age.' Anneke's eyes blazed.

'But what about *their* children?'

'I am not going down in history as a monster,' Anneke hissed. 'Or having my family stigmatised by what has happened.'

Everything around him narrowed into a pinpoint of concentration. There was nothing but the metallic taste in his mouth, the pounding of his pulse in his ears.

It wasn't the first time he'd faced death. But it was the first time he was going to die with his wife and daughter, and his newly born son waiting for him.

Fury burned. He couldn't see the finger tightening on the trigger but he knew that's what was happening, and he pushed his left foot hard against the ground, dropping his right shoulder, already plunging to the ground, when another figure appeared at a run.

'MAMA! NEIN!'

Anneke fired once. The compressed *thump!* of the shotgun reverberated through Dan's body but he didn't feel any shot piercing him, tearing him apart, and as his shoulder smacked against the wet paving, he kept rolling until he collided with a bin, toppling it with a crash.

Lungs heaving, blood pulsing, he scrambled up to see Anneke sprawled on the ground. Sophie was above her, pistol against Anneke's head.

Gustav was holding the shotgun. He was shaking.

'Du wollten ihn erschießen. Sie waren wirklich.' You were going to shoot him. You really were.

'Es war um Sie zu beschützen.' It was to protect you.

Anneke's voice was pleading.

Gustav didn't look at his mother. His hands were unsteady but he managed to break the shotgun, ejecting the spent cartridge as well as the one that hadn't fired. His face was ashen.

Dan went and stood over Anneke.

'You killed my father.'

She pulled her lips back into a snarl. 'He was going to destroy everything we've worked for, everything we've built up. The Klinic, our reputation, all our life *work*.'

Dan became aware of a figure approaching from the shadows. They held a pistol in both hands. Detective Superintendent Didrika Weber.

'He wouldn't drop it.' Anneke squirmed. 'He wouldn't let us continue our research. He wanted to destroy *everything*. Don't you see? He wouldn't have just ended our lives, but Gustav's also. Our entire family would go down in history not as one of ground-breaking scientists finding the solution to a worldwide problem, but as Nazi-like monsters experimenting on humans.'

Dan looked her in the eye.

'How did you inject the babies in Duncaid? What excuse did you use over there?'

A flash of satisfaction filled her face. 'Oh, that wasn't me. That was Gordon Baird.'

CHAPTER SIXTY-EIGHT

'Gordon?' Sophie's eyes were wide.

'Who else would it be?' Anneke said nastily.

'But Gordon wouldn't do that.'

Arne stumbled into view at the side of the house. Didrika Weber went to him, gripping his arm as he stood swaying beside her, glassy eyed. The DSI didn't say anything. No matter that Sophie was armed. Didrika was, Dan realised, wanting to see how this unfolded.

'He didn't do it himself.' Anneke made it sound as though she was talking to someone particularly stupid. 'He got the nurse to do it at Duncaid's surgery. Told her it was a trial vaccination for measles.'

'She wouldn't have just done what he said, surely,' Sophie protested.

'It was 1958,' Anneke hissed. 'Doctors were revered in those days. They could do anything.'

Dan couldn't stop to listen to any more. He had to call DI MacDonald and fill him in. With the hour time difference, it was 2.15 a.m. in the UK, but he didn't think the man would complain.

'MacDonald,' he answered fast. He obviously hadn't been asleep.

'Go and pull Gordon Baird in. I think he knows where Lucy is.'

'How come?'

'He's trying to protect a project he and two old university friends have been conducting over the past six decades.'

'Which friends?'

As Dan explained, he could hear MacDonald was on the move. He heard doors banging down the receiver, footsteps. He paused when he heard the DI talking to someone else, realising MacDonald was on another phone barking orders to Murdoch. When he came back, he said, 'They all worked at Porton Down?'

'Yes.'

'As a pathologist he could easily cover up causes of death. And then there's the small fact that Gordon Baird's nephew is Procurator Fiscal of the area. Oh, and the Duncaid funeral director is related to them too.'

'A real family affair,' said Dan and at the same time he thought, *what about Christopher?* Was his friend involved as well? After all, Christopher had never volunteered the fact he was related to the fiscal. Had he been trying to cover things up? And what about Connor? Why had he been murdered? Had he uncovered something to do with Snowbank?

As they talked, Dan rubbed a hand over his stomach where the scar was throbbing after the unusual activity. He watched another two police cars arrive. Sophie had kept her weapon on

Anneke until Didrika Weber had handcuffed her and also handcuffed Arne.

After he'd finished the call, Dan went and joined Sophie. She was pale but she was still functioning, still operative. She had guts, as well as an inner strength that kept her chin high despite her father's death and despite having learned what Rafe had apparently been involved with.

'Where did you get that?' Dan asked, looking at her pistol.

'Gustav. He's a member of a gun club. They have shooting competitions.'

Gustav looked shell-shocked. He was still trembling.

'I'm sorry,' he said to Dan. 'I suspected something was going on, but I didn't know what.'

'Why did you follow me?'

'Ah.' Gustav exhaled, ran a quivering hand over his head. 'My father was always anxious about where you were going, what you were doing. I didn't know for sure that he'd killed your father, but if he had . . . I didn't want him to do the same to you.'

'You were trying to protect me.'

Gustav grimaced. 'I didn't do a very good job.'

'You probably saved my life.' Dan gripped Gustav's arm briefly. 'Thank you.'

'I can't believe it. My mother?! She is crazy. She has to be.' He put a hand across his eyes. 'My God. They are both crazy. Rafe and Gordon too. How did they even *think* they'd get away with it? And all those poor people . . . Their children . . .'

A tear rolled down his cheek. Sophie came over and took him into her arms. She looked at Dan over Gustav's shoulder. Her pistol, Dan noticed, was now tucked into her waistband.

'HMIC trained you well,' he told her.

'I took the odd weapons course. Livened things up a bit.'

'Sorry about your dad.'

Sorrow filled her face. 'I got your message. Thanks.' She rocked Gustav close, kissed his cheek. 'I came here to be comforted, and now look at me.'

He decided not to mention her husband, or go into her father's history or Project Snowbank and how it had led to this, and she seemed to realise it because she gave him a rueful smile. 'It's going to be awful. I might go overseas until 2028.'

There would undoubtedly be a global media feeding frenzy when all this came out, and as the children of the scientists involved, they'd be in the spotlight.

'I'll probably join you,' Dan said.

Heading overseas wasn't such a daft idea, he thought. At least until the media interest died down. Persuading Jenny to undertake a two-month long holiday somewhere like Australia, however, would be another matter.

CHAPTER SIXTY-NINE

In the pitch dark, Mac drove straight to Glenallen Lodge. He'd already rung Murdoch and told him to meet him there with all the back-up he could find, and now he pushed his car as hard as he dared, wanting to find out where Lucy was, wanting to see her, wanting to know she was safe.

His headlights swept over a handsome granite lodge standing at the entrance to a drive. A green and white sign read GLENALLEN ESTATE. Murdoch had told him that the Bairds' old lodge, a huge pile with turrets and sweeping lawns, was a mile down the drive. When the estate had been sold, the family had moved into the smaller lodge near the estate's entrance.

How the mighty have fallen, Mac thought. He pulled over, reversing in behind a Land Rover and making sure he could get away easily if he needed to. He knew he should wait until Murdoch arrived, but how could he sit around doing nothing while Lucy was still missing?

Grabbing a torch from the glovebox, he scrambled outside. When he closed his door and the interior light went out, the darkness was complete. He waited a few seconds for his night vision to kick in. Not a pinprick of light showed anywhere.

Something rustled nearby and he stepped away, turned on the torch. He didn't want a broken ankle walking to the front door.

As he walked along the front path a security light came on and at the same time, dogs began barking. He switched off the torch. Went to the door and raised his fist.

Bang-bang-bang.

His policeman's knock.

The dogs went crazy.

He thumped again.

Bang-bang-bang.

Lights came on upstairs. Then one downstairs.

The dogs continued to go insane.

A man called out in broad Scots, 'Who is it?'

'The police.'

'Let me see your warrant card. In the window to your left, if you please.'

Mac turned to see another light snapping on inside. Then a beaky old man in a tartan dressing gown appeared, standing expectantly next to the bay window. Mac pushed his warrant card against the glass. The old man nodded.

'Just a minute.'

He flung the door open. Two dogs launched themselves outside and for a moment Mac felt a surge of horror – why the fuck hadn't he waited for Murdoch? – but the dogs wound themselves around him, sniffing, growling half-heartedly, their tails wagging.

'They're all bark,' said the man.

'Gordon Baird?'

'Aye.' He stepped back, opening the door wide. 'Come in. Don't be standing there in the dark like some kind of ugly night creature.'

Mac walked inside. Heard the door shut behind him.

'I'm looking for my colleague, DC Lucy Davies. She went missing two days ago.'

At that, Gordon Baird's eyes widened. 'Lucy Davies? She's a policewoman?'

'Yes.'

'I thought there was something about her.' He was shaking his head. 'But I never knew she was from the polis.'

Mac stepped close to the man. He didn't do it consciously, but his muscles filled out, making him look bigger and more forceful.

'I want to know where she is.'

Absolute confusion rose in Baird's eyes. 'Why would I know where she is?'

'Don't fuck me around,' Mac snapped.

'I'm not.' The man's expression turned bewildered. 'I swear it.'

Mac drew back his fist. 'If you don't tell me, then so help me God I will pulverise you until you are nothing but a bloody mush.'

'You can hit me all you like but I won't be able to tell you anything *because I don't fucking know!*'

'I don't care that you're a pensioner,' Mac snarled. 'Nor do I care that I'll lose my job, go to jail even, because I WANT TO KNOW WHERE SHE IS!'

The dogs suddenly erupted into another round of furious barking and rushed to the door where someone was thumping.

'Why the fuck don't you lot ring the fucking doorbell?' Baird said, stalking to the door and flinging it open. 'Come on in and join the fucking party,' he told Murdoch.

'Where is she?' Murdoch asked.

'For Chrissakes, how many times do I have to say it?! I don't fucking know!'

Dan strode back to the old man. 'You wanted to get rid of her because she was going to expose Project Snowbank.'

Baird's eyes just about popped from his head. 'Project *what*?'

'Snowbank.'

'How the fuck do you know about that?' He was staring at Mac as though he'd seen a ghost.

'Tell me where Lucy is, and I'll tell you how we found you out.'

The old man glanced at Murdoch, then back at Mac. 'Do you really think I'd be stupid enough to disappear an attractive woman like that? Let alone a fucking DC. I'd have to be completely off my trolley.'

For the first time, Mac began to realise that Gordon Baird was telling the truth. He looked at Murdoch. 'Bring him in.'

Baird looked horrified. 'What the fuck for?'

'Injecting dozens of babies with some experimental shit in the 1950s, for a start.'

CHAPTER SEVENTY

When Dan told Sophie he was heading to Duncaid to see Christopher, she said although she'd like to come too because 'us kids should stick together', she wanted to be with Gustav for a bit.

'He's really shaken up.'

'He's not the only one,' Dan replied, looking at her pale skin and haunted eyes.

'I'll be OK.' She gave him a brave smile of old that reminded him of the little girl who'd scraped all the skin off her knees but refused to cry. 'I'm tough, me.'

All three of them had spent the remainder of the night at Polizeiwache Isterberg being debriefed, and by the time they'd signed their statements and been released it was 10 a.m.

Outside, Gustav shook Dan's hand and Dan surprised himself by pulling Gustav into a hug, clapping him on the back. He must be getting old. Or sentimental. Or maybe a bit of both.

It was the first time Dan had seen Gustav give a smile since they were kids. It was weary, but it was still a smile.

'Look after yourself, Dan.'

There were no flights from Hanover to Inverness or Aberdeen until late evening, so Didrika Weber offered to drive Dan to Berlin.

'No baby on the way this time,' she said. 'Which means I won't get hauled in front of my boss and bawled out for abusing my position.'

'No,' Dan agreed.

'Is your wife talking to you?'

'No.'

'Flowers, chocolates, an expensive holiday, all those have their place, but in this case I think there's only one thing for it.'

Curious, Dan said, 'What's that?'

'Diamonds. Lots of them.'

'Diamonds?' A startled laugh broke through. 'You really think something as cheesy as that would work?'

She turned her head briefly to look at him. 'Us women like cheesy.'

He didn't think even a lorry load of diamonds would help matters. He'd broken his promises to Jenny time and again, and this time he thought it was probably too late. She would have had enough and he couldn't blame her. He'd tried to change, he honestly had, but when the whistle of a mission shrilled, when people needed him, called on him, he just couldn't help it. He had to join the chase. It was imprinted on his DNA as well as his psyche. It was who he was.

As Didrika pulled her Beetle outside departures, he said, 'Thanks.'

'You may not thank me when you see the prices.' She grinned.

Dan spent the journey to Scotland alternately napping and thinking. He still couldn't see how Connor's murder tied into all this. Or Lucy's disappearance. Gordon Baird wouldn't kill his own grandson, surely, and Mac had already called and said he was fairly sure Gordon Baird hadn't disappeared Lucy either. Christopher had a listening device in his car. What did that mean? Who was listening to him? Why?

Dan was convinced that if he could find who'd put the device in the car, he'd uncover the person who was behind all this. The person who'd put Joanna Loxton on his tail and then moved her out of sight. The person who'd set Sirius Thiele onto Jenny and onto the journalist Murray Peterson.

All he had to do was find them.

CHAPTER SEVENTY-ONE

Lucy awoke from her dream, and for a blissful moment she didn't know where she was – she thought she might be in her old childhood bed in Southwark – but then reality crashed in.

A pale light filtered down from the patch of sky. Dawn had come.

She tried to go back to sleep. Anything but look at her prison, but she was too cold, too uncomfortable, her mouth too dry. She struggled up. She felt slightly sick and very tired.

She trudged around the bottom of the well. Two steps forward. Two steps to the side. Two steps back. It required effort and she wondered why she bothered. Nobody was going to find her. She knew she wasn't going to make it. She may as well lie down and give up. Would death come faster if she willed it? She wished she could fall asleep and die without knowing it. She didn't want to slowly rot to her death down here, frightened and alone. She'd much rather get shot or even eaten by a shark. At least it would be quick.

Three days without water.

Today was the last full day she would be alive.

*

She had been dreaming for hours, weaving fantastic plans of what she'd do when she got out of here, when the longing for a full English breakfast struck her.

Sausages, black pudding, fried bread, fried eggs, baked beans, no tomatoes. She liked tomatoes very much, but not when they were cooked and went soggy.

Oh, and some mushrooms too. Preferably those really big field mushrooms that went almost black when they were cooked.

Her stomach rumbled noisily.

She was so thirsty, her mouth so dry, she felt as though she could drink a river dry and she'd still be dehydrated.

She was slurping down her third mug of imaginary tea when she became aware of a distant drone. A plane, she thought. Several had gone over, including a couple of fighter planes, no doubt practising out of RAF Lossiemouth. She discounted it, having heard a variety of imaginary engines, cars and jeeps coming to rescue her.

The drone grew louder.

It wasn't an aircraft. In fact, it sounded like a car engine and it was getting louder and louder. She leaped to her feet, ignoring the stab of pain in her ankle. The engine was loud and real.

Please God someone's come to rescue me!

The engine was abruptly shut off.

'Help!' she yelled, but her throat was so dry, hardly any sound came out.

Frantically she swallowed, desperate to lubricate her throat but she had no saliva.

'HELP!' she shouted, hoarse and weak.

She thought she heard a noise from above and stopped trying to shout for a moment. A soft scraping sound, as though something or someone was walking through the heather.

It grew louder. It was heading her way.

Lucy began to yell. 'HELP ME! HELP, HELP!'

Pain shot through her nose and into her head as she shouted, but she didn't stop.

'HELP, HELP!'

After a little while she paused but couldn't hear anything, so she yelled some more, praying it was a farmer come to check his sheep, a hiker, a photographer wanting to take pictures of the rotting farmyard.

'HELP!' Lucy screamed.

The next second something peered down at her.

Big ears, broad head, long pink tongue.

It was a dog.

CHAPTER SEVENTY-TWO

Mac was questioning Gordon Baird, desperately trying to find a clue that would lead him to Lucy, but he was struggling.

The man had already confessed to being part of Project Snowbank. He'd also confessed to persuading the practice nurse at Duncaid's surgery to administer the injection to the town's babies under false pretences.

'We didn't know that DNA methylation was going to occur in the next generation.' He suddenly looked very tired. 'We were horrified, to be honest, but couldn't think of anything to do aside from letting them die, and hope that they didn't have children who might die even younger.'

Mac was having trouble keeping a neutral expression. These men had played God with people's lives. Children's lives. It made him feel physically sick.

'Didn't you try and find a solution?'

'Of course.' Baird looked affronted. 'What do you think we are? Animals?'

Something worse, thought Mac, but held his tongue.

'I took blood samples from patients. I sent them to Arne. He has a huge laboratory in Isterberg. But we couldn't find any kind of cure. We decided to let nature take its course.'

'And let everyone die.'

'That way their genes wouldn't be passed on to do further damage.'

'No chance of that,' Mac said harshly.

Gordon Baird lifted his chin. Held Mac's gaze with steady purpose. He exuded dignity and gravity that Mac may have admired had they met elsewhere.

'You forget what we were trying to achieve,' he said.

Mac ignored him. 'You got your nephew, Brice Kendrick, to cover up the early deaths.'

'He didn't cover up anything,' Gordon Baird protested.

'He just refused to authorise any autopsies on anyone from Duncaid. You can't say he didn't know about it.'

Gordon Baird's face turned flat. 'I decided to tell certain members of the family what we'd done. A lot of people wouldn't. But I wanted to take on the responsibility.'

'And cover it all up.'

The man's mouth tightened.

'And Connor?' Mac said. 'Your own grandson?'

'What about him?'

'Who murdered him?'

A look of pure disbelief appeared. 'Why the fuck would I know that?'

'Considering you murdered umpteen innocent people without batting an eyelid, I thought you might have an opinion.'

'Well, Detective Inspector MacDonald, I don't, and you can get off your fucking high horse because you forget our original goal. To give people a choice about how they wanted to age. We were doing this for *humankind*. Look at our elderly population at the moment. How lonely they are abandoned by their children. Three point nine million elderly people say television is their main company. How sad is that?'

'How sad is it that Alistair Tavey's daughter, Sorcha, who was a budding biology student, has Alzheimer's?' Mac snapped back.

Gordon Baird blinked. 'You know about that?'

'Dr Grace Reavey called me earlier. I know about everything. And I mean *everything*.'

Gordon Baird didn't look regretful or ashamed. He said, 'We had government backing, don't forget.'

'But not when you got Belinda McCreedy to inject Duncaid's babies.'

The shock on Gordon Baird's face was real and Mac felt a surge of satisfaction.

'I told you I knew everything.'

Baird's gaze grew sly. 'Except where your little DC is.'

The officer sitting next to Mac in the interview room had to physically restrain him from leaping over the table and flattening Gordon Baird's beaky nose.

CHAPTER SEVENTY-THREE

'HELP! HELP!' Lucy called out.

The dog vanished.

'Come back! Please, come back! Nice doggy, don't leave me!'

'Hello?' A man's voice.

'Help! Please help me!'

A silhouette appeared. 'Hello?'

'Oh God, please help me, please get me out of here. Please, please . . .'

'Lucy?' The man sounded shocked. 'Is that you?'

'Yes, yes. Please help me, please.'

'Jesus Christ. I knew you were missing but what the . . . you're *here*. I don't believe it. Jesus . . . Let m-me . . . Let me get a l-ladder or something.'

His figure vanished.

'Don't leave me!' she yelled.

'Christ. C-christ. S-sorry.' In his haste he was stammering in fear, and she suddenly realised who it was.

'Christopher?'

'Y-yes. Jesus, Lucy. Everyone's been going crazy looking for you. Are y-you all right?'

'Just get me out of here!'

'OK, OK. But I have to leave you to find—'

'Give me your phone,' she said. 'Please, don't leave me here without your phone.'

'Yes, yes. Good idea. Hang on . . . Here it is . . .'

She stepped back as his phone fell towards her. She caught it. Moved to the middle of the well and held the phone to the sky, praying she'd get a signal.

The screen lit up, demanding a code.

'Your code!' she yelled.

'Treble three, nine six one.'

When the screen lit up into a blissful welcome page, she could have wept in relief.

'I'll get a ladder, OK?' he told her. 'I'm sure there's one in the barn, or something anyway. Hang on, Lucy. I'll be back as soon as I can.'

Lucy would have called Mac immediately, except she didn't know his mobile number off by heart. She could recite her childhood landline off without a problem, but the instant mobiles had come in she'd simply stored everyone's number in her contacts list and never learned any by rote.

She dialled 999.

'I'm a police officer,' she told the dispatcher, and recited her name followed by her warrant and collar numbers. 'I need DI Faris MacDonald's phone number urgently.'

'Sending it through now.'

Ting.

Lucy dialled his number. She could have screamed when it went to his mailbox. She tried to remain calm but quickly dissolved into a hiccupping, sobbing mess.

'Sorry, Mac, sorry,' she said. 'I'm OK, really. Christopher's gone to g-get a ladder to get me out. Thank God he found me. His dog found me . . .'

'Lucy,' Christopher called. 'Watch out.'

She hung up the phone as he lowered a rickety ladder that was missing two rungs and was rotten as hell, but it could have been a treasure chest filled with jewels for the joy it brought her.

She clambered up and then Christopher was reaching down and gripping her wrists and helping her. Hot tears streamed down her cheeks. She was holding on to him – this wasn't a dream, it was *real*, he was *real*. She was safe now. The tears kept pouring down. Christopher was also in tears. They held each other tightly for a long time, unable to let go.

CHAPTER SEVENTY-FOUR

When Lucy saw where she'd been on the map, she said, 'For God's sake. What were you doing all the way out here?'

He looked away. Swallowed. 'I'm trespassing actually. But when I know the coast is clear, that the landowner and head keeper are out of the way, I like to take a walk on our old land. I miss it, you see. Terribly.'

He'd led her to a burn that ran behind the abandoned farm-yard, with clear, cold water. Lucy folded on to her front and scooped handfuls into her mouth. She lay there for a long time, drinking. Finally, she had rolled on to her back and looked at the sky.

I'm alive.

Now, they were in his VW Polo jerking and bouncing down a rough farm track. It had to be the same route her kidnapper had taken. The dog was in the back, panting. Christopher wound down his window.

'Sorry,' she said. 'I must stink.'

He looked across. He smiled. 'You smell terrific. You smell of *life*.'

She dropped her sun visor. Looked in the vanity mirror.

'Oh my God.'

Her nose was black and swollen. There were purple and black bruises under her eyes, hanging like over-ripe plums. Her nostrils were caked with dried blood, and there were more flakes of blood stuck around her mouth and chin.

She looked down at her hands. They were covered in dirt and her nails were bloody and broken from trying to climb out of the well.

She began to shake.

'I'll take you to Elgin,' Christopher said. 'To the hospital.'

'No,' she said. She didn't want to go somewhere impersonal. She wanted to be with friends, to feel safe and protected. 'Take me to Grace.'

CHAPTER SEVENTY-FIVE

Grace took one look at her and burst into tears.

'Sorry,' she said. 'God, I'm so unprofessional . . .'

Lucy said, 'I'd hug you, except I reek.'

'I don't care what you smell like.' Grace went to Lucy and held her close. Tried not to sob, failed. 'Sorry,' she said again. She looked at Christopher as she wept. 'Thanks.'

'I was walking the dog . . .' He made a helpless gesture. 'I can't believe it.'

Grace finally leaned back, wiping the tears from her face. 'Let me have a look at you.' She held Lucy's chin between her fingers and turned her face from side to side. 'It doesn't look deformed. When did the nosebleed stop?'

'The day before yesterday.'

'Any whistling sound when you breathe?'

'No.'

'Pain in your sinuses?'

'Not nearly as bad as they were.'

Grace was relieved the skin and septum wall appeared to be intact. 'Home treatment will be fine. Ice packs for ten minutes every few hours for the rest of the day will help. I'll clean you up and give you some paracetamol. Tonight, make sure you prop your head up in bed with lots of pillows, to help reduce the swelling. In a month or so no one will be able to tell it was broken.'

'Thanks, doc.' Lucy gave a smile.

'Keep your fluid levels up.'

Grace gently bathed Lucy's face before turning her attention to her bloody fingers. She applied antiseptic and bandaged the worst ones leaving the others to heal naturally in the open air.

'I'll strap your ankle for now,' she told her, 'but, like your face, it needs ice packs and to be elevated. When did you last eat?'

'Breakfast Monday.'

Grace nipped outside and came back with a chicken and mayonnaise sandwich, and a Mars bar. 'Courtesy of the practice manager. She'll get herself another lunch in a moment.'

Lucy devoured the sandwich and started on the Mars bar.

'Does your boss know you're OK?' Grace asked. 'Mac?'

'I've left a message.' Lucy looked at Christopher. 'He'll call you because he'll see your number come up.'

'Yes.' Christopher's voice was quiet.

Grace took in the slight sheen of sweat on his skin. 'You look like a ghost. Are you all right?'

'I think it's the shock.' He glanced at the door then away. Rubbed the back of his neck. 'I can't stop thinking that if I hadn't walked the dog where I did . . .'

He closed his eyes and swayed. 'And then there's Dad . . . The police took him away this morning.'

Grace went to him and grabbed an elbow, steered him to a chair. 'Sit down,' she commanded.

He sat.

'I did that particular walk because . . . I thought I might never be able to do it again. It's one of my favourites.' His eyes were still closed.

'I'm glad you did.' Grace touched him gently on the shoulder.

'Why you?' Christopher asked Lucy. It seemed a rhetorical question, but she still answered it.

'I'm not sure,' she said. 'But I think it was a combination of things. He kidnapped me after I'd met Dan's contact. We didn't talk at all, but the kidnapper wouldn't have known it. I also re-traced the route I thought Connor may have taken. I think he got lost in the fog and the rain, and ended up at the wrong end of town. I tried it and came out at the Blackwater Industrial Estate. Slap bang outside Green Test Lab. There was what looked like a mortuary van outside. I hung around for a bit but I didn't see anyone.'

'A what?' Christopher's voice was faint.

'A mortuary van.'

Christopher ran a finger between his neck and shirt collar. 'Are you sure?'

'Pretty sure, yes.' She swallowed. 'I don't know what's going on in that lab, but I think Connor saw something. And was killed for it.'

He looked at Lucy. And as he looked, the blood continued to leave his face until he was bone white. Was he going into shock? Grace wondered, and she was going to suggest he lie down when he jack-knifed to his feet.

'I've got to go,' he said.

'You know something?' Lucy asked.

He didn't respond. He headed for the door.

'No, wait!' Ignoring the stabs of pain in her ankle, Lucy hared after him. 'Did you know you have a listening device in your car?'

He stopped dead. Turned around. 'What?'

'A bug. In your Polo.'

For a second he looked as though he hadn't heard her but then he said, 'Fuck.'

As Grace watched him, the colour began to return to his face, filling the muscles with blood. She was relieved. She'd honestly thought he was going to pass out.

'Tell me what's going on,' Lucy said.

'I can't.'

'TELL ME!' she yelled. 'Because whatever it is nearly got me killed!'

'Sorry.'

He headed outside, Lucy hot on his heels. Anxious, Grace looked through the window to see Christopher was heading to his car. Lucy was right alongside, still badgering him.

It was only because Grace was at her window and facing the rear of the surgery's wheelie bins that she saw him.

A man in his fifties, dressed in a double-breasted camel coat. Long pale face. His gloved hands held a pistol with a long snout. A silencer.

Sirius Thiele.

He was stalking Christopher and Lucy.

CHAPTER SEVENTY-SIX

Grace went completely light-headed.

What was Sirius Thiele doing here?

She dropped down out of sight. Tried to focus. She couldn't ring Lucy and warn her as Lucy didn't have her phone. She didn't know Christopher's number, but since it should be on the surgery's system . . .

She crept to the windowsill.

Sirius was now walking openly towards Christopher and Lucy. He held his pistol behind his back. They hadn't seen him. He was going to walk up to them, really close, and shoot them. He wouldn't miss.

Panic and fear surged through her.

Oh, God.

She had no time.

No time to dial 999. No time to think.

Grace exploded for the door. Yanked it back. Tore down the corridor. She smacked into a patient who grabbed her arm, saying, 'Whoa there,' and shoved him aside. Pushed on by terror, Grace threw herself at the surgery doors and flung them open, leaping down the steps three at a time. She sprinted across the car park.

If she ran fast enough, she'd cut him off. She was almost between him and her friends. She just had to get there first.

Sirius's gait was smooth and steady. He was closing in on Christopher and Lucy. But she was closer. If she could run just a bit faster . . .

Lucy began to turn as she heard running footsteps. Christopher faltered too, but Sirius kept walking. In a single, smooth movement Sirius brought up his gun.

'Sirius!' Grace yelled. 'Stop!'

He didn't falter, didn't pause. He took aim. He was going to take Christopher down first. Then Lucy.

Grace saw Lucy was already moving, sprinting away but Christopher stood paralysed. He was staring wide-eyed as though he couldn't believe his eyes.

Grace could see Sirius's finger around the trigger and knew he was going to fire at any moment. Without thinking, she flung herself in front of Christopher.

'Stop!' she gasped. Her heart hammered against her ribs, her blood humming in her ears. 'Just stop.'

She heard a car driving down the road in front of the surgery. A crow cawing. But otherwise everything was quiet.

'Grace.' Sirius's expression was sombre. 'Please move out of the way.'

'No.'

His eyes held hers. The same black, wet pebbles from her nightmares.

'I won't ask a second time.'

'Then you'll have to shoot him through m-me.' Her voice wobbled.

'Christopher,' Sirius said quietly. 'Do you want Grace to be shot while protecting you?'

Christopher didn't move or speak. Grace didn't look at him. She'd already diagnosed him as temporarily unable to function – he was frozen with fear.

'Let him go,' she said.

Sirius shook his head, making a tsk-ing sound. 'If I do that, then I may as well retire.'

'Retire then.'

'It's not as easy as you may think.'

'Why not?'

'There's my reputation to think of.'

He took a step forward but Grace pressed herself against Christopher, putting her arms behind her and around Christopher's middle.

'What's wrong with being seen as merciful?'

'In my business, everything.' His voice was dry.

'Please.'

He leaned slightly to the side. Was he looking to see if he could get a clear shot at Christopher? Grace leaned in the same direction.

Sirius leaned to the other. Grace mirrored him.

'Christopher's a friend,' Grace begged. 'You can't kill him.'

He sighed.

'Then you leave me no choice.'

Grace felt a sudden urge to urinate. She gave a small whimper but she didn't move.

The gun didn't waver. His eyes gleamed.

He sighed again.

To her astonishment, Sirius withdrew one hand from his gun and brought out a phone. Dialled.

'It is with regret that I cancel my current contract with you with immediate effect.'

He listened for a few seconds then said, 'Permanently.'

He lowered the gun. Began to step backwards. Grace didn't trust him. Was he pretending so that she'd move and he'd get a clear shot at Christopher? But he kept backing away. When he was six or seven yards from them he turned. His steps were brisk and he reached the far end of the car park within seconds.

'What the hell?' Lucy arrived in a rush.

Grace was still staring at the spot where Sirius had been standing. Her ears were ringing and she felt dizzy. Slowly, she folded to her knees.

'He cancelled his contract,' she whispered. 'I don't under-stand why.'

She glanced at Christopher, who was staring at her with a peculiar expression on his face.

'Am I the only one who sees it?'

'Sees what?' asked Grace.

Christopher looked at the space where Sirius had vanished and then back at Grace.

'Did you notice he had a birthmark on the side of his neck?' he said. His voice was calm. 'Below his right ear?'

Grace stared at him.

'Shaped like an ivy leaf?'

Her hand went to her neck. Something inside her started to crawl.

He held her eyes. 'Birthmarks can be inherited,' he said in the same calm tone. 'Some marks may be similar to marks on other family members. And when you take in facial shapes, skin and eye colour, freckles, body type, height . . .'

Her ears were ringing. She opened and closed her mouth but no sound came out.

'If you don't mind my saying,' Christopher said, 'you certainly have some interesting relatives.'

'I'm *related?*'

'You could get a DNA test done, but in my opinion you'd be wasting your money. It's obvious.'

CHAPTER SEVENTY-SEVEN

Lucy helped Grace inside the surgery. 'I know you've had a shock,' she said, 'and I wish I could stay with you . . .'

Over her shoulder, Lucy saw Christopher had climbed into his car and was buckling up.

'But I want to see where Christopher's going. Something's wrong, I need to find out what.'

Grace's lips were trembling, her skin cold and waxy. She looked as though she might throw up. 'I'm related to a mass *murderer*?'

'You don't know that for sure.'

'Mum told me Dad died when I was a baby, drowned at sea . . . what if that's not true?'

'He could just be a distant cousin or something,' Lucy tried to reassure her. 'Or related by marriage.'

Lucy heard the Polo's engine start.

'When he handcuffed us to the radiator,' Grace said. Her voice was distant. 'Do you remember he gave me one of Mum's big squashy cushions to sit on? And how when he handcuffed me he told me he'd done it so my muscles wouldn't freeze up as quickly?' Her gaze was wild on Lucy. 'He knew back then we were related. *He knew*.'

'Get yourself a shot of brandy,' she told Grace urgently. 'Anything. I'll be back as soon as I can. OK?'

Grace nodded but Lucy knew she hadn't heard her. She was deep in her own mind, struggling with what could turn out to be a potentially horrifying revelation. She'd just see where Christopher went and then she'd come back to Grace.

'Can I borrow your car?' Lucy asked.

'Keys are on my desk.'

Lucy sprang up and grabbed them. Refusing to let her ankle slow her down, she raced outside to see Christopher's Polo turn right out of the car park. Jumping into Grace's car, she started the engine. Rammed it in gear and tore after him.

Thankfully he hadn't put much distance between them and was barely half-way down the street. He was over the speed limit, doing forty miles per hour in a thirty zone, and as she followed him she felt her breathing begin to level out, her pulse settle.

She kept an eye out for Sirius. Grace's relative or not, she'd love to arrest him, throw his sociopathic backside behind bars. But she had more important things right now. Sirius would have to wait.

Christopher drove down Duncaid's high street, turning right at the clock tower and continuing for half a mile. Just past the Beanscene Café he turned right again, and she knew where he was going. To the Blackwater Industrial Estate.

She dropped back a little. He was out of sight when she turned into the estate. Instincts screaming with danger, she checked the Green Test Lab first, but he wasn't there. Nor was he at the

Biofoods lab. She trickled to the other side of the industrial estate to see he'd parked outside the Duncaid Environmental Research Centre.

Lucy left Grace's car around the corner and out of sight. She approached on foot. Ankle now blazing with pain, she hobbled into the little reception area. Empty. Tiptoeing into the corridor with its long window that overlooked a laboratory, it too appeared empty but she had to assume people were around. It was midday on a Thursday after all. Or had everyone gone into town for lunch?

She crept down the corridor. As she approached the door at the end, she heard shouting. Christopher. Yelling at the top of his voice.

She opened the door. Tiptoed into a small hallway with offices on each side. One of the doors was ajar. This was where the shouting was coming from.

'She would have died if I hadn't found her! What the hell do you think you were trying to do? She's a policewoman! She's a *friend*!'

'No friend of mine.' Jasmine's voice was curt. 'She's a cop, so what? Plenty more where that comes from.'

'Jesus Christ. You're a piece of work, you are. I can't believe I thought you were special. You're nothing but a cold, murdering bitch.'

'A bitch who protected you.'

'I didn't ask for your protection!' he shouted. 'I didn't ask for you to kidnap Lucy and try to murder her! Christ, I even showed you that well during what I thought was a romantic stroll!'

'When you told me about that sheep that had fallen in and you didn't know about it for two weeks by which time it was well and truly dead. Do you really think you're innocent here, Christopher?'

'I could show you a car but I don't expect you to run someone over with it,' he snapped. 'I went there this morning, not really thinking she'd be there, but something niggled at me and I just wanted to check. Thank Christ I did. Thank Christ.' He sounded close to tears. 'I don't want anyone dead.'

'You just want the money. To buy the Glenallen Estate back.'

'Yes, I want my home back. But not if it means people get killed for Chrissakes!'

'You are like a child.' Jasmine was dismissive. 'You should grow up. Real life isn't full of roses. It has thorns too.'

There was a clatter. It sounded like something plastic had been thrown down. 'Is this yours?' he asked.

'No,' she said.

'You're lying.'

'I did not bug you, Christopher. Why would I? I had you eating out of my hand. Now, tell me where you found it.'

'Why should I?'

'Just tell me.' Jasmine sounded irritated.

When Christopher didn't respond, she made an angry sound in the back of her throat. '*Poq Gai*. Go die on the street. You make things so difficult when in reality they are so easy.'

'Like body snatching?' His voice went stiff.

'We had to conduct our tests. I explained it to you.'

'But Nimue Acheson? Christ, Jasmine . . .'

'You are so sentimental. She was just a corpse. A cadaver we needed to examine.'

'You have no soul.'

'I don't need a soul. I have my country.'

Sudden silence.

'I no longer want to do business with you,' he said. His voice was flat and calm. 'From now, I terminate our arrangement. I want you to fuck off back to China and take that slimy, nasty little Bao Zhi with you.'

'You cannot terminate it. You have signed the agreement.'

'I don't care. It's finished. Over. You don't have the formula, and I won't give it to you.'

'You think I don't have it already?' Her voice was smug. 'I know your passwords, I know all your codes. You think you're so clever, but I have everything we need to take Snowbank to China. Thank you, Christopher.'

Lucy felt light-headed. Bao Zhi wasn't here to test Christopher's strong rice for the Kou Shaiming Company. He was here to test *Snowbank*.

Christopher laughed, but it wasn't a laugh of amusement. It had the ring of triumph.

'You really think I'm that stupid that I didn't suspect you might be seducing me for my father's technology? Jesus, Jasmine. And to think at one point I considered you intelligent.'

'What do you mean?' Alarm filled her voice.

'The formulas on my computer aren't the same ones that came out of Porton Down. They're similar enough to fool someone not cognizant of the structures, but trust me when

I say they won't work. It will be like injecting a person with glucose.'

At that moment, a mobile began to ring.

'Don't answer it,' Jasmine said warningly.

'It's Sam,' he told her. 'We don't want her coming here, do we?'

Jasmine gave a grunt of what could have been agreement.

'I'll just text her. Tell her I'm at the lab.'

Lucy thought she heard a whisper behind her and for a moment, she thought it was just a draft coming from under the door, but then she sensed movement.

She planted her good foot on the ground and she was spinning around when something kicked her injured ankle very hard. She cried out, off-balance, about to fall to the ground but Bao Zhi caught her. He snaked an arm around her neck and brought a knife to her throat.

A hunting knife.

'Keep still,' he hissed.

CHAPTER SEVENTY-EIGHT

When Mac got Lucy's message, for a moment he didn't know what to do. He stood there like some kind of dumb bullock, relief flooding every vein in his body like morphine and making him feel euphoric but shockingly weak.

He rang the number she'd called him on but it went straight to the messaging service. Christopher's voice, *Sorry I can't take your call* . . .

Christopher had found Lucy? Hastily, he called Grace.

'Hello?' One word and he knew something was very wrong. She sounded dazed.

'Grace. It's Mac here. DI MacDonald. What's happened?'

'Oh. Hello. Well, Lucy's OK. That's the main thing. She's OK. She's er. . . a bit bruised but she'll be all right. Christopher found her in a well. In an abandoned farmyard. I gave her a chicken and mayonnaise sandwich and a Mars bar. It was Susan McCreedy's sandwich but she said she didn't mind . . .'

She was drifting, obviously in shock.

'Grace,' he snapped at her, wanting to clear her head.

'I just saved Christopher's life. Sirius was here.'

His heart clenched. Lucy had told him about Sirius Thiele, the professional assassin.

'Where is she now?'

'She followed Christopher. She's in my car. She told me he could be a cousin twice, maybe three times removed, but I'm not so sure . . .'

'Where are you?'

'The surgery.'

'Tell someone what's happened,' he ordered. 'Call the police. OK?'

Small pause.

'You're right.' Her voice suddenly strengthened. 'I ought to call the police. I should have done it earlier but there was no time. Absolutely none. He was going to kill Christopher, you see. And if I hadn't stopped him, he'd be dead. The police. I'll do it now.'

He hung up and at that moment, a text came through from Christopher.

At the lab.

He wanted to text back asking if Lucy was with him, but if she was following Christopher she might be doing it clandestinely, so he held fire and drove there instead.

CHAPTER SEVENTY-NINE

'*Tā mā de.*' Fuck. Jasmine stared at Lucy. 'What are you doing here?'

With Bao Zhi's arm crushing her windpipe Lucy couldn't speak.

'She was spying,' Bao Zhi said.

'That's all she ever does.' Jasmine came close. So close that Lucy could see a scattering of blackheads crowding the woman's nasal creases. 'Spying. And look where it's got her! Ha! Not looking so clever now, are you?'

Christopher was on his feet. 'For God's sake, Bao Zhi. Put the knife down.'

'No.'

Lucy was struggling to breathe. Her fingers were clawing at his arm but it was like scratching an iron band.

'Little bitch,' said Jasmine. 'You've caused us nothing but trouble.'

Lucy could smell the Chinese man's breath. Onions and garlic and something sweet, like fruit lozenges.

'PUT THE KNIFE DOWN!' Christopher suddenly shouted, making them all flinch.

Bao Zhi's grip slackened fractionally and Lucy took a huge gulp of air. As she did so, she felt a stinging sensation. Warm liquid trickled down her neck. Blood.

She couldn't help it. She gave a whimper.

'I told you to *keep still*,' Bao Zhi hissed.

'Jesus Christ,' Christopher said. 'She's bleeding . . .'

He made to turn, to get a cloth, a bandage, *anything*, when Jasmine snapped, 'Stay where you are.'

Christopher fell still.

Jasmine looked between Christopher and Lucy. A calculating look came into her eye.

'You move one inch,' she told Christopher, 'and Bao Zhi will draw his blade across her throat. She will drown in her own blood. He will then cut her stomach. He will open her abdomen to make sure her organs spill across the floor. She will die in immense pain and without dignity. And it will be your fault.'

'No.' Christopher paled.

'We will let her go, if you do as I say.'

Christopher's mouth opened and shut. He sent Lucy a desperate gaze. She wanted to tell him not to trust Jasmine, to run while he could, but she still couldn't speak against the pressure on her throat.

Jasmine stepped to a computer terminal. Moved the mouse. Brought up a page, then another. She tapped on the keyboard.

'Where is the formula for Snowbank?'

'No,' Christopher whispered.

Jasmine gave Bao Zhi a nod. He pressed the knife against Lucy's throat. The stinging sensation increased and she said,

'No, no . . .' but all that came out was another frantic whimper. The warm trickle increased. Tears began to run down her cheeks. 'Please . . .'

'OK, OK.' Christopher's voice trembled. 'Let me—'

'No.' Jasmine's voice was hard. 'Tell me how to access it. I don't want you secretly sending someone a message.'

'I won't, I promise. Please don't hurt Lucy . . .'

Jasmine looked at Bao Zhi and gave him another nod. His grip lessened a little.

'OK.' Christopher took a breath. 'It's only available on the iCloud. I created a separate account. It's got several firewalls. If you go to an account called Council Bills, the first password is X0NGGL4C7BBT.' As he spoke, Jasmine tapped. Tensions lessened. Bao Zhi may not have realised it but his grip eased further.

'Why?' said Lucy softly.

Jasmine looked up with a frown. 'What?'

'Why is Snowbank so important to you?'

'I don't have to explain anything to you.' Jasmine turned back to the computer.

'No, you don't,' Lucy agreed. 'But it would be nice to know why I nearly died for it.'

When Jasmine remained silent, Christopher ran a hand down his face.

He said, 'Kou Shaiming is one of the biggest pharma companies in China. It's really competitive over there. If they have Snowbank, they'll be way ahead of everyone else. They want to use Snowbank to give them guidance on how well an individual is ageing and reduce the risks of diseases associated with old age. With the research team they've got – it's massive – they'll be able to predict which diseases they might suffer from, and help prevent them before it's too late.'

Jasmine paused and looked at Christopher. 'You really believe that shit?'

'What?'

She shook her head. 'You are so naive it is unbelievable. Stupid man.'

'What?' He was bewildered.

But Jasmine turned back to the computer.

I must get her talking, Lucy thought. *Divert her.*

'If you're not going to use Snowbank as Christopher thinks, then what plans do you have for it?'

'Guess,' she snapped.

'Um . . .' Lucy pretended to think of something intelligent to say to keep the woman engaged.

'It could be a secret assassin's tool,' Lucy suggested. 'But it wouldn't be much use if you had to wait years for it to work.'

Jasmine turned and looked at her. 'Not bad.'

'An assassin's tool?' Christopher repeated, looking horrified. 'What an awful thought! Kou Shaiming are only interested in helping humanity, not destroying it. Snowbank is there to do good.'

'Aiyee!' Jasmine flung up her hands. 'I can't take this any longer! Snowbank is for humankind, civilisation, charity, compassion, ha! You try living with terrorists on your doorstep for generation after generation.'

Jasmine had turned her back on the computer and was intent on Christopher.

'The Uyghurs have been a thorn in our side for hundreds of years,' she spat. 'They have refused to integrate into Chinese society. They are unpatriotic separatists who threaten the stability of our country. They detonated a bomb on a city bus in Urumqi only this morning. Twelve people died, ten of which were children. They are animals. They are *worse* than animals. A baby boosting injection for every Uyghur child will eventually solve the problem. They will never know they have been exterminated. Is this not better than going in with tanks and soldiers? The Uyghurs will die out peacefully, each generation dying younger and younger until they are no more.'

Christopher stared. 'You're talking about genocide.'

'So? Without the Uyghurs, we Han Chinese will be able to live peacefully again. In harmony.'

'But all they want is their culture, their heritage, without being annihilated by the State.'

'Then they should stop making bombs.'

Christopher looked bewildered. 'But we *talked* about this. I thought you were *on their side.*'

'You still don't get it, do you?' Jasmine's voice became a shout of frustration. 'I told you what you wanted to hear, you imbecile!'

Lucy had to do something while everyone was distracted, but she didn't know how. Bao Zhi still had his arm around her neck and although she couldn't feel the knife against her skin, it would take a millisecond for him to cut open her throat.

I have to move, Lucy told herself. *You know they won't let you out of here alive. They will kill you. YOU HAVE TO DO SOMETHING!*

She felt the pressure of fear building. Her nerves tightening. Her pulse began to lift as her adrenalin started to activate.

'We have to stop them!' Jasmine went on. 'Or the Uyghurs will continue killing shopkeepers, innocent street traders and children unless we do something about it. Like implement Snowbank.'

JUST DO IT!

CHAPTER EIGHTY

Bracing her right foot, Lucy pivoted swiftly to her left, away from the knife, swinging her shoulder anti-clockwise, push-ing *into* Bao Zhi's grasp and not away. For a split-second he was caught unawares and she kept spinning, bringing her left elbow hard into his stomach.

She felt the knife draw over her shoulder. Felt it cut through her fleece and shirt, but it didn't hurt.

She smashed the heel of her boot down on his instep. There was a cracking sound. She heard him grunt and she slipped out of his grip, tumbling to the ground.

Bao Zhi swarmed over her.

She locked her hands together and smashed her fists into his face but he kept coming. He was bringing up the knife and he was going to stab her. She squirmed and fought to get away, lashing her feet out, trying to kick him, hurt him, but she could have been fighting a brown bear for all the effect she had.

She heard Jasmine shouting and Christopher's screams high pitched with terror and panic.

There was a flurry of movement behind Bao Zhi but Lucy couldn't see what was happening. Her eyes were glued to the knife. She crossed her arms in front of her to defend herself.

'No . . .' she managed, fighting with all her might.

At that moment Christopher appeared behind Bao Zhi. He held a computer monitor in both hands. He smashed it down on the man's head.

Bao Zhi looked at Lucy as though surprised. His eyes widened. His mouth opened. And then he collapsed on top of her, the monitor crashing to the side.

'Jesus, oh Jesus.' Christopher was standing over them, shaking.

Lucy pushed and shoved Bao Zhi's form aside. Scrambled to her feet.

Jasmine was nowhere to be seen.

'Police,' Lucy said. Lunged for a phone. Dialled 999. Requested police and an ambulance.

She hung up. She was panting and felt dizzy.

'You're bleeding,' Christopher told her. 'A lot.'

She reached her left hand around to her right shoulder. It was wet and warm and when she brought her hand back, it was covered in blood.

'We need to get out of here,' she said. A wave of weakness folded over her and she swayed.

Christopher came to her. Put an arm around her waist. 'Let's go.'

They'd barely taken three steps when Jasmine appeared. She was holding a syringe.

She said, 'Christopher. Leave Lucy. This is all her fault – can't you see? We'll tell them it was Lucy who killed Bao Zhi because he kidnapped her. He's a crazy man. He wanted Snowbank for himself so he could get all the accolade at home. Become rich and famous. Come.' She clicked her fingers at him.

To Lucy's dismay, he dropped his arm from her side. Moved away from her.

'What is it?' he asked, sounding interested.

She didn't say anything.

'It's phenol, isn't it?'

Jasmine gave a nod.

'You killed Connor.' His voice was quite calm.

'It was an accident.'

He said, 'My boy.'

'I'm sorry,' Jasmine held Christopher's eyes. 'I was examining Nimue Acheson . . . Bao Zhi didn't know who it was . . . he just saw a child who would have told someone what he'd seen . . .'

Christopher looked at Lucy. His eyes were clear of shadows. He looked almost beatific. 'Get ready.'

He caught Lucy by surprise because the next thing he yelled was, 'GO!'

She responded a heartbeat too slow because he was already lunging for Jasmine, both arms wide, encompassing her in a giant bear hug.

Jasmine was shouting as she struggled to break free, but Christopher was silent as he hugged her.

Lucy staggered forward. Dodged past them. Pushed open the door. Ran across the hallway and down the corridor, ankle scorching. She battled a wave of dizziness as she lurched through reception. Nausea roiled through her. And then she was outside and stumbling for Grace's car, fumbling for the keys, but her legs were trembling, her vision wavering.

You're nearly there. Don't stop.

She beeped open the Golf. Only ten yards to go.

She heard footsteps behind her and glanced over her shoulder.

Jasmine was coming for her, hard and low. Her face was split in a snarl. She held the syringe at her side as she ran.

Dan's voice in Lucy's mind: *Approximately one gram is sufficient to cause death . . .*

Lucy put every ounce of effort into her run, but she was weak after her incarceration, her body exhausted, her damaged ankle and bleeding shoulder slowing her even further. Jasmine was catching up.

The car came from nowhere. Engine roaring, it squealed around the corner and accelerated hard.

Lucy turned her head.

She saw a grey sedan going flat out. Headed straight for Jasmine. She saw Jasmine try to dodge away but she was too late. The car hit her without slowing. Lucy heard the soft thud of flesh against metal.

Jasmine's body tumbled over the sedan's bonnet, smacked into the windscreen and slid away, slamming on to the asphalt.

The car shrieked to a halt.

A man leaped out and ran to Jasmine. Stamped on her hand. Kicked the syringe aside. Kicked it again and again, until it was beneath the car and out of reach.

Then he turned to her.

Broad shoulders. Curly brown hair. Mismatched grey eyes.

Mac. Her DI was here.

Faris.

Lucy's legs gave way. She folded to the ground.

Mac pelted for her. Skidded to her side.

She looked into his eyes. She wanted to say, 'I love you,' not because he'd saved her life but because she'd promised it would be the first thing she'd say to him if she got out of the hole alive, but her lips wouldn't work properly.

She tried to speak but whether she said anything she never knew because a violet cloud started to close in on her vision and as it grew darker and darker, bright bolts of white lightning sparked through and it was so beautiful she reached out a hand, wanting to touch them and when she did, she was surprised at how warm they were.

CHAPTER EIGHTY-ONE

Three days later (Sunday)

Lucy lay curled on the sofa in Grace and Ross's kitchen, reading the newspapers. It was chucking rain outside but with the Aga and log fire blazing, the cold and darkness of the stone hole where Bao Zhi had thrown her felt a million miles away. Grace was at the surgery, Ross was insulating the roof of one of the cottages.

She'd been discharged from hospital on Friday. They'd given her twenty-five stitches across her shoulder and told her she was lucky the knife hadn't lacerated any tendons or done any lasting damage. They'd washed and bathed her. Put antiseptic cream on her hands and arnica on her bruises. She hadn't cared she was in a busy, noisy ward. It made her feel safe. She spent most of her time dozing in between meals and hospital visits.

Mac had come to see her several times. Grace and Ross too. And Dan. He'd been with her for ages. After he left, she slept solidly for two hours, exhausted not just with talking, but from all the revelations in Germany and how they tied into Connor's death in Scotland.

Four university friends, and now there were two: Gordon and Arne. Arne was in police custody along with Anneke, as was Gordon Baird. Gordon had been devastated when he had learned how his son and grandson had died. Gordon had, albeit unwittingly, orchestrated both their deaths. Poetic justice for all those innocents he'd played God with, Lucy decided, not feeling much sympathy.

Jasmine had suffered two broken legs, a broken pelvis and a fractured collarbone. Her wrists were both fractured and she'd sustained a brain injury when her head had hit the ground. She was in the same hospital but under guard. Lucy had no intention of visiting her.

Bao Zhi was dead, his head caved in by the computer monitor Christopher had smashed against his skull. Christopher had died saving Lucy. He'd taken most of the syringe of phenol and when Mac got to him, he was no longer breathing. His heart had stopped. Lucy wasn't sure how she felt about Christopher. It was because of him that all this had started. Or should Gordon take the blame? After all, it had been Gordon who'd told Christopher all about what he and his fellow colleagues at Porton Down had been working on all those years ago.

Gordon hadn't wanted Snowbank to be forgotten, at least that's what he said, 'I just wanted Christopher to know there was a whole project to draw on if he wanted to look at the subject of ageing, to help people in the future.'

Christopher, however, had seen his chance to make a fortune.

'You just want the money. To buy the Glenallen Estate back,' Jasmine had said.

Christopher's hunger for the past, to walk his childhood moors and fish the same rivers, had in effect, killed his son.

Lucy flipped the page on her tablet. More comment on Project Snowbank. It had certainly fired up the public imagination. Some advocated it, others abhorred it. Everybody had a view. It made for some interesting reading. Rain rattled against the windows. Her neck and shoulder ached. She was still very tired. Her eyes began to close.

The next thing she knew, Mac was there, droplets of rain in his hair and on his coat.

'Hello, sleeping beauty.' He was smiling and looked as handsome as hell.

'I'm not sure about the beauty bit.' Her face was a mess, her nose still swollen, the skin around her eyes coloured green, purple and blue.

'Shame Halloween's not for a bit.' His smile broadened. 'You wouldn't need to dress up.'

'Thanks a bunch.'

He took off his coat, hung it over the back of an armchair. Came over and to her surprise said, 'Budge up.'

She raised her legs to make room. He sat down with a sigh. She was going to curl her legs beneath her but he caught them and gently hooked them across his lap. Stroked her calves then her instep. He looked into the flames of the log fire, seemingly content.

Heat flushed her skin. A combination of nervousness and discomfort. Had she missed something? She knew she'd promised to declare her feelings for him if she got out of the hole, but since her release all they'd talked about was the case. And the more they'd talked about Murray Peterson, Jasmine and Bao Zhi, the more she realised she didn't have the guts to say anything.

He was her DI. Full stop.

She had to respect that.

'Er . . .' She suddenly felt exquisitely embarrassed. 'Boss?'

He quirked an eyebrow at her. 'Something wrong?'

'You're, ah . . . being quite intimate.'

He looked surprised. 'Am I?'

'Well, yes.' But she didn't move. It felt so good to feel his thighs beneath her calves, his hands on her legs, her feet; she felt as though she could stay like this for ever.

'Don't you remember what you said to me?' He was frowning.

She stared at him. 'When?'

'After I hit Jasmine Zhang with my car, I ran to you and you reached up and touched my face and told me . . .'

He looked at her expectantly.

Her cheeks flamed red. 'I didn't know I said anything.'

'Oh, but you did.' He quirked an eyebrow at her. 'Do you fancy saying it again, maybe? I'd quite like to hear it a second time.'

You can do it, she told herself. *You promised yourself, remember?*

She licked her lips. Looked into his eyes. Took a breath.

'I love you.'

'Well, DC Davies.' He held her gaze solemnly. 'That's good to know because as it happens, I love you too.'

CHAPTER EIGHTY-TWO

Grace hooked her arm under Ross's and walked with him across the car park to the crematorium where Christopher's funeral ceremony was to be held. Lucy and Mac were just ahead. They were holding hands. Grace wasn't sure if she'd ever seen Lucy so happy, and Mac obviously adored her, which was a relief. She couldn't have borne it if her friend had given her heart to someone who didn't give theirs back.

They passed a couple of police officers at the door, another two inside. They'd had to show their IDs to more officers at the crematorium gate thanks to the hordes of media that had descended on the area. Grace had reluctantly sold her story to one of the national newspapers, but only because by signing up to an exclusive it meant that other outlets would leave her alone.

Project Snowbank was on the front page of every newspaper, headlined on radio and TV. They'd had French, American and German journalists in Duncaid as well as Chinese, and even someone from the Xinjiang Uyghur Autonomous Region had turned up. The effects of Project Snowbank were of global interest, and there was constant debate over the ethics of it, the moralities and principles of such a scheme, which was keeping just about every journalist in the world occupied.

Gordon Baird had been devastated and delighted.

Devastated that his past had caught up to cause his son and grandson's deaths, but delighted that the project was finally getting the attention and dialogue it deserved.

Grace had gone to see him in prison where he was awaiting trial.

He'd been surprised to see her, but pleased too.

'You're not taking the job in Edinburgh then?'

She'd surveyed him at length. 'You wanted me out of the way, didn't you?'

He raised his hands as if to say, *what choice did I have?*

'You flattered and manipulated me.' Her voice was flat.

'Hardly,' he snorted. 'You're a top GP and that's the honest truth. But yes, you're right in that you were making me slightly nervous with all those autopsy requests. You knew something was up.' He nodded in approbation.

'And Brice Kendrick?'

'He didn't want the stigma of Snowbank on him or the family. Nobody did.' His expression distant. 'If Christopher hadn't missed Glenallen quite so much, then none of us would be here.'

'Did you know he was selling Snowbank?' Grace asked curiously.

He looked shocked. 'Absolutely not. And if I *had* known, I would have put a stop to it. It's not for *sale*. It was a government project don't forget. It was designed for *the people*.'

'What about Peter Kendrick? The funeral director?'

'He always was a greedy little man. I've heard through my solicitor that Jasmine bribed him to supply her with corpses so she and Bao Zhi could conduct post-mortems. See exactly how Snowbank had worked.'

'So the coffin's buried were—'

'Empty, yes.'

Forensics had already found trace evidence of body fluids, hair and fibres in the Green Test Lab – Jasmine and Bao Zhi's secret research centre for the Kou Shaiming Company.

Grace couldn't think of any other questions so she'd looked at him squarely.

She despised him, *loathed* him for what he'd done to all those people, her *patients*.

'Hey,' he said, his hands were rising in protest but she let the full force of her disgust for him show before she rose and walked out of the room without looking back.

A low rumble came from above and a smatter of raindrops fell. Ross flipped open the umbrella he'd brought and sheltered them as the rain began to fall harder. Ahead, Mac snapped open his umbrella and did the same for him and Lucy.

'All right, Gracie?' Ross looked down at her, solicitous and loving.

'Yes, thanks.' She squeezed his arm.

She'd told Ross about Sirius and what Christopher had said about sharing the same birthmark, and he'd immediately suggested she ring Bernard Gilpin, the Director General of MI5.

'He was a good friend of your mother's for a long time,' Ross reminded her. 'If anyone knows whether Sirius is related to you or not, it would be him.'

It had been a strange phone call. The last time she'd seen Bernard had been ten days after her mother had died, when he'd explained a lot about her mother's past. He'd sounded surprised to hear from her, but not unfriendly, and when she asked if it was possible she might be related to Sirius Thiele, he fell silent.

Grace didn't say anything to prompt him. She sat in her country kitchen, skin prickling with nerves, waiting for him to say something.

'Whatever makes you think that?' he eventually asked.

When she described what had happened, how Sirius had treated her with an odd respect, Bernard said, 'I don't know anything about his past, I'm afraid. I don't know where he came from, or who his parents are. Nobody does.'

'Did you know my father?'

'I'm afraid not.'

There was a small silence.

'Without a DNA test,' Bernard said, 'you'll never know if you're related to him. Do you really want to undertake such a thing?'

'No, not really.'

The realisation that she didn't need to know if she was related to Sirius suddenly lifted the anxiety that had been dogging her, pressing her down into depression. If she *was* related to such a person, it wasn't as though she could do anything about it.

And if she wasn't, well . . . she shared a birthmark with a trained assassin, a killer, that was all.

'Then let's leave it like that,' Bernard told her.

'Yes.'

Grace eased her clasp on Ross's arm as they walked into the crematorium. She saw Sam and her mother in the front pew, little Dougie on Sam's lap. Grace had prescribed a short-term sedative for Sam, to help her sleep as well as function for the funeral, but she'd advised not taking it for long or it might interfere with the ability to grieve. Both Sam and her mother were seeking counselling.

Several patients came up to greet them. Disa and Sorcha hugged her – both were now getting support for Sorcha's Alzheimer's. Iona Ainsley's husband also came over. Lachlan, the paramedic, gave her a wave. Constable Murdoch nodded at her but he was still unable to hold her gaze. She may have done the right thing requesting all those autopsies but it didn't mean he liked it.

Grace wasn't sure whether they were there to pay their respects to Christopher or to get some sort of closure, but most of the village was there.

Gordon Baird had been told he couldn't attend. He may have been Christopher's father, but if he'd turned up, he probably would have been lynched.

Murderer.

The word had smoldered through Duncaid's streets, swirling around its residents like a poisonous gas.

How the town was going to come to terms with Snowbank was anyone's guess, but given how tough, strong and compassionate its inhabitants were, she reckoned they'd pull together to create some kind of new way of living.

Her heart bled for the descendants of the babies who'd been injected in Duncaid and Braunschweig all those years ago. Duncaid's GP records showed that the practice nurse's grandmother, Belinda McCreedy, had injected twenty babies with Gordon Baird's experimental serum. Between them, those babies had eventually had thirty-two children, which made a total of fifty-two people who were going to die young thanks to Snowbank.

So far eighteen had died.

The remaining thirty-four, mostly in their teens and early twenties, were being counselled by psychotherapists, psychiatrists and every mental health expert in between.

There was talk of government compensation. Insurances were cancelled. Scientists were working frantically to find a way of halting the ageing process, keep everyone's telomeres long. But nobody was holding out any immediate hope, least of all her friend Ben at Barts.

'I'm so sorry, Grace,' he'd said. 'It's awful.'

'You'll get your Society membership.'

'Christ, I was only joking about that. Those poor people.'

Through it all, Grace talked to her patients. She visited them at home, walked with them, held them when they cried.

She confessed to Ross that she could now see how shallow she'd been by being tempted to work in Edinburgh.

'And now?' His eyes were keen on hers.

'I'm not going anywhere. I'm here to stay.'

CHAPTER EIGHTY-THREE

Dan sat with Gustav and Sophie inside the crematorium, watching Christopher's coffin being brought inside. He'd been asked by Sam to carry the coffin and although he'd been honoured by the request, he'd had to decline. He didn't say why, just told her he'd explain later.

He opened the Order of Ceremony. Saw one of the hymns was 'All Things Bright and Beautiful', which had been their favourite as kids. Dan hadn't appreciated nature before he'd been introduced to the Bairds. He'd been a city boy, with no real understanding of animals and birds or the cycles they lived. How salmon out at sea returned to the river of their birth to spawn. How stags and hinds lived in separate herds for most of the year. He could understand Christopher's passion for the land and how his soul felt as though it atrophied living on the edge of what he believed was his and being unable to set foot upon a single square inch of its moss, a single stem of grass.

His friend had made a catastrophic error trying to sell Snowbank to a Chinese pharma company. He'd been blinded by what he wanted to hear – that the Kou Shaiming Company was going to do nothing but good with the science – against the reality of a highly competitive business in a morally unscrupulous country.

Christopher had died to protect Lucy. But he'd also died to atone.

Sophie reached across and put her hand over his. Gave it a squeeze. He squeezed back. For the first time since his son Luke had died, he felt like crying.

Out of the corner of his eye, he saw Gustav lean forward a fraction, past Sophie, and look at him. Dan swallowed. Gave a nod. Gustav leaned back.

Four of them, childhood friends. Now three.

'Please stand,' the minister bade the congregation.

Dan let the ceremony wash over him. He stood and prayed, sang and listened to the music. He felt numb and hollow. Infinitely sad.

After seeing Lucy in hospital, after being debriefed by Police Scotland and Philip Denton in London, he'd talked with Mac who, given half a chance, would have liked to kick him squarely in the balls for endangering his DC. If the man didn't realise he was in love with Lucy, then maybe it was time someone told him, but when Dan saw them arrive at the crematorium together, hand in hand, it seemed things had finally been resolved.

The concluding hymn was sung. The minister said the last words. Dan watched the committal take place, and then Christopher's coffin was obscured by curtains closing around it. Sophie wiped her eyes. Gustav cleared his throat and held Sophie's hand.

Jenny had wanted to come but when Dan explained why it was probably a good thing if she stayed at home, she'd seen the sense of it. 'I'll send him a prayer,' she told Dan. 'You too.'

When he'd eventually arrived home, he'd expected the cold shoulder. Maybe a demand for divorce. Instead he'd found his home bright and welcoming with a fire blazing in the sitting room and what smelled like slow-cooked beef in the oven. His favourite.

He'd gone into the kitchen, where Mischa was in his baby carrier and Aimee at the table colouring in a colouring book of horses. After greeting the children, he'd taken Jenny into the hall. He said, 'I know it's not much, but I saw it and thought of you.'

He passed her a jewellery box.

She gave him a sideways look. Untied the ribbon and gently raised the lid.

Inside was an enamel and silver pendant in the shape of a white heather.

'Dan,' she said, lifting it up. 'It's beautiful.'

'White heather brings luck and protection.'

'How appropriate.' Her voice was dry but her eyes were warm.

'It also signifies one's wishes will come true.'

He took a deep breath. Looked her in the eyes. 'What do you wish for?'

He hadn't needed to say more. She knew him well enough that those five words covered a great swathe of meaning.

'I wish . . .' She thought a little longer. 'For you to be happy. But me too. I know I can't stop you going on mad missions. It's who you are. I realise that. I also realise that these were exceptional circumstances and that I had to go somewhere safe. Yes, I hated it, but yes, it was necessary. That said, I really don't want anything like it to happen again, especially with two children . . .' She sighed. 'But I can't stop you doing something you love any more than you can stop me from getting my private pilot's licence.'

He blinked. 'What?'

'A client of mine has offered to teach me how to fly.' Her eyes had flashed wickedly for a moment. 'Just think of the perks! You'll be able to hire me at a brilliantly exorbitant rate to fly you across the Channel any time you want.'

He was a very lucky man, he thought now. Very lucky indeed.

He watched the row in front of him leave. People around them started to get to their feet. As Sophie made to rise, he said, 'Wait.'

He didn't look at her.

He felt Sophie look at Gustav, but Gustav was staring straight ahead, his skin pale. He didn't move either.

They sat together, the three of them, as the rest of the congregation filed outside.

Finally, the room was empty.

'It's time.' Dan led the way through the double doors, followed by Sophie and Gustav.

As soon as he stepped outside, he saw them. Two men in jeans and wind breakers next to a beech tree on the right. Two more stationed at the car park's exit on the left.

A stiff breeze lifted Sophie's hair so it blew around her face. Leaves rustled around their feet.

Gustav said, 'Goodbye, Sophie.'

His footsteps were clipped on the paving as he walked away.

There was a long silence. Dan didn't look at Sophie, nor did she look at him.

'How did you know?' she asked.

CHAPTER EIGHTY-FOUR

'The only people,' Dan said, 'who were aware of my affair were in the firm. And Jenny would never have told you.'

'No,' Sophie agreed. 'She wouldn't.'

'And nor would I.'

'No.'

Silence.

'And to think I thought I covered it up so well. I didn't think you'd realised.'

'I didn't,' he admitted. 'Not until later.'

'Me and my big mouth.'

One of the men made to move towards them but Dan held up a hand. *Wait.* The man stopped.

'So, you're not with the HMIC.'

'No.'

'Did we cross paths when I worked for the firm?'

'Yes. But you wouldn't remember.'

Another memory lost to him. No point in belabouring the point. His memory was what it was.

'You had Joanna Loxton follow me.'

'Yes.'

'Why?'

'I didn't trust your dad not to have told you something. He was a wily old fox, wasn't he? He'd set up that newspaper ad with Dad . . . what if he'd done the same with you? I wanted to know what you were up to. I didn't want you putting two and two together . . .' She took a breath. 'And just so you know, I didn't have any idea that Bao Zhi killed poor Connor.'

Dan stared straight ahead as he spoke.

'You put a tracker on my car.'

'Correct.'

'You got me pulled in at Hanover Airport. Set the BND on Didrika Weber.'

'Dan, I was trying to fucking *protect* you.'

'You and Christopher were in it together. He wanted the money to buy back the estate, and you because . . . well, you like being spoilt.'

'I certainly do,' she sighed. 'To my detriment.'

She tucked a lock of hair behind her ear. Dan saw she was wearing Gustav's diamond earrings.

She said, 'Christopher wanted to ask you to join us in selling Snowbank, but I told him you'd say no. You're too upstanding. Too principled.'

'What about Gustav?'

'He refused. He said it was immoral.'

'You had an affair with him to stop him giving you away.'

She was silent, pursing her lips before she spoke.

'Yes. I told him we weren't going ahead with the sale, but I was never sure he believed me. Keeping him close meant he'd stay loyal.'

'And my dad?'

'I thought Arne had killed him. Not Anneke, the mad bitch.'

Dan looked at the men, waiting patiently. 'You put a listening device inside Christopher's car.'

'I was worried for him. Jasmine and Bao Zhi were incredibly slippery. Ruthless too. I didn't trust them an inch. They kept tabs on Murray Peterson in case he stepped out of line. Bao Zhi followed him to the pub. I'm sorry your friend Lucy got caught in the crossfire but he was convinced Murray had told her everything . . . Psychopathic bastard.'

'Who you were doing business with.'

She opened her palms. 'Come on, Dan. I tried my best to safeguard you! Every step, every inch of the way.'

'By using Sirius Thiele?' His voice rose a little. 'Jesus, Sophie, did you have to go that far?'

She rounded on him. 'You wouldn't stop, Dan! You were like a fucking dog with a bone. You kept plugging away and I knew that unless I did something serious, you'd get to the bottom of it and ruin it all. Nobody was meant to get hurt. We were going to sell Snowbank, make a nice packet, and then Christopher could have his precious Glenallen and Nick and I could buy our ocean-going yacht and sail around the world . . .' She paused, closing her eyes.

'Nobody was going to get hurt?' he repeated disbelievingly. 'What do you think the Chinese pharma company were going to do with Snowbank? Use it to save the world?'

'Oh, don't be so sanctimonious. They're already engineering genes like you wouldn't believe. Snowbank's just one of many projects flying around.'

Dan felt part of his soul fall away. 'This whole thing was concocted by you, wasn't it? Without you, Christopher would never have known how to contact the Chinese pharma company, let alone organise such a deal.'

He looked at her, his childhood friend who he'd laughed with, played with and shared glasses of Ribena with. He had to force himself to harden his heart.

'You told Sirius to kill Christopher.'

She stared straight ahead.

'You wanted Christopher dead because he was the only person who knew you were involved in the sale of Snowbank.'

She turned to him, her eyes vivid and bright. 'It's all conjecture, you know.'

Dan gave the men a nod. Two started forward. The other two shifted on their feet. One reached round to the base of his spine as though he had an itch, but Dan knew he was checking his weapon.

'I'll send you a postcard,' she murmured. She turned and rose on her tiptoes and kissed his cheek. She smelled of rose and ginger. Sweet and bitter.

He watched her walk away, her black stilettos clipping, her cashmere coat swaying with her hips. He saw the men approach, saw her greet them. The men stepped into position on either side of her. Escorted her to an unmarked grey Volvo. She climbed into the back where another man waited. The door closed.

He watched the Volvo move off. Watched another car fall in behind. He thought he saw Sophie wave her fingers at him through the rear window but he couldn't be sure.

Four friends. Now two.

EPILOGUE

Sam wheeled Dougie and his pushchair up the hill to the local Costcutter. She needed milk, bread and bleach. She also needed some fresh air.

Seagulls reeled above her, their calls echoing around the stone cottages. Such a foreign sound compared to what she was used to. It smelled different here too. Of salt and seaweed, and fried chips.

It was good being able to walk down the street without being stared at. As the wife as well as the daughter-in-law of two of the most newsworthy people in the country – if not the world right now –she hadn't been able to open her curtains in Duncaid without seeing a dozen cameras pointed at her.

It had been Lucy's idea to move out of the area for a bit, and at first she hadn't been sure. She was Duncaid born and bred. All her relatives were in town, along with all her friends, but although the idea had been frightening, the appeal of starting again had become more attractive with each day that passed.

Not that she was running away or anything. She hadn't changed her name and she certainly wasn't going to cover up or lie about her past, but this way she had more control and could tell people what had happened in her own way rather than have them gossip behind her back, staring at her and pointing a finger. *That's her, the wife.*

Besides, she may well move back to Scotland after a while but for the moment, it was just a relief to be herself with her little boy. The cottage she'd rented was tiny but what it lacked in space was made up for by the view of the sea. She could sit in the garden for hours looking at it, and even though she hadn't been here long, she'd begun to feel that the future may not be as bleak as she'd once thought. She'd even started to look at getting a job locally and had an interview lined up with Yorkshire Cozy Cottages with a view to housekeeping the local properties on their books.

Regardless of whether she eventually returned to live in Duncaid or settled elsewhere, she would have to tell her son one day. Her mum advised her to start telling parts of the story as early as possible so that it would become a comfortable part of his life even if he didn't fully understand it. Then he wouldn't have a horrible shock when he was older, and she wouldn't spend her life dreading that the truth would come out. Because of course it would. It was too big, too horrendous to hide from.

She hadn't seen Gordon since his arrest. She blamed him for everything. If he hadn't told Christopher about Snowbank, Christopher would still be working on his strong rice and Connor would be alive. Jasmine would never have come into their lives and she and Christopher would have grown old together, been buried together. Except, of course, she would have died before him because tests had shown that she had what was now known as the Snowbank gene. She'd be lucky to make it to her sixties and there was nothing she could do about it.

Except live her life as well as she could. Bring up her boy as best she could. And keep her head high and her shoulders back, because for all his faults, Christopher had been a good man. After all, he'd made the ultimate sacrifice, dying to save another person's life, and she was going to make sure that his son would grow up being proud of him.

The sun came out as she passed the Friendly Bean Café. Life was about moving forward. Since she'd relocated, she could feel how much stronger she was. How she could hold Christopher and Connor close, keep her memories of them vivid and clear without drowning in them.

In the distance she could see a fishing boat and a yacht in full sail. They ducked and bobbed on the ocean and like her, they were moving forward.

AUTHOR'S NOTE

This book is a work of fiction. However, the science behind Project Snowbank came from researchers at King's College London, who recently announced they have developed a way of testing how well, or badly, your body is ageing. They say the test could help predict when a person will die, and identify those at high-risk of dementia and Alzheimer's. The team said looking at 'biological age' is more useful than using a date of birth.

The test uses a process called RNA-profiling and looks at 150 genes that are activated in healthy 65-year-olds in the blood, brain and muscle. From the age of 40 onwards, you can apparently use this to give you guidance on how well you're ageing. Or not, as the case may be.

The wide-ranging consequences got me thinking. What would you do if you discovered that although you appeared fit and healthy at sixty, you were in fact biologically aged 80? Would you spend your pension travelling the world? Cancel your life insurance? The ramifications were far more complex than I first realised, and became one of the main themes in the story.

ACKNOWLEDGEMENTS

I would like to thank Angela Harper, Scenes of Crime Officer, for her expert input on forensic evidence and a variety of police practices and methods in the UK, and also Peter Hinrichs, Polizeihaupkommissar a.D., for allowing me to badger him across the airwaves about police procedures in Germany.

I was introduced to the idea of Project Snowbank by the remarkable Professor Randall Smith, whose insights made a deep impression on me. His keen interest in older people and social care, ageing and maintaining dignity in later life sparked the inspiration for this book.

I am incredibly lucky to have a family of scientists on hand who I can go to with some crazy story ideas and they help me make it all real: Patrick Seed, Christina Seed, Dr Janet Seed and Professor Michael Seed. You really are my brainstorming gurus and I can't thank you enough for your creative contributions as well as all the cake.

I owe thanks to Peter and Geraldine Wolstencroft for giving me the idea of setting the book partly in Scotland and for filling in any gaps. RIP, Peter. You're very much missed.

To Jo Brandie, landlord of The Fiddichside Inn, I was so sorry you died before you could see yourself in print. You're a local legend and I only hope the fishing's as good where you are.

Thanks also to my editor, Katherine Armstrong, not just for her professional, perceptive eye, but for the title. Zaffre continue to be a publishing dream to this author, and I would like to give heartfelt thanks for all their support. I am truly proud to be part of the Zaffre team.

As is customary in these cases, I must now say that any mistakes that remain will be my own.

Always grateful thanks to Rowan Lawton, my agent, and Steve Ayres for their continued and much appreciated support. Thanks to Tai Lichtensteiger for drinks in her beautiful apartment which, quite unplanned, took centre stage in Chapter Ten.

Thanks to all the bloggers and reviewers out there for your enthusiasm, and also for finding me a plethora of new readers. You've been fantastic.

Lastly, a massive thanks to my readers. I hope more than anything that you enjoy this novel, because I wrote it for you.